"My dance, I believe?"

"Are you sure you've danced with every other female in town, from the oldest to the youngest?" Sarah asked archly.

He raised a brow, and in that moment she knew she'd made a mistake.

"Ah, so you were watching," he said, grinning.

"I most certainly was not," Sarah insisted. "I never sat down myself, except when the musicians took a break. I only just realized that you hadn't made good your threat to claim a dance."

"'Threat?'" he echoed. "I believe I only requested a dance, as proof of your goodwill. And I was waiting for a waltz, Miss Matthews."

"Oh? Why?" she asked. Was this girl asking the daring questions really her?

Again, the raised brow. "If you have to ask that, Miss Sarah Matthews, then it's no wonder the South lost the war."

Laurie Kingery

and

Pamela Nissen

The Doctor Takes a Wife

&

Rocky Mountain Redemption

Recycling programs for this product may not exist in your area.

ISBN-13: 978-1-335-45479-9

The Doctor Takes a Wife &
Rocky Mountain Redemption

This edition published by arrangement with Harlequin Books S.A.

For questions and comments about the quality of this book, please contact us at CustomerService@Harlequin.com.

Love Inspired
22 Adelaide St. West, 40th Floor
Toronto, Ontario M5H 4E3, Canada
www.Harlequin.com

Printed in U.S.A.

CONTENTS

Laurie Kingery is a Texas transplant to Ohio who writes romance set in post–Civil War Texas. She was nominated for a Carol Award for her second Love Inspired Historical novel, *The Outlaw's Lady*, and has written a series about mail-order grooms in a small town in the Texas Hill Country.

Books by Laurie Kingery

Love Inspired Historical

Hill Country Christmas
The Outlaw's Lady

Bridegroom Brothers

The Preacher's Bride Claim

Brides of Simpson Creek

Mail Order Cowboy
The Doctor Takes a Wife
The Sheriff's Sweetheart
The Rancher's Courtship
The Preacher's Bride
Hill Country Cattleman
A Hero in the Making
Hill Country Courtship
Lawman in Disguise

Visit the Author Profile page at Harlequin.com for more titles.

THE DOCTOR TAKES A WIFE

Laurie Kingery

For God has not given us a spirit of fear,
but of power and of love and of a sound mind.

—2 *Timothy* 1:7

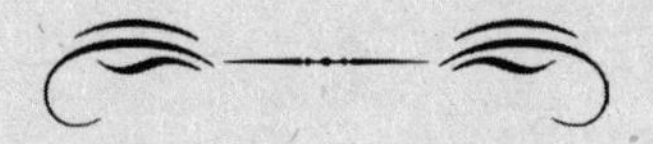

To the wonderful people of San Saba County, Texas,
and in memory of the real settlement
of Simpson Creek, and as always, to Tom.

Chapter One

"You look very lovely today, Miss Matthews," said the voice in an accent that was as far from the usual drawl Sarah heard around her as Maine was from Texas. She stiffened, schooling herself to assume a polite expression as she looked up into the blue eyes of Dr. Nolan Walker.

A lady, she reminded herself sternly, did not make a scene in public, and most certainly not while standing in the receiving line at the wedding of her sister. Even if the speaker was a Yankee outsider who had no business being here.

"Thank you, sir," she replied in a carefully neutral voice, and did not quite meet his gaze. "May I present Lord Edward Brookfield, Viscount Greyshaw, the groom's eldest brother, come all the way from England?" She watched out of the corner of her eye as the Yankee doctor shook hands with the English nobleman next to her.

The men exchanged greetings.

"And may I also present—" she began, intent on passing the Yankee on down the line away from her.

Nolan interrupted her. "Miss Matthews, I was wondering if we might sit together while enjoying the refreshments?" He nodded toward the punch bowl and the magnificent quadruple-tiered wedding cake that Sarah considered the crowning achievement of her baking career. "I… I'd really like to get to know you better." He had dropped the "g" on "wondering," while "together" and "better" came out "togethah" and "bettah," and yet his accent was wholly unlike a Southern drawl.

The utter effrontery of the man! Hadn't she already made it clear back in October, when he'd come to town to meet her that she Was Not Interested in being courted by a Yankee and a liar? He'd written her a handful of letters telling all about himself, except for the one fact that made him Unacceptable—that he was Yankee. She'd only found out when he'd come to meet her on Founders' Day—right before the Comanche attack.

"I'm afraid that's impossible," she said crisply. "I'll be busy helping to serve the cake and the punch. Now—"

"Perhaps a dance, then? I understand there'll be dancing later."

She glared at him. "Out of the question," she snapped. "Now, *if I may be permitted to continue,* you're acquainted with Miss Caroline Wallace, aren't you, the bride's best friend?" She gestured to the bridesmaid standing next to her.

She didn't miss the surprised look Lord Greyshaw

gave her, nor the sympathetic one he bestowed on the Yankee. Perhaps there would be a chance later, after the wedding, to explain to Nick's eldest brother why a properly brought up young lady of the South did not encourage familiarity with pushy northern interlopers?

Mercifully, the doctor now allowed himself to be handed on down the line. The next person to approach was Mrs. Detwiler, an elderly widow, resplendent today in deep purple bombazine. Sarah hoped the woman had not heard what had passed between her and the Yankee doctor, for Mrs. Detwiler was sure to have an opinion on it, likely one contrary to Sarah's.

But luck was with Sarah—the older lady had indeed missed hearing the Yankee's words and Sarah's tart replies.

"You girls all looked lovely up at the altar," she proclaimed. "Was it dear Milly's idea to have her attendants decked out in different fall hues? She certainly picked colors that looked good on each of you."

Sarah smiled and glanced down at the gold *Gros de Naples* fabric she wore, knowing it complimented her blond coloring just as the mossy green cloth complimented Caroline Wallace's brunette hair and as the rust color played up Prissy Gilmore's strawberry-blond tresses. "Yes, and she sewed them all, too, as well as her bridal dress," Sarah said, gazing at Milly who was at this moment sharing a happy smile with Nicholas Brookfield, her English groom.

"My, her fingers must have been busy!"

Mrs. Detwiler didn't know the half of it, Sarah thought. Milly had not only had all that sewing to do, but had also determinedly learned how to cook under Sarah's tutelage. While she wasn't yet the confident cook and baker that her sister was, Sarah thought it wasn't likely Nick and the rest of the men would starve with Milly minding the ranch kitchen once Sarah moved in to town. Now that Milly was a bride, Sarah had wanted her sister to be free to manage her house, and she had wanted to try her own wings, too. So when Prissy had begged Sarah to teach her cooking and the other housewifely arts, Sarah found a way to kill one bird with two stones and had agreed to move in with her.

"I declare, it's the wedding of the decade for Simpson Creek," Mrs. Detwiler gushed.

Sarah nodded. At the very least, it was the first wedding since the war ended, as well as the first which had resulted from Milly's founding of the Society for the Promotion of Marriage—or, as it was more commonly known, the Spinsters' Club. Milly deserved to be the very first bride, and the happiest, Sarah thought, growing misty-eyed with love and pride.

"Now it's *your* turn," the old woman announced, cupping Sarah's cheek affectionately.

Sarah cringed inwardly, hoping no one else had heard. "Oh, I don't think so, ma'am. Several others in the club have made matches and are engaged to marry, and I don't have a beau at the moment. But I'm in no hurry," she added in the most carefree tone she could manage. She wouldn't want Mrs. Detwiler to guess that her words had made Sarah remember Jesse, her fiancé who hadn't returned from the war.

"Pshaw," the older woman retorted. "A pretty girl like you? You should have beaux by the dozen. Why don't you see if you can catch the bouquet when your sister throws it, hmm?"

"I—I'll see what I can do," Sarah mumbled, feeling the crimson blush creeping up her neck and into her cheeks. "Um…may I present Viscount Greyshaw, the groom's eldest brother?"

Mrs. Detwiler allowed herself to be distracted, and gazed up at the Englishman. "I've never met a real lord before," she burbled. "Am I 'sposed to curtsy?"

Edward Brookfield smiled graciously. "We could just shake hands if you like."

Everywhere she went during the post-wedding festivities, Sarah felt Dr. Walker's gaze upon her—when she helped Milly cut and serve the bridal cake, while she ladled out cups of punch, during her chats with other guests, such as Nicholas's visiting English brothers, the viscount and the vicar.

"So you're going to move into the cottage with Prissy when we come back?" Milly was asking. She and her groom were spending their wedding night in the hotel, then leaving in the morning for a week's honeymoon in Austin.

"Yes, Prissy's very excited about it," she said, seeing her friend laughing and talking across the room with some of the others from the Spinsters' Club. "Well, we'll see how it works out. You'll take me back if I don't like it, won't you?"

"Of course," Milly and Nick said at once, then Milly added, "The ranch will always be your home, too—but I think this will be good for you. Sarah, you *will* write down all your recipes as you promised before you go, won't you? You know them all by heart, but it's not so simple for me."

"You'll do fine," Sarah assured her. "And don't you worry about a thing while you're gone, you two," she said. "I'll keep Josh and the rest of the hands well fed and looked after, I promise you."

"I'd never doubt it," Milly said. "Sarah, who do you keep glaring at?" she said, following the direction of her sister's gaze.

"That…that Yankee!" Sarah sputtered. "He keeps staring at me. He's got nerve, coming here just as if he belonged!"

"We *did* invite the entire town," Milly pointed out mildly, looking surprised and somewhat disappointed at her sister's outburst.

Sarah couldn't blame Milly for her reaction. Sarah *had* always been the meek one, the quiet one. She'd never exhibited such a dislike of anyone, so her open dislike of the doctor was bound to attract her sister's attention.

"And he *is* the new town doctor," Milly added.

Sarah sighed. If Dr. Harkey hadn't been one of the few casualties during the Comanche raid on Founder's Day, when everyone was gathered in town to celebrate, Nolan Walker might have ridden right back out of town after she refused to talk to him. But now it looked as if he was going to stay forever.

"He does rather look like a hungry lion who's spotted a lonely gazelle," Nick said with a grin, after glancing at the man. He turned back to Sarah. "Would you like me to go have a word with him?" he asked, assuming a fierce expression and clenching fists. "You're my sister now, and I won't have blackguards bothering you."

Sarah tried not to laugh at his mock-menacing features and failed. "No, thank you. I'll take care of it," she muttered, rising to her feet.

"Sarah—be nice, please," Milly said in a warning tone. "Just for today, at least."

"I won't challenge him to a duel, I promise," Sarah said, and stalked across the floor full of milling guests.

She saw him watching her advance, as he leaned negligently against the wall in his black frock coat and trousers, sipping a cup of punch.

"I won't have you staring at me," she announced. "Stop it immediately!"

A slow smile spread over Nolan Walker's angular, high-cheekboned face, making him even more handsome than he had been a moment ago, blast the man. "But you're the most beautiful woman in the room, Miss Matthews. You even outshine the bride. So why wouldn't any normal man want to look at you?"

She blinked in astonishment at his audacity, hating the flush that crept up her neck again. "In the South, we're taught staring is ungentlemanly and rude. So I'd like you to desist—please." She resented having to add that polite word.

"Tell me, Miss Matthews, just why *do* you dislike me so much? You hated me on sight."

Not on sight, she thought. *On hearing.* She'd been more than pleased with her first sight of him, happy and relieved that he had proven to be every bit as appealing in person as he had seemed in his letters. Then he'd spoken, dashing her hopes with the evidence of his deception. He was worse than just a Yankee—he was a Yankee who had almost tricked her into caring for him. And yet his outlandish accent was curling around her heart in such a dismaying way.

"I don't *hate* you," she argued. "It's wrong to hate. But it ought to be very obvious why you're not welcome here."

A spark flared in those blue eyes. "I'm not? Your sister invited me here today. The other single ladies speak to me. Townspeople with ailments and injuries have shown no hesitation to come to my office. The South is a hospitable region, I've always been told, and so I'm finding it here. Only you, Miss Matthews, have been openly hostile to me. Why? Or are you too cowardly to tell me?"

Sarah felt her fists clenching at her sides. She took a quick look around her, to make sure no one else was watching them, but the other conversations buzzed on, unabated. Even Milly's face was turned away from them, however Sarah suspected that to be a deliberate act on Milly's part rather than lack of curiosity.

Sarah drew herself up. "This is neither the time nor the place," Sarah said, falling back on her dignity.

"So you will tell me, some other time?" he challenged, his blue eyes dueling with hers, and finally, making her look away first.

"If it's so important to you."

"Oh, it is, I assure you, Miss Matthews, or we would not be having this conversation. But I have a suggestion to make to you."

"And that is—?" she asked, wary. He was leading her into a trap.

"Why don't we make a truce, just for today, at this special occasion? Your sister's been giving us these worried little glances the whole time we've been talking."

Sarah jerked her head around, only to see that Milly was in deep conversation with Nick's middle brother, Richard. Was Dr. Walker lying about Milly, in an effort to make Sarah feel guilty?

"Why don't we agree to be civil, even pleasant, to one another today?" Dr. Walker went on. "We can go back to being best enemies tomorrow, if you like."

"'Best enemies?'" she repeated, and sternly smothered an impulse to laugh. "What an absurd man you are, Dr. Walker! Very well, just for today I'll pretend I don't wish you'd ride out of town and never come back."

She'd thought her last words would make him flinch, but he only grinned. "If you mean it, you have to agree to dance with me, Miss Matthews. Just one dance."

Chapter Two

She opened her mouth to reply—to refuse, Nolan was sure—but she was interrupted by Prissy Gilmore, who dashed up to Sarah and tugged at her arm.

"Sarah, come on! Your sister's going to throw her bouquet!"

Sarah looked back at him, as if she still might toss off a refusal before joining the gathering group of women and girls in the far corner of the church social hall, but he spoke before she could.

"You won't catch it," he told her, as if it was an accomplished fact.

His words stopped her, made her go rigid—just as he expected.

"Oh? And why is that, Dr. Walker?" she inquired, giving each word chilly emphasis.

He gestured at the women. "Look at them. Lots of tall ladies there. Besides, you don't want it badly enough."

As he'd hoped, she responded to his words as if they had been a dare. Raising her chin, she demanded, "Is that so? Well, we'll see about *that.*" She whirled around and caught up with Prissy.

He grinned when the mayor's daughter, unnoticed by Sarah, smiled conspiratorially at him over her shoulder.

"Prissy" was short for Priscilla, he knew, but what an inaccurate nickname. There was nothing the least bit prim and proper about the cheerful, outgoing girl. She'd been so kind to him after Sarah had taken to him in such dislike the day he came to town, and had helped him save face by letting him escort her to the picnic. He guessed with a little effort on his part, she would have been willing for him to court her instead. But it had been just his luck that the moment he had spotted the willowy golden Sarah, he'd lost his heart.

He wished it wasn't so. It made no sense. He'd never been one to chase disdainful women just to see if he could change their minds about him, merely because it was a challenge. But he'd begun falling in love with Sarah Matthews when he'd read her letters, and once he'd laid eyes on Sarah, Prissy Gilmore could be nothing more than a friend to him—and he was glad to have her friendship, for he sensed that she'd be willing to do whatever she could to help him win Sarah.

He wasn't sure anything would work, though. He faced the fact that he might eventually have to give up and admit Sarah would never do more than despise him. And then he'd have a choice to make—stay in town and watch her choose someone else in time, or leave Simpson Creek and go back home to Maine. He had no one there any longer who mattered to him, though.

Did she hate him because he was a Yankee? Was that all there was to it, a rebel Southerner's reflexive dislike because he'd been part of the Union army?

Nolan had been charmed by her first letter, introducing herself as a representative of the ladies who'd advertised for bachelors for the small Texas town. He knew he ought to have told her which side he'd fought on in one of the letters he'd written from his friend Jeff's home in Brazos County. But he'd been aware of enough anti-Yankee sentiment in Texas to think he'd have a much better chance of acceptance if Sarah got to know *him* first through his letters. They were getting along very well as long as they communicated by letter, but as soon as he'd uttered his first syllables in her hearing, she'd backed away in disgust.

He sighed, watching as the guests fell silent, and the bride turned her back to the clump of unmarried ladies of all ages and heights. Sarah had made her way to the front. He thought he saw her dart a glance in his direction, but then the bride made a few feints at throwing her flowers, and Sarah Matthews became all business, staring at the silk bouquet with the intensity of a sheepdog spotting a straying ewe.

Milly flung the bouquet, and Sarah leaped for it, catching it despite the efforts of a taller girl behind her trying to lean forward and snatch the prize while it was still airborne. The bride ran over and embraced her sister, followed by the groom, while everyone cheered and gathered around them. Sarah was soon hidden from his sight—but not before he saw her shoot him a triumphant look.

It was a start, he thought. Even if she'd sought his

gaze only to mock him, it was better than the icy way she had ignored him ever since he'd arrived in town. Now she had caught the bouquet, though, and tradition decreed that meant she would be the next to be married.

"And now we'll have the throwing of the garter," Prissy announced, cupping her hands to project her voice over the hum of conversation. "Would all the unmarried men please gather at this end of the room?"

Nolan walked toward the gathering throng made up of grinning young boys, a couple of graybeards and men whom he knew were courting various members of the Spinsters' Club. As he approached, he spotted the new Mrs. Brookfield and her husband leave the social hall, but by the time he had positioned himself behind a short youth not old enough to grow a beard, they had returned. Smiling, Nicholas Brookfield waved a circlet of blue, lace-trimmed ribbon over his head.

"Catch it, Pete!" called one of the bridesmaids, the one who had been standing next to the English lord in the receiving line. "I want us to get married next!"

A dark-haired fellow on the left side of the group called back, "I'll try, sweetheart!" and everyone laughed.

Nolan surveyed the crowd. Was Sarah watching? She was, and pretending not to care, he noticed with amusement.

The Englishman turned his back to them, just as his bride had done to the ladies. "Good luck, gentlemen!" he cried. "Who'll be the next lucky groom?"

Nolan dared a wink at Sarah, but before he could see her reaction, Nick Brookfield tossed the garter. It flew through the air, and Nolan launched himself upward as the tiny missile flew straight and true as if the groom had been aiming it precisely at him.

And perhaps he had. Brookfield met his gaze and grinned as Nolan waved the bit of ribbon and lace above everyone's heads as they applauded and clapped him on the back.

"Thanks," Nolan murmured, handing the garter back to Brookfield, who returned it to his blushing bride before turning back to him.

"Don't mention it, old fellow. And don't give up. Sarah's a good woman—I think you'll find she'll be worth a bit of persistence on your part."

Nolan's eyes sought and found Sarah, who was watching him with an unreadable expression on her face. Then she turned away, pretending a great interest in something her sister was saying to her.

It means nothing, Sarah told herself. She wasn't a believer in omens, so there was no significance to Nolan Walker catching the garter as she had the bouquet. It was all just part of the traditional tomfoolery at weddings. Catching the bouquet or garter guaranteed nothing. Anyone could see that Caroline Wallace and Pete Collier would be the next bride and groom, despite not winning those prizes.

At the opposite end of the room, the fiddlers were tuning up for the dancing. She supposed she *would* have to dance with the cursed Yankee, if only to spare herself the scene that might follow if she refused.

The first dance, of course, was the bride and groom's dance, and the musicians struck up a waltz. Sarah forgot all about the Yankee while watching

Nicholas Brookfield, her new brother-in-law, whirl her sister ever so gracefully across the floor as if they had been dancing together all their lives.

They were so perfect for each other, she thought, seeing the loving way Nick gazed down at her sister, and she up at him as if no one else existed in the universe. She felt the sting of tears in her eyes. She remembered how he had only had eyes for Milly from the first day he had arrived. *Lord, please grant them a long and happy life together, and lots of children.*

She felt a twinge of aching sadness, too. Milly's happiness also meant changes for Sarah's life. It would never again be Milly and Sarah, two sisters alone against the world. Milly now had a husband to tell her deepest hopes and secrets to. *Please, Lord, if You see fit, find me a husband, too, a good man who also loves You. I know that if it's Your will for me to marry, You'll send a man who's neither a liar nor a Yankee!*

Almost against her will, her eyes searched the hall for Nolan Walker, but she didn't see him. Had he left? *Good*, she thought fiercely. She could relax and enjoy herself if she knew he wasn't here to plague her any more.

Then someone tapped her on the shoulder. She started, giving an involuntary cry that came out soundng remarkably like a mouse's squeak, thinking Dr. Walker had managed to circle his way around to her without her noticing his approach and was now claiming his dance. But it was only Edward, Viscount Greyshaw.

"Oh, I *do* beg your pardon, Miss Sarah," he said, looking as startled by her reaction as she felt. "I—I didn't mean to take you unaware. It's time for us to join in, I believe," he said, nodding toward the pair still waltzing in the middle of the hall.

"O-of course," she said, giving a weak laugh. "I didn't mean to jump. I'm afraid I was so intent on watching my sister and your brother dance, I didn't see you coming."

"They *do* make a handsome couple, don't they?"

Fitting her gloved hand to his, she joined him on the floor, thankful that she had lately practiced with Nick and could give a competent accounting of herself. It would not do to tread on a lord's feet.

In a few moments, Caroline Wallace and her counterpart among the groomsmen, Richard Brookfield, joined them in their waltzing, and then Prissy and old Josh, the foreman of their ranch. They certainly made an odd couple, the old cowboy and the young, vivacious Prissy, and Sarah knew that old Josh would have rather faced a horde of Comanches again than be dancing in a fancy frock coat. But Nick had become like a son to him, so he'd been honored when Nick and Milly had asked him to be in the wedding. Sarah saw him laughing at something Prissy had just said, and figured Prissy's lively chatter was keeping Josh's self-consciousness at bay.

A Virginia reel followed next. Lord Edward remained with her, remarking, "You know, we call this one 'Roger de Coverley' at home." He was a good dancer, and so was his younger brother, Richard, who claimed her for the Schottische which followed. He drew back when a square dance was called after that, though, unfamiliar with the American dance. Josh came to Sarah's side and asked her to partner him.

Sarah had seen Dr. Walker in the crowd during the waltz, and when the band struck up the reel, she saw him ask Jane Jeffries, one of the Spinsters who had been widowed by the war, to dance. To Sarah's surprise, Jane accepted, a smile lighting her usually somber face. *Didn't she know that Dr. Walker had served in the same army responsible for her husband's death?*

Nolan sat out the Schottische, taking a chair next to Maude Harkey, another of the Spinsters. Maude wasn't dancing tonight, for she still wore deep mourning for the death of her father, Dr. Harkey. How did Maude feel, speaking to the man who had taken her father's place as town physician? Yet she seemed pleased that Dr. Walker had sat down with her.

How kind of him to keep Maude company since she can't dance tonight, a voice within Sarah whispered, but Sarah firmly squelched it. *He probably just feels guilty that he's the town doctor only because her father died.*

Sarah was even more surprised to see him up again when the square dancing began, partnering Faith Bennett. *Well, aren't you the ladies' man?* The spiteful thought distracted her and caused her to stumble in the "Allemande left" the caller announced.

Pay attention to your steps, Sarah. Did you expect him to gaze longingly at you until he finally gathers his courage to claim his dance? Of course she wasn't jealous, she told herself. One wasn't jealous over someone one didn't want. His behavior just proved he was a liar and a deceiver—a typical Yankee, in short!

Chapter Three

The lead fiddler announced the last dance of the night, a waltz. After this, Milly and Nick would go to the hotel for the night, and the guests would all disperse to their homes.

By this time, Sarah's nerves were raw, expecting at the beginning of every dance that Dr. Walker would come to claim her, but so far he hadn't. She had not lacked for partners, for someone else always asked her, but dancing with others did not mean she avoided him. Every dance but the waltz meant being passed to other dancers for at least a few seconds. Still, Dr. Walker had seemed intent on charming every woman in town except her.

Once, he had even managed to get Mrs. Detwiler up on the floor, and the older lady had clearly enjoyed it, though she was red faced and out of breath by the end of it. Sarah saw him fetching her punch while she sat and fanned herself. Sarah wouldn't have minded spending some time in a chair herself, being fetched a cool drink, for her feet were aching from all the dancing and her hair had long since fallen from its elegant knot.

Now, though, she felt a kinship with the gazelle Nick had mentioned earlier as she saw Dr. Walker crossing the floor toward her.

"My dance, I believe?"

"Are you sure you've danced with every other female in town, from the oldest to the youngest?" Sarah asked archly.

He raised a brow, and in that moment she knew she'd made a mistake.

"Ah, so you were watching," he said, grinning.

"I most certainly was not," Sarah insisted. "I never sat down myself, except when the musicians took a break. I only just realized that you hadn't made good your threat to claim a dance."

"Threat?" he echoed. "I believe I only *requested* a dance, as proof of your goodwill. And I was waiting for a waltz, Miss Matthews."

"Oh? Why?" she asked. *Was this girl asking the daring questions really herself?*

Again, the raised brow. "If you have to ask that, Miss Sarah Matthews, then it's no wonder the South lost the war."

She felt herself flushing so hotly that it took all her strength of will not to open the fan that dangled from her wrist and start using it. "If we stand here arguing all through the dance, Dr. Walker, we will miss it altogether."

The couples had just arranged themselves on the floor, and the fiddlers had struck only the first notes, but he took her hand without another word and led her onto the floor. In a moment they were gliding over the floor with the rest of the dancers.

Sarah saw Milly, waltzing with Nick, watching her,

her smile even brighter than before because her sister was dancing with the Yankee doctor. *Good for you,* Milly mouthed. She probably thought Sarah and Dr. Walker had agreed to bury the hatchet. Sarah smiled back, not wanting Milly to worry that she'd only agreed to postpone the battle, not call it off.

She found to her surprise Nolan Walker was an excellent dancer, better even than the Brookfield brothers, who had probably been taught to waltz in their English nursery. His steps were so smooth he made it easy to follow him, so she was never in any danger of treading on his toes.

"Thank you, Miss Matthews," he said when the last notes died away and the other couples drifted off the floor. "I enjoyed that very much."

She couldn't say she'd enjoyed it as well; she'd been too conscious of his nearness and his gaze trained on her the whole time. "You're welcome, Dr. Walker. You…you're an accomplished dancer," she said, determined to give credit where it was due.

"Surprised?" he asked. "I assure you, Miss Matthews, we Yankees do not all live in caves, coming out only to devour raw fish."

Before she could catch it, her mouth fell open at his gibe. "Are you making fun of me, sir?"

He grinned. "Not at all. I was only teasing you, my thorny Southern rose."

How could one man be so infuriating? "I'm not 'your' anything, Dr. Walker. And now that you've had your dance with me, you must excuse me while I go see if my sister needs any help before she leaves."

"Very well, but don't forget about that talk we're going to have."

His blue eyes dared her to claim she didn't remember what he was talking about, but Sarah was not a dishonest person and she remembered all too well that he'd demanded she tell him sometime why she was so hostile to him.

"Oh, I won't. I'll look forward to it," she said.

He bowed, but Sarah felt his gaze on her as she walked away.

The next morning, Sarah met Nick's visiting brothers outside the church. The newlyweds were not with them, but Sarah hadn't really expected them to be up this early. They were to meet after church in the hotel's restaurant for Sunday dinner. After that, the newlyweds would depart for Austin in a specially hired coach, accompanied by Edward and Richard, who would pay their respects to the embassy branch in the Texas capital before journeying back to the coast and boarding a ship for home.

"A pity my wife's so near her time," Lord Greyshaw remarked as they walked up the steps that led into the church. "She'd have loved your Texas, Sarah." Amelia, Viscountess Greyshaw, was only a couple months from delivering their second child. It had been felt the ocean voyage and overland travel would be too risky for her, and Richard's wife, Gwenneth, had remained at Greyshaw to keep her company in their husbands' absence and to watch over Violet, their younger sister.

"Yes, such mild weather, for late autumn, to be sure," Richard agreed, looking up appreciatively at the blue sky. "At home we'd be gathered around the hearth complaining of the dank cold."

"Oh, it'll get colder closer to Christmas," Sarah replied. “Every few winters, it actually snows. You gentlemen must come again and bring your wives and children.”

“Eddie’s already taken me to task for not bringing him,” Lord Edward said, grinning as he mentioned his son. “He’d like to meet a wild Indian. Oh, dear,” he murmured, seeing the shudder Sarah hadn’t been able to suppress. “I do apologize. I had forgotten all about the attack. How dreadfully clumsy of me.”

“That’s all right,” Sarah said, gazing behind the church where, on Founder’s Day, the Comanches had come galloping across the creek and into the town. “Hopefully, now that we have the fort, it won’t happen again. There’s a cavalry regiment that patrols the area regularly and in any case, the Comanches are in their winter quarters now, up on the Llano Estacado, the Staked Plains. We’d better go in, gentlemen,” Sarah said, as the bell began to toll from the steeple above them. She played the piano for the services every Sunday and knew Reverend Chadwick would be waiting on her to begin the service.

She was relieved to see that once more, Dr. Nolan Walker did not grace a pew. She had never seen him attending services since his arrival in Simpson Creek. *He must be an unbeliever. Just one more reason not to be friendly to him.*

Sarah would have been surprised to know that Dr. Walker was seeing a patient in his office at this very hour.

“Th-thank you for seeing me at this time, Doctor,” said the pale, mousy little woman who’d entered his waiting room. "I—I wouldn't want to come when you had other patients coming and going…."

She'd knocked so softly at his door he almost hadn't heard her from his quarters behind the office. He had only just arisen from bed, the tolling of the church bell having awakened him from the sleep he'd finally achieved at dawn.

"And why is that, Miss Spencer? Surely you have a right to consult a physician as much as anyone else in Simpson Creek."

"I… I don't want anyone to know I'm seeing a doctor," she whispered, eyes downcast. "They might wonder why. I—I'm expecting a child, you see."

He looked at her quickly. If Miss Ada Spencer was pregnant, it was not obvious, as yet. But that explained the reason for the furtive visit, if it was true.

"Are you certain? That you're…ah, with child?" he said, wondering for the thousandth time why women in this day and age spoke of it in hushed tones or euphemisms and couldn't use the correct term for something which was, after all, a natural thing and should be a happy event—unless, of course, a woman was unmarried.

"Yes, I'm sure," she insisted, and told him all the symptoms she had been having.

"I'll need to examine you," he said. "Would you be more comfortable if there was another woman present? Would you like to come back when you can bring someone?"

Still looking down, she shook her head. "I haven't told Ma," she said. "She'd be ashamed of me. She'd want me to keep to home now that I've 'disgraced' myself. She's in church now, so she doesn't know I'm here."

Was Mrs. Spencer a church-going hypocrite, praying for the heathen in Africa while oblivious to the trouble within her own house? He was familiar with the type, but he hadn't met the woman so he shouldn't assume that was the case. Did Ada Spencer have no friends, then? But perhaps she had no one with whom she was willing to trust her secret.

"I just want to make sure the baby's healthy," she murmured, glancing timidly up at him, then away again.

"Where is the father?" he asked, careful to keep his tone neutral.

"Dead," Ada said, her tone as lifeless as the word. "He died when the Comanches attacked in October."

"I see." Simpson Creek had suffered half a dozen casualties that memorable day he'd arrived. And now there would be a child born who would never know his father because of it, and a woman who might be bowed down with shame the rest of her life. "I'm sorry."

A tear trickled down Ada's sallow face. "He wasn't going to do right by me anyway," she said. "He was leaving town that morning. It was his bad luck he happened to run into those savages."

Nolan remembered the man who'd appeared at the church, tied onto his horse, who'd lived only long enough to give a few moments' warning of the impending raid.

"And what do you plan to do, Miss Spencer? It's none of my business, of course, but if you stay around town, people will eventually know that you're with child. Have you considered relocating to another town—even another state, where you could say you were a widow?"

Again, she shook her head. "Ma and Pa are old. I'm the only one left at home to take care of them. They won't turn me out, even once they know."

But they won't give her emotional support, either. He sighed, and wished he had a nurse he could call on to be present.

"Very well, let's have a look," he said, opening the door to his exam room and beckoning her inside.

Afterward, he waited for her at his desk in the adjoining room.

"If you're expecting, it's very early," he said, after she came in and sat down. "At this stage, I can't be certain. When did you…that is…" He stopped, aware of the awkwardness of his question and wishing he could just spit it out instead of having to dance delicately around the point. He'd been so much more comfortable around soldiers, saying what he meant without having to think about it so carefully.

"In September," she said, thankfully sparing him having to come up with another euphemism. "It…it was only once or twice…."

Nolan Walker sighed. Obviously once or twice had been enough. It was useless to wish the dead man had behaved honorably and married the girl before leaving her with child and getting himself killed.

She wasn't a bad-looking woman, he thought, though in her present depressed, shame-faced state it would be hard for a man to see her better qualities. How did one go about suggesting to a woman in this predicament that if she held her head high and was pleasant and charming, some good man might well come to accept her *and* the coming baby?

Ah, well. He was a physician, not a counselor or matchmaker. Perhaps he could persuade her to trust Reverend Chadwick with her secret. The minister seemed like a decent man who wouldn't shame this poor woman still further, but could give her good advice. And perhaps in time, she would trust one of her friends enough to enlist another's company at her appointments with him, if her mother wasn't willing once she knew the truth. Ada Spencer belonged to that Spinsters' Club, didn't she? So she must have some acquaintances, at least. He'd feel a lot more comfortable when he needed to examine Miss Spencer if she brought another female with her.

"Very well, Miss Spencer," he said. "If all goes well between now and sometime in the middle of June, I see no reason that you cannot deliver a strong healthy child. I'll need to see you a few times before then, of course."

"The middle of June? That's when my baby will come?" A spark of joy lit the woman's narrow face, and he marveled. Even while she risked disgrace, a woman could find joy in the thought of a coming baby.

"Based on what you told me about when the child was conceived, yes. Though babies, of course, have a mind of their own and can come earlier or later than when a physician predicts."

"Thank you, Doctor."

"You're quite welcome, Miss Spencer." He rose to

indicate the appointment was over, and she moved quickly toward the door.

"Oh, and Miss Spencer," he said, trying to make his request sound casual, "why don't you bring a friend with you next time you come? I'm sure it would be wiser for the sake of your reputation." *And mine.*

She looked back at him, then bolted out the door without another word.

Chapter Four

"My message," Reverend Chadwick began, "is one I have felt compelled to preach today, the subject of forgiveness. Certainly this is a timely subject, in view of the recent national conflict that nearly tore our country in two forever. Maybe the Lord wanted me to speak on this because *one person* present is struggling to forgive another. But really, it doesn't matter whether one person or twenty needs to hear it. I take my text from Matthew Chapter Eighteen, in which Peter is asking Jesus how many times he should forgive his brother."

Sarah winced inwardly. Of all the subjects for the pastor to preach about! And just after she had been thinking that his failure to attend church served as an additional reason why Dr. Nolan Walker deserved neither her forgiveness nor her friendship…

Reverend Chadwick went on to describe how Jesus had decreed one should forgive seventy times seven. "Now, does the Lord mean we are only to forgive four hundred and ninety times? No, dear people, He means *infinitely.* If we don't forgive, we aren't forgiven—simple as that."

Sarah shifted uncomfortably in the pew, hoping the elegant Lord Edward and his kindly brother Richard didn't notice. The white-haired pastor seemed to be speaking straight to her, though he wasn't looking in her direction.

"In fact," Reverend Chadwick went on, "the Bible goes so far as to say if we take our gift to the altar, and discover we have something against our brother, we're to go and make things right with him first."

Very well, then. She had brought a tithe of her profits from her bakery sales to put in the collection plate, but she'd hold on to the coins until she'd had a chance to speak to Dr. Walker. That was the right thing to do. It wouldn't be easy—much would depend on how he responded, but surely Pastor Chadwick's choice of this topic meant that she was to forgive Nolan Walker for serving with the Union Army. She could pay him a visit this very afternoon, after she and the Brookfield brothers met with the Milly and Nick for dinner and she saw them all off to Austin. After all, she was already in town, and had left dinner on the stove for the cowhands, so she didn't have to get back to the ranch soon.

She sighed, at peace with herself now, and admitted she was even looking forward to seeing the blue-eyed doctor and hearing him talk in that outlandish accent again. With some difficulty, she forced her attention back to the sermon.

"Time to go see the newlyweds," Edward murmured, after they had shaken hands with Reverend

Chadwick and had spoken with several members of the congregation.

"Yes. I think marriage will be good for Nicholas, especially marriage to your dear sister," Richard told Sarah. "He's made an excellent choice. Just think, Edward, now there's only Violet for us to see safely married…."

"As she's hardly out of the schoolroom, I hope that will be some time from now," his brother said, but Sarah was no longer listening.

Instead of gazing down the main street of Simpson Creek to her right, toward the hotel where they would meet Nick and Milly for dinner, she had glanced to her left, where a low white picket fence surrounded the doctor's office.

Just as she looked, the door opened. Perhaps Nolan had peered out, seen her emerge from the church and was coming to greet them? Perhaps she could say something to indicate she would like to talk to him later?

But instead of Nolan Walker, she saw a female figure emerge, glance furtively at the townspeople strolling away from church, then turn away and walk quickly down the alley that ran past the side of the doctor's office. A dark bonnet hid her features as soon as the woman turned her head, but in those brief seconds when she had been facing toward the church, Sarah recognized Ada Spencer.

What is she doing there? Doctors don't have office hours on Sunday mornings. Therefore she must have been there for a completely nonmedical purpose.

Thinking about Ada's secretive manner, Sarah was suddenly sure the two had been Up to No Good.

She thought back to the summer, when Ada had been giddy with excitement over being courted by that Englishman Harvey Blakely. Blakely had come to try to blackmail Nicholas about his past or, if he wouldn't cooperate, to expose Nick's disgrace in India, but after failing to discredit Nick, Harvey had been the first casualty on the day of the Comanche attack. Ada had been a virtual recluse ever since, and never came to the Spinsters' Club meetings. When she thought about her, at all, Sarah had assumed Ada was still mourning her English beau, scoundrel that he had been. In the excitement of her sister's wedding, Sarah had forgotten all about Ada.

Now, though, it seemed that Ada had set her cap at a new bachelor, and perhaps Nolan Walker was all too willing to meet with the vulnerable woman in his office at a time when they wouldn't likely be interrupted by patients.

They probably hadn't even remained in the office. Behind it was the doctor's private living quarters—Sarah knew this from her long friendship with Maude Harkey, the late doctor's daughter and also a member of the Spinsters' Club who had shared those quarters with her father until his death in the Comanche attack. When Dr. Walker had taken over as town physician, he had been offered the space, and Maude had moved in with a married sister in town.

Sarah's heart sank. Though she had been looking forward to clearing the air with Dr. Nolan Walker, and perhaps more, she knew now she had been right all along about him.

Dr. Walker was nothing but a Yankee opportunist—little short of a carpetbagger. And now, it seemed, he was a womanizer as well, and was engaged in an improper relationship with a woman who had already proven she was more than willing to go to any lengths to have a suitor.

Resolutely, Sarah turned her face away from the doctor's office, and gazed directly ahead of her toward the hotel. She'd go straight home after her dinner with Milly and her new husband. She'd cook a fine supper for the cowhands and perhaps begin planning for her move to the cottage she would be sharing soon with Prissy.

It was a good thing she'd found out about Dr. Walker's true character before she'd made a fool of herself. Perhaps she should warn the others in the Spinsters' Club, she thought, firmly ignoring the ache in her heart.

The time had gone by quickly. Milly and Nick had arrived home December 23, and Sarah welcomed them back with a wonderful supper.

"Oh, Sarah, why don't you stay till after New Year's?" Milly said the morning after Christmas. "It doesn't seem right, your moving out right now. Why not stay till then?"

"It was a wonderful Christmas, wasn't it?" Sarah said. "Your first one as husband and wife," she said, smiling at the couple across the table. "But Milly, I can't keep putting it off. Today's the perfect day. Bobby and Isaiah are already set to load up the buckboard right after breakfast, aren't you?"

Down the table, the two cowhands nodded.

Sarah looked forward to sharing the cottage with Prissy, for her lively and vivacious friend knew no strangers. It would be fun teaching Prissy how to cook and manage a household. And what would it be like, not having to cook three square meals a day for hungry cowboys, and hitch up the horse whenever she had baked goods to deliver?

An hour later, all was in readiness for her departure.

"Now remember, you—"

"Can always come back," Sarah finished for Milly, from her perch on the driver's seat of the wagon loaded with her bed and chest of drawers, as well as a pair of chairs Milly said she could spare. "I know. And perhaps I will, after I teach Prissy a few basic kitchen and housekeeping skills."

"She couldn't possibly be any slower to learn to cook than I was," Milly said. "Now, with the fried chicken, you dip it in the beaten eggs, *then* the flour and spices, right?" She was to cook her first dinner without help tonight, and she'd already admitted she was nervous about it.

"Right. Actually, I'm more worried about teaching Prissy how to launder clothes than the cooking," Sarah said. "She still thinks doing the laundry consists of handing her dirty clothes to the housekeeper. But don't worry, your first supper will be fine."

"Of course it will, darling," said Nick, who'd been helping Bobby and Isaiah load the wagon. He put an arm affectionately around his wife's waist.

Sarah watched them with a certain wistfulness. She was so happy for her sister, yet wondered if she would ever know this happiness herself.

She straightened and nodded to Bobby, sitting next to her and holding the reins, and Isaiah, who waited on his horse beside them. They were coming along to help her move her furniture into the cottage. "We're burning daylight, as Josh would say. I reckon we'd better get going."

By noon, the men had unloaded everything on the wagon, placed it all wherever Sarah and Prissy had directed in the little cottage, rid the house of a mouse that had sent Prissy shrieking in panic out into the yard and departed. Now Sarah and Prissy sat down and enjoyed the sandwiches Sarah had packed for their midday meal.

"It's shaping up well, isn't it?" Prissy said, surveying with satisfaction the room that served as a combined dining area and parlor. They had arranged the round oak table between the kitchen and the couch and chairs, and there was a fireplace along the back wall. Behind the dining room and parlor, a short hallway divided the two bedrooms.

"Small, but cozy," Sarah agreed. "But I just realized something I should have thought of before..."

"What's that?"

"Now that I'm here, I won't have the wagon to deliver my baked goods to the hotel and mercantile. It's a lot to carry, so I'm either going to make at least a couple of trips back and forth to the cottage, or—"

"I could help you carry your pies and cakes," Prissy offered.

"Thanks, but it's not fair for you to have to do that several times a week. I think I'll just go see if Mr. Patterson has a little pull-cart he could trade me for this week's pies." She arose, and took her woolen shawl and bonnet from the pegs by the door. "I need to discuss with him and the hotel owner when I can start delivering again, anyway." She had notified her customers she would not be baking again till after the move. "Do you want to come with me?"

"No, I think I'll work on arranging my bedroom," Prissy said. She stretched and rubbed the small of her back. "I have a feeling my bed's going to feel very good tonight, after all the boxes we've been carrying and the furniture we've been arranging and rearranging. Oh, and while you're there, would you look and see if they have anything lighter for curtain material? Mama's castoff damask curtains are just too dark and heavy for this room, don't you think?"

Sarah nodded her agreement. "I'll look at the bolts of cloth while I'm there. Perhaps a dotted swiss..." Sewing was Milly's area of expertise, but surely she could sew a simple pair of gathered curtains.

It only took her five minutes to walk from the cottage on the grounds of the mayor's property, out the wrought-iron gates and down Simpson Creek's main street to the mercantile. The weather was cool, and lowering clouds in the north promised colder weather still, perhaps even a "blue norther." Might they even have some snow? It was too bad it had not come in time for Christmas, if so...

Distracted by her thoughts, she didn't remember

to look out for the warped board that lay halfway between the hotel and the mercantile—

—and suddenly she was falling headlong, her arms flailing in a vain attempt to regain her balance. She cried in alarm as her shawl slid off backward and her forearms skidded along the rough boards. The fabric of her left sleeve snagged on a protruding nail which sliced a three-inch furrow into the tender flesh of her arm, leaving stinging pain in its wake.

And blood. A crimson trickle, then a rivulet welled up from the lacerated flesh, staining the cloth. Dizzy and nauseated at the sight, she closed her eyes, hoping she was not about to faint.

Then there were voices and running footsteps from inside the store, and a pounding on the boards as someone ran up the walk from behind her. "Miss Matthews! Are you all right? I saw you fall."

Sarah recognized the voice of Mr. Patterson, the owner of the mercantile. She heard another voice asking, "Wait, don't try to move her. Can you hear me, Miss Matthews?" She recognized that voice, too—that of the very last person she wanted to have witnessed her humiliation, Dr. Nolan Walker.

Her recognition galvanized her and kept her from giving into the blackness that she might well have surrendered to otherwise. She opened her eyes. "Of course I can. I'm fine. Just…give me a minute."

She opened her eyes, and saw that he was kneeling beside her.

"Can you move your limbs, Miss Matthews?"

"Of course I can," she said again, and to prove it, struggled to sit up.

"Wait. Just lie there a moment, get your bearings." he commanded her, coolly professional. "Lift your head." He wrenched off his coat, and laid it under her head.

"I assure you, Dr. Walker, I *have* my bearings."

He ignored her. "Mr. Patterson, could you please get me some clean cloths and water?"

By now a trio of curious cowboys riding by, and a couple of small boys who'd been shooting marbles across the street, had stopped to gawk at her, and she felt her face flaming with embarrassment. "Please, I don't want to be a public spectacle." She reached out a hand. "And it's cold. Help me inside."

"Very well, just sit up for a moment, don't rush—"

She was not about to act the fragile, swooning belle in front of this man. Paying no heed to his injunction, Sarah used his hand to pull herself to her feet. Then she accidentally caught a glimpse of her bloody sleeve. Her head swam, and the black mist threatened to swamp her again. If only she had a vial of smelling salts in her reticule, as proper ladies did! Suppressing a shudder, she looked away from her injured arm and allowed Dr. Walker to help her into the mercantile.

Inside the store, Mr. Patterson had set out a chair in front of the counter, and Mrs. Patterson bustled about, setting a bowl of water and some folded cloths on top of the flat surface.

She sank gratefully into the chair, and felt the soothing, cool wetness of the cloth the mercantile owner's wife wiped on her forehead, murmuring, "You poor dear, that was a nasty fall!"

"Thank you, Mrs. Patterson, I—I'll be all right,"

she felt compelled to say, though she still wasn't completely certain.

"You'll want to look away," she heard Dr. Walker saying, as he peeled back the blood-stained, ripped sleeve from her injury. He then took another cloth and soaked it in the water, wrung it out, used it to sponge the blood away. The cut stung like a hundred red ants were biting her at once, and Sarah bit her lip, determined not to cry out.

Then Dr. Walker patted it dry, and used a long dry cloth to wrap around her arm, ripping one end of it into two strips to tie it expertly, binding the bandage.

She had to admire his cool professional manner. He'd done it all in less time than it took for Mrs. Patterson to stop clucking over her.

"Thank you, Dr. Walker," she said, standing. "I—I appreciate what you've done. I'm sure it will heal up nicely now." She'd have to return another day to see about the curtains and the wagon. Right now she wanted nothing more than to escape his gaze and that of the Pattersons and go back to the cottage. She'd doubted he'd accept payment for his impromptu doctoring, but perhaps she could bring him a cake by way of thanks.

"It's a blessing he was there," Mrs. Patterson murmured in agreement.

"Oh, I'm not done, Miss Matthews. That's a nasty gash you have, and it's going to need proper disinfectant and some stitches to heal properly. You need to come down to the office with me where I can do it properly."

Her eyes flew open. “Oh, I’m sure that’s not necessary,” she protested.

“And I’m sure it is. Come along, Miss Matthews,” he said, tucking her uninjured arm in his.

“But—”

“Best listen to the doctor, dear,” Mrs. Patterson was saying.

“Yes, he’s treated wounds on the battlefield, after all,” her spouse added.

She felt herself being pulled out the door, willy-nilly. She trusted his medical judgment, but she wasn’t sure she was ready to be alone with him, even if she was only a patient to him in this instance.

Chapter Five

His hand under her elbow, and keeping his eyes on her still pale face, Nolan led Sarah carefully down the steps to the street. Behind them, a dog had found the bonanza of apple pie splattered against the wall and on the boardwalk and was happily lapping it up.

It was the coldest day he'd experienced since coming to Texas, but it was still nothing to what the weather would be like in his home state at this time of year. Back in Maine, there might well be a foot of snow on the ground and a bitter wind blowing. Folks would be swathed in heavy coats, hats, boots and knitted scarves. Perhaps he'd miss seeing snow eventually, but right now he savored the warmth of the sun on his face.

Then he felt Sarah shiver.

"Are you cold?" he asked.

"No, I—I'm fine."

Nolan whipped off his frock coat again anyway and settled it around her shoulders over her shawl. She had sand, he thought—real courage and grit. She hadn't given in to her faintness when many ladies would have, but he had to remember she'd just had a traumatic experience and had lost some blood.

Sarah blinked at the gesture, and a little color crept into her cheeks. "Th-thank you."

They said nothing more during the short walk to his office. He ushered her inside, seating her in his exam chair which had a flat surface extending over each arm. He was thankful he'd had sense enough to clean and boil his suturing instruments last night, even though the hour had been late—after he'd finished taking care of a cowboy who'd been cut by flying glass in a ruckus at the saloon. The instruments lay on a metal stand, concealed by a fresh cloth, but he wouldn't bring them out yet.

"I'll be right back. I'm going to put a pot of water on for coffee when we're finished," he said, deliberately not giving her the chance to demur before he walked down the hallway that led to his living quarters. She'd need something hot and bracing when he was done.

Returning, he stepped over to a basin, poured a pitcher of water into it and began to scrub his hands and forearms with a bar of soap, remembering all the times the other field surgeons had made sport of him for what they called his "old maid fussiness" when he was preparing to operate. "I can amputate twice as many legs and arms as you can in half the time, Walker," one of them had boasted. "And I don't use gallons of carbolic, either." News of the use of carbolic acid's role in preventing infection had come from Europe in the last year of the war, but only a few doctors in America believed in it.

"Yes, and you lose most of them to infection days later," he'd retorted, "while most of mine live to recover. So I still come out ahead."

He felt her curious gaze on him, watching as he scrubbed up and down, the harsh lye soap stinging his skin. Then he poured diluted carbolic acid over his hands. When he looked back while he was drying his hands on a clean towel, though, he found her staring at his open rolltop desk. He'd been looking at a small framed daguerreotype he normally left hidden in a drawer, and when he decided to stroll over to the mercantile, he'd absentmindedly left it out on the desk.

"That's my wife and son," he said, when he could find his breath. "They died the summer before the war began."

Her eyes widened and grew sad. "Oh, I'm sorry," she said quickly, then seemed to hesitate, and he knew she was trying a polite way to ask the question.

"Cholera," he said, sparing her the need.

"Oh…how terrible," she murmured. "You had no other children?"

He shook his head, firmly suppressing the old pain within him. "No. Now you're going to have to be brave," he said, knowing his words would distract her from further questions. He brought the bottle of diluted carbolic acid and a basin to the armrest. Pulling a stool over, he sat, then carefully unwrapped the bandage around her arm. He held her arm over the basin, and caught her gaze.

"This is going to sting," he warned. "You want a bullet to bite?"

He'd hoped his little attempt at humor would make

her smile, at least for a moment. but she only shook her head and looked away, putting her other hand to her mouth.

"Go ahead," she whispered.

He poured the carbolic acid over the wound, wincing inwardly as she gasped and clamped her free hand over her mouth.

"Sorry. I don't want you to get blood poisoning or lockjaw from that rusty nail."

After removing the basin, he rolled over the tray of instruments on its stand and unscrewed his jar of boiled catgut suture in alcohol, pulled out a couple lengths and laid them on the stand among his instruments. Then picking up a suture needle, he threaded it.

"This is going to hurt, too, I'm afraid, though not as much as that carbolic."

"Do what you have to do," she said, tight-lipped, her face as white as the unbloodstained part of her bodice.

He bent his head to his task. She couldn't know how much harder this was for him than it had been to suture a soldier's cuts, knowing his touch was inflicting more pain on the very woman he cared about so much. He had to steel himself to ignore her wince each time he inserted the needle into her flesh. Thanks to his experience in battlefield surgery, he was able to close this relatively uncomplicated wound quickly. When he was finished, he looked at his patient.

Her head lay back against the headrest of the chair, her eyes were closed. Pearls of sweat beaded her pale skin.

"I'm done," he said, wondering if he ought to get

out the vial of hartshorn he kept in his desk for swooning ladies. "You were very brave, Miss Matthews."

She opened her eyes and smiled wanly at him. "Thank you."

He saw her dart a glance at the neatly sutured wound before she raised her gaze back to his face.

"This may scar a little," he said, "but not as much as if we'd just bandaged it. And you're going to have to watch it for infection. Any red streaks or swelling or drainage, you come back to see me immediately. I'm going to rebandage it," he said, and took up a roll of linen, which he circled around her forearm and tied by the ends as he had at the store. "Now I'll get that coffee I promised you."

"Oh, but you needn't bother—" she began, but he cut her off.

"No bother, I want some, and I need to see a little more color in those cheeks before I let you out of that chair. If I let you get up now, you'll collapse like a wilted lily." Wishing he could invite her back to his kitchen but knowing it would seem improper to her, he left without waiting to hear any further protests.

He returned a moment later, carrying two sturdy crockery mugs full of steaming coffee.

"I took the liberty of putting sugar in yours," he said. "I didn't know if you take it that way, but you need the sugar for energy right now." Then, a little less certainly, he said, "It's probably a little strong for you. I could get some water—"

"No, it's fine," she assured him. "Josh, our foreman, always says it isn't ranch coffee unless it's so strong the spoon stands up in the cup." She took a tentative sip, then another deeper one before he spoke again.

"Is this a good time to have that talk?"

"T-talk? What talk?" Sarah stammered. She should have known he would take advantage of being alone with her like this to claim the fulfillment of her promise. She could hardly refuse to talk to him, now that he'd played the Good Samaritan and taken care of her wound.

His expression told her that he knew she'd been playing for time to think, that she knew exactly what talk he meant. "The talk you promised me at the wedding, even said you'd look forward to, and have avoided ever since. The talk in which you're going to explain why you don't like me."

"I haven't avoided you," she protested. "I've been very busy at the ranch, what with Milly being off on her honeymoon and all. I haven't come into town except to deliver my pies and cakes, go to church and attend a meeting of the Spinsters' Club."

He raised an eyebrow as if to imply that if she could do all that, she could have made time to talk to him. "So why don't you? Like me, that is. You seemed to like me well enough when we were corresponding, but as soon as you set eyes on me, you no longer did."

Sarah sighed. She was trapped and there was no getting around it. She'd promised to do this and she had to honor her word. She owed him her honesty, at least—but now that it came down to it, and especially after what he'd done for her today, she didn't feel as righteous about her dislike as she had before. Or as certain.

"Perhaps you find me a homely fellow, not much to look at," he ventured, but there was a twinkle in his eye.

She met his gaze head on. "Dr. Walker—"

"Nolan," he corrected her. "We're not speaking as doctor and patient now."

"I'm sure you have some sort of a mirror," Sarah said, "so you know very well you're not ugly." Quite the contrary, she thought, looking into his deep blue eyes and studying his strong, rugged features. She took a deep breath. "All right, but remember you asked to hear this. I didn't like you because you're a Yankee."

Understanding dawned in his eyes. "So you thought well enough of me until I spoke to you."

"Yes, and that's your fault. You never said you were a Yankee. By writing to me from Brazos County, you allowed me to believe you a Texan."

"So you dislike me strictly because I come from the North," he stated. "Doesn't that sound rather arbitrary on your part, seeing as the war's over? As I mentioned, it hasn't prevented the rest of the townsfolk from accepting me. Why is it so important to you?"

Sarah sighed again, steeling herself to the pain of talking about Jesse. "I was engaged to a wonderful man before the war began," she said. "Jesse Holt. He… he died in the war—at least, I have to assume that, since he never came back. The men who did come back said…" She looked down as she struggled to finish. "Sometimes when men were killed, they…they… couldn't be identified."

Nolan's eyes, when she looked up, were unfocused, haunted, as if he was remembering that and worse.

"I loved Jesse," she said simply. "I… I can be your friend, I suppose…that is to say, we don't have to be enemies. But you came in town to court me, isn't that right? How can I keep company with someone who fought with the Union, when they killed my Jesse? And don't tell me that you were just a doctor, caring for the wounded," she said, when she saw he had opened his mouth to speak. *"You wore blue."* All the old grief swept over her, threatening to swamp her, and she bent her head, struggling against tears that escaped anyway. She put a hand to her mouth. "I'm sorry," she said. "I… I thought I was over it."

Now it was Nolan's turn to sigh. "I know," he said, shifting his gaze to the daguerreotype on his desk. "Mostly, I only have pleasant memories about Julia and Timmy…but once in a while someone will walk like her, or a little boy will remind me of him… But I know they wouldn't want me to mourn forever, Sarah."

She noticed he had switched to using her first name, but she didn't correct him.

"It's been over five years now since they died," he said. "I want to go on with my life. I…know it might be too soon for you."

"I wanted to go on with my life, too," she said. "Meet a good man, get married… That's why I agreed to join the Spinsters' Club when my sister started it."

"But you didn't want to meet a Yankee."

She let the statement stand. "You're free to court any of the other ladies in the group, or find someone elsewhere, you know."

"I know," he said. He raised his head to look at her,

and it was a long silent moment before she found the strength to look away.

"We're friends, at least. That's something." He gave her a half smile. "Here's some bandages," he said, reaching inside a box and taking out several rolls of bleached linen. "Keep the arm clean and dry and change the dressing every day. Will you come back in a couple days, so I can satisfy myself that it's healing properly?"

She nodded, thinking she could bring him that cake then, and offer to pay him something, also. "Do you have to take out the stitches?"

He shook his head. "No, they're catgut—made of sheep intestines, really—so they'll absorb on their own inside, and the part that's showing will disintegrate and fall out."

She stared at the bandaged wound and shuddered. "Sheep intestines?"

He chuckled. "I'm sorry. I shouldn't have told you that."

Then he smiled at her, and she was so struck by what a compelling smile he had that she forgot all about sheep and their insides.

Chapter Six

"Oh, Sarah, that looks divinely delicious!" Prissy gushed two days later, watching as Sarah put the finishing touches on her blackberry jam cake with pecan frosting. "Will you teach me how to make that one for the New Year's Day party?"

Sarah looked up from her work, pushing back a stray curl which had escaped from behind her ear. "What New Year's Day party?"

"The one my parents are giving. Remember the afternoon party on New Year's Day my parents always gave before the war? The whole town came, and everyone from the nearby ranches. Papa wants to start having it again as a sign that things really have gotten back to normal. I meant to mention it sooner," Prissy said with an airy wave of her hand. "You know, it's really the last *big* social event till spring for the whole town, if you think about it," Prissy went on. "You can't plan on anything big for certain, what with the unpredictability of winter weather, though we might manage something smaller with the Spinsters' Club, if some candidates show up. *Que sera, sera,* as the French say."

What Prissy was saying was true. The Spinsters' Club had been started in the summer, when it was relatively easy for an interested candidate to travel to Simpson Creek. They had a taffy pull coming up, but that was all until at least March.

Oh, well, it didn't matter to her anyway. Even before her sister had founded the Spinsters' Club, Sarah had been a homebody, content to wait on the Lord to provide her a beau if He willed it so.

"But at least all the ladies of the Spinsters' Club will be coming, and the ones who are being courted will bring their beaux. You never know who might bring an eligible man to the party as a guest," Prissy said, still thinking out loud.

"Oh, and I told Mama we'd bring a couple of desserts." It was a typical Prissy-style change of subject. "Why don't you bake your cherry upside-down cake, and I'll make one like this—" she pointed to the one Sarah was completing "—if you'll teach me, of course."

"Sure I will." Sarah vaguely remembered attending some of those extravagant open-house parties the mayor and his wife had hosted in those halcyon prewar years, though she had barely been old enough to put up her hair before the last of them.

Mentally, she readjusted her plans. She'd been thinking of asking Milly if it was okay if she and Prissy came out to the ranch for dinner for New Year's. Now, of course, she'd have to think about what she was going to wear, as well as making a dessert to contribute. Perhaps Milly and Nick would come into town for the party.

"Or maybe you should make the biscuits. I declare, yours are the lightest, the fluffiest… I don't think I'll *ever* be able to make biscuits like that." Prissy let out a gusty, dramatic sigh.

"Oh, I don't know…the ones you made this morning were…um, much better," Sarah told her with a grin.

"You mean they were almost edible this time, as opposed to the lead sinkers I made last night for dinner," Prissy said, with a rueful laugh. "Your sisters' pigs probably wouldn't eat them."

"It just takes practice. You'll be making fine biscuits before long, I promise."

Prissy seemed reassured. "Is that for the mercantile, or the hotel?" she asked, gesturing at the cake.

"Neither. I promised to see Dr. Walker so he could check my wound, so I'm going to take it with me when I go to the office this morning."

"Ohhhhhhh!" Prissy said, drawing the syllable out, her eyes dancing with glee. "So your heart has thawed toward the handsome Yankee."

"It's done no such thing," Sarah said quickly. "At least not the way *you* mean." She avoided her friend's knowing gaze. "It's just the polite thing to do. He was very kind to me that day."

"Hmm," Prissy murmured, clearly unconvinced by Sarah's casual words. "It must be nice to have a knight in shining armor. Oh! You might as well deliver his invitation to him personally," Prissy said.

"Invitation?"

"To the party, silly. Mama had asked me to take the invitations around town this afternoon, but you can save me that stop, at least."

Before Sarah could say anything else, Prissy dashed into her bedroom and was back in a couple of minutes, waving the cream-colored vellum envelope with its handwritten invitation inside. *Of course Dr. Nolan Walker is to attend the party like everyone else.* Suddenly attending the party had become much more complicated. How was she to act around him?

"So what are you going to wear?" Prissy asked.

Sarah shrugged. "I don't know… I suppose you have a suggestion, now that you've seen the entire contents of my wardrobe?"

Prissy giggled. "I think you should wear that lovely red grenadine dress with the green piping. Very festive. And men like red dresses."

"I don't give a fig what color Dr. Walker likes!"

"Ah, but *I* said 'men.' *You* applied my generalization to Dr. Walker."

Caught. Sarah tightened her lips and glanced at the clock on the mantel as she reached for the cake cover. "This is a silly conversation, Prissy Gilmore," she said primly, "and I'm going to be late if I don't leave now."

The sound of her friend's giggles followed her out into the street.

Really, she was going to have to warn Prissy to cease and desist with her matchmaking efforts, Sarah thought as she walked down the street, avoiding ice-rimmed puddles—she didn't want to fall again. She was *not* going to change her mind about Nolan Walker, she really wasn't, and the sooner her friend understood that, the better. She didn't want to be embarrassed at the party. Perhaps she *would* wear the red and green dress, but really, her selection had *nothing* to do with the town doctor… When she'd pointed out he was free to court anyone else, he'd simply said, "I know," so surely that meant he realized she was never going to reconsider her position with him, and he was now considering other options….

She'd said they could be friends, hadn't she? Had she been too hasty to indicate there could be nothing more? Even with all she'd had to do in the last few days because of her move into town, Nolan Walker had seldom been far from her mind.

So intent on her thoughts was she as she turned and strode up the walk that led to the doctor's office that Sarah almost bowled right into a figure descending the steps.

"Oh!" she cried, tightening her grip on the cake plate and looking up at Ada Spencer. "I'm sorry, Ada, I didn't see you. I'm afraid I was lost in thought."

The other woman gave a short laugh. "That was certainly obvious!" Her eyes narrowed as they focused on what Sarah was carrying. "A treat for the good doctor? My, my, he's going to grow fat with all the goodies the ladies of the town are bringing him," Ada said archly. "Why, just the other day I brought him pralines myself. Have a nice visit with Dr. Walker. I must be getting home—we spent far too long chatting, the doctor and I. I don't know where the time went."

Sarah stiffened as the other woman stepped past her and went out into the street. So "all the ladies in town" were bringing treats to the doctor, were they? Or was it only Ada? Suddenly Sarah felt foolish and pathetic carrying the beautiful cake, like a schoolgirl with a silly infatuation. She could turn around now and take the cake back down the street to the mercantile and sell it. Yes. That's what she'd do, and then return to the doctor's office and have him check her wound, as she had agreed.

"Well, good morning, Miss Sarah," Dr. Walker said, opening his door. Through the window, he'd seen her coming up his walk right after he'd just closed the door on Ada Spencer. Surely Sarah's coming was his reward for being patient and kind during Ada's unexpected visit, made under the pretext that she'd felt something was wrong with the baby. It had taken him an hour to calm her and send her on her way, and now here was Sarah Matthews, looking lovely in her loden green shawl and navy holly-sprigged wool dress. And bearing a gift, he thought, spotting the covered plate she carried. *Well, well.*

He saw her start. Clearly, she hadn't been expecting him to open the door before she'd even had the chance to knock.

"G-good morning, Dr. Walker. I… I've come to have you check my arm, if you have the time."

"Please, call me Nolan," he said, guessing she called him "doctor" to maintain a distance between them. "And of course I have time. It will only take a minute. Come in," he said, opening the door and gesturing for her to enter. "And what is that you're carrying?"

Two spots of pink bloomed on her cheeks. "I brought you a cake, to thank you for your kindness the other day when I fell—as well as the dollar I owe you for the doctor visits," she said, pointing to the placard that indicated his prices. She set the cake on a chair next to his inner office door and began to fish about in her reticule.

"Please forget about the fee." He put out a staying hand. "I'm sure this cake will be quite enough in the way of payment, and how thoughtful of you to bring it. May I?" he said, putting his hand on the lid of the cake plate.

"Of course. But I've been told you've been receiving quite a lot of such things," she said, "so it won't be all that special." Her tone strove to be unconcerned, but he heard the disappointment underneath.

His hand stilled and he gazed at the entrance door. He'd seen Ada and Sarah exchange a few words on the walk, and hadn't missed the quickly suppressed dismay which had flashed across Sarah's features. What had the other woman said to her?

"Nonsense," he said, going ahead and lifting the top and staring at the delicious-looking confection it had concealed. "This looks wonderful, Miss Sarah. I've been told you're quite a cook—and now I'll be able to discover that for myself."

She looked at him as if she wondered where he could have heard such a thing or if he was trying to flatter her, but said only, "Well. I hope you enjoy it. But I don't want to waste your time, Dr. Walker. Why don't you have a look at my wound and then I'll be going?"

He followed her into the office, closed the door behind him, then gestured for her to sit in the chair. He began to unwrap the linen roll, noting with satisfaction that as he had instructed, the bandage had obviously been changed from the one he had applied, and once he had completely removed it, the wound itself proved to be free of redness, swelling and drainage. His sutures had held. He pressed a finger into either side of the wound, and was pleased to see that she did not flinch.

"It's no longer painful?"

She shook her head.

"It appears to be healing well," he said. "I want you to continue to keep it clean and dry, and change the bandage every day, and by, say, New Year's Day, you can leave the wrapping off, get it wet and so forth." He saw a flush of color rise in her cheeks again and realized he no longer needed to hold her forearm. He released it.

"Oh, that reminds me," she said, once again reaching for her reticule. "Prissy asked me to give you this for her parents." She held out a vellum envelope.

Curious, he opened it, and saw that it was an invitation to an open-house party at the home of the mayor and his wife on New Year's Day. "A party," he murmured. "Are you going?"

"Of course. I live right on the grounds now, you know, in that little cottage with Prissy."

She'd mentioned her move when she'd been in his office the last time, after her fall. She would have been surprised to know he thought of her every night when he went into the hotel restaurant right across the street from the mayor's house for his supper. If he had been on better terms with Sarah, he would have called to bring her some little thing as a housewarming present, but he hadn't thought she'd welcome such a visit.

"Good. I'll see you there, and I'll bring your cake dish and cover with me—unless you need them before that?"

She must have thought it was a dismissal, for she arose and said, "No, at the party will be fine. Good day, Doctor."

He couldn't bear for her to leave so soon, but he had

no good reason to keep her here—unless she would allow him to share the concern that had been weighing on his mind. He'd thought about waiting to bring it up till he knew her better, but after Ada's disturbing visit, he wanted to speak of it now.

"Please," he said, rising, too. "If you have a minute, may I discuss something with you?"

She glanced at him sharply, her eyes wary. Probably she feared he was going to revisit their conversation about why she would not let him court her. He sat back down, and as he was hoping, she sank back into her seat, too.

"I'm worried about the lady who just left, Miss Spencer. How well do you know her? Are you friends?"

She blinked. "Friends?" She gave a shrug. "I used to think so… I've known her for years, and she was a part of the Simpson Creek Spinsters' Club when it started, but lately…"

Her voice trailed off, and her eyes looked troubled. He wondered if that meant she knew about the baby.

"Why do you ask?" Her tone was curious, but not guarded. No, Ada hadn't told her.

Here was the tricky part. He wanted to make sure Ada Spencer had friends to help support her, but he didn't know if she'd told anyone about the baby she claimed to carry. He was no more certain than he had been at Ada's last visit that she actually *was* with child, and had been troubled to see that once again she'd come alone, disregarding his request to bring another female with her. And she'd seemed even more brittle, emotionally, when she'd come today than she had before.

He took a deep breath. "It's difficult for me to say," he began, "without violating her confidence…but I will say she seems troubled. I—I'd hoped she had friends to confide in." He waited to see what she would say.

She hesitated, but at last she said, "Ada's been keeping mostly to herself lately. She used to seem as carefree as any of us, but…that all changed after that Englishman came to town—the first man who was killed the day of the Comanche attack, remember?"

He nodded. Despite all the horrors Nolan had seen in the war, the image of the arrow-riddled, bloody figure slumping on his horse was a sight he'd never forget.

"They were courting," Sarah said. "She stopped coming to the Spinsters' Club meetings once that began. Afterward, we all assumed she was grieving, but then…" Her voice trailed off and she bit her lip, looking away.

"Then?" he prompted.

"Forgive me, Doctor… Nolan… I, uh…thought that you—that is, the two of you—were…um…"

Her face was scarlet now, and he guessed what she had been thinking. It was exactly as he had feared, and he could guess Ada Spencer had given Sarah that impression.

"I'm not sure what you thought, exactly, Miss Sarah," he said carefully, "but Miss Spencer is my *patient. Only* my patient."

"I… I see."

Did he imagine it, or did she appear slightly less distressed?

"She's going through a difficult time," he said. "I think she's in need of friends, Miss Sarah. I know it's asking a lot, but would you perhaps be willing to…be a friend to her?"

Chapter Seven

He held his breath as he watched her eyes widen in surprise, but to his relief, he saw no immediate resistance there.

"You think she needs my friendship? What makes you think she would accept me as her friend after distancing herself all this time?"

"I don't know why anyone wouldn't be glad of your friendship, Miss Sarah. I know I am." He locked his gaze with hers.

Her lashes dipped low over her eyes. "Thank you, but I'm not sure Ada would feel the same, given the way she's been acting lately. Perhaps you should approach Reverend Chadwick—"

"I thought about that, but I really think she needs to speak to another woman at least to begin with," he said quickly. "All I'm asking is that you try."

She was touched by his trust in her. "And you cannot say what is troubling her?"

He shook his head. "That'll have to come from her, if she chooses to take you into her confidence. If she won't open up to you, perhaps she will to another of the ladies, but please use discretion in who you ask."

Sarah studied him. "Why do you care so much about this?" she asked.

"Because I know what it's like to feel friendless."

She looked as if she'd like to ask him more, but just then the bell over the entrance tinkled, announcing the arrival of another patient. The whimpers of a fretful child penetrated through the door between the waiting room and the inner office.

"Duty calls," Sarah said with a wry smile, rising again. "I—I'll try to talk to Ada. And thank you for looking at my arm," she added, formal once more.

"You're very welcome." He placed the cake inside his rolltop desk and closed the cover over it. No sense giving anyone anything else to gossip about.

She opened the door, and Nolan saw that one of the young married women of the town stood in the waiting room, holding a red-faced, squirming toddler, while another child not much older clung to her skirts.

"Howdy, Sarah."

"Lulabelle, looks like you've got your hands full," Sarah observed.

The young mother gave her a flustered smile before turning to Nolan. "Doctor, Lee here stuck a black-eyed pea in his ear and I can't get it out nohow," the exasperated mother told him.

"Well, bring him in, I'm sure we can remove it," he said, but his eyes lingered on Sarah's graceful figure as she exited.

Because I know what it's like to be feel friendless. His answer reverberated in her mind as she stepped into the street. There were so very many things she wanted to know about him. Why would Nolan Walker ever have been friendless? He'd made friends effortlessly soon after arriving in town, and just look how easily he'd managed to talk her into being friends, if they could not be more than that. Had he meant the loneliness he'd felt when his wife and son had died?

She would have asked him if Lulabelle Harding hadn't brought her child in just then, and she still wanted to know. Perhaps she could ask him about it some other time. And he had never told her what he'd been doing in Brazos County during the time he had been corresponding with her—had he been assigned with federal occupying troops? He must have been. What other reason could he have had for being there?

Sarah had been surprised by Nolan's request that she try to be a friend to Ada. Thinking she should go talk to her now while the resolve was fresh in her mind, she started to turn down the road that led past the doctor's house to the home Ada shared with her parents, then hesitated. If she went there now, Ada would realize she had come straight from the doctor's office and guess that Nolan had put her up to it. She might even jump to the wrong conclusion that the doctor had violated her confidence. And Ada's parents would be there, which meant that she and Ada might not have any privacy to talk.

No, it was best that she encounter Ada casually in town, if possible. Perhaps she could talk to Milly about it? Milly always seemed to know everything about everyone around Simpson Creek, though she did not gossip. But if Sarah were to tell her that she had reason to be concerned about Ada, Milly might have some insight about what could be troubling the woman. Perhaps she would think it was a simple matter of grief over Ada's slain beau and what to Ada had been a promising courtship cut tragically short. Milly and Sarah, however, had learned the truth about the man's character from Nick, who had known Harvey in India.

Sarah thought about riding out to the ranch. She'd love to see her sister, and inquire how she was doing now that the cooking chores were all up to her. Prissy's father had made it clear that Sarah was free to borrow a riding horse from the stable any time she desired.

She cast an eye at the sky. Gray clouds still hung over the western horizon, threatening rain, and by now it had to be nearly noon. By the time she walked back to the cottage, changed into her riding skirt, had Antonio, the Gilmores' servant, saddle a horse for her and rode out to the ranch, it would be midafternoon. And she still needed to stop into the mercantile and hotel restaurant and promise their respective proprietors that she would be baking again starting tomorrow, and Prissy had asked her to look at lighter curtain material for their main room… No, she would not go today.

But she could always pray about the matter, she realized, feeling guilty that she hadn't thought of that first. No matter when she spoke to Ada, it was best to do so after seeking heavenly guidance, not before. She needed to stop using prayer as a last resort, after she had exhausted all her own efforts, and think of it first.

Father, I'm concerned about Ada Spencer. I don't know what's troubling her, but You do, Lord. Please help her to realize You are always with her, wanting to aid her. Help her to look to You for her needs. And please show me how to be a true friend to her...

She found a bolt of white dotted swiss in the mercantile that would be perfect for their curtains. While Mr. Patterson was wrapping it up, Mrs. Detwiler came in and made a beeline for Sarah.

"Hello, Sarah! Did you and the newlyweds have a nice Christmas? How do you liking living in town? Are you coming to the New Year's Day party at the Gilmores? Well, of course you are, you're living right on the grounds."

Sarah had started to ask about the Detwilers' Christmas, but when the voluble older lady chattered right on as if she wasn't expecting a question in return, Sarah smiled and said, "Yes, we did, and yes, I am liking it and yes, of course I'll be at the party."

"Good! I reckon you'll be on the arm of that fine Yankee doctor. My, you two made a handsome couple dancing at the wedding. You and he have probably been sparkin' ever since, haven't you?" she asked with a cackle of laughter.

Sarah felt herself flushing and shook her head. "No, Mrs. Detwiler, we're not courting. We just danced one dance together...."

"Not from any lack of 'want to' on his part, I'll warrant. It was plain as the nose on my face. Now, don't you let one of your Spinsters' Club friends snatch up that fine man first," she admonished, shaking a gnarled finger at Sarah. "You be like your sister—Milly knew a good thing when she saw it and she didn't dillydally and let some other woman get close to that handsome Englishman a' hers!"

Sarah marveled inwardly, thinking how disapproving the older woman had been of Milly when she'd founded the Spinsters' Club, and how Nicholas had won her over. "Yes, ma'am, and perhaps when the right man comes along, I'll—"

"You might not recognize it when it happens. I didn't, when my George first started coming to call. You think again about that Dr. Walker, miss. I know what I'm talking about."

"Yes ma'am," Sarah said obediently. It never did any good to argue with Mrs. Detwiler.

When she reached home, she found Prissy stirring a pot over the kitchen stove, and upon inspection found her friend hadn't managed to burn the beef stew Prissy, with Sarah's help, had started simmering before Sarah left the cottage. "Mmm, that's going to be good," Sarah said, sniffing the air.

Prissy grinned. "Perhaps there's hope for me yet." She put down the large spoon. "Sarah, I've been thinking, why don't we invite someone over for supper sometime soon? Wouldn't that be fun?"

Sarah nodded, thinking this might be her opportunity. Prissy could be the very person to help the withdrawn woman open her heart. "How about Ada? She's been through a lot lately, and perhaps she'd be grateful for some company other than her parents—"

Prissy wrinkled her nose. "Sarah, Ada Spencer's been downright *odd* lately. Just the other day I waved hello to her from down the street and she turned and slunk off in the opposite direction. No, I meant someone enjoyable to be around, like your sister and her husband. Or maybe we should invite a couple of the other ladies from the club—or all of them! Let's do it after New Year's Day."

Sarah sighed inwardly. She was all for a dinner party, but this meant she was back where she started, needing to find an excuse to talk to Ada.

The next three days provided no opportunities, either. She didn't encounter the woman while delivering her baked goods, nor did Ada appear in church on the morning of New Year's Eve. It seemed Sarah would have to go to the Spencers' house after all. But now it would have to wait until after the Gilmores' party the next day, for she was going to be busy this Sunday afternoon helping Prissy and her parents get ready for the event.

"Dr. Walker, good of you to come," the walrus-mustached rotund man said, shaking his hand enthusiastically. "Happy New Year!"

"Happy New Year to you, Mayor Gilmore, Mrs. Gilmore," Nolan said, smiling at him and his plump pigeon of a wife, fighting to keep his gaze directed politely on them while he longed to look over their heads for Sarah. "It was kind of you to invite me."

"Of course, of course. Everyone in Simpson Creek comes to our open house on New Year's Day. It's a tradition, you know."

Not only was all of Simpson Creek milling around in the elegantly appointed, brocade-wallpapered ballroom, it seemed as if half of the rest of San Saba County was, too, all of them dressed in their best finery. The scent of rose and lavender water mingled with savory odors of food and the strains of music played by the fiddler.

"Please, help yourself to the some refreshments, sir," Mrs. Gilmore said, gesturing at the overloaded table in the far corner of the room. And there his gaze found the woman he sought, for Sarah was standing next to a huge haunch of roast beef, slicing it for a handful of people who were lined up.

He headed in that direction, but he was intercepted midway across the room by half a dozen people, the last of whom was the mayor's daughter.

"My, aren't you looking handsome tonight, Dr. Walker," Prissy said, her eyes sweeping over him admiringly. "Just wait till Sarah sees you."

He was thankful he had two black frock coats, one for doctoring calls, the other kept for fancy occasions such as this, and that he'd had time to bathe and shave after delivering Mavis Hotchkiss's baby at a ranch west of town. "Why thank you, Miss Priscilla," he said, "You're looking very fine yourself."

She dimpled and fanned herself, then leaned close to sniff the air. "Thank you, sir. *Mmm,* and you *smell* quite handsome, too."

He'd dabbed on some bay rum after he'd shaved. He'd hoped at the time that a certain lady would appreciate it…but his thoughts had been on Sarah, not Prissy. "Miss Priscilla, I didn't know it was possible to smell handsome," he said, amused. "You must have a discerning nose, to be able to detect such a thing over the delicious scents wafting from the food table."

"Oh, go on over there, you know you want to," she

said, waving him on with a knowing wink. "Doesn't our Sarah look absolutely wonderful in red?"

He was glad that with Prissy, at least, he didn't have to pretend he wasn't longing to stand here and continue making small talk. "As you do in gold, Miss Priscilla," he said. "Thanks."

He crossed the remaining distance to the food table, and seeing that Sarah was still busy slicing beef for the guests in the line, took selections from the other dishes on the groaning board, for he had been at the delivery since dawn and hadn't eaten since the night before.

At last he came to the head of the line. "May I have some roast beef, Miss Sarah?"

She looked up from her carving tools. "Why, Nolan, I didn't see you come in. Happy New Year to you."

May the new year bring about a change in your heart. "Will you have to remain at carving table?" he asked. "I was hoping you could sit down and eat with me." He gestured at the small tables scattered around the sides of the room.

"No, I'm only carving until Antonio can come back," she said, "And here he comes now," she said, indicating a liveried manservant approaching with a clove-studded ham. "So, yes, I can sit down and eat with you. As it happens, I've become very hungry, standing here watching the food go by."

He waited while she selected some food, and then they found a vacant table not far from the door.

"I stopped at your cottage to see if I could escort you to the party, but no one answered," he told Sarah when they had settled themselves.

"No, Prissy and I have been here since early morning, helping them get the food set out," she told him.

"So I figured. Anyway, I left your cake plate and cover at your doorstep. Best cake I ever had," he told her.

"Then you'll have to try my Neopolitan cake that's over on the dessert table to see if you still think so," she said. "And be sure and try the pecan fruitcake Prissy made—please be sure and tell her it's delicious, for she needs confidence in her baking skills. Oh, there's Milly and Nick!" She waved at the couple who had just entered the ballroom.

It was foolish to hope to be alone with a particular woman at a party, he told himself. "It looks like marriage agrees with you two," he told the couple when they joined them a few moments later, along with Reverend Chadwick.

"Yes, I quite recommend it," Brookfield answered, grinning. ""How's the doctoring business?" he asked in return.

"For a small town, it certainly keeps me busy. I've already helped usher Simpson Creek's newest citizen into the world today, out at the Hotchkiss ranch."

"Ah, a new baby for the new year," Sarah said, her face brightening with pleasure.

"I trust Mavis had an uncomplicated lying-in?" Milly asked. "That's her fourth, you know."

Nolan had just opened his mouth to answer her when a shrill cry rose over the hubbub of chattering and the clinking of silverware against china.

"So there you are, Nolan!"

Chapter Eight

Ada Spencer pointed at him, her tone shrill. Her other hand fluttered down to her abdomen. She wore a green hooped gown that would have been the height of fashion before the war, but now it looked decidedly out of place. Her mother was a larger woman, so perhaps it had been hers, for it hung loose as a sack on Ada. Her hair had been pinned on top of her head in a parody of an upswept chignon. Her eyes were unnaturally bright. Two hectic flushes of color blotched her pale cheeks.

Antonio, the Gilmore's manservant, hovered uncertainly behind her as if he hadn't wanted to admit her to the party, but he hadn't known quite how to stop her.

Conversation hushed and people turned to stare. The fiddler stopped playing.

Nolan stared, and darted a glance back at Sarah. "Excuse me..." he whispered. "Reverend, perhaps you'd better come with me," he added in an undertone, and started across the room, feeling as if he had blundered into a nightmare.

Sarah rose. If there was trouble from Ada Spencer,

she didn't want Nolan to face it alone. Milly stood, too, and they followed Dr. Walker and the preacher.

"Miss Spencer, what's wrong?" Nolan said, when he reached Ada, "Are you ill? Is it—" He kept his voice down, wishing they didn't have such a large, curious audience.

"Ill? No, Nolan…the baby's just fine, kicking away," Ada announced in tone of brittle gaiety that was audible to at least half the room. Her hand remained protectively over her abdomen. "Naturally, since you and I…well, I thought you would be by to escort me to the party, but you never appeared. And here I find you consorting with another woman!" She stared at Sarah as if she had never met her.

"Ada, we were only talking… Nolan?" Sarah said uncertainly, even as Milly put a cautionary hand on her shoulder.

"Miss Spencer is ill," Nolan said, making sure his tone was firm and would carry at least to the closest fringe of people who were avidly listening. He figured they could inform the rest. "Miss Sarah, Mrs. Milly, Reverend Chadwick, would you mind coming with me? We're going to help Miss Spencer home."

"But, Nolan, I came for the party!" Ada protested, looking over her shoulder at the party behind her. "I haven't wished Happy New Year to anyone, or had any of the food over there on the buffet table, and our child makes me so hungry!"

Nolan felt the blood drain from his face. He fought the impulse to recoil from this woman. "Come with us, Miss Spencer, please," Nolan said in the kindest, gentlest tone he could muster, the kind of voice one used with a fractious animal—or the insane.

"Nolan, we really *are* on a first-name basis aren't we? After all…" Ada glanced meaningfully downward and laughed. Her eerie merriment made his skin crawl.

"We'll take you home. You want to take good care of yourself, don't you?" What must Sarah be thinking? If he'd ever had any hope that Sarah would change her mind about him, it was surely lost now.

They managed to herd Ada out into the vestibule, and while Reverend Chadwick was wrapping Ada's shawl around her shoulders, Nolan turned to Sarah, hoping to whisper that he'd be back later to explain.

But Ada must have seen him out of the corner of her eye, for she whirled away from Reverend Chadwick, fury in her eyes.

"Is it too much to expect you to be faithful to the *mother of your child?*" she demanded. "You stay away from him, you—you—" Thankfully, words failed her then, but she started gathering herself as if she meant to lunge at Sarah.

Nolan and the reverend took a firm grip on the struggling woman, and suddenly Nick Brookfield was there too, helping them, putting himself between Ada and his wife and Sarah.

Nolan wanted to shout at the crazed woman, "Be quiet! You know that's not true!" but all he could do was turn to Sarah, and let his eyes plead with her to understand. "I'll be back as soon as I can," he managed to say, even as he struggled to keep a hold on Ada.

"Now, Miss Ada, you mustn't excite yourself, you know it's not good for you…" Reverend Chadwick was saying in his soothing voice, but it was obvious she wasn't listening. The mayor, his wife and Prissy hung back at the entrance of the ballroom, their eyes wide, obviously unsure what to do. All the partygoers were gathered behind them, their mouths hanging open in fascinated horror.

Sarah was pale, but to his relief, Nolan saw no suspicion or condemnation in her eyes, only pity as she gazed at the thrashing crazy woman, then back at him. He thought she saw her nod, but he couldn't be sure.

Shaken, Sarah watched the door close behind the three men herding Ada Spencer.

"Well, I never," breathed Prissy, who had come up beside her. "It's not true, is it? What Ada said about a baby—hers and Dr. Walker's?"

"No, I'm sure it's not," Sarah said quickly, though she could not have said why she felt so certain. She didn't know Nolan Walker that well, she reminded herself. Was this why Nolan had thought Ada needed a friend, because she was expecting a baby and had no husband? Or because Ada was losing her mind? Or both?

"No, it's not true," Milly said behind her. "Sarah, let's walk to the cottage, shall we? I think it's time to discuss something with you. You don't want to stay longer at the party anyway, do you?"

"No, I… I don't," Sarah agreed, feeling perilously close to tears. "You don't mind, do you, Prissy?"

"Of course not. If it's all right—" her gaze sought Milly's permission in addition to Sarah's "—I'll come, too. Mama and Papa will understand."

* * *

Revisiting in her mind the October day the Comanches had attacked in the midst of the Founder's Day celebration was hard for Sarah, but she felt relieved when Milly had finished speaking.

"So Ada had just told you and Nick that Harvey Blakely had abandoned her while she was with child when his horse brought him, mortally wounded into town?" Sarah murmured. The saucer rattled as she set down her cup of tea with a shaking hand. "How dreadful."

"And you never told a soul her secret," Prissy breathed. "You're so good, Milly."

Milly shrugged. "It wasn't my secret to tell. I intended to be a supportive friend to her, but I hardly saw her after that. And what with getting ready for the wedding and all..." She threw up her hands.

"I know what you mean," Sarah said with a guilty sigh. "I meant to do the same when she started acting so oddly...."

Milly's brow furrowed. "You know, for a woman who's four or five months along... I wonder if that's why she wore that loose gown..." Her voice trailed off and she refused to elaborate. "Never mind, I was just thinking out loud. It's none of my business."

"Poor Ada," Sarah said, her heart aching as she remembered the wild look in Ada's eyes.

"I think you'd better stay away from her, after how she acted tonight," Prissy muttered.

"But now she needs friends more than ever!" Sarah cried.

"I'm afraid what she may need is an asylum, dear,"

Milly said, putting a comforting hand on her sister's shoulder, "since Harvey's death seems to have unhinged her mind. And if anyone's foolish enough to believe Ada's wild accusations even a little, it'll be Dr. Walker who may be needing friends."

Sarah stared at her sister. As usual, Milly was right. "I won't stop being his friend," she said. "He's a good man."

"I agree," Prissy said.

Sarah sighed. "What we *can* do for Ada is pray for her," she said.

"You're right," Milly said, and joining hands with her sister and Prissy, they did so, right then, asking the Lord to give Ada a clear mind so she would know what was true and what wasn't.

Nick arrived at the cottage shortly after that to collect his wife, reporting they'd succeeded in getting Ada home, and that Dr. Walker and the reverend had stayed to explain what had happened to her elderly parents. Then he and Milly left, wanting to reach the ranch before darkness fell.

"Looks like almost all the guests have left," Prissy remarked, standing on their porch step after she and Sarah had waved goodbye to Milly and Nick. The drive that curved in front of her parent's large house and the street beyond was now nearly bare of carriages.

"I imagine Ada's outburst put a damper on the festivities," Sarah said. She could imagine all too well that the scene Ada had made would be the talk of the town for a long time to come. *Please, Lord, don't let anyone believe Ada's unbalanced raving.*

"I think I'll go help Mama and Papa finish up for

a while. I'll bring back some of the leftover food for our supper," Prissy said.

"I'll come help, too." Sarah reached for her shawl.

Prissy put out a staying hand. "You'd better stay here, in case Dr. Walker comes back soon. I have a feeling he's going to need to talk."

Sarah paced the cottage restlessly after Prissy left, dusting furniture that didn't need it, rearranging things, going to the window to stare out into the gathering dark.

Nolan arrived, looking haggard and careworn, about an hour after the Brookfields left.

"Ada's sleeping. I gave her a sedative and her mother put her to bed," he replied to her wordless question as she let him in. "No, I won't stay that long," he said, when she would have taken his coat. "I just wanted to come and see if you were all right, after what happened, and to explain...."

"I'm all right," she assured him, touched by the anxious look in his eyes. "And perhaps it will make it easier if you know that Milly told me and Prissy about Ada's being...um...with child," she said, feeling herself flush as she spoke about the delicate matter, "and that Ada told her the father was that Englishman, Harvey Blakely. Then the Comanche attack happened and he was killed...."

Nolan sighed, clearly relieved. "Yes, that does make it easier. Then you know there's no truth to what she said about me being the father."

"Of course. Nolan, at least come sit by the fire and have a cup of tea before you go," Sarah insisted. "You look exhausted."

Following her to the settle in front of the fire, he admitted he was. "The reverend and I stayed awhile to talk to her parents after she finally fell asleep."

"How are they?" Sarah asked.

"Worried, of course," he said, giving her a grateful smile as he accepted the cup of tea she had poured. "They've been concerned about her odd behavior for months now, and didn't know what to do—they were too ashamed to speak to anyone about it. I think as much as they were embarrassed to learn that she had sneaked out of the house in that outlandish dress and made a scene at the open house, they were relieved to know there was a cause for Ada's…shall we say, unusual behavior. Reverend Chadwick and I assured them we'd help in any way we can." He took a breath and added, "Your pastor is a good man."

"Yes, he is."

Nolan stared into the fire. "They didn't know about her claim that she's expecting."

"They didn't?" Then her mind focused on the way he had said it. "Why did you put it that way, Nolan—'her claim'? You don't think she's with child?"

He shook his head. "I didn't want to talk about this, but after what happened, and especially the way she acted toward you, I think the time for silence is over—for your safety, if for no other reason. I examined Ada once in my office, and I wasn't sure she was with child then. I helped her mother get her to bed tonight, and… well, to put it as delicately as I should to a lady, there's no changes to her body that should be there by now, if her story was true."

"There aren't? Then why would she tell such a

story?" Sarah asked. "She has to know the truth will come out eventually when there's no baby."

"Because I think she believes it's true. It's my opinion she has what's called a hysterical pregnancy, Sarah. Throughout history some women who wanted a child badly enough have somehow tricked their bodies into displaying some of the symptoms of pregnancy. I don't know if you ever read any English history, but Queen Mary, sister of Queen Elizabeth, suffered from this delusion too, back in the sixteenth century."

Sarah stared at him, trying to take it all in. "Did you tell this to her parents?"

Nolan nodded. "I've urged them to consult another doctor in the closest town, just to confirm what I'm saying. I've told them I'll remain her doctor if they're willing, but her mother must come with her to her appointments."

"Now I understand why you said she needed a friend to confide in," Sarah said. "Nolan, I tried, but I never had the chance to speak to her," she admitted. "I'm sorry."

"No, I'm the one who should be sorry for even suggesting it," he said. "I didn't realize until the scene at the party how brittle her hold on sanity is. It might have been dangerous for you to reach out to her."

"You meant well," she told him. "Nolan, Milly says she might need to be in an asylum."

He sighed again. "It's possible, though I hope not. Mrs. Spencer told me that there's been a history of insanity in the family tree. Her grandmother died in an asylum." Then he studied her for a long time. "Perhaps I shouldn't have told you all that, but after the way she reacted toward you, I thought it was best that you know." His gaze locked with hers. "And I find you so easy to talk to, Sarah."

She looked down, her heart beating faster at the directness of his gaze. "You may trust me not to gossip, Nolan," she assured him.

"I knew that," he said. The clock struck the hour. "And now I must bid you good night." He rose.

She stood up, too, and went to the door with him.

He looked down at her as he opened the door, the planes of his angular face shadowed by the darkness. He smiled.

She had the oddest feeling he had wanted to kiss her. She couldn't have allowed it, of course. They had agreed to be friends, but even if she was willing to forget he was a Yankee, she reminded herself, he wasn't a Christian. The Bible warned against being unequally yoked in marriage, so friends was all they could ever be.

How silly of you, Sarah. Just because a man has a certain look in his eye, that doesn't mean you need to think of why you can't marry him!

So why did she feel a moment of regret as she watched him walk away?

Chapter Nine

Nolan was thoughtful as he made his way back home. He'd been pleased and relieved that Sarah, though she'd blushed and looked embarrassed, was willing to speak with him about such a frank subject. Most women wouldn't have spoken about pregnancy to any male except their husbands. And many women might have believed Ada's ranting.

He'd been surprised by Reverend Chadwick, too. He'd been introduced to the town's preacher when he arrived in town, of course, and became more relaxed when the minister didn't seem inclined to pester him about coming to church. He'd assumed the cleric had written him off as a potential member of his congregation.

But tonight he'd been impressed by Chadwick's overwhelming patience toward Ada. Despite the vile names the madwoman called him as she tried to bite and scratch him and the two other men, Reverend Chadwick had never shown himself the least bit angry or even exasperated with her, continuing to speak kindly and calmly to her as they struggled to take her home. He'd been a rock of support to her elderly parents, too, when they'd huddled, bewildered and distraught, to hear what Nolan had to say about their daughter's condition.

What a difference existed between Reverend Chadwick and the chaplain who'd served with Nolan. Though the chaplain had been a favorite of the men of the regiment, he'd avoided the captured, injured Confederates he was also supposed to minister to as if they had the plague.

Nolan had once taken him to task about it.

"What an idea, Doctor, that I should treat those rebels as if they deserved the same as our boys in blue!" he'd cried, recoiling at the idea. "Why, at home in Illinois, my wife and I ran an underground railroad station. You should have seen some of the poor creatures who came to our house, running for their lives away from cruel slave owners. And you're telling me that you think I should speak of God's mercy to the very men who held them in bondage?"

Nolan had very much doubted most of the scary, skinny men and boys in the tattered remains of gray uniforms had ever owned slaves, let alone the ones who'd come to the chaplain's home, but he didn't trouble himself to argue with the man. He didn't think wounded, dying rebels would find much comfort in anything that man had to say.

Reverend Chadwick lived in a small house behind the church, so he and Nolan walked together when they'd left the Spencers' house and Nick had gone to fetch his wife.

"That was very troubling," Chadwick said, as they walked. "I'll be praying for her."

Nolan sensed the man was hoping Nolan would say he would pray for her, too, but he didn't want to tell the preacher how little he believed in prayer. "Have you known the Spencers long?" he asked instead.

Chadwick nodded. "They moved to Simpson Creek when Ada was a babe in arms. She was just like any other young lady before that Harvey fellow came to town—happy, but wishing for a beau. It's very sad to see her like this now." He was silent for a few strides. "I'll be praying for you, too, son. That can't have been pleasant, having such an accusation leveled at you in front of all those folks."

"No," Nolan agreed. He was touched by the reverend's caring. Though Nolan didn't think the prayers would accomplish anything, he could still value the kindness of the gesture. "You don't think anyone will believe it, do you?"

"Sensible people, no," the reverend said. "Though there are always a few who are willing to believe the worst rather than the best. But the people around here need a doctor too much to ride that high horse for long. Oh, your ears may burn for a few days until some other topic becomes a nine days' wonder. That's the way of small towns, I suppose."

"I'm surprised you're not telling me the best thing I could do to dispel the rumor would be sitting in a one of your pews every Sunday," Nolan said. He watched for the man's reaction.

Chadwick gave a chuckle. "There are probably better reasons for coming to church than as an antidote to gossip," he said, unoffended. "But you know you're welcome, Nolan. And whether you come or not, I'm always here to listen if you need to talk. You minister to bodies, while I minister to souls—but both can be lonely at times, I think."

Nolan had heard the reverend was a widower, but he thought Chadwick meant more than that.

"But as for church, if you don't come to hear me preach, you might come to hear Sarah play the piano. She's very gifted."

Sarah played the piano? It was something he hadn't known about her. But then, she wasn't one to boast of her accomplishments.

The reverend was watching him with a knowing twinkle in his eyes. "Ah, perhaps I've given you a good reason," he said with another chuckle. "I heard you say you were going to go back and tell her what happened. Perhaps you ought to do that now, son, before it gets any later. She looked worried."

Now, having finished his talk with Sarah, he let himself inside his dark house and reached for the match safe so he could light the lamp on the entry table. His mind turned back to his talk with the reverend.

Even when Nolan had steered the conversation toward the church, Chadwick had never once made him feel that he thought less of him for not attending. Interesting.

His thoughts turned again to Sarah. Before the scene at the party, he had decided to gently pursue her, and gradually try to break down her resistance against him courting her. But now that Ada Spencer had made a public accusation against him, and had included Sarah in her venomous attack, he wasn't sure what to do. Perhaps he should just let things lie for a while until the gossip died a natural death.

He couldn't stop his eyes from searching for her, though, during the next fortnight, as he walked to the hotel for some of his meals and to the mercantile for supplies. But he didn't encounter the shy, golden-haired beauty making her rounds of deliveries to either place.

The number of patients coming to his office had dwindled since the party. He'd gotten some pointed looks by a few townspeople on the street, people he remembered seeing at the New Year's Day party, and two or three times conversations had ceased just as he'd entered the hotel restaurant or the mercantile. He'd tried not to let it bother him, supposing they'd realize they were wrong when Ada Spencer never gave birth, but after his initial warm reception when he'd first come to Simpson Creek, he'd be lying if he told himself their reaction didn't hurt.

But there were still those who either hadn't heard about Ada's wild accusation or needed doctoring too much to care, such as the elderly widow who came in because of catarrh, the near-deaf old man complaining of rheumatism, a young mother bringing in a fretful child with quinsy throat or a cowboy "all stove up" after being thrown from a horse he was trying to break.

He looked up each time the bell at the door of his office tinkled to announce an arrival, hoping against hope it was Sarah coming to visit, but he was always disappointed. At least, if it wasn't Sarah, it wasn't Ada Spencer, either. He hadn't seen the unstable woman since the New Year's Day party, though he had seen her mother walking past his house with a basket in her hands as if she was doing some errands. He supposed he should call and inquire about Ada's welfare, but he wouldn't go alone, he'd take the reverend with him. It was just common sense.

Finally, curiosity got the best of him one morning when he spotted Prissy coming out of their cottage as he walked by on his way to the mercantile for a new can of Arbuckle's coffee. He waved and called out to her.

"Fine weather for January, isn't it, Miss Prissy? Back home in Maine we'd likely be wading through a foot of snow," he began, wondering how soon he could inquire about Sarah and still sound casual.

"I sure wouldn't want it to be any colder than this," Prissy said, shivering and pulling her coat more closely about her. "Though I would like to see snow, just once. You just never know about winter in this part of Texas—some days it can feel like spring, and then a norther will blow in. But you're not really interested in the weather, are you? You want to ask me about Sarah, so why don't you go ahead and do that?" Her eyes danced with mischief.

He couldn't help but laugh. "As always, Miss Prissy, you see through me all too easily," he said. "How *is* Sarah? I haven't seen her around for a few days."

"That's because she's been out at the ranch almost since the party," Prissy said. "Her sister's found out she's expecting a baby, and she's had a rough time of it with morning sickness. Sarah went out to help with the cooking till Milly's feeling better because she couldn't even brew the coffee without being ill. I've really been missing Sarah—I've had no one to test out my cooking on but Mama and Papa, and Papa says he'd rather eat Flora's—that's our cook—meals until I get a little better," she said ruefully.

"Hmm, perhaps I should pay Mrs. Brookfield a call," Nolan murmured, thinking he could kill two birds with one stone—offer any medical help that the first-time mother needed, and see Sarah at the same time. "If you don't think that would be presumptuous, that is, since she hasn't sent for me."

"You could, and of course it wouldn't be presumptuous, you silly Yankee man, it would be neighborly," Prissy said, chuckling.

Not expecting any patients, Nolan had gone straight home, intending to hitch up his buggy and drive right out there after dinner. But as soon as he'd finished eating, Ed Thompson, who owned a nearby ranch, arrived at his office with a boil that needed to be lanced.

Nolan drove out to the Brookfield ranch after that, only to be told that Sarah had just left the ranch after dinner, for Milly was feeling well enough to cope with the cooking again. Milly Brookfield was radiant with happiness that she would give her Nick a child in the early fall. She thanked Nolan for the kindness of coming to check on her.

He promised to deliver her baby when it came, of course, even while he thought of how Sarah must have ridden back to town while he was eating his dinner, or perhaps while he was attending to Thompson.

It seemed if he was to see her, he must take Chadwick's suggestion and come to church after all. He hoped God—if there was a God, which he very much doubted—wouldn't mind that he was trespassing in His house just to see the golden-haired beauty who played piano every Sunday.

Too bad it was Monday. Sunday had just passed and he would have to wait until it rolled around again. But perhaps he would get lucky and see her before Sunday, and not have to go to church after all. Prissy would have told her that he'd been looking for her—perhaps he could contrive to "accidentally" encounter Sarah instead of attending church to see her. He'd rather not be a hypocrite if he could help it.

But the next day marked the beginning of a disaster, and after that he was much too busy to think about maneuvering a chance meeting with Sarah Matthews, or going to church just to see her.

Chapter Ten

A pounding at the door roused Nolan from a sleep filled with uneasy dreams.

"Sorry to wake you like this, Doc, but please, kin you come out to the ranch?" the distraught-looking man on his porch pleaded, when Nolan went to the door. "I'm Hal Parker's son, Hank. Pa's took real bad with a fever, and he says he kin hardly catch his breath.

"Pa caught cold a week ago," the middle-aged Hank Parker went on while he helped Nolan hitch his horse to the buggy. "He was sneezin' a lot an' didn't seem too bad at first, but now it seems like he jes' cain't shake it. He's achin' all over, feverish and his breath's rattlin' in his chest...we were gonna wait till mornin' t'call you, but he says he can't get no air..."

"No, no, you did right," Nolan assured him, and soon they were on the road heading eastward to the ranch that lay between Simpson Creek and San Saba, Parker riding alongside Nolan's buggy. Nolan feared the old man's condition had gone into pneumonia.

When they arrived at the ranch house, Hank escorted him into the retired rancher's bedroom, where his father lay in the bed, propped up by pillows and surrounded by his anxious old wife, the son's wife and a quartet of sleepy-looking children of various heights. All of them edged politely back against the wall as Nolan entered the room with his black doctor's bag.

Hal Parker labored for each rasping breath. The sound of it filled the small room.

"Pa, we've brought the doc," his son announced, as Nolan went toward the bed, but if the old man heard, he gave no indication.

"Hello, Mr. Parker," Nolan said as he leaned over the bed. "I'm Dr. Walker."

The old man opened clouded eyes and tried to focus on Nolan, then closed them wearily again. "Where's… Doc… H-Harkey?" he managed to say, but the effort sent him into a spasm of coughing when he finished.

"Hal, he's dead," his elderly wife told him loudly. "He died when those Comanches attacked last fall, remember?"

Nolan studied Parker. He was red-faced and clammy, his pulse thready and rapid. His eyes seemed sunken. His mouth gaped wide like a fish's with his attempts to draw in enough air.

Nolan opened up his bag, took out his stethoscope and listened for thirty seconds. Just as he had feared, the moist rattling within the man's chest filled his ears. It was definitely pneumonia.

Mr. Parker's daughter-in-law had already given him willow bark tea for the fever, and to this Nolan added a dose of morphine, trickling the draft in cautiously lest the delirious man choke. He directed the daughter-in-law to sponge him with a cold wet towel.

Nothing they did worked, however, and the old man breathed his last just as the sun was rising over the distant blue hills.

"He's gone," he told the white-faced son, and closed the old man's eyes. The man nodded grimly, unsurprised, and put one arm around his weeping mother, the other around his wife. The children clustered around them, some crying, some solemn-eyed in the presence of death.

"Thank ya. Ya done all ya could," the old woman murmured, tears sliding down the weathered grooves of her cheeks. "Hal's with the Lord now, and someday soon I'll join 'im."

Nolan inclined his head respectfully. However accustomed he was to death, he could never understand this calm, patient acceptance. He was angry when he lost a patient, angry at himself and against an implacable foe that fought without scruples. When Jeff had died despite all his efforts, he'd raged for days, finally seeking oblivion at the bottom of a whiskey bottle but finding no relief.

Death was the end. There was nothing more. When his wife and son had died, Nolan had received no echoing sense that they were alive on any other plane of existence. Nothing he had seen in the war had taught him any different.

"I'll inform the undertaker when I get back to town," Nolan told them, gathering up his black bag.

"And Reverend Chadwick, too, if you'd be so kind, Doc."

Hal Parker's death was Nolan's first since becoming

Simpson Creek's doctor, he mused as he drove back to town. The few deaths on the day of the Comanche attack didn't count—he'd only taken over, as any doctor would, when the town's physician had been felled by an arrow.

He tried to be philosophical as he drove back to town. Pneumonia was always a danger to the elderly, especially in winter. A doctor couldn't expect to be in practice and not see death.

The funeral was held two days later in the churchyard, where all the Simpson Creek inhabitants had been buried ever since the town had been founded back in the 1850s. Fortunately it was a mild day—cold enough to require a coat, but without any wind or rain. The whole town attended, for Hal Parker had been one of the first settlers of Simpson Creek. Nolan went too, in part out of respect to the family, but also because he knew he'd see Sarah there. With the loss of his first patient in town weighing on him, the pleasure of some time in Sarah's company would be a comfort, indeed.

She stood near the coffin, her golden hair a lovely contrast to the somber black dress and coat she wore. She caught his eye and nodded slightly as Maude Harkey joined her, then the two began an a cappella duet of "I Know that My Redeemer Liveth." Maude's voice was a reedy soprano; Sarah's clear notes soared above it in perfect pitch, though she sang no louder.

He decided that he'd speak to her after the service—casually of course. But while Reverend Chadwick read a passage from the Bible in which Jesus said He was the resurrection and the life, Nolan became distracted when he noticed that the deceased's widow was absent from the gathering, as was the daughter-in-law. Half of the Parker brood were coughing, and one of them, a little girl of perhaps six, looked especially sallow and wan and leaned against her older brother for support. Had they caught their grandpa's illness?

"I would also ask your prayers, good people, for Hal's widow, who took ill yesterday," Reverend Chadwick announced as he closed his Bible at the pulpit. "Sally Parker is home taking care of her. Under the circumstances, rather than having the usual dinner in the social hall following the burial, we're going to send the food y'all have so generously provided home with the Parkers, so they can get back to the ranch sooner."

It was a very good idea, Nolan thought, though the dinner would have given him a longer time to be in Sarah's company. It seemed like illnesses spread like wildfire among large gatherings in the winter, so he figured it wouldn't hurt if a cold spell kept Simpson Creek folks in their homes for a while. When he'd taken his medical training back east, he'd seen that whenever there'd been a milder winter and people were able to gather together often, there were more cases of chest colds, catarrh and influenza.

When the funeral service was over, some headed for their wagons or their homes down the road, while others lingered in the churchyard to talk. Nolan discreetly made his way toward Sarah, who along with Prissy had just helped the Parker family arrange the covered dishes of food into the buckboard among the children.

"Mr. Parker, if there's anything more I can do, please let me know," he said, before turning to Sarah. He'd be called out to see the little girl soon, unless he missed his guess.

"Thanks for what ya done, Doc," the drawn-faced

young rancher said as he climbed into the driver's perch. "No one could have tried harder to save Pa. It was jest his time, I reckon."

Nolan touched the brim of his hat to the man as he clucked to his horses and drove out.

"Sarah, your song was lovely," he said. *Though not as lovely as you.* He supposed Sarah Matthews would be beautiful in any circumstances.

Pink bloomed in her cheeks. She looked down, then back at him. "Th-thank you," she said. "It…it's always been a favorite of mine… I hope it blessed the Parkers…."

Nolan was conscious of all the people passing by them, of Prissy standing by Sarah, trying to appear as if she was not listening. They had probably come together. If only he had some excuse to take Sarah where they could talk.

"I… I hope you've been well…" he said, and thought immediately how ridiculously trite it sounded.

"Yes, of course… I'm usually healthy as a horse," she said, then chuckled. "Oh, my, that didn't sound very ladylike, did it?" she said, glancing at Prissy to include her in the conversation. "Ladies are supposed to be delicate flowers, aren't they?"

He appreciated a woman who could laugh at herself. "There's nothing wrong with having a sound constitution," he told her, and then silence reigned again as he tried to let his eyes speak for him.

Prissy took it upon herself to rescue them. "Dr. Walker, you *are* coming to the taffy pull the Spinsters' Club is holding on Friday night, aren't you? Seven o'clock, in the church social hall."

"I… I didn't know about it," he said. "I—"

"I hope it doesn't sound like a childish pastime, but it's hard to find things to do in the winter," Prissy said.

He didn't miss the surreptitious nudge Prissy gave Sarah. Obviously she thought Sarah should chime in on the invitation. But Sarah's gaze had strayed toward the road.

"Not at all," he said, wondering about the way she seemed to be sidling away from them—*as if she wants to be away from this place...or me. Does she not want me invited?*

"I confess I have a bit of a sweet tooth, so thanks for the invitation," he said. He wanted to ask Sarah if she would be there, too, but first he had to see what reaction she had to his acceptance of the invitation.

But her gaze remained fixed on the road before her. At last his gaze followed hers, knowing and dreading what he would see.

Ada Spencer was standing at the entrance to the churchyard, glaring at them, her eyes like drawn daggers. Her mother stood next to her, her expression worried, one arm anxiously draped around her daughter's shoulders as if to make sure Ada did not move any farther into the churchyard. She was obviously trying to urge her away, but Ada seemed glued to the spot.

Nolan fought the urge to give in to frustration and struggled to keep his face serene. What right did this disturbed woman have to destroy their peace, to ruin an innocent relationship?

"I'll leave first, and try to draw her away," he whispered to Sarah and Prissy. "I'll talk to you later, Sarah." He strode toward the road, lifting an arm in greeting, "Hello, Mrs. Spencer, Miss Spencer," he called, trying to sound as if he was genuinely glad to see them. "How have you been? Are you feeling well, Miss Spencer?" he said, as he reached them.

Ada smiled a strange smile, then let her coat fall open. She was wearing another oversized dress whose waist tie outlined the curve of her supposed pregnancy. "Oh, I've been feeling *very* well, dear Nolan," she said, in a weirdly cheerful voice that was loud enough to be heard by those still in the churchyard.

"You should call him Dr. Walker, Ada," her mother admonished. "He's a physician, and he deserves respect—"

"Oh, but we've been using each other's given names in private for a long time now, haven't we, Nolan? I suppose it *is* time for me to come see you in the office again," she said, patting her abdomen as she had at the New Year's Day party. "We do want to take proper care of our child, don't we?"

Nolan glanced at her mother, who only grimaced in pained ruefulness.

Why couldn't the woman control her daughter? Biting back the reply he wanted to make, he focused on Ada again. "That would be fine," he said carefully. "As the town doctor, I'm always happy to care for its inhabitants. Be sure to bring your mother with you, all right? I'm sure you'd be more comfortable that way. Good day to you both," he added, touching the brim of his hat and hurrying past them.

Reaching his yard, he opened the gate, then pretended he had dropped something until he could be sure Ada didn't linger to accost Sarah.

Chapter Eleven

Sarah couldn't stop looking over her shoulder every few yards as she and Prissy walked home, still not sure she wouldn't see Ada following them with some weapon raised high to attack her.

For God hath not given us the spirit of fear, but of power, and of love, and of a sound mind, she remembered from the New Testament, she thought, and felt the fear lift away from her as if someone had removed a thirty-pound sack of flour from her back.

Lord, please heal Ada and restore her sound mind.

They reached the wrought-iron fence that surrounded the mayor's house and grounds. "Thank God that crazy Ada didn't try to follow us, although I'm sure Dr. Walker wouldn't have let it happen," Prissy said, lifting the heavy iron latch that opened the gate. "Oh, I wish something could be done with her so she wouldn't keep popping up like that, when you least expect her! It's positively spooky," she grumbled on. "Why can't her parents see she needs to be in an institution? There ought to be a law."

"I'm sure that poor old couple can't bear the thought," Sarah said. "From everything I've ever heard about such places, it's like putting someone in a cage. You don't hear of anyone ever emerging again in his right mind."

Prissy rolled her eyes. "That may well be true, but I think you're being entirely too generous about this," she said. "Next, you'll say we need to keep praying about it."

Sarah grinned, for she had indeed been about to say that very thing. "Of course I wish Ada weren't acting like this—for Dr. Walker's sake, if not for mine. He looked so tired today at the graveside, so sad. I'm sure losing a patient must be very hard on him."

Prissy sighed. "See, you do care about him! Sarah, what Nolan Walker needs is a good *wife* to encourage him, to see that he eats properly, make sure he gets his rest."

The picture Prissy had painted of Sarah as devoted wife, caring for Nolan, was a very appealing one. But she couldn't dwell on it, because Prissy wasn't done.

"When are you going to get off your lofty perch and let yourself love him?" she went on. "That excuse that he's a Yankee's wearing a little thin by now, don't you think?"

Sarah stared at her as they had reached their little cottage and went in. She hung up her coat with a sigh, then took Prissy's coat and hung it up, too. "Dr. Walker and I *have* become friends. But how can he and I be anything more if he's not a believer? The Bible warns about being unequally yoked, you know."

Prissy groaned exasperatedly. "Sarah Matthews, if

you gave that man the *slightest* bit of encouragement, he'd be sitting in the front pew every Sunday morning, and you know it."

"Having him come to church with the wrong motive is not the answer," Sarah said. She knew she sounded prim and she didn't want to, but if Nolan came to church, she wanted it to be for the right reasons.

"Maybe he'd start off coming to see you, but while he was there, he'd have to hear the preaching," Prissy pointed out. "That's the way *I'd* do it, anyway."

Sarah sighed again. Could Prissy be right?

"You don't mind me inviting him to the taffy pull, do you?" Prissy asked. "I mean, I wasn't inviting him for my sake, but you were distracted by seeing Ada staring at you, which I didn't realize at the time, and I—"

"No, I'm glad you did," Sarah assured her. She couldn't deny she'd be glad to see Nolan there. Unless someone brought some unattached male guests, she and the other Spinsters would be watching the ones who were courting bill and coo with their beaux, something that was becoming harder and harder to do without feeling a very human envy. "With no family here in town, he probably doesn't take very much time to enjoy himself," Sarah murmured. "And perhaps he and one of the other Spinsters will discover a liking for one another..." She busied herself with lighting the stove and putting the teapot on top of it, activities that didn't require her to look Prissy in the eye.

Prissy gave a low whistle. "Sarah Matthews, you can just stop saying such silly things that you don't even believe. I'm not fooled for a minute."

Sarah couldn't help but smile. "I'm glad you always tell me the truth, Prissy," she said, and gave her friend an impulsive hug. "We'll see what happens. Now, why don't we get back to your cooking lessons? If your mama and papa are coming to supper tomorrow night, we'd better see if you can make some edible dumplings, and then we need to do a bit of housekeeping."

"Ever the taskmaster," Prissy groused goodnaturedly.

Nolan didn't show up at the taffy pull. Sarah told herself it didn't matter, that she hadn't been expecting him to, and tried to keep herself from watching the door every time it opened to reveal a new guest's arrival. She even had a good time, laughing and singing with the others as they stretched and pulled the sugary, sticky confection into pieces of candy. A wiry ranchhand from Cherokee glued himself to her side during the early part of the evening, and he was pleasant enough company, but when he left later without asking if he could call on her, she was only relieved.

Had Nolan been called out to see a patient, or had he decided a taffy pull was just too childish for a professional man such as himself to bother with? Perhaps he wasn't interested in her after all.

In actuality, Nolan had been summoned back to the Parker ranch that morning, for both the little Parker girl and her grandmother, Hal Parker's widow, were abed with the same high fever and coughing that had felled the old rancher. Hank Parker's wife was staying out of bed by sheer will to take care of them, for she was feverish and coughing, too.

By nightfall he'd forgotten all about the taffy pull, immersed as he was in the struggle to save the old woman and the child. He stayed out at the ranch for twenty-four hours, alternately medicating the grandmother and the granddaughter and helping the younger Mrs. Parker sponge both of them down. He finally sent the exhausted young wife off to bed and instructed her worried husband to heat up some of the broth left on the stove for her. By morning, the little girl seemed as if she would survive with some careful nursing, but the old woman had followed her husband into death.

He drove home the next day, aching in every joint, as weary and discouraged as he'd ever been in the war after hours in the casualty tents.

But when he arrived back at his office, there was already a man sitting on a horse in front of it, waiting for him. There would be no rest for him yet.

He visited two ranches and three houses in town that day, and all of the patients he saw were suffering from the same chills, fever, coughing and body aches. He dosed them for their fevers and coughs, instructed their families on nursing them and giving them lots of water and nourishing broths and reassured them the best he could. He advised the still-healthy inhabitants of each house to stay home so as not to spread the contagion.

Of the patients he saw that day, only two were advanced in years, so with any luck the others would recover. But it was clear that Simpson Creek was in the throes of an epidemic. And all of them had been at the funeral of Hal Parker.

Each time he returned to his office, someone else

was waiting to bring him to another sick person, or had left a note in his door that he was needed at such-and-such a house. He wished he could split himself into several doctors, so he could be in more places at one time, or at least had a trained assistant who, in his absence, could dispense medications, or take care of someone until he could get there. A nurse—yes, that's what he needed. A nurse. Or several nurses.

He finally fell into bed without eating supper, for he was too tired to make himself anything and it was too late to walk down to the hotel restaurant. He slept dreamlessly until the sound of church bells woke him the next morning.

Got to tell Reverend Chadwick he ought to call off Sunday services until this epidemic dies down, he thought groggily. People didn't need to be congregating in small places, spreading the sickness. If there was a God, wouldn't He understand?

He'd barely completed the thought before the sound of his office bell jangled him fully awake. Apparently he wasn't going to have time to have a proper breakfast and shave before his patients needed him again.

"I declare, I've never seen so many cases of the grippe," Mrs. Gilmore said Wednesday afternoon over dinner. Sarah and Prissy were dining with them, as they did at least twice a week. "Why, just in town yesterday I heard of half a dozen people down with it."

Sarah thought of Milly. They'd just been together at church Sunday, but perhaps she ought to ride out to the ranch this afternoon and check on her and Nick. If they were fine, she was going to tell them not to come into town, she decided. A woman with child didn't need to be exposed to sick people.

Before she left, she'd set a pot of vegetable soup to simmer on the stove, enough for their supper and to take some down to leave at Nolan's office. The poor man was likely working such long hours that he probably wasn't taking the time to eat properly. But could she trust Prissy to mind it so that it didn't boil down to nothing and scorch the soup into a charred mess? The girl could be so forgetful sometimes....

"And someone said it's really bad down at Burnet," Prissy's mother went on, helping herself to another serving of scalloped ham. "I'm going to have to write your Aunt Vira, Prissy, and make sure she's all right. She lives in Burnet, you know," she said to Sarah.

Sarah did know, for Mrs. Gilmore spoke incessantly about her older sister Vira. It sounded as if the woman was quite a character, and a hypochondriac to boot.

"Speaking of Vira, I stopped by the post office on my way home, and there was a letter from her," Mayor Gilmore announced, breezing into the dining room, late as usual, and waving an envelope.

Seizing the envelope, his wife dropped her fork on her china plate with a clatter and tore it open. She held out the unfolded page for a moment until her eyes found their focus, then scanned the page.

Sarah saw the color drain out of her normally florid cheeks.

"Oh dear," she murmured, and stared at the page again.

"Mama?" inquired Prissy. "Is Aunt Vira sick?"

"No, but she says everyone else in Burnet is, so she

thought it best to come here for a visit. She plans to stay until the influenza's all gone from down there. Anson's going to bring her, she says."

"Mama, you've got to write and tell her not to come!" Prissy cried. "It's no safer here, with people falling ill left and right."

"I can't," her mother wailed. "You know Vira—she never waits to hear an answer. She's probably already on the way!"

"Nevertheless, Martha, we ought to try," Mayor Gilmore said. "There's probably more risk of her bringing the contagion here than of her contracting it in Simpson Creek. Write out what you want to say after dinner, and I'll see if we can send a telegram—or if the wires are not working, maybe I can pay one of Andy Calhoun's boys at the livery to ride down with the message."

"Well, if you're not able to stop her, it'd be fun to see Anson, at least," Prissy said. "I've been writing him to persuade him to come visit with his mother ever since we started the Spinsters' Club, but he kept giving me excuses. I think the idea of all those single women scared him," Prissy said with a giggle. "You'd like him, Sarah."

"Didn't I meet him a long time ago? Before the war?" Sarah asked. She had a hazy image in her mind of a boy with dark brown hair some six years older than her who'd taken delight in tormenting the girls at a church picnic.

"That's right, you did—I remember now. Oh, he's changed since then," Prissy assured her. "Last May when we went down to Burnet to welcome him home from the war, I swan, he'd grown a foot taller while he was away," Prissy enthused. "And that military bearing..." She pretended to fan herself. "If he wasn't my cousin..."

Sarah laughed at her friend, and then everyone was quiet as the clatter of horses' hooves and carriage wheels on the driveway outside reached their ears.

Mayor Gilmore got to his feet and peered out the window. "Well, you needn't bother writing the message. She's here, she and Anson. And from the amount of trunks and boxes, she means to stay for a while."

Chapter Twelve

With an excited shriek, Prissy sprang up from the table. She ran to the window to confirm her father's words, then out of the dining room, her shoes clattering on the flooring of the hallway. Mayor Gilmore and his wife hastened after her in a more decorous fashion. Sarah followed them, lingering in the doorway, not wanting to intrude too soon on a family reunion.

"Aunt Vi! Anson!" Prissy called, running down the steps. The young man assisting his mother out of the landau had his back to them when Sarah reached the doorway, but Sarah could see that he was tall and solidly built. Aunt Vira was plumper than her sister, indeed quite rotund, and possessed of at least two chins. She was dressed in a matching violet coat and bonnet which clashed violently with the maroon wool dress beneath it.

Sarah saw the old woman look up to see her niece rushing at her, but before she opened her arms to her, Aunt Vira pressed a rumpled lacy handkerchief to her mouth and gave a gusty sneeze.

"Oh, my dear girl! Martha, Herbert! I certainly hope you have a roaring fire going, for I declare, I've never been so chilled in all my born days!" she cried, embracing Prissy, and then her sister. "Anson put a hot brick at my feet when we left, but it didn't stay hot very long, I can tell you. And that road! My poor bones have never been so rattled about in my body! I felt as if my brain was about to shake right out of my skull!" She sneezed again.

"I told Mama the trip would be hard on her, and that we should keep to home, but she insisted on coming," said the young man, who had finished giving Antonio directions on stabling the horses and had now come to join his mother. "Why, cousin Prissy, you're looking all grown up!" he said with raised eyebrows.

Sarah understood instantly why Prissy had hinted that her cousin was handsome. With those dark eyes and hair and that broad-shouldered frame, she could well imagine he could make quite an impression on the Spinsters' Club if he stayed long enough.

"Oh, pooh, I don't look any different than I did in May when we came to see y'all," Prissy pouted prettily, and her cousin gazed down at her, enchanted.

As long as there were women like Prissy, Sarah thought with amusement, there would always be Southern belles.

"But who's this?" Anson said, tearing his gaze away from Prissy and toward Sarah.

Prissy didn't seem to mind relinquishing the spotlight. "Aunt Vira, Anson, this is my best friend, Miss Sarah Matthews. Sarah, my aunt, Mrs. James Tyler, and my cousin Anson."

Anson strode forward and bowed to Sarah. "Miss Matthews, I am charmed to meet you," he said, turning the full force of his smile on her. *"Charmed."*

Sarah could no more have stopped the smile which spread across her face at this fulsome greeting than she could stop breathing, but even as her eyes catalogued his features, she was thinking how Nolan's angular face appealed to her more.

"Mrs. Tyler, Mr. Tyler, nice to meet you," Sarah murmured.

"Oh, no, that won't do, Miss Matthews," protested Anson smoothly. "Please, call me Anson."

Aunt Vira smothered a cough before saying, "And where do you live, Miss Matthews? Are you visiting with Prissy?"

"That's the best part, Aunt Vira!" Prissy interrupted. "She lives right there," she said, pointing beyond the older woman toward the cottage, which was nearer to the road. "With me! Mama and Papa are letting us use the old cottage!"

Vira Tyler's jaw dropped open. "Whatever for? Why would you choose to live away from your dear mama and papa, niece? That makes no sense."

Prissy giggled. "Oh, Aunt Vira, we're just across the lawn from the big house!"

"Actually, it makes perfect sense, Vira," Mayor Gilmore put in smoothly. "Martha was at her wit's end trying to teach Priscilla all the housewifely arts when our daughter would much rather think of feminine fripperies, but her friend Miss Matthews seems to have perfected all the skills and virtues that a young lady should know to manage her own house. So we thought it a fine idea to let them live in the cottage for a while, where Miss Matthews can teach her all these things. I fear we have been too indulgent with our only daughter, Vira, but she learns willingly from Miss Matthews."

Unseen by her parents and her aunt, Prissy rolled her eyes at Sarah before interjecting, "Aunt Vira, she's teaching me how to cook! I've learned to make delicious stews and light-as-a-feather cakes and mouthwatering fried chicken and—"

"Yes, yes," Vira Tyler said, waving one hand and dabbing her forehead with her handkerchief in the other. She sneezed yet again. "That's wonderful, dear niece, and you must tell me more later, but right now, I need to get inside by the fire. I am chilled to the bone, I tell you! If there's been a colder day this winter, I can't remember it."

Sarah saw Prissy's parents exchange a look. Though overcast, the weather had been very mild for January. Without another word, they helped Aunt Vira into the house.

Anson tucked Prissy's arm in his as they strolled toward the house. "Perhaps you'd like to demonstrate your newfound prowess in the kitchen for me while I'm here, cousin."

"What a good idea! We'll make a party of it! I'll invite the ladies in the club who have not yet found a beau, and—"

"*Whoa,* cousin! What's wrong with just the three of us, you, me and Miss Sarah?" He winked at Sarah over his shoulder. "I believe I'd like to become better acquainted with your friend, not be subjected to a passel of females all aiming their wiles at me at once."

Prissy let out a peal of laughter. "Why, Anson, who's to say our friends are going to fall all over you, you conceited thing? And if you hadn't interrupted me, I was going to say I'd be inviting Nolan Walker, our new town doctor. He would like very much to court Sarah, but she's still making up her mind about him—"

"Prissy, you're talking about me as if I weren't here," Sarah complained. "And I'm very sure your cousin isn't interested in my personal business," she added with a quelling glare at her friend. Prissy could be such an artless chatterbox at times!

Anson was about to mount the first step up into the house, but at that, he let go of Prissy's arm and turned around to grin at her. "Oh, but I *am* interested, Miss Sarah. A man likes to know at the outset if he has a rival."

Sarah took a step back, unsure how to politely discourage Prissy's cousin's flirtatiousness. Perhaps, if she had not met Nolan first, she might have found Anson Tyler's confident charm appealing. The thought startled her—she had insisted she wasn't interested in Nolan, and yet again she found him preferable to another man?

Even as she made this startling realization, Prissy gave her cousin a light, playful slap on the cheek. "Now you *stop* that, Anson! You'll frighten Sarah away, and she'll move back to the ranch, and Mama and Papa will make me live in the big house...."

Anson raised his hands in mock surrender. "All right, all right," he said. "I hope I haven't offended you, Miss Sarah? I promise to behave myself during my stay here. Pax?"

Sarah smiled in spite of herself. "Pax."

"Wonderful," Prissy said. "You must be hungry, Anson. I'm sure Flora is putting dinner together for you at this very moment. Let's all go inside and chat. You can tell us what's become of all those handsome boys you mustered out with, Anson."

"Y'all go ahead," Sarah told them. "You'll want to spend some time with your relatives, and I have some things to do."

"But—"

"I'll be back by supper," she assured them. "Prissy, I'm sure you'll want to show Anson our cottage—could you just check on the soup I'm going to put on the stove to simmer?"

Sarah headed for the stable, where she requested Antonio saddle the horse she usually borrowed. Then she went to the cottage, where earlier she had diced some carrots, onions and the remains of some chicken they'd had last night, added some dried beans she'd soaked overnight and some pepper, salt and dried chilies and mixed it all in a pot of chicken stock. Then she set it on the stove to simmer before changing into her riding clothes.

Within half an hour she was riding toward the ranch.

She found Milly in her kitchen, stirring her own pot, but hers held chili. The room was redolent with the savory, spicy smell.

"Oh, I was just thinking about you!" Milly cried, rushing forward to embrace her sister. "I heard someone ride up, but I thought it was just one of the men coming in from the pasture. They're all out checking fence and tending stock, but they'll be so glad to see you!"

Roses bloomed in Milly's cheeks once again, Sarah noted, and if she could stand the smell of chili cooking, she must be feeling better.

"You'll stay for supper, won't you?" Milly burbled on. "I'll have one of the men ride back with you, or you could even stay the night… I'm so happy to have some female company after all these men!"

Sarah shook her head. "I'm sorry, I promised I'd be back at the cottage for supper." She told Milly about Prissy's aunt and cousin showing up unexpectedly, but didn't mention one of the reasons she wanted to get back was to deliver soup to Dr. Walker. "I really just came to see how you were doing, to see if everyone was well."

Milly blinked. "Fine as frog hair split three ways—even me," she said with a grin, patting her abdomen, "though I've had to let out my dresses in the waist a bit. Good thing I'm handy with a needle, hmm?" She studied Sarah more closely. "Why shouldn't we be well?"

"The influenza's getting really bad in town, Milly," Sarah told her. "Several folks have come down with it since old Mr. Parker died. I see Dr. Walker's buggy going back and forth all the time, and it seems like there's always a horse or a wagon parked in front of his office. I came to tell you as long as everyone's healthy out here at the ranch, you'd better not come into town. No sense in risking your health, Milly, especially now that you're expecting."

Milly frowned and her shoulders sagged. "But I was just planning to go to mercantile, now that I'm feeling better," she said. "Bobby's grown out of all his shirts again," she said, referring to their youngest cowhand. "And what about church on Sunday?"

Sarah was thoughtful. It was now Wednesday. "You'd better stay home, Milly. Send one of the men to the mercantile if you absolutely have to have something, or send them to me. As for church, I'm sure the Lord will understand."

"Well, at least sit down with me for a few minutes and have a cup of tea and some of these cookies I made," Milly said, pointing to a crockery jar on the table. "Tell me all about Prissy's aunt and cousin. The middle of January seems like an odd time to come for a visit."

Sarah nodded. "The influenza's hit Burnet very hard, so she wanted to get away from it, I expect." She thought Prissy's aunt was coming down with something, too, what with the way she couldn't stop sneezing and coughing when she arrived, but she didn't mention it, not wanting to worry Milly.

"And is her boy Anson as ornery as ever? I imagine he's all grown up now, isn't he?"

Sarah nodded. "He's grown a foot since he went away to war, and filled out some. He's quite the handsome charmer now."

"Ohhhhh?" No one could inject such a depth of meaning into a single syllable and a lifted brow as her sister.

"He tried flirting with me, but I indicated I wasn't interested," Sarah said loftily, pretending a great interest in brushing a cookie crumb off her bodice. "Though I imagine the Spinsters' Club ladies will be."

"Why?" Milly said, ignoring Sarah's second remark for the first. "Because of our Yankee doctor?"

To her dismay, Sarah felt a blush spreading up her cheeks. "Of course not. I don't know why you and Prissy keep trying to pair us off."

Milly only smiled.

"We agreed to be friends," Sarah said, "and then he didn't even show up at the taffy pull, and hasn't mentioned it since. Though I imagine it was because he was so busy taking care of all those sick folks," she admitted, determined to be fair.

"And how's Ada?" Milly asked.

Milly had been to the Parker funeral, but she had left before Ada had shown up and glared at them. Sarah told her sister about the incident, finishing with "But I haven't seen her since, fortunately."

"You be careful if you do," Milly said. "I'll pray for her."

The grandfather clock in the parlor struck the hour. "Goodness, it's getting late," Sarah said, rising. She wanted to return in time to deliver that soup to Nolan so he'd have it before he was ready for his supper. "I've got to be going. Please tell Nick and the men I'm sorry I didn't get to see them…."

As much as she cared about Molly and the rest of the ranch's inhabitants, she felt pulled back to Simpson Creek as if by a magnet. For that was where Nolan was.

Chapter Thirteen

No light showed through the windows, either in the doctor's office or the connected house in the back as Sarah strode up the walk in the gathering dusk. Setting the heavy pot of soup on the step, Sarah walked around the yard toward the back, her high-button boots crunching the dead brown grass. A quick glance around showed the buggy parked, its traces empty, but just to be sure he hadn't ridden the horse, she stepped into the small barn and found his chestnut gelding in his stall, busily devouring his oats. The beast looked up, snorted at her, then dipped his head to his feed once more.

Had Nolan already gone down to the hotel for supper? A glance at the watch pinned to her bodice had told her it was only five, but perhaps he'd missed the midday meal and had gone early. She'd knock, just in case.

Repeated knocking produced nothing but an answering silence. She was about to turn and go, but on an impulse, stooped to peer through the waiting room window.

In the dimness she could make out the shape of a man sprawled in one of the chairs, his feet propped up on another chair, shirtsleeved arms splayed out limply beside him. Nolan's mouth gaped open slightly.

It was his utter stillness that alarmed her. Through the window she could not see any rise and fall of his chest, any movement of his jaw that would indicate Nolan Walker was alive. Oh dear, what if he had died, a victim of the very epidemic he was trying to combat? Could the influenza work that fast? Perhaps it could, if someone was utterly exhausted from his work, as Nolan must be.

With a cry of alarm, she tried the knob and found it unlocked. Maybe she was not too late. Perhaps if he was still breathing, and she summoned aid—Reverend Chadwick would be the closest—they could get him to bed and nurse him back from the brink… She crashed into the room.

The "dead" man came instantly awake, throwing himself into an upright position before his blue eyes were even fully opened.

"Are there wounded, corporal?" he barked out. "How many? How bad off? Are we in retreat? How close are the rebels?"

She uttered a shriek of surprise and jumped back at his rapid-fire questions and sudden violent movement, even as relief flooded over her that he was not dead or dying. "Dr. Walker—*Nolan*—it's me, Sarah Matthews," she said. "The war is *over*, remember? You're in Simpson Creek, Texas."

She watched him guardedly as Nolan struggled to focus on her, saw when the realization hit him that he'd been dreaming, and when recognition dawned in his sharp blue eyes.

"Ayuh," he said, his voice thick with his "downeast" accent and the remains of sleep. He stood up. "Of course. I… I dozed off for a moment. Just needed a catnap… What time is it?" he asked, rubbing his eyes and then his chin.

"Going on five-thirty."

He blinked, reminding her of an owl.

"Wh-what are you doing here, Sarah? You—you're not ill, are you?" he asked, a touch of anxiety in his voice. He peered at her closely. "Or are you here for someone else?"

"No, I'm not sick, and I'm not here for anyone else," she said, seeing the weariness lining his face, and his pallor. "But you're going to be soon if you don't start taking better care of yourself, Nolan. I—I brought you some soup," she added.

"Soup?" he muttered, looking confused as his gaze fell on her empty hands.

"I left it on the step." She went out to get the pot.

He was alert enough by the time she came back in to open the door for her. "But why—?"

"Because I guessed that you might have been so busy that you weren't taking time to go to the hotel for a proper meal."

"You'd be right about that. I was going to walk down there, after I shut my eyes for a minute…that was an hour ago, I think." He lifted the lid and sniffed the pot's contents, gazing into the mixture of chicken, vegetables and broth like a child might look at a gingerbread house at Christmas. "*Mmm,* still warm." His face relaxed from its tense lines and his mouth broadened into a smile. Then his stomach rumbled, loudly, and they both laughed.

"Sarah, I think you arrived just in the nick of time and probably saved my life," he said. "Will you come into the kitchen and have a bowlful with me?" He took the heavy pot from her and set it on the chair beside him.

She looked at him, wanting to say yes, but knowing it wouldn't be quite proper to be alone with him in his private quarters. She didn't want to keep Prissy waiting for their supper, either, though her friend still hadn't returned from the big house when Sarah came in from the ranch.

"I… I have to get back to the cottage," she said. "Prissy will be waiting for me, and we're to have company, Prissy's cousin." She explained again about the unexpected arrival of Prissy's relatives from Burnet, but unlike when she had told her sister, she told Nolan how Vira Tyler had seemed to be in the early stages of an illness.

"Of all the fool things to do!" he snapped. "The newspaper editor was just telling me today how he's had word that the influenza's hit Burnet badly, and Prissy's aunt's came from there, probably bringing it with her. You must stay completely away from her, Sarah, do you hear? You and Prissy both."

His sharp tone took her aback. "I—I'll try, Nolan, but I don't know if Prissy will. It's her aunt, after all," she said, her tone mildly reproving.

He sighed. "I'm sorry," he said. "I didn't mean to sound as if I was issuing orders. It's just that this influenza's the most virulent I've ever seen, and in case that's what she's got instead of an ordinary catarrh, I don't want your health endangered. Or Prissy's either, for that matter."

The caring in his tone, and blazing from his blue eyes, touched something deep in her soul.

"There are a lot of people stricken with it around Simpson Creek?"

He nodded, his face grave. "There've been a handful of deaths already between Simpson Creek and San Saba," he told her. "People who woke up feeling well enough, just a bit tired, who've been on their deathbeds by the next morning. Mostly old folks, though I've seen plenty younger who were hard hit. It starts with the same sneezing and coughing that you said Prissy's aunt is doing. And like anything contagious, it spreads quickest when people are gathered together. I'm going to have to speak to Reverend Chadwick about canceling church services till this is over."

Her mouth fell open. "Canceling church?" she repeated, aghast at the idea. "How could coming together to pray and sing be harmful?"

His brows knit together and his eyes grew stormy. "Everyone coming to gather in that little building is the very worst thing that could happen. It would only help the sickness spread," he said, as if incredulous that she would have to ask.

He shrugged. "We physicians don't know how illnesses like this spread, only that they do when people congregate together like that. There's no need to make my job that much harder."

The condescension that flavored his Yankee voice

lit a spark of irritation in her. "You might consider that the town coming together to worship could make your job easier," she said.

"And how could *that* possibly be?" he demanded.

"We could pray for you, and for those who were ill," she said. "Or haven't you ever heard of praying for the sick?" There—she could be patronizing, too.

He blinked. "Yes, of course, and I used to believe in it," he said.

"'Used to?'" How could she have forgotten that however friendly they had become, they were poles apart in matters of faith? "You think it's impossible that the Lord could care about an influenza epidemic in a little Texas town?"

His face softened, and his gaze fell. "I… I'm sorry, Sarah. I don't mean to quarrel with you. I fear I'm too tired to remember my manners. Please forgive me."

"Of course," she murmured, seeing anew the lines of weariness that creased his forehead and cheeks. "And I'm keeping you from eating the soup. But before I go, I had another reason for coming," she said. "Prissy wanted me to invite you to come down to the cottage for supper tomorrow," she said. "I imagine you and Anson would have a lot to talk about, since you both served in the war, though of course he was a Confederate. I hope that's not a problem for you?"

In actuality, she thought it might be more of a problem for Anson, so she'd have to make sure he was prepared to be civil to their Yankee doctor.

"And we were going to ask a couple of the Spinsters' Club ladies, those that aren't attached to anyone…" She didn't say other females were being invited to discourage Anson from flirting with her, for she thought Nolan's presence might be sufficient to accomplish that.

His expression told her that he realized the significance of her inviting him somewhere, but it was followed by one of regret.

"I thank you for the invitation," he said, "but even if I weren't on a call when suppertime comes, I have to tell you I think any social gatherings are ill-advised right now, for the same reason I believe church should be postponed for a while."

Her gaze met his, and she saw the pleading for her to understand in those blue depths.

"I suppose you're right," she said with a sigh. "Very well, if Prissy hasn't already invited the other ladies, I'll tell her not to. But I suspect she's afraid Anson will be bored, and go home to his farm, leaving Vira with them for too long a visit," she confided. "Why don't you just come, if you're not on a call? We'll leave the invitation open. You have to eat, and so will Anson," she pointed out reasonably. "We'll understand if you don't stay late afterward, I promise."

"I really think you ought to go back to your ranch till the threat is over."

"I just came from there," she said. "I told Milly not to come into town, since she's expecting, but I can't go running back to the ranch every time something happens."

He sighed. "Very well, I'll be there if I'm able, Sarah. And thank you again for your thoughtfulness," he added, gesturing toward the soup.

Sarah had only gone as far as the millinery shop,

which lay midway between the doctor's office and the cottage, though, when she saw Prissy and Anson coming toward her. Even in the gathering darkness, she could see their faces were grave.

"I'm sorry, did you get impatient waiting on me for supper?" she called. "Didn't you see the note I left that I was delivering some of the soup to Dr. Walker?"

Prissy shook her head. "No, it's not that. We've come to fetch the doctor."

"What's wrong?" Sarah asked, stopping stock-still. She had a feeling she already knew, however.

"Mother's taken very ill, Miss Sarah," Anson told her, his flirtatious manner gone as if it had never been. "She began having shaking chills while we were eating, and Aunt Martha put her to bed with a hot brick at her feet. She woke up with a high fever just a little while ago. And she's short of breath."

"Flora said her forehead was so hot she was afraid the sheets would catch fire," Prissy said, her eyes wide in the shadows. Since both the Mexican housekeeper and Prissy had a penchant for dramatic exclamations, Sarah didn't take the statement at face value, but she knew the situation was serious.

"Mama's staying with her, sponging her forehead and trying to get some willow bark tea into her. Oh, Sarah, please say you found Dr. Walker at home."

Sarah nodded, reversing her direction and beckoning for them to follow. Poor Nolan. He probably hadn't even had time to eat a bowl of the soup before he'd be forced to leave his home once more.

Chapter Fourteen

Too hungry to bother reheating the soup, which was at least still tepid, Nolan was just lifting the first spoonful to his mouth when the bell at the door tinkled yet again.

Smothering a most unphysicianly curse, he let the spoon drop with a clatter back in the bowl and got to his feet. If it was anything less than a dire emergency, he promised himself as he trudged down the connecting hallway that led to the waiting room, he was going to tell whoever had come he'd be along in a few minutes after he'd finished his meal. A doctor had to eat, like everyone else. Or perhaps, if he was required to go some distance, he could put some soup in a big mug and gulp it as he drove. It was better than nothing.

When he recognized Sarah's anxious face in the window, however, thoughts of his interrupted meal fled.

He opened the door quickly. "Sarah? What's wrong?" He saw that Sarah was flanked by a worried-looking Prissy and a somewhat younger man he didn't recognize—her cousin from Burnet?

"Oh, Nolan, I'm so sorry to bother you again so soon, but on my way back to the cottage, I met Prissy and her cousin on their way here. Prissy tells me her aunt's taken very badly since I went out to the ranch this afternoon. Oh…sorry," she added, with an apologetic glance at the other man on the steps. "This is Mr. Anson Tyler, Prissy's cousin. Anson, Dr. Nolan Walker."

"Mr. Tyler," he said, acknowledging the other man, and pretending not to see how Anson Tyler had stiffened at the sound of his voice.

"Please, will you come to the house, Dr. Walker? Aunt Vira's burning up with fever, and she's short of breath—" began Prissy.

But Anson Tyler was putting up a hand to stop his cousin's flow of words. "Prissy, we won't be needing this man's services after all," he snapped, his body rigid, his voice shaking with indignation. "You didn't inform me the man was a Yankee. I won't have him touching my mother, do you hear? I take it there is no other physician in Simpson Creek? I'll escort you ladies to the house, and then I'll saddle a horse and ride for San Saba. There must be a doctor there we can trust."

Nolan felt his temper kindle at the stiff-necked rebel's foolishness. If not for Sarah's and Prissy's presence, he might well have told Anson Tyler to come back when he was prepared to be sensible and closed his door on him.

But before he could say anything, Nolan saw anger storm over Prissy's normally cheerful features. She rounded on her cousin, stamping a tiny booted foot as she exploded. "Anson Tyler, don't be a fool! The war is over and Nolan Walker is a fine doctor!" She shook her small fist at him.

Then Sarah chimed in. "Anson, it would take you an hour or more to saddle up and ride in the dark to San Saba, longer still to return with its doctor, even assuming you could find him. What would you do if you found him gone, out tending some sick person there? You'd lose time your mother may not have!"

Prissy turned her back on Tyler and stepped closer to Nolan. "Please forgive my witless cousin, Dr. Walker—we'd be very grateful if you'd come see what you can do for my aunt."

Sarah looked as if she would very much like to box Tyler's ears, but she turned her pleading gaze on Nolan, too. "Please?" she murmured, and he knew in that moment he could refuse her nothing. He waited for consent from Anson Tyler, though. He could see pride and loyalty to the lost cause of the South warring with filial love and practicality, and he saw the moment the latter virtues won.

"Very well, Priscilla, Sarah, perhaps you're right in this matter," he conceded. "Under the circumstances, I will set patriotism aside *for the moment*—" he said, his dark eyes warning Nolan "—and let this Yankee sawbones see what he can do for my mother. But take care, Yankee—I'm putting you on notice that we'll not accept any stinting in her care."

Nolan set his teeth to prevent a contemptuous retort, saying only "If you'll excuse me, I'll just get my bag."

As he retraced his steps down the passageway, he heard Prissy snap, "Anson Tyler, if you don't stop being such an *idiot*, I'm never going to speak to you again!"

Nolan grinned. Texas women might appear fragile, but they had backbones of steel, and they didn't suffer fools gladly.

Sarah waited with Prissy, Anson and Mayor Gilmore in the parlor at the foot of the stairs while Mrs. Gilmore accompanied Nolan up the stairs to the guest room where her sister lay. They were gone, it seemed, for an eternity; when he returned to the parlor alone, his face was bleak.

Anson had jumped up when he came into the room. "How's Mother doing? What do you think about her chances, Dr. Walker? You didn't leave her alone, did you?" he asked, with a trace of his previous suspicion.

"She's sleeping at the moment, sir. Your aunt is staying with her while I speak to you. I've given her something for the fever and the cough."

"You can save her, can't you?" Anson pleaded, his eyes wide with dread.

Prissy patted his shoulder soothingly. "If anyone can, he can, Anson."

"I don't know," Nolan said honestly. "Tonight will be critical. Much depends on the lady's constitution."

Sarah thought Anson looked even more frantic when he heard those words. Prissy had already told her that Aunt Vira suffered many ailments, and her heart wasn't strong. The excess weight she carried probably wasn't helpful, either.

"Have you applied a mustard plaster? The doctor in Burnet swears by them," Anson said eagerly.

Nolan shook his head. "I haven't, but when I arrived, the housekeeper informed me she had. I left it on—it will do no harm."

"How about a purgative?" Mayor Gilmore suggested. "Calomel syrup?"

Again, Nolan shook his head. "A lot of physicians use it, but I see no value in a medicine whose chief ingredient is toxic mercury."

"How about bleeding her?" Anson said. "Surely you've thought of that."

Sarah thought she detected a flash of impatience in Nolan's face, but it was gone too quickly to be sure. His next words, uttered flatly, though, tended to confirm what she'd seen.

"The option crossed my mind, yes, but it's my belief it only weakens the patient," he said. "Some of my fellow doctors did it during the war, when they could think of nothing else to do. Their patients died, for the most part."

"But—surely there's something you can *do?*" Anson demanded indignantly.

"Mr. Tyler, in the Hippocratic oath, physicians are instructed 'First, do no harm.' I realize it's difficult to wait out the hours, but I've treated her fever and her cough, and propped her up on pillows so she can breathe more easily. It's called supportive therapy. I will continue to watch over her. After that, it's up to the patient."

"And up to the Lord," Sarah said, startling herself when she realized she had spoken out loud. "I've been praying… I'm sure we all have been," she said, looking around the parlor at the others. “Perhaps we could send for Reverend Chadwick.”

“I’ll send Antonio,” Mayor Gilmore said, getting heavily to his feet. He appeared relieved to have something to do. Anson sank back into the chair, nodding in acceptance.

Nolan’s eyes met hers, and in them, she saw gratitude that she had calmed those in the room with her words.

Lord, please, if it’s Your Will, save Mrs. Tyler and show Nolan that You are indeed the Great Physician. Help him to realize that You are present, working alongside him.

He was awake, but in that not-fully-focused state in which one part of his mind watched the labored rise and fall of the elderly woman’s chest and heard the whistle of her breathing, while the rest of his mind roamed free, visiting the past, pondering the future, when some slight sound—a rustle or the creak of a floorboard behind him—brought him to full alertness.

He turned, and saw Sarah standing there, a candle in its holder in one hand, a plate with a covered bowl in the other.

A glance at the clock told him it was midnight. “Sarah? Sarah, you should not be here,” he said softly, rising with the stiffness that long stillness brought and coming to meet her. He’d thought she must have gone back to the cottage long since and be fast asleep.

She came into the circle of light provided by the lamp on the bedside table. “I couldn’t sleep,” she confessed in a whisper, her gaze going to the woman on the bed. “How is Mrs. Tyler?”

“About the same,” he said. “Soon it will be time to give her some more of the willow bark tea, if I can arouse her enough for her to safely swallow. She was cooler for awhile, but now her fever’s climbing again. What is this you’re carrying?”

“I got to thinking about how you never did get to eat your supper,” she said. “I thought I’d warm up some of that soup and offer to sit with her while you eat it.”

“Dear Sarah,” he said, smiling at her in the flickering light. “You are determined to feed me, aren’t you? I’m so tired I’m almost past the point of hunger, but this will be very welcome,” he said, taking the plate from her. He saw that there were also sandwiches next to the covered bowl of soup. “But come back into the anteroom, here, and sit with me while I eat. I don’t want you exposed to her illness any more than you have already been.”

She hesitated. “But Mrs. Tyler—”

“Will be well enough for a few minutes,” he finished for her. “I’ll be able to hear any change in her breathing from here,” he said, gesturing her into the adjoining room, where a small table and a pair of chairs stood.

“Who came in, after I came upstairs?” he asked her. “I heard the door open and close, and voices.”

“Reverend Chadwick,” she told him. “He’s downstairs, keeping a prayer vigil. He said to call him if you needed him.”

He absorbed the fact. “He’s a good man. Did you tell him what I said about canceling church services?”

She nodded. "He said he'd pray about it tonight. If he does decide to cancel them, he could put out the word around town, but there's always a chance people from the outlying ranches wouldn't hear and would show up anyway."

"But there'd be fewer of them. Did the Gilmores and Mrs. Tyler's son go to bed?" he inquired in between spoonfuls of soup. "Prissy, too?"

She nodded.

"That's good. They're going to need their rest tonight, in order to be strong enough to combat this influenza if and when it strikes them. After being around Mrs. Tyler so closely today, I fully expect one or more or them to come down with it," he told her. "Especially her son, who's been around her from its onset."

"I'll be here to help take care of them," she told him, her gaze meeting his steadily.

She was as brave and selfless as any of the sturdy male assistants who'd served with him in the battlefield tents, he thought, though slender and dainty. No wonder he was falling in love with her.

"I don't want you ill, Sarah, but I may have to take you up on that. So you'd best go now and get some rest yourself, in case I have to call on you for nursing care."

"I will in a minute, Nolan, but before I go, I have a question for you, something I've been wondering about for a long time now."

"Yes?" He could not imagine what it was, but her lovely face was serious.

"Will you tell me what were you doing in Brazos County, after the war, when you wrote me from there?"

Chapter Fifteen

She saw his blue eyes widen a bit, and thought he was going to assent, but then, from the other room, she heard Mrs. Tyler cough and utter a little moan.

To Sarah's disappointment, he shook his head.

"It's too long a story. There's no way I could summarize it in a few short sentences and send you on to your rest." Then he reached out and took her hand. "But I promise I *will* tell you one day, Sarah, when all this is over. I want to tell you about it."

She would have to be content with that for now.

"All right, Nolan. I'll say good night. Prissy and I will go back to the cottage to sleep, but Mrs. Gilmore told me there's a bellpull by Mrs. Tyler's bed that will summon Flora if you have need of anything. We'll see you in the morning. The guest room's been made ready for you down the hall," she added, pointing. "When I relieve you in the morning, you can sleep."

He shook his head wearily. "I'll have to go back to the office in case anyone else is seeking me."

She nodded, realizing she had forgotten in the last

few hours that many others in and around Simpson Creek were also suffering from the influenza epidemic. How could one doctor take care of all of them? When could Nolan rest?

Her fears must have shown on her face, for he reached out a hand and cupped her cheek. “Don’t worry, dear Sarah,” he said, in that flat downeast accent she was coming to love. “We doctors learn to doze in chairs, eyes closed, but with our ears attuned to any change. I’ll manage. Now go sleep—doctor’s orders.”

She managed a weak smile at his words and left, sure she would never sleep a wink for worrying.

For God hath not given us the spirit of fear...

She fell asleep praying.

Sarah woke the next morning with Prissy shaking her arm. “Come on, we’ve got to go to the house.”

“Is your aunt—?” Sarah could not put her dread into words.

“She’s no better—no worse, either—but Mama and Papa both came down with fever and chills during the night.” Prissy’s eyes were wide with anxiety. “Anson’s wild with worry.”

Sarah dressed hurriedly and followed Prissy out of the cottage. On the way, Prissy explained that Nolan had gone back to his office to get more medicine for them and would be back as soon as he could.

Going up the walk into his office, Nolan noticed that there was already a sign posted in front of the church:

SUNDAY CHURCH SERVICE CANCELED UNTIL FURTHER NOTICE DUE TO INFLUENZA OUTBREAK. PLEASE PRAY FOR THOSE SUFFERING.

A good, sensible man, the reverend.

Once inside, Nolan bent over his open black bag, replenishing his supplies of willow bark extract and morphine, conscious of the need to hasten back to the Gilmores'. He hadn't been surprised to learn that the mayor and his wife had come down with the first symptoms of influenza during the night; it often took hold quickly like that and this was apparently quite a virulent epidemic. He was concerned for them, for neither was young nor of a particularly sound constitution, and Prissy had mentioned her mother had a weak heart just as her aunt did. Both the mayor's wife and her sister, he suspected, were subject to dropsy. Perhaps Mrs. Gilmore and Vira Tyler would benefit from a little digitalis.

He sighed. There was so little in his bag that really helped with influenza. He could treat fever and pain, but after that, it was up to the body to recover—or not. He refused to buy the patent medicines that were advertised in the newspapers as the answer to every ill. He knew they contained little but flavoring and opium or alcohol. Nor would he use the drugs his colleagues had relied on but which he knew to be dangerous, such as calomel.

He was running low on morphine. Simpson Creek wasn't big enough to boast a druggist's shop, but perhaps he could persuade Anson Tyler to use some of his nervous energy to ride to San Saba's chemist for some—it would give the man something to do besides pacing the floor outside his mother's room and glaring at Nolan.

A movement at the window caught his eye and he turned his head, but before he could focus on it, it was gone. It may have been only a bird perching on his windowsill, but might it be some patient peeking in to see if he was present before he knocked?

There was no one at the door, however. Going to the side yard where the window was, he looked down the street and was just in time to see a female figure in a green dress disappearing into the Spencers' house.

Had Ada been spying on him through the window? He felt a flicker of annoyance, then pity for the madwoman.

He thought for a moment of going to inquire at the Spencers' to see if they were well, and by so doing make it plain to Ada that she had been seen, but he decided against it. He needed to get back to the Gilmores' house, and didn't have time today for Ada and her pregnancy fantasies.

He didn't wish influenza on his worst enemy, but the thought occurred to him that if Ada Spencer contracted it, he'd at least have the opportunity to examine her—properly chaperoned by her mother, of course—and prove once and for all she was not with child.

For Sarah and Prissy, the day blurred into a nightmare of sponging the feverish Gilmores and Mrs. Tyler with cool water, changing their sweat-dampened sheets and covering them with blankets when the chills rattled their teeth. They made sure the patients were propped up with pillows to help their labored breathing. They emptied basins. Sarah was glad when Nolan sent Anson after some additional morphine, for his constant barging into his mother's sickroom to check on her condition was making Prissy jumpy as a cat.

She supported both women and helped Prissy hold her father in a leaning position while Nolan thumped their upper backs rhythmically. This was called chest percussion, he told them, and helped loosen the mucus that congested their lungs.

It was clear to Sarah from the first, though, that the two women were taken worse than Mayor Gilmore. Though he coughed hard enough to rattle the windows, at least he *could* cough and clear his lungs, while the women both seemed unable to mount a defense against the rattling congestion in their chests and their raging fevers. Though Prissy's father complained of a pounding headache and stabbing pain when he breathed, they only moaned weakly, while he finally drifted into a peaceful, snoring slumber. He was, in fact, asleep when the sun rose the next morning and both Mrs. Tyler and Mrs. Gilmore died within minutes of one another.

Sarah held Prissy while she sobbed, her own tears blending with those of her grieving friend's. Though it had been years since her own mother had died, she clearly remembered the knifelike sorrow that had lacerated her then.

A stricken, pale Anson joined them in the parlor, followed by Nolan. Sarah released Prissy into Anson's embrace.

Nolan caught Sarah's gaze, his eyes somber. "I'll go notify the reverend," he said. "I'm sorry, Sarah, but I've had word of another influenza patient in town. I'm going to have to go there, but I'll come back when I can."

Numb, Sarah nodded dully.

Flora entered the room, her own eyes already swollen from crying. "Senorita Matthews, I've closed the curtains and hung a black wreath on the door. If you will write the message, I will send Antonio to the telegraph office to notify Senorita Prissy's brothers in Houston and San Antonio of their mother's passing."

Prissy pulled away from her cousin. "They won't be able to come in time. I wouldn't want them to risk their health coming here, anyway. Tell them to stay at home and I'll write when I can."

Sarah saw Anson wince, and guessed he must be wondering if Prissy would eventually blame his mother for bringing the fatal illness into their home, even though there were so many already ill here in Simpson Creek.

"Prissy, why don't you come lie down for a while?" Sarah murmured, urging her friend toward her old bedroom. "As soon as I compose the telegram, I'll sit with your father, and Flora will take care of what's needed for your mother."

To Sarah's surprise, Prissy let herself be put to bed.

The rest of the day, Sarah remained by the mayor's bedside, with Flora and Antonio assisting in his care. She stepped away only to take a little nourishment brought by the housekeeper at noontime. She hoped it wouldn't be left to her to tell the mayor his wife had died, but in the afternoon Mr. Gilmore's fever soared, bringing delirium with it. He was incapable of asking questions.

She was left with a new fear—would he die, too? How would Prissy survive losing both her parents and her aunt?

Nolan returned at five, and was invited to join Sarah and Prissy for a simple cold supper in the dining room of the big house while Anson sat with the sleeping mayor. Now dressed in mourning, a hollow-eyed Prissy ate little and said nothing.

Anson came into the room when they were almost finished.

"Your father's awake, Prissy, and clearheaded. He's asking for you and about your mother," he said. "I—he saw my black armband and asked about it, so I told him…about my mother. I think he's guessed about Aunt Martha, but he'll want to hear it from you."

Prissy rose, looking almost relieved now that the time had come to share the burden of grief with her father. Sarah rose also, intending to go with her as support, but Anson put out a staying hand.

"I'll go with her, Miss Sarah. You look exhausted. Finish your supper, and keep Dr. Walker company." All hostility toward the Yankee doctor appeared to have vanished in the wake of Anson's grief.

Gratefully, she watched Prissy and her cousin go, then turned back to Nolan, only to find him studying her.

"He's right, you know," he said. "The old sergeant who was my surgery assistant would say 'you look as if you've burned all your wood.' Sarah, you must get some rest tonight."

Sarah managed a tired smile. "Thank you, Doctor, but no more so than you. Who was the new influenza patient you went to see today in town, may I ask?"

His brow furrowed. "I'm afraid it's your old friend Mrs. Detwiler."

She uttered a cry of alarm, and would have jumped to her feet, but he took gentle hold of her wrist.

"Sarah, there's no need for you to go charging out of here to nurse her, too. Her family is taking care of her very capably, and she doesn't seem to have a very bad case."

"But she's old…" Sarah said, still gripped by fear for the feisty old lady who had been so opposed to the Spinsters' Club but who had become her and Milly's close friend this past year.

"I imagine if you were to call on her tomorrow you would find her much improved, unless I'm sorely mistaken," Nolan said. "She's already been through the worst of it, and her daughter only just contrived to sneak out to ask me to call on her, just to be certain."

Sarah felt her lips curve up in a smile in spite of the exhaustion that threatened to swamp her. "That sounds like her. Perhaps if I organized the Spinsters' Club ladies, we could provide nursing during the epidemic for those who aren't blessed with families like Mrs. Detwiler's…" she said aloud. Her mind already raced ahead to think how it could be done.

"Sarah, I've been so impressed with how you've shouldered the responsibilities here," he said. "Prissy would have been lost without you. You're quite a lady, do you know that?"

She could only stare at him, for she had felt totally inadequate to the demands and sorrows she had faced this day. She only knew Prissy and her family had needed her, and she was there.

"When I met you," Nolan went on, after taking a sip of the coffee Flora had brought them, "I heard you were a very talented cook but got the impression Milly always made the decisions. It was Milly who ran the ranch, who started the Spinsters' Club..."

"She did," Sarah agreed, not sure what he was getting at.

"I think she will be quite proud to hear what you've taken on here," he said. "But I must tell you, the very first thing I had to learn as an army surgeon was that I could only concentrate on one patient at a time. No matter what they brought in after I had begun to remove a bullet or—well, you can imagine, there were worse injuries—I had to finish what I was doing before I could take on something else."

"What are you saying?" Sarah asked him. She was sure his point must be plain, but her exhausted brain was too tired to glimpse his meaning through the fog that surrounded it.

"Prissy isn't as strong as you," he said simply. "She's just lost her mother, and her father won't be healthy again for a long time. She's going to need to lean on you in the next few days and weeks."

She could only stare at the table, her gaze unfocused, as realization dawned of what Mrs. Gilmore's death would mean. "Prissy won't be able to stay in the cottage—she'll have to move back into the house to look after her father." Her shoulders sagged in discouragement. "I can't stay there alone, so I'll have to move back to the ranch. How can I help her then? Poor Prissy—so much for her learning independence and the housewifely arts. Flora manages everything in the house." Secretly, Sarah felt a little sorry for herself, too. She'd enjoyed living in town with Prissy. And she loved her sister, but Milly didn't need her as she once did.

"I hope you don't have to move back to the ranch, Sarah," he said. He looked as if he wanted to say more, but he didn't. "Nothing needs to be decided tonight. As soon as Prissy retires for the night, please, I want you to, also."

Chapter Sixteen

On the day after Prissy's mother's funeral, Anson left to take his mother home to Burnet to be buried.

During the farewells in the courtyard, Anson said, "Dr. Walker, would you mind if I spoke to Miss Sarah for a moment?"

Sarah saw Nolan blink in surprise, but after darting a glance at Sarah to see if it was all right with her, he nodded slowly.

Anson took Sarah by the elbow and steered her just out of earshot of the others.

"Miss Sarah, I hope you'll forgive me if I speak frankly, since I'm about to leave," he said, gazing down at her, his dark eyes earnest. When she said nothing, he went on. "I—I'm sorry we didn't get to know one another better, that I didn't meet you before you met that Yankee doctor." He nodded toward Nolan, who stood by Prissy's father, who was still so weak he'd been pushed outside in a wheeled chair. Nolan was trying very hard to keep his eyes averted from them. Sarah could tell, but there was a certain tenseness about him that told her he was very aware of them.

She wouldn't have been female if she wasn't at least a little flattered by the ruefulness that tinged the eyes of Anson Tyler, who remained handsome even in his grief. She couldn't help wondering, if she hadn't already met Nolan, if she would have found Anson more appealing. But it was no use pondering the matter. She *had* met Nolan first, and because of that, her heart was already occupied.

"Anson, I—" she began, struggling to find the right words, but he interrupted her quickly as if to spare her.

"But I know I'm leaving you in good hands," he said. "I've come to respect your Dr. Walker. He's a good man, even if he *is* a Yankee."

The admission touched her, for it represented a complete reversal of his earlier, automatic enmity toward Nolan.

"Thank you, Anson. And I believe there's a wonderful lady out there, just waiting for you to find her. Perhaps you ought to come back to Simpson Creek some day—she could be part of our Spinsters' Club."

"Maybe I will." A spark of the charm that was so much a part of Anson Tyler reappeared in his eyes.

Once Anson had departed, and Nolan had helped Prissy's father back inside, Nolan took his leave, for he had many ill people to attend to.

Mayor Gilmore called his daughter and Sarah into the parlor.

Sarah was braced for this talk. Prissy's father would express his thanks for her help nursing the family and for what she had taught his daughter, tell Prissy he needed her in the house and offer Sarah the help of Antonio and the use of the wagon to move her things back to the ranch.

Mayor Gilmore cleared his throat and dabbed at red-rimmed eyes with a rumpled handkerchief. "Sit down, both of you girls," he said, then waited as they did so. "Your mother was so proud of you, Prissy—proud of how sweet and lovely you are, and especially about all you'd learned in the short time you and Sarah have been living in the cottage. But a little bird told me—" his gaze now wandered to Flora, who stood by the door in case she should be needed "—you thought it was your duty to reside again in the house and take care of your old papa. I want to tell you that I don't feel it's necessary."

"But Papa," Prissy protested, surprised. "Of course I'm going to move back in! I want to look after you!"

"Your mother would not want you to give up all you were learning just to keep an old man company day and night. Flora and Antonio will still be here, and with you living just across the grounds, you're close enough to take suppers with me whenever you like—even cook the meals yourself—right, Flora?"

"Oh, *sì,* senor, I would enjoy the two senoritas taking over the cooking whenever they wish," Flora agreed.

"I have to face the fact my little girl has grown up, just as her brothers did," Mayor Gilmore said, dabbing at his eyes again.

"Oh, Papa, you're the best father a girl could ever have!" Prissy said, throwing her arms around his neck.

Sarah saw a proud tear trickle down the mayor's

cheek as he hugged his daughter. “And you’re the best daughter. But once this blasted influenza lets up, I need to get back to governing the city, eh? I’ve got a reelection campaign to run this spring, remember?”

“Oh, Papa, as if any man in town wouldn’t vote for you!” Prissy cried.

“Assuming there’s anyone left to vote,” he added, shaking his head sadly. “At the funeral, I heard Mr. Patterson died the day before yesterday, and Andy Calhoun the day before that.”

“And Miss Mary, the millinery shop owner,” Prissy said. “And Pete Collier, Caroline Wallace’s fiancé. Poor Caroline! Their wedding was to be in March!”

“Reverend Chadwick looks worn to a frazzle,” Sarah murmured, mentally saying a quick prayer for the gentle old shepherd of their church.

At least word from the ranch was good, Sarah thought, reaching into her pocket to feel the note Milly had had Isaiah drop off this morning. No one at the ranch had been ill, and she had to think it was because they’d stayed away from town. Isaiah had waited outside while Sarah had written a note back to Milly, then gotten back on his horse and rode out again.

Mayor Gilmore stifled a yawn. “Why don’t you girls plan on coming for supper tonight? I’ve asked Flora to make your favorite tamales, Prissy.”

“Wonderful, Papa! We’ll be there, won’t we, Sarah?”

“Good, good. Right now, though, your old papa is tired and needs a nap.”

* * *

"That was very generous of your father," Sarah murmured as they walked back to the cottage.

Prissy sighed. "He's being so brave."

Sarah agreed. Even as she mourned for the dead and fretted about the continuing ravages of the epidemic, though, she felt a sense of being reprieved. She would not have to move back to the ranch—*away from Nolan,* her heart whispered.

The thought stopped her short. Hadn't she decided that no matter how she admired his fierce dedication to healing, he was not for her, because he was not a man of faith? But her heart didn't seem to be listening.

"What shall we do this afternoon?" Prissy asked. "I feel as if we've been cooped up in the big house forever. I don't want to sit in the cottage and just think about how I miss Mama. But it's not a good time to go visiting, and all the shops are closed…."

"I had an idea," Sarah told her, remembering the thought she'd first broached to Nolan at dinner after Prissy's mother and aunt had died. Perhaps now was the perfect time to transform her thought into action. "Let's go brew a pot of tea, and I'll tell you all about it."

Prissy thought her idea was wonderful. By suppertime they had visited all the Spinsters in town who weren't already nursing family members or mourning a loss, like Caroline, and enlisted their aid. Then they called on Nolan to inform him. And so the Spinster Nursing Corps was born.

Nolan's first impulse, when he found Sarah and Prissy waiting at his office after he returned from yet another call upon a new influenza victim, was to forbid Sarah to have anything to do with nursing the sick. She'd done more than enough already in her care for the Gilmores. She was too sheltered, too fragile...*too precious to him.* He did not want her exposed again to the ravages of influenza.

Yet he realized even as his mouth opened to form the words that he couldn't forbid her to do this. He had no authority over her. She'd accepted him as her friend, but he was nothing more to her, and she'd do this thing with or without his blessing, he could tell by the determined jut of her jaw and the warlike glint in her eyes. He couldn't very well permit Prissy to nurse the sick and not allow Sarah to do so, also.

And he had to admit he desperately needed help. Each day brought word of new influenza cases. There were so many down with it in and around Simpson Creek that it was no longer practical to remain at the bedside of each one until they passed the crisis and either gradually got well or developed a fatal pneumonia. He needed capable assistants whom he could trust to watch over feverish patients and dose them with medications according to instructions, and who could judge when it was necessary to summon him back to the bedside. In short, he needed nurses, and here were two young women saying they wanted to be just that, and had enlisted others, too.

He met with them at his office just after sunrise the next morning, and smiled in spite of his fatigue to see the row of earnest-looking young women. All of them were clad in dark, practical clothing, either actual mourning or somber-hued skirts and blouses.

"Good morning, ladies. I'm thankful you're here, and I applaud your dedication to your community and your willingness to place yourselves at risk. You do understand, don't you, that you could be putting yourself in a position to contract the infection?"

To a woman, they all nodded, their faces solemn. His eyes lingered on Sarah, who nodded again, almost imperceptibly. He could imagine what she was thinking—*if I didn't catch it nursing Mr. and Mrs. Gilmore, or Mrs. Tyler, surely I'm not going to.*

"Very well, then, before I send you out," he said, "we shall just cover a few basics, with which some of you may already be familiar." Then he spoke of providing warmth for patients who were chilled, but not over-blanketing them, which slowed down the body's natural cooling mechanism, the specific diet for those able to eat, the brewing of willow bark tea, accurate dosing of the morphine and laudanum he would send with them.

"In regard to these medicines, it is not a case of 'if a little is good for the patient, a lot is better,'" he cautioned the would-be nurses. "These drugs can be deadly if not properly used, so you must adhere strictly to the guidelines I have given you for indications, amount and frequency."

He saw them all taking it in. Sarah and some others took notes.

"Lastly, the most important preventative measure you can take for your own health is to *wash your hands vigorously with soap and water* after touching a patient. If they're able to follow instructions, tell them to cover their coughs and sneezes. And get the proper rest and nourishment. If you fall ill yourself—" He could not look at Sarah as he said those words. Visions of his wife and son, dying so quickly and miserably in the cholera epidemic, swam before his brain. Once again he wished he could forbid her to expose herself to this danger.

He cleared his throat with difficulty. "If you fall ill yourself," he began again, "then someone must nurse *you*, so do not allow yourselves to become exhausted or go without eating and resting. You must let me know immediately if you develop chills, fever, headache or sore throat—promise me, ladies?"

There was an answering chorus of yeses.

"Very well then. We shall move on to assignments. In some cases, I will send you out in pairs if there is more than one family member ill at a residence. In other cases, only one of you will go. Miss Harkey and Miss Thompson, I'd like you to go to the Fedders' house, where both Mr. and Mrs. Fedders are ill. Miss Jeffries, to the Hotchkiss ranch. Miss Shackleford, to Mrs. Brenner…" He allowed himself to look at Sarah again, toying with the idea of asking her to accompany him on calls as his assistant, a way of keeping an eye on her and making sure she did not overtire herself in her zeal to help. But he knew it might cause talk, and worse, she'd see right through his claim of needing a nurse to accompany him and resent his ploy.

"…Miss Gilmore and Miss Matthews, to the Poteets—both the sheriff and his wife are ill."

At this point the bell over the door tinkled, and Nolan looked up to see Reverend Chadwick entering, wearing his care like a heavy frock coat.

He didn't wait to be greeted. "Dr. Walker, I'm sorry to interrupt, but you're needed at the Spencers."

"Ada's ill?" Sarah asked, before Nolan could form the question. "Or is it…"

He knew she was trying to ask whether it was influenza, or her supposed pregnancy, but didn't know how in front of the other ladies, some of whom still believed Ada's story.

"Both her parents have come down with the influenza," the minister said. "Miss Spencer seems…well enough…"

Nolan guessed Chadwick didn't want to add *physically, at least.*

Sarah and Prissy exchanged glances, as did the other ladies. Ada had been their friend and part of the Spinsters' Club, after all, before she had started acting so strangely.

Nolan rubbed his chin. "Well, then, that means a change of plans. I was going to keep you, Miss Bennett, and you, Miss Lassiter, in reserve, to take over when the others need to be relieved or if new cases should arise, but instead I'll need you to come along with me to the Spencers."

He sought and found Sarah's gaze. She would understand why he dare not have her come to the Spencers, after the way Ada had acted toward her at the Gilmores' New Year's Day party. He sensed that her thoughts mirrored his. What might her parents' illness—or worse, their deaths—do to Ada Spencer's already troubled mind?

Chapter Seventeen

Nursing Sheriff Poteet and his wife was much harder than taking care of the Gilmores and Mrs. Tyler had been. At the Gilmores' luxurious, stately home, at least, she and Prissy had had Flora and Antonio to assist them and take over when they needed to rest or take their meals. Here at the sheriff's far humbler abode, which was actually connected to the jail, they were completely on their own, and had only each other to rely on.

They soon developed a system—Sarah kept vigil by the ailing lawman and his wife, dosing them with willow bark tea and morphine and bathing them with tepid water, while Prissy kept chicken broth simmering on the cookstove and boiled the soiled bedding over a fire outside; then they traded off. In the evening, Prissy would go home to check on her father, who continued to progress slowly in his convalescence. During the night one girl slept on a pallet in the small kitchen while the other sat between the beds of the sheriff and his wife, and they'd switch in the middle of the night.

Sarah had not forgotten the middle-aged sheriff's complicity a few months ago with those who would have persecuted the former slaves now working as Matthews Ranch cowhands, but she could not find it in her heart to hold that against him as he struggled for each breath. Each paroxysm of coughing turned his lips blue, a ghastly sight against the florid heat of his face. The once-paunchy man looked sadly diminished in his nightshirt.

"I'm gonna die, ain't I?" he rasped on the third full day they had spent there, after a spasm of coughing left the pillowcase blood flecked.

The sight of the crimson spots made Sarah queasy, but she steeled herself to ignore her churning stomach. She couldn't help the desperately ill man by giving in to squeamishness. "Sheriff, you've got to keep fighting," Sarah said, sponging his sweaty brow. "If we can just get this fever down..." But she feared he was right. He kept coughing, but it didn't seem to relieve the increasing rattling in his lungs.

"Better send fer th' Rev'ren'...got a lot to atone for... I ain't always been the best sheriff I coulda been. Git Mabel in here, will ya?"

"I'll go fetch him, Sarah, and leave a message for Dr. Walker, too," Prissy said. She had just come in the room with a couple of sheets she'd dried in front of the fireplace. Snatching up her cloak, she strode back through the door that led through the jail to the street. Thank God there were no prisoners awaiting trial in either of the jail's two cells. The criminals must be either holed up for the winter or had heard of the influenza outbreak and decided to give Simpson Creek a wide berth.

Sarah noticed Sheriff Poteet hadn't asked for the doctor. He'd already given up hope, and probably nothing further she said about his recovery would sound convincing.

"Sheriff, your wife's already here—she's sick, too," Sarah reminded him, moving aside so the ill man could see his wife lying on the trundle bed across the room. With some effort, Mrs. Poteet turned on her side and faced them, a tear trickling down her gaunt cheeks.

"Robert, you…got t'…hang on, y'hear?" she said, in between her own spasms of coughing. "I need you… Simpson Creek needs you."

"Dunno…if I can, Mabel," the sheriff mumbled, as his eyes drifted shut. "You been a good wife…"

Those were his last words. He drifted into insensibility and was unaware of Reverend Chadwick's arrival or his bedside prayers. He lasted until sunset. Nolan arrived just as he heaved his last breath.

Out of the corner of her stinging eyes, while she and Prissy did their best to comfort the new widow, Sarah saw Nolan close the sheriff's eyes and cover the body with the bedsheet. She kept Mrs. Poteet shielded against her body while Nolan, aided by Prissy, carried the sheet-covered form out of the bedroom and into the office so the ill woman would not have to witness her husband's removal whenever it took place. Nolan had told her the town's undertaker could hardly keep pace with the number of victims the influenza epidemic had claimed.

When he was done, Sarah left Prissy with their

remaining patient and went outside with Nolan into the winter darkness. Fatigued by her ordeal and the overheated bedroom, she'd been craving fresh air and news of the "outside world," as she had begun to think of Simpson Creek, but she longed to spend a moment with Nolan even more.

Their breaths formed clouds in the chill night air.

"Sarah, you look so tired," he said, stepping close and smoothing away an errant strand of hair that had plastered itself to her forehead. "Are you sure you're getting your fair share of rest?"

His fingers felt blessedly cool against her aching head, and it was all she could do not to lean into his caress. Her head pounded and she was too tired to examine the significance of his touch, and why she appreciated it so much.

She nodded. "Oh, Prissy's doing her share and more. In fact, I caught her trying to let me sleep through my shift. She said she couldn't bear to wake me." She gazed up at his earnest face, lit only from the kerosene lamp shining through the jail window. "I wanted to ask you about the Spencers, Nolan. How are they? Is Ada still well?"

His gaze fell, and she knew before he spoke what his answer would be. "Mr. and Mrs. Spencer died this morning, Sarah."

She couldn't stifle the gasp. "Both of them? But what of Ada? Is anyone with her? She didn't catch it, did she?"

Nolan shook his head. "The last time I saw her, she was as she has been, physically hale but still insisting she is pregnant."

Something in his eyes alerted her. "The last time you saw her? What do you mean? Where is she?"

He shrugged. "I wish I knew, Sarah. Mr. Spencer died first, then his wife, and when I told Ada her mother had expired, she ran out the door, shrieking, and I haven't seen her since. The reverend has a couple of neighbors out searching for her, but though they've caught glimpses of her, running behind houses and dodging down alleys, they haven't been able to get close to her. It's as if she's become a wild creature… We left the house open—I hope when she gets cold and tired enough, she'll come back and take shelter."

Even in the shadows, she could see his eyes were troubled.

"Poor Ada," she murmured. "What will become of her? At least, when her parents were alive, she had a reason to stay around home, people to watch over her and love her…."

He rubbed his forehead. "I wish I knew what was best to do. I'm going to have to speak to the reverend as soon as I can to learn if she has any relatives who could be sent for. If not, I'm afraid an institution may be the only answer."

"How awful." She had a sudden sense of how blessed her own life had been, how relatively carefree, and shivered.

He misunderstood. "You're cold. Let's go back inside," he murmured, gesturing toward the door, but he stopped with his hand on the doorknob. "Sarah, now that the Spencers have died, either Miss Bennett or Miss Lassiter are free to take over here. I believe I'd better send for one of them to relieve you and Prissy—"

Sarah couldn't hide her dismay. "No, not tonight, Nolan, not when Mrs. Poteet's just lost her husband. She's used to us. It wouldn't be right to turn her care over to someone else when her grief is so new, so raw."

"Tomorrow morning then," he said firmly. "I won't have you overtaxing yourself, Sarah. You…you're too important to me."

She froze in the doorway, caught by his words and the intensity in his eyes. "Nolan…"

He raised a hand to ward off her objection. "I know, I know. We agreed not to speak of this. But I won't let you endanger yourself any more than you already have, Sarah."

Her eyes stung with unshed tears. Her throat felt thick with words she wanted to say. "I…that is, thank you, Nolan. For caring about my welfare."

"I would do more than *care*, Sarah. You know that."

Impulsively, she reached out a hand and touched his cheek, bristly with the beard he hadn't taken time to shave this morning. "Yes. I know, and I—" She caught herself, not wanting to blurt out something she hadn't thought through. "We'll talk, Nolan, when this is over…."

He covered the hand that still cupped his cheek. "Yes, we will. It seems we're always postponing our talks."

"You can send Faith or Bess over tomorrow morning, and Prissy and I will go home and rest, I promise. Mrs. Poteet needs us with her tonight."

He gave in with a sigh, perhaps recognizing she was right.

When he had gone, Sarah returned to the bedroom where Prissy sat with Mrs. Poteet. Nolan had given the woman a sleeping draft, and she snored softly now, her breathing still labored and congested, but clearer than it had been yesterday. Her fever had been down all evening. Mrs. Poteet would recover, Sarah realized, though in her grief, there would probably be times the sheriff's widow would wish she had died, too.

Prissy studied her in the lamplight. "Go lie down for a while, Sarah," Prissy said. "I'll sit up with her. You look done in."

She wanted to argue, to point out that her friend looked just as tired, but she ached in every bone, and her head was throbbing. Maybe a few hours of sleep was a good idea. "As our old foreman Josh would say, I feel tired as a mule that walked a mile in spring mud. But—"

Prissy interrupted. "I'll come wake you when it's your turn, I promise." She made shooing motions with her hand. "Now *go*."

Nolan laid down the straight razor and rinsed the remaining soap from his face, then straightened and studied his image in the mirror above the basin to make sure he'd hadn't missed any spots.

After restocking his black bag, he'd slept straight through the night, for no one had come to summon him. It was the first time he'd had a solid night's sleep since the influenza had struck. Was it too soon to hope the epidemic was starting to abate?

He'd stop first by Miss Bennett's to ask her to relieve Sarah and Prissy, and then he'd drive around in his buggy, checking on all his influenza patients to make sure they were recovering. Pneumonia was always a threat in the wake of influenza, especially if a person tried to rise from his bed too soon....

Then he heard the light thudding footsteps running up the stairs, followed in short order by pounding at his door.

He grimaced. *No, the epidemic isn't over yet,* he thought, striding down the hall to his office. This would be yet another frantic relative of a new influenza victim, reporting that his wife, or her pa, or grandma, or child, was coughing and feverish....

Through the side window, he saw that it was Prissy standing on his porch, her shoulders heaving with her efforts to catch her breath, her eyes wide in her flushed face.

He threw open the door. "Prissy, is Mrs. Poteet worse?"

She shook her head, still panting. "Nolan, you've got to come! I-it's *Sarah!*"

Chapter Eighteen

"She's coughing and her forehead is so hot…and she says her chest and her head hurt…"

"Sarah?" An icy fist seized his heart and squeezed it. *No, it can't be.* He'd just seen her last night, and while she was clearly fatigued, her eyes had been clear and she hadn't mentioned any discomfort… But it was often thus, he reminded himself. A person went to bed merely tired, and woke up ill. Sarah might not have recognized the first symptoms, the aching bones, the throbbing headache, as being anything more than fatigue.

"When did it start?" he demanded, mechanically throwing on his coat and spotted his doctor bag where he'd left it by the door, his mind racing ahead.

"She took over for me at Mrs. Poteet's bedside about midnight, and she didn't mention anything…but when I woke up this morning, I heard this steady rattling from the floor in the bedroom… It was her chair, Nolan, shaking from the force of her shivering in it!"

"I'll go to Sarah," Nolan told Prissy as they rushed

out of the office. He had grabbed an umbrella from the tall hook on the wall as he left and handed it to Prissy. Big fat raindrops had begun to fall, and one landed with chilly precision on his left ear.

"Would you run home, please, and tell Flora to prepare a sickroom for Sarah, then go to Miss Bennett or Miss Lassiter—whoever's closer—and tell her to come to the Poteets' to take over there as quickly as she can? You may return home as soon as your replacement's arrived, but be sure to bathe and change your clothes before you come in contact with your father—we don't know what might trigger a relapse."

"Do you want Antonio to hitch up the carriage to bring Sarah down to the house?"

Nolan nodded as they reached the street. "I could carry her there quicker, but getting drenched in this cold rain is the last thing she needs. Tell him to hurry!"

They ran their separate ways in what was now a downpour. Fear lent wings to his feet, and in his headlong rush, he skidded into an icy puddle between the hotel and the mercantile, lost his balance and fell flat in the mud. Heedless of the mud that now splotched both coat and trousers, he picked himself up and rushed on.

Within seconds of arriving at the Poteets', his eyes confirmed the truth of Prissy's report. Sarah lay propped up on the Poteets' horsehair sofa in their sitting room, swathed in a thick blanket, her eyes slitted open and dull with fever. A hectic flush bloomed on each cheek.

Her teeth chattered against themselves. "C-c-*cold,*" she muttered when the sound of his footsteps caused her to open one eye a trifle wider. "Tell N-Nolan… sorry."

She doesn't even recognize me.

"I *am* Nolan, sweetheart," he said, "and you have nothing to apologize for. I'm going to take good care of you," he told her, leaning down close so she could see him. "You're going to be fine, sweetheart," he promised, though he had no idea if he was telling the truth or not. He reached out a hand and touched her forehead, intending only to brush away a lock of damp, dull gold hair plastered there, but it was like touching the inside of a pot from which boiling water has just been poured.

He wanted to wrap another blanket around her, scoop her up in his arms and run out of the house, but the rain still drummed steadily on the tin roof overhead, and he forced himself to remain calm and wait for the promised carriage. Reaching in his black bag, he pulled out his stethoscope and listened for a moment, hearing the rhonchi, abnormal whistling sounds, and rales, a noise that proclaimed congestion in the breathing passages.

"Do you think you could drink some willow bark tea?" he asked her. "I'll just go set the kettle on the stove."

"I'll…t-try…but wh-what…about Miz… P-Poteet…?"

"I'll check on her," he promised, but he put the kettle on to boil before he did so.

The sheriff's widow opened her eyes when he peeked into the bedroom. They were reddened and puffy from weeping and her sallow features wan, but the light of full awareness shone from them.

"Doctor…"

"How are you today, Mrs. Poteet?" he said, forcing himself to come to the bedside and inspect her more closely when all he wanted to do was go back to Sarah.

"Better…." she rasped. "Sorry… Sarah's sick now…."

He had left his stethoscope in the other room, but he could tell even without it that her breathing was much less labored than it had been yesterday. Sarah and Prissy had nursed her back from the brink, and now it might cost Sarah her life.

"I'm going to take good care of her," he promised again. "You just rest, Mrs. Poteet. With some watchful nursing, I believe you'll be just fine. Miss Bennett or Miss Lassiter will be here in a few minutes to help you."

Sarah had fallen into slumber by the time he returned with the tea. He had to shake her awake to take it, and when she drank the hot brew, her teeth rattled against the crockery cup. *Where is Antonio with that carriage?*

Oh, God, make him hurry! He was hardly conscious of addressing the Lord, whom he had not talked to since his wife had died—except when he had prayed, in vain, that Jeff be made well. *And please heal Sarah. Don't let her die like You did Julia and Timmy, please…*

While he waited, he laid Sarah out more fully on the couch, yet keeping her propped up so she could breathe, and pushing up the sleeves of her blouse, bathed her arms, her face and her neck in tepid water to bring down the fever. Sarah seemed barely aware of his efforts, her only reaction to shiver as the heat of her skin evaporated the moisture left by the cloth almost before he could dry it. Was he winning against the heat that burned within her, or merely keeping pace with the inferno?

"Please, Lord, let her live. Take me instead," he prayed aloud, willing the carriage to appear, along with one of the other Spinsters.

It seemed an eternity before the creak of wheels and the slowing *splosh* of hoofbeats heralded the arrival of the mayor's brougham.

For Sarah, the day passed in a series of confusing, unfocused images—being swaddled in blankets and carried outside, the rhythmic turning of carriage wheels, the soft touch of feminine hands as she was undressed and placed in sweet-smelling, warmed sheets, of Nolan's "Downeast" accent as he barked out orders for cool water, another blanket, willow bark tea. She heard Prissy's voluble chatter, too, shrill with fear, Flora's melodious Spanish…and was that Milly's worried voice? But how could that be? Hadn't she firmly told her sister to stay on the ranch, away from the contagion that plagued Simpson Creek?

She was aware of each breath rattling in her lungs, shaking the thick fluid that threatened to smother the life-giving air, the knifelike pain with each inhalation that stabbed into her ribs like thin spears heated over a fire, the paroxysms of coughing that racked her body until she had to stop and gasp for air so she had the strength to cough some more, the headache that was like a white-hot hammer pounding on a red-glowing anvil, producing multicolored sparks that flared against her eyelids. Her throat felt like a raw wound that had been rubbed with salt, too sore to swallow the liquids that she nevertheless sucked down greedily whenever she was awake enough to take them. She had to have water, for her skin felt like the parched sand of the desert, and then, in the next instant, she felt as if she lay in a snowbank, with more feathery-cold flakes drifting down on her, her skin turning blue against the icy crystals.

Then the fever soared even higher, and the voices around her faded, and other voices and figures swam hazily into view—her mother, her father, smiling at her. She saw a figure standing with them, and wondered if it was Jesse, her dead fiancé, and whether she would see him soon.

Then she looked closer, and saw that it was not Jesse—the Figure that stood between her father and mother was much taller, and wore a long robe so dazzlingly white between them that she couldn't look at Him, but she knew who He was. He smiled, too, but He held up a nail-scarred palm.

"Not yet."

And she knew nothing more for a while, sinking back now into a dreamless sleep.

Later, the voices she knew swirled around again—the voice of Reverend Chadwick, praying and reading aloud from the Psalms, and Prissy's voice, saying she'd heard that, sometimes, the only way to decrease a fever for a woman was to cut her hair as close as possible to the scalp. The idea was so horrifying to her that she raised up, swinging and shrieking, until she heard Nolan's voice promising they wouldn't cut her hair if she'd only calm down, for her frenzy was raising her fever still higher.

Then darkness fell—for the first time? the second? the third?—and the light in the room was reduced to the glowing circle cast by the single lamp on the bedside table. Her bones ached as if someone was grinding them to powder, inch by inch. At intervals, liquid was trickled down her throat. Sometimes the liquid was bitter, and though the pain slid into the background then, the sleep that followed was full of horrifying images—of the terrifying, war-painted faces of attacking Comanches splashing across Simpson Creek on their Paint ponies, of arrow-studded, bloody bodies of the Indians' victims....

"Are you praying, Reverend?" she heard Nolan's voice, the vowels flat and harsh, demand. "Why isn't she getting better? Why isn't your God doing something to bring her out of this? Doesn't He care?"

"Are *you* praying, son?" came Chadwick's gentle answer. "We all need to be praying, I think."

"Oh, He doesn't want to hear from me, Reverend, I promise you. If He did, He wouldn't have let Julia and Timmy die in that horrifying way."

"'Julia and Timmy?'"

"My wife and son. They died in a cholera epidemic. Have you ever seen someone die of cholera, Reverend? You'd never—" she heard his voice catch "—forget it..."

Is Nolan crying?

"Easy, son, easy...it's going to be all right," she heard Chadwick say, his rusty old voice soft and soothing.

"No, it won't, Reverend," Nolan snapped. "It wasn't all right for them, or for so many of the men I tried to save, men in blue *and* gray—I didn't care! It wasn't all right for Jeffrey Beaumont… No, He doesn't listen when *I* ask. I'm nothing to Him."

He expected the preacher to challenge him on his last remark, but instead Chadwick asked, "Who's Jeffrey Beaumont, Nolan?"

"A colonel who was brought to my tent during one of those last battles, after the war should have been long over, but it wasn't yet. He wore gray, Reverend—I cut away what was left of his uniform and found a minié ball had penetrated his spine. He couldn't move his legs. He begged me to let him die, but I wouldn't listen. Maybe I should have…"

"So he lived?"

She heard Nolan's short, harsh laugh. "He lived. Long enough for them to threaten to haul him off to Libby or someplace like it where he'd just lie there, helpless, until some fever took him. I held them off at gunpoint one time, and told the pair who came for him I'd send them both to perdition before I'd let them take him. Jeffrey and I had become friends by that time, you see."

"Yes, I can well imagine," the minister said. "I'd want such a staunch defender as a friend, too."

"He told me he knew he was going to die, but he just wanted to get home to Texas. I couldn't imagine what difference that made… I hadn't been home to Maine since the war broke out and I'd seen so many states by then I couldn't even remember where I was by that time. I told him that he wasn't going to die, that with some devoted nursing care he could live out his life in a wheelchair, though it was sure he'd never walk again. He told me there was no one at home who could do that for him—his parents were dead, you see—but he wanted to make it to Brazos County. He said he'd die happy if he could take his last breath under that big cottonwood tree on the bank of the Brazos River that flowed past his land."

"So what happened?"

"About the time I was sure they were going to court-martial me and ship him off to prison by force, the war ended, and I resigned my commission and told Jeffrey Beaumont I was taking him home. So I rode with him on the train, and took care of him. Sometimes I had to defend him against arrogant Federals who wanted to take his seat on the train—for I had to purchase extra space for him so he could lie down. Other times, once we left the train and were traveling over the road, he had to tell suspicious Southerners that the Yankee with him was trying to help him reach his home."

So that's what he'd been doing in Texas, Sarah thought, and felt guilty about all the times she'd imagined him being part of the occupying troops, or some sort of carpetbagger....

"So you took him home," the minister's voice gently prodded.

"Yes. I took him home to Beaumont Hall, his plantation on the river. And I met his cousins and his elderly aunt, who wept on my shoulder and thanked me for bringing him home. We were there for weeks, and he was doing well. He could still use his hands, even if his legs were becoming withered and contracted, despite my efforts to exercise them and massage them. He'd gotten used to his chair on wheels, and the necessity of accepting help with so many everyday things…." Nolan's voice trailed off as if he was remembering.

A moment passed, and then he went on. "The girl he loved chose to marry another man, a man who could walk and ride and give her children, and he didn't become bitter—he accepted it with such grace and generosity…he even gave them his blessing." Again, the bitter laugh.

"He sounds like a very good man."

"He was. A better man than I'll ever be, Reverend."

"'Was'?"

"Was," Nolan confirmed. "He died, Reverend. A fever took him, and nothing I did made any difference. Not even when I prayed for him. He died just as he wanted to, under that cottonwood tree on the banks of the Brazos River."

Chapter Nineteen

"So that's how you came to the great state of Texas," Pastor Chadwick murmured, when Nolan finished speaking.

"Yes," Nolan said. He lowered his gaze to Sarah, lying so flushed and still, her eyes closed, her perspiration-damp hair confined in a dull yellow braid lying beside her on the pillow. He wondered what she would have thought of his tale. "Jeff was the brother I never had, and a better friend than any I'd met among those wearing blue."

"And yet, once your responsibility to your friend, the Confederate colonel, was ended, you didn't return east to your home."

Nolan shrugged. "Oh, I could have gone back to Maine, I suppose—a medical college there had already sent me word that they'd love to have a physician of my experience teaching medicine. I'm sure my experience as a battlefield surgeon would have benefited the medical students. But Maine didn't feel like home anymore."

"So you remained in Texas," Chadwick prodded gently.

Nolan shook his head. "By that time, I'd grown to love Texas…her vastness, her big sky, her interesting, warmhearted people with their drawling accents… Jeff told me about mountains here, and tropical palm trees, and deserts, and it made me curious. I'd like to see the rest of it someday." He sighed. "I knew Jeff would never be the one to show me. He had been growing more frail for a long time, but rather than admit to myself that he was going to die, I buried my head in whatever books and newspapers were available…."

He glanced back at Sarah then, for it was the part of the tale where she began to be the reason for his stay, but she just lay there, her shoulders rising and falling beneath the sheet, her breathing harsh and labored. Pearls of sweat beaded on her forehead. As soon as he finished telling this saga, he would have to see if he could rouse her enough to sip some more fever-reducing tea—perhaps verbena this time.

Chadwick's eyes remained bright with interest, so Nolan went on. "And in one of those newspapers, I saw an advertisement for the Simpson Creek Society for the Promotion of Marriage."

Chadwick's lips broadened into a smile. "Ah, the Spinsters' Club. The advertisement piqued your interest?"

In spite of the apprehension that held him in its icy grip, Nolan chuckled. "I admired their pluck in seizing the initiative, to advertise for what they wanted—husbands—rather than staying meekly at home and waiting for them to simply show up on their doorsteps. I thought if one of these spirited women would have me, she might make a good doctor's wife, and I'd take it as a sign that I belonged here. I sent an inquiry. And in a couple weeks or so, Miss Sarah Matthews started corresponding with me."

He'd lived for those letters, he remembered. He'd imagined meeting and marrying Miss Sarah Matthews, and bringing his bride up to meet his friend at Beaumont Hall. But the visit was not to be—Jeff died, despite Nolan's care and desperate prayers, and once he was gone, there was no real reason for Nolan to remain at Beaumont Hall. The "Spinsters' Club" had invited him and a couple other candidates to come for Founders' Day. He'd ridden southward, knowing Sarah Matthews would be as beautiful in person as she was interesting in her letters, and hoping she would not hate him because he was a Yankee.

"Thank you for telling me, Nolan," the preacher said, rising stiffly. "It's getting late, so perhaps I'd better be going, though of course you can send me word at any hour if you need me."

"Thank you, Reverend. Be careful going home tonight—Antonio said the temperature had dropped, so watch for icy patches in the street."

"I'll do that, thanks. And know that I'll be praying."

Nolan rose with him. "When you do, perhaps you could ask that no one else will need a doctor around here tonight." He wasn't sure he'd be willing to leave Sarah's side, not even if the most experienced doctor in the world could take over.

"I'll do that, son—"

Just then, a harsh, gutteral cry erupted from the

woman on the bed. Her spine arched like a tightly drawn bow.

“She’s having a seizure!”

Sarah’s slender frame threw itself into a racking series of alternating contractions and relaxations. The bed frame thudded in a horrible rhythm against the wall with the force of the convulsion.

Nolan’s hand dived to her forehead, and flinched as he felt the heat there. She was as hot as if the very sun had taken up residence within her.

“Dear God!” Chadwick cried.

“Help me turn her on her side, Reverend!” he said, fearful that Sarah would choke.

Prissy ran into the room, perhaps drawn by the noise of the bed shaking, and screamed when she saw Sarah convulsing.

“Prissy! Go out and see if there’s ice in the rainbarrel—or in a water trough in the stable. I need it to get her fever down!” Nolan wasn’t even sure if she could get it in time to help her friend, but he sure couldn’t think with Prissy’s shrieking reverberating in his ears.

He was dimly aware of the preacher trembling and sinking to his knees on the other side of the bed, his hands clasped, his head bent.

The seizure went on for an eternity, though in actuality it probably only lasted thee minutes. Then her body sagged in limp exhaustion and a faint pink crept back into Sarah’s chalky, blue-white lips. Nolan felt engulfed by hopeless despair flooding through him. It was never good when a fever soared so high the patient convulsed. He was going to lose her. Perhaps he should have let Prissy cut her hair…

"Reverend, please, pray harder!" he whispered desperately. It was all he knew to do.

Chadwick raised his head, the silver hair gleaming in the lantern light. "*You* pray, too!" he commanded, his voice gentle but strong as granite.

"But I can't… He doesn't listen to me," Nolan protested, knowing he'd said it before. Hadn't the old preacher been listening?

"Hogwash!" Chadwick retorted, his eyes burning a hole into Nolan's soul. "He's *always* heard you. Sometimes the answer is 'wait.' Sometimes it's 'no,' and we won't know this side of Heaven why that is, but He's always heard you, son. The answer may be 'no' this time, too, but it sure doesn't hurt to ask Him—and it would help *you*. I know our prayers together would be stronger than any I can say alone—and stronger still if you believed in the One you're talking to."

Nolan felt his knees bending as if of their own volition, and he sank down by the bedside opposite Chadwick and bowed his head, too.

"Lord, please," was all he said at first, but he knew he couldn't leave it at that. "I don't have any right to come to You, I know that," he went on, his voice hoarse and ragged with the desperation of his need, "but the reverend here says it's all right to ask. I'm begging, even. Please save my Sarah. Take me, if You want to, but please heal her. I… I'll accept Your decision if the answer is no—at least, I'll do my best to—but please save her. I guess I've never *not* believed in You…but I just didn't think You cared one way or the other about me or anyone I loved. Reverend Chadwick says You do care, and I've got to believe that. Please, Lord, save Sarah...." He felt the tears, thick in his throat, hot on his face.

"Nolan, I've got ice!" Prissy shouted from the stairway, and ran into the room, her breath heaving her shoulders. She carried a huge bowl of chunks of ice. Her fingers were wet and blue. She'd apparently broken it out of the rain barrel or trough and fished it out with her own hands.

Nolan rose. "Get me some thin cloth, please—handkerchiefs, rags, whatever you have."

Prissy ran from the room and returned with a two or three delicate lawn handkerchiefs. He wrapped the cloths one layer thick around the chunks so that the ice wouldn't directly touch Sarah's skin, and with Prissy helping him, he stroked the ice over Sarah's forehead, her arms, her neck.

His prayers were silent now, but he continued them. *Lord, please, save Sarah. You are the Great Physician, after all. I'll do anything You want, just save her, please.*

Will you serve Me, Nolan? No matter what happens?

Yes, Lord. I'm Yours, from now on.

Gradually, he felt a peace descending, relaxing his shoulders, quieting his pounding heart. He let his forehead relax against the side of the bed.

He must have dozed for a few minutes, for he awoke to Prissy gently shaking his shoulder.

"Go lie down for a while, Nolan. You're exhausted."

He shook his head vehemently, his gaze flying to the motionless figure on the bed. "No, I can't, she might have another convulsion—"

"No, she's cooler now, see?" Prissy said, as he reached out a shaking hand to touch Sarah's forehead to verify her words. "I'll watch over her, and I won't close my eyes even for a second, I promise. I'll call you if there's *any* change, no matter how small."

He wanted to argue, but he was too fatigued to form the words, and let her lead him to the guest room down the hall.

Sarah felt like a swimmer who had dived deep into a silent, bottomless pool, now rising slowly to the surface, but not by any efforts of her own, for she was too weak to use her arms to propel herself upward. As if from a great distance, she heard Nolan pleading for her rescue. And then Someone was calling her, telling her to let go, to float to the surface.

Her head still throbbed, her throat remained like sandpaper, but the inferno within had banked its fires. She lay there for an endless time, trying to recall where she was, and what she'd been doing before her body had betrayed her and surrendered to illness.

She had been at the Poteets' home. The sheriff had died. Nolan had been there… She remembered her insistence on staying the night to help the widow, and her first suspicions that all was not right within her….

Tentatively, she opened an eye, squinting against the flaring light of the candle.

"It's about time you came around, Sarah. You've given us all quite a scare," Prissy said.

Prissy had just finished helping her brush her hair, wash her face and put on a pretty robe when Nolan entered the room the next morning.

"See? I told you that she was better," she crowed, grinning.

"So you did," Nolan said, his gaze fastened only on Sarah. "How do you feel, sw—Sarah?"

He'd been about to call her *sweetheart.* The thought sent hot color racing up into her cheeks and her gaze dropped shyly into her lap against the earnest intensity of his blue gaze.

"Like a butterfly left out in the desert after it's been trampled by a maddened bull," she confessed, smiling and raising her eyes to him again. "I hurt *everywhere,* Nolan, but not as bad as I did yesterday. And I can't seem to get enough to drink," she added, glancing longingly at the water pitcher on her bedside stand.

He took the hint, and poured her a glass of water, sitting down in the nearby chair as if his knees were suddenly wobbly.

"Thank God," he breathed, his eyes suspiciously wet.

"Ah, the senorita is much improved today, *sì?*" Flora called out as she entered the room, bearing a tray of steaming broth. "I expect she might be ready for some soup, eh? You eat that, Senorita Sarah, and I will bake you my best *pan dulce,* no?"

"Yes, *please,*" Sarah said. "I can't think of anything I'd like more."

Flora turned to Prissy, saying, "Mees Prissy, your papa wants to see you. Probably he wants to hear how Mees Sarah fares, eh? Shoo now, I will stay with her," she added, nodding toward Sarah and settling into a chair.

She had appointed herself as her duenna, Sarah realized, amused, because after a glance in the mirror

Prissy had brought, she thought she could hardly be considered a female in need of being chaperoned, with her bloodshot eyes, her hair in a lank braid and her skin pale as milkweed blossoms. She wished she could have had a bath, she thought, even though she realized she would have been too weak to get in and out of it.

"Sarah, I..." Nolan seemed unsure of what to say, which he had never been before. "I...well, I thought you should know that seeing you like this is an answer to prayer."

She blinked. "I heard you," she said, even as she realized the fact. "Thank you..."

"I meant every word," he told her. "Even if you... well, if you had not...not survived, Sarah..." He looked away, as if he needed to collect himself. "I said I would believe. But I asked Him to save you, and He did. And now that He has, I'm going to need your help on this road of believing, Sarah."

She reached out her hand to him.

Chapter Twenty

It was a week before Sarah felt strong enough to leave the big house for their little cottage on the Gilmore grounds. During that time Nolan came to check on her twice every day, morning and evening. At first he seemed fearful when he came into the room, as if he worried that the progress she had made since his last visit—eating solid food, initially getting out of her sickbed, being able to sit up in a chair for longer and longer periods, descending the stairs to eat in the dining room with Prissy and her father—had been only a dream, and he would find her once again lying helpless and insensible, burning with fever. But as each day drew to a close, she grew stronger and coughed less. The bone-deep aching ceased. The anxious look in his eyes each time he beheld her faded.

He stayed only briefly in the mornings, for although the number of new cases in and around Simpson Creek was decreasing, those whom influenza held in its awful grip were still very ill, and some of them died. Every morning Nolan saw the undertaker and his assistant digging new graves in the church cemetery. And of course, the more ordinary business of a small town doctor continued, as he treated illnesses, broken bones, headaches, belly pains and wounds.

Sarah slept much during the first few days after passing the crisis, letting her body regain its strength. Then sometimes she was wakeful during the night, and she passed those hours praying for those she loved and reading the books Prissy would bring her from her father's library.

In the evenings, after his house calls were finished, he left a notice on his office door that he could found at the mayor's house, and came to spend a few hours with Sarah, cheering on her progress and telling her about his day. Sometimes Prissy sat with them, sometimes she left them discreetly alone, though she was always nearby.

They spent time, during his evening visits, reading the Bible together and discussing what they had read. He had questions, and she did her best to answer them, though sometimes she had to suggest Reverend Chadwick might be able to explain a point of doctrine better than she could.

The day came when she was finally strong enough to make the short journey across the grounds to the cottage, leaning on Prissy for support. When Nolan came that night, they celebrated with a meal that Prissy had cooked of Sarah's favorites, fried chicken, black-eyed peas, biscuits and apple custard pie.

Nolan was pleased to see that Sarah's appetite, which had been poor when she first left her sickbed, had returned and she was enjoying her food. The pink was returning to her cheeks, too, and the golden gleam to her lovely hair—thank God they hadn't cut it.

"That was wonderful, Prissy," Nolan praised, when he finished his dessert. "You've turned into quite an excellent cook."

Prissy beamed with pleasure. "I *have* come a long way from the girl who couldn't figure out how to light the oven, haven't I, Sarah?"

"That you have. Pretty soon you won't need me at all," Sarah said with a laugh.

Prissy chuckled. "Not so fast! Nolan, she still has to sit there and help me figure out how to get everything ready at the same time," she confessed, rising. "And now why don't you two go over and sit by the fire, while I redd up these dishes?"

Nolan was glad to comply, and assisted Sarah to the horsehair couch. He suspected Sarah only pretended to need to lean on his arm, and the knowledge that she liked doing so warmed him inside.

"Is that a new dress?" he asked, indicating the flower-sprigged lavender dress she wore. "It's beautiful." *You're beautiful,* he thought, loving the way her green eyes glowed at the compliment.

She nodded. "Milly brought it by—though I distinctly remember telling her to stay at the ranch until the epidemic was completely over. But she said she'd had time on her hands out there on the ranch, so she made this to celebrate my recovery."

"I haven't seen any new cases today," he told her, "and no one awakened me through the night. I think this epidemic is finally on the wane. I believe among those who still have it, all should recover."

"Thank God."

He nodded his agreement. "And thanks to the Spinster Nurses," he said. "I appreciate you organizing them to help. But you know what I *did* see today, Sarah? Buds on the trees! And Mrs. Detwiler has crocus and tulips beginning to poke up through the soil in her flower beds! And it's only February! Back in Maine, the ground would still be covered in a foot of snow!"

Sarah laughed. "I like your appreciation for our Texas weather, Yankee doctor. Let's see if you're still so enthusiastic about Texas summers."

It was an unspoken acknowledgment, he thought, that he had come to stay. Her amusement lit her entire face.

Then her expression sobered. "Nolan, have you seen Ada around town?"

He nodded. "In the mercantile, just today. She was dressed in mourning—not the loose garments she'd been wearing lately."

Nolan saw the spark of hope light her eyes. "Did you speak to her? Are you saying she's returned to her right mind?"

He hated to douse that spark. "Yes, I spoke to her. I asked her how she'd been feeling lately, and she announced that the influenza had caused her to lose our baby, though she knew I'd be relieved to hear it."

"Oh, *Nolan!*" she cried, putting out an impulsive hand to touch his arm in sympathy. "Did anyone hear her?"

"Only the three ladies gossiping by the pickle barrel. I don't think I've met them. They gave me scandalized looks as I departed."

"Surely Mrs. Patterson set them straight after you left," she declared with a confidence he was far from feeling. "I know she was one of others who realized Ada's stories were moonshine from the start."

He sighed. "I don't know if Mrs. Patterson even heard them. She seemed more than a little absent-minded when I paid for my purchases. She even called me Doc Harkey."

Sarah remembered Mr. Patterson had been one of the influenza victims. "The poor woman. She and her husband were married for thirty years."

The clock on the mantel chimed nine times, and Nolan rose. "It's late. I'd better go."

"I'll walk you to the door."

He had hoped she'd say that. "Do you think you'd feel strong enough to go to church with me on Sunday?" he asked, when they reached the shadowy vestibule.

Her face lit with pleasure. "Oh, Nolan, are they holding services again?"

"I told the reverend I thought it'd be safe by then. He told me to tell you not to worry about the music just yet—we can sing without the piano this week." He couldn't imagine a better way to start attending church again than with her sitting in the pew next to him.

"I have three days to gather my strength, then," she said with a grin, for it was Wednesday evening. "Shall I meet you there?"

"No, I thought I'd pick you up, and then we'd have dinner in the hotel and perhaps go for a buggy ride afterward, weather permitting. We can look for more signs that spring is on its way."

Her eyes sparkled, though he wasn't sure if it was at the prospect of escaping the indoors, returning to church or spending time with him. He hoped it was at least a combination of the three.

"I can hardly wait," he said, meaning it. At church, the town of Simpson Creek would finally see them as a courting couple. Perhaps that meadow west of the creek would be the perfect setting for their first kiss.

"Oh, Nolan, neither can I!" she exclaimed, and before he knew what she was about, stood on her tiptoes and kissed him.

Ah well, if his Sarah decreed their first kiss should be now, who was he to want to postpone it till Sunday? He returned her kiss with enthusiasm, savoring the honey sweetness of her mouth.

When they drew apart at last, he looked down at her and said, "Good night, sweet Sarah."

"Until Sunday," she whispered.

She dreamed of Jesse that night, her fiancé who'd never returned from the war.

She faced the gaunt, hollow-eyed figure in the ragged gray remnants of a uniform.

"It's time," she told him. "I loved you, but now I have to go on." She was relieved to realize she didn't feel guilty.

That was what it meant to fall in love again, she realized. Now that she loved Nolan, her love for Jesse Holt was relegated to a memory, a reality that was no more, just as his time on earth was no more.

* * *

Sarah woke at dawn the next day, conscious of a bubbling energy surging through her. It was high time, she thought, that she began baking again. She could barely suppress a happy hum until a sleepy-looking Prissy entered the kitchen and poured a cup of coffee.

"Being in love agrees with you," Prissy observed with a wry smile. "It's about time." Sarah had told her about the plans for Sunday, and while she hadn't spoken about the kiss, she thought her friend may well have guessed, judging by the knowing look in her eyes.

"Now, don't overdo it," Prissy said an hour later, as she was leaving to check on her father. "Remember, Nolan told us about the danger of a relapse."

"I'm fine," Sarah told her. "A little baking will hardly exhaust me." She wouldn't tell Prissy that she meant to deliver them, too.

By noon, she had dropped off her first armload of baked goods at the hotel restaurant, and was planning to return to the cottage just long enough to pick up several pies for the mercantile, which lay in the opposite direction.

Coming out of the hotel, Sarah ignored the lone cowboy lounging in front of the Simpson Creek Saloon. Probably suffering from spring fever, she mused absently, for the day was warm enough to be March rather than February. Perhaps he'd been given an errand in town, and he was lingering, reluctant to return to his duties…

"Sarah?" The voice came from the direction of the solitary cowboy.

She stared, transfixed, into the lean, beard-shadowed face of Jesse Holt.

Chapter Twenty-One

For a moment she forgot to breathe. It couldn't be. It was what she had prayed for for so long. She took a step forward, another, then stopped, expecting the figure in front of her to dissolve into nothingness as he had done in her dream last night. She'd been ill, and she'd dreamed about Jesse. Perhaps that was why she was now transferring Jesse's features, Jesse's *voice*, onto the figure on the bench. If she just waited for a moment and blinked a few times, surely he would fade away again.

Her mind had played tricks on her like this before, when the war was newly over and she had begun to realize that the continued lack of letters and his failure to return meant Jesse was really dead. She'd seen his face in every dark-haired, dark-eyed stranger, and thought for a few precious heartbeats it was Jesse, until a closer look disappointed her each time.

But this hallucination had risen to his feet, his heavy canvas duster flapping in the breeze. He moved slowly forward, pulling off his hat, as if he too were in a dream.

"Sarah Matthews, is that you?" the man repeated again, using Jesse's beloved slow drawl. "Don't you know me, Sarah-girl?"

"Jesse? Jesse Holt?"

A smile spread across the lean, beard-stubbled cheeks. Jesse's smile. "The very same."

She tried nonetheless to hold on to the reality she had known for almost a year now. "You can't be Jesse, mister. Jesse Holt is dead. Jesse never came back from the war."

The stranger masquerading as Jesse had the grace to look ashamed. Taking his eyes off her face, he stared at the line he was toeing in the mud in the street.

"Yes, well, I'm sorry about that. I never meant to make you wait that long. I can tell you're surprised to see me. How are you, Goldilocks?"

She had never liked this nickname Jesse had given her, but his use of it established beyond all doubt that the man walking toward her, so near now that she could almost reach out and touch him, was really her long-lost fiancé Jesse Holt.

"Where have you been?"

She was surprised at the surge of anger she felt within her, and she could tell by the way his eyes widened, then narrowed, that he was, too, for he lost his confident grin for a moment. But then he found it again.

"Well, now, I'll tell you all about that, Goldilocks, I promise I will. What are you doing in town? I thought I'd find you out on your pa's ranch. As a matter of fact

I was just waitin' for my horse to have a shoe replaced down at livery yonder, and then I was goin' to ride out and surprise you." He must have remembered his unshaven face, for he added, "Though I 'spose I should've made a stop at the barbershop first."

She remained speechless, and he tried another tack, maybe thinking she needed more reassurance that he was no imposter. "How's your pa? And that sweet sister of yours—Milly, isn't that her name? Is she bossy as ever?"

"Our father's passed on. Milly's married and she and her husband live on the ranch," she said stiffly.

"I'm sorry about your father," he said. "So Milly's got the ranch. What about you? You—you're not married, are you?" He lost that perfect assurance for just a moment.

"No, I'm not married," she said. "I'm living with Prissy Gilmore in a cottage on the grounds of the mayor's house." She didn't jerk her head backward to indicate it; Jesse had grown up in Simpson Creek just as she had and he would remember where the mayor's grand house stood.

He blinked, and looked as if he'd like to ask why. "Don't that beat all?" he said at last. The wind ruffled his hair at that moment. "Hey, you must be gettin' cold, aren't you?" He looked around him as if deciding something. "Why don't you invite me in for a cup of coffee and I'll tell you what I've been doing since the war's been over?"

She stiffened. "I don't think that's a good idea. Prissy's not there right now." She assumed Prissy had not returned from checking on her father, but she wouldn't have invited him even if she had been certain Prissy was there. Too many months had gone by, and now he had appeared without a word of warning, out of the blue. Later, she promised herself, she'd examine why the thought of Jesse in her house no longer appealed to her. Once, she knew, she would have invited him in and been glad that Prissy's absence gave them the privacy to exchange a kiss or two.

He chuckled, rubbing the back of his neck as he glanced behind him at the saloon. "And I reckon it wouldn't be fittin' to invite a lady into the saloon, either, to tell you my tale. Say, does the hotel still have that restaurant? Let me buy you dinner."

"No thank you, I'm not hungry," she said. It was the truth. Her stomach was churning.

"Coffee, then. You can keep me company while I eat. I've been on the trail since mornin', and I'm hungry enough to eat a longhorn steer, hide, horn, hoofs and beller."

Even as she smiled automatically at his joke, she decided he deserved to be heard out, at the very least. They'd once been engaged to marry, after all. And sitting together in a public place was certainly better than inside the cottage.

"All right," she said, and led the way back into the hotel.

Jesse drank a swallow of coffee to wash down the mouthful of roast beef he had chewed. "Right after we were taken prisoner, we were sent to Camp Chase in Columbus, Ohio. We figured we could escape from there and then it'd only be 'bout a hundred miles to the Kentucky border, but before we could do that, they transferred us to Johnson's Island in Lake Erie."

"Was it awful there?" Sarah asked. "We heard horrible things about Libby Prison...."

He shook his head. "Not so bad, except in the winter, when those winds came whistlin' outa Canada. We about froze our Southern hides off. Then in September of '64, a bunch of us tried to seize one of the boats that made stops at the islands, and pretty near got away with it too, but we found out we'd been betrayed and had to hightail it to Canada instead."

"You've been in Canada since the year *before* the war ended?" Sarah cried, unable to hide her indignation. "Why didn't you make your way back to the South, or at least write me from Canada?"

"Now, don't go soundin' all righteous, Sarah," he said with a flash of irritation as he speared another hunk of beef. "We had good reason to lay low. There were spies swarmin' all over northern Ohio and southern Canada lookin' for us, and the war was goin' bad. Someone might've intercepted my letter. We figured there was no use bein' cannon fodder in a lost cause and decided t' wait out the war where it was safe."

While other boys in gray kept dying. "Well then, where have you been since then? The war was over last April."

He sat back, studying her, grinning. "You look good, Sarah."

She recognized a dodge when she heard it. And what nonsense. Her mirror had told her only this morning how pale and thin she looked after her battle with influenza, but then Jesse Holt always had been a silver-tongued rascal.

"Livin' away from that bossy sister must agree with you," he said with a wink. "I'm glad I didn't have to ride out there and argue my way past that dragon. She never did like me, you know."

No, she hadn't known that, but it was just like Milly to have left her sister to make up her own mind. Sarah bit back the impulse to defend her sister and kept waiting, unwilling to be distracted.

The waiter returned to their table. "More coffee, folks?"

Sarah shook her head. Jesse said, "Sure, and we'll have some of that chocolate cake when we're finished. We're celebratin', you see.

"Where have we been, you asked," Jesse said, after the waiter had gone. "Well, while we were in Canada, we worked here and there, did a little a' this and a little a' that, to keep food in our bellies…."

"'We'?"

"Me and the boys from Johnson's Island who escaped together. Some of 'em were officers, some enlisted, but once we got outta that prison, we were equals. An' we figured it was time to get even with those Blue Bellies that put us in that blasted cold prison. So we've been makin' our way back t' Texas, stoppin' t' make life miserable for the Yankees whenever we could." He winked. "We've found it can be mighty profitable, mighty profitable indeed. And quite amusin'."

Mystified, she stared at him. "Jesse, whatever do you mean?"

He smiled that lazy smile again. "A little raiding, a holdup or two of stages bringin' the payroll to those blasted Federal troops who got no business occupyin' our fair state, a bit a' rustlin' of carpetbagger cattle..."

Sarah felt her jaw drop. "You're an *outlaw?*"

He laughed. "Nah, nothin' like that, Sarah. I told you, we're only harrassin' Yankees. We don't bother honest Southerners. High time we made up for all those years those b—those Yankees stole from us."

While she was still staring at him, her mind reeling at what he was so proudly telling her, he reached out and seized her hand, which had been clutching her coffee cup, and leaned across the table, his eyes intense.

"Sarah, they stole those years from *us,* from you an' me. If they hadn't tried t' bully the South, you an' me'd be married for three or four years with a passel a' kids. With your pa dead, I could've taken over the ranch and we'd have been sittin' pretty, yes siree. You know that's what would've happened."

Yes, they'd have married, she thought, but she was no longer sure she would have been happy. She pulled her hand away from his slowly, trying not to seem as if she was repelled by his touch.

"Jesse, the war is *over,*" she said. "The other men from Simpson Creek who survived came home and took up their lives again."

"Aw, Sarah, we were cooped up for so long, we were just havin' some fun before we settled down," he protested. "You always used to like havin' fun, so I figured you'd understand."

She felt her temper spark. "Jesse, I wore *mourning* for you. Your poor mother died thinking she'd see you in Heaven. You couldn't have written to say you were *alive?*"

Finally, he had the grace to look ashamed. "You know I never was much for book learnin'," he said. "I think I gave that schoolmarm we had—what was her name? Miss Russell?—most of her gray hairs. But I never meant to make you sad, Sarah, honey."

He looked at her with puppy-dog eyes, a look that used to melt her heart. "I'm here to make it up to you, Sarah. Run away with me, and we'll get married, and I'll introduce you to th' boys. We'll have a fine life—you'll see. A couple of 'em are married, too, or they have lady friends here 'n' there that ride along with us from time to time."

She couldn't believe her ears. "You think I'd even *consider* leaving with you to live an outlaw's life, always on the run?"

"Aw, Sarah, we have a grand time, livin' high off the hog. We're free to do whatever we want, whenever we want. We eat the best food, drink the best wine—our ladies are drippin' in jewelry and fancy clothes. But I'm willin' to leave it all if you insist."

"'Leave it all'?"

"Sure. That's how much I love you, sweetheart. If you don't want to live free as a bird, I'll come back and have that ranch with you. We'll let Milly stay there, too, of course, but it ain't fittin' for no lady to be runnin' a ranch anyway."

"I told you, Milly's married now," she managed to say, in the midst of the temper that was threatening to boil over into angry words. "I think her husband might take exception to that idea."

"We'll buy him out, then," he said grandly. "They can go find some other ranch. I know you always set great store by that old place."

She was conscious of the handful of other diners in the restaurant, and remembered again that her mother said ladies did not make a scene in public.

She folded her hands in her lap and looked away. "I'm sorry, Jesse. I loved you, and I prayed every night during the war for your return, but now—"

He straightened. "*Loved* me? You don't love me any more? There's someone else, isn't there?" he demanded, his narrowed eyes twin smoldering fires.

She looked away from his glare. She didn't want to tell him about Nolan, didn't want to hear his reaction to the news that his former fiancée was in love with one of the very Yankees he hated so much, especially since she and Nolan hadn't even had the chance to explore their new feelings for one another yet. But she wouldn't lie, not about the relationship that had come to mean so much to her. She just wouldn't say any more than she had to.

"Yes," she said. "Yes, I'm sorry, there is. I wish you well, Jesse. And now I'd best be getting home." She rose. The encounter—preceded by her busy morning of baking—had exhausted her, and she just wanted to reach the sanctuary of the cottage and lie down for a while.

Chapter Twenty-Two

Nolan whistled as he walked across the muddy street toward the hotel. It had been a busy morning, but a good one. All of his influenza patients seemed to be on the mend, and there continued to be no more new cases. And just as the sun rose, he had helped usher a new baby into the world. He couldn't wait to tell Sarah about it.

He glanced over his shoulder at the cottage, which sat diagonally across from the hotel, wishing he could drop in and see her right now, then decided against it, hoping Sarah was following his instructions and resting.

No, instead of knocking on Sarah's door, he'd have his dinner and then return to his office, where he'd restock his bag and "redd up" the office, as Prissy would say. Perhaps he'd even get a chance to catch up on his professional reading.

He was still whistling as he walked through the hotel lobby and into the restaurant, nodding a greeting at the waiter as he headed for his usual table by the window, but then he stopped stock-still.

Sarah was just rising from a table against the wall, and as he watched, the rangy-looking saddle tramp who'd been sitting opposite her jumped up, too, and grabbed her hand with a familiarity only a man who knew a woman well would dare.

Had he been completely wrong about Sarah Matthews? He'd thought she loved him, too. Was it possible she had other suitors, just as in love with her as he was?

"Sarah, you can't leave like this," the man said in a disbelieving voice, his rough features stricken. "I left the boys and came all this way to see you—I even offered t' leave 'em for good, and you're going to just walk out?"

"Jesse, *please,*" Sarah said in a low, distressed voice, pulling her hand away. Her back was to Nolan so she hadn't seen him, so he remained where he was. "Don't make this harder than it is. Please just accept what I've told you, and go on your way. But I beg you, if I ever meant anything to you, leave those bad men and start your life back on an honest path. I don't want you to die like outlaws do, from a bullet or at the end of a rope."

The man gave a harsh bark of laughter and his features hardened into something ugly. "Leave them? You make it sound like I'm some homeless cur, Sarah, going along with anyone who'll spare me a crumb. Sarah, I'm the *leader* of the Gray Boys gang. Me, Jesse Holt—the leader!"

Jesse Holt. Wasn't that the name of Sarah's fiancé, who'd died in the war? Apparently he hadn't died. Had

Sarah known that all along? Had they met in secret before, and now were becoming bold enough to meet in a public place?

"And I was willing to give all that up for you," the man went on, his face hardening into an angry mask, "but you're throwin' it back in my face and tellin' me you've fallen in love with someone else. Who is it, Sarah? That's what I want to know, and I think I have a right."

He *hadn't* been wrong about Sarah. He didn't know where this Holt fellow had popped up from, or if Sarah had known he was still alive, but obviously Holt didn't mean anything to her anymore, because she loved *him.*

By now, everyone in the restaurant was staring, townspeople and travelers alike. While Sarah had spoken quietly, Holt hadn't bothered to keep his voice down, so everyone in the room was now absorbed in the dramatic scene.

Sarah's voice shook, but her stance was no-nonsense as she said, "It's none of your concern anymore, Jesse. Goodbye."

The saddle tramp thrust his hand out as if he meant to stop her by force. It was time to step in.

"Is this man bothering you, sweetheart?" Nolan said, coming forward and placing a proprietary hand on her shoulder.

Sarah half turned and jumped, clearly startled. "*Nolan!* I'm glad you're here. Please, just take me home." Her face was flushed dully red with misery as she reached for his arm and took hold of it.

He looked down into her eyes, hoping she read the love in them. "Of course." Then he looked back at

Holt, making sure the man wasn't going for a gun. He wasn't, but if looks could kill, Nolan knew he would have been sprawled on the floor.

Clearly conscious of his enthralled audience, Holt's face screwed itself into a mask of scorn as he looked him up and down. "*This* is the fellow you left me for? This Yankee swell in a frock coat? How could you, Sarah? Your ma an' pa must be rollin' in their graves, knowin' their daughter's cozy with a Yankee."

"That's enough," Nolan snapped. "The lady's leaving, and you're not to bother her further."

Holt cocked his head and drawled, "I declare, he talks funny."

A few of the onlookers chuckled.

Nolan clenched his fists, but Sarah's hand tightened on his wrist. "Please, let's just *go*."

They turned and started for the door, but Holt wasn't done.

"You'll be sorry, Sarah! This whole town's gonna be sorry you threw me over!"

Nolan felt her shaking as they hurried across the road. Fortunately, Prissy still hadn't returned to the cottage, for Sarah managed to hold it in only until they crossed the threshold before she threw herself into his arms in a torrent of tears.

"Oh, N-Nolan!" she cried, her whole body heaving with her sobs. "He j-just appeared out of n-nowhere!"

"Did he come here to the cottage, looking for you?" Nolan asked, chilled at the thought of that man knowing where his Sarah lived.

"N-no..." she said against his coat as he held her,

her voice thick with tears. "I was coming out of the hotel—I'd delivered some baked goods, you see..."

So she hadn't been resting as instructed, but Nolan hadn't the heart to reprove her about overexerting herself.

"...And he was sitting outside the saloon," she continued, still shaking. She told him how Holt had escaped to Canada during the latter part of the war and had been running with a gang of outlaws ever since returning across the northern border. "He thinks it's all right because they're 'only stealing from Yankees,'" she cried. "Oh, Nolan, he's *nothing* like the sweet young man I loved before he went to war!"

"Ssssh, sweetheart," he soothed, still holding her and resting his face against her hair. "War has a way of changing men, and frequently not for the better. But it's over now. You're safe."

"But you heard him! He didn't just threaten me, he threatened the whole town!" she wailed. "What are we going to do?"

"We won't have to do anything," Nolan assured her. "Those were empty threats. Some men don't take rejection very well, that's all."

"But it's so unfair, Nolan! I mean, I'm glad he's not dead, but he never sent a word to tell me he was still alive! And then to show up out of nowhere, almost a year after the war was over, and get angry because I'd gone on with my life. Can you imagine, Nolan, he tried to talk me into running off with him!"

Nolan wanted to growl in rage at the thought of that saddle tramp inviting Sarah to join him on the run. He was relieved to see that Sarah was no longer weeping, but angry.

"Or if I wouldn't do that," she went on, pulling away to pace back and forth, waving her arm in a furious gesture, "he very nobly offered to give all that up and take over the ranch!"

"I reckon Nick Brookfield would have something to say about that, as well as Milly," he said drily. "Just picture Holt trying to waltz in there and persuade Milly to give up her ranch."

She gave a watery laugh and swiped a hand at her eyes. "She wouldn't even need Nick to defend it," she said. "She'd get out the shotgun herself."

"That's the spirit," he told her, stroking her cheek. "Now, don't worry about Holt anymore. Likely as not he's already ridden out of Simpson Creek and you'll never see him again."

"I hope you're right," she said, twisting a fold of her grenadine cloth skirt.

"You weren't tempted—even for a moment, before he told you what he'd been doing?" he asked her curiously, then wished he could call back the question as soon as he asked it. He had no right to probe her heart like that.

But Sarah apparently didn't mind. She shook her head, her eyes unfocused as she seemed to look within herself. "Not for a moment," she told him. "There was something about him that had just changed too much. And he wasn't *you,* Nolan." She went back into his arms and offered her lips for a kiss, and he was more than glad to take her up on it.

"But Nolan," she began when he let her go at last, "seriously, what if it wasn't an empty threat?"

He sighed. "Perhaps you shouldn't go anywhere alone for a while, even in the daytime," he said. "If I can't be with you, take Prissy."

"I meant his threat to harm the town," she said. "After all, the sheriff is dead, and his old deputy, Pat Donovan, has never been up to anything more than whittling while he guards someone already locked up."

It was a sobering thought. Nolan sighed. "I'll speak to Prissy's father. Now that the flu epidemic is over, we need to remind the mayor the town needs a new sheriff."

The next morning, Sarah, accompanied by Prissy in accordance with Nolan's request, headed to the mercantile to deliver the pies and cakes she'd baked yesterday.

"I feel silly asking you to come along like some sort of guard, Prissy," Sarah said as they walked. "It's not as if it's even likely I'd see Jesse between the cottage and the mercantile, even if he did stay in town. And I don't think he'd do anything more than ignore me, anyway."

"Oh, just think of me as someone to help carry your wares," Prissy said cheerfully. "Papa was wanting some peppermint drops at the mercantile anyway. And besides, it couldn't hurt to be careful—why, you could have knocked me over with a feather last night when you told Papa and me about Jesse showing up alive, and then acting the awful way he did."

"Yes, it was the last thing I ever expected," Sarah said. "I was never so glad to see Nolan in my life!"

"See, I told you that he was the one for you," Prissy said smugly as she held open the door of the mercantile to let Sarah in.

As they entered, Sarah spotted Mrs. Detwiler and Mrs. Patterson with their heads together at the counter.

"Good morning, ladies," she called out. "Good to see you up and about, Mrs. Detwiler, after your illness. Mrs. Patterson, I have some baked goods for you."

Both ladies jerked upright at the sound of Sarah's voice, looking so guilty Sarah knew they must have been talking about her. She felt a sinking in her stomach as if she'd eaten one of Prissy's early practice biscuits.

"Good, Sarah, I'll be glad to have them," Mrs. Patterson said quickly, trying to assume a businesslike manner. "It's been so long since anyone dared venture out, even if they were well, and now they're starting to ask where your cakes and pies have been. Of course, I told them you'd been very ill yourself...."

"Sarah, I was about to come see you," Mrs. Detwiler said, as if perhaps she realized Sarah saw through Mrs. Patterson's chatter. "There's something Mrs. Patterson and I thought you ought to know—"

Sarah raised her chin as Prissy quietly laid her share of the baked goods on the counter. "That Jesse Holt is alive and came to town yesterday? Yes, I'm aware. We ran into one another."

Both women looked distinctly relieved at not having to break the news to her.

"I imagine that was quite a shock, seeing him alive

after all that time," Mrs. Patterson said, peering curiously at her through her spectacles. "You didn't have any idea? He never wrote to tell you?"

As if the whole town wouldn't know if I'd received a letter from him, Sarah thought, remembering that Postmaster Wallace loved to gossip as much as the women did. "No," she said quietly. "But of course I'm glad he isn't dead, even if our lives have gone in different directions."

"Then you don't mind that he and Ada Spencer were cozyin' up with one another?"

"Jesse? And *Ada Spencer?*" Prissy exclaimed, while Sarah was still trying to find her voice.

"They met in front of the mercantile yesterday—I saw it from that very window," Mrs. Patterson said. "I thought he looked familiar but then Ada came along and went flyin' into his arms and squealin' in delight, callin' his name."

"Well, she knew him, too, of course, before the war," Sarah reminded her. "We all knew Jesse—we'd grown up together."

"Well, they came in here for a while, seein' as it was a mite chilly outside still, and stood and talked for the longest time. I heard bits and pieces here and there—"

"You don't need to tell me, Mrs. Patterson. I've already wished Jesse well, but explained that I've come to care for another very much—"

Mrs. Detwiler interrupted, "And that 'another' is Dr. Walker, isn't it? Took you a while, but you always were a smart girl. I'm right happy for you two."

But Mrs. Patterson was not about to be distracted. "Then you won't mind that Ada practically threw herself at him, and Jesse Holt looked mighty pleased to catch her," Mrs. Patterson said, as if Sarah hadn't hinted she'd heard enough. "Miz Powell, the cook at the hotel, said those two took supper there last night, and Ada was all gussied up," Mrs. Patterson said with a cackle that would have put one of Milly's hens to shame. "Not a sign of mourning on that one. Scandalous! And when they were done eating, Miz Powell said, they went off down the street arm in arm."

Sarah couldn't help but wonder if Ada had told Jesse about her recent "pregnancy."

"Ada's had a rough time lately," she said, aware that both ladies were waiting for her reaction and hoping this would satisfy them. "Perhaps she and Jesse would be good for one another." *And perhaps Ada can persuade Jesse off the outlaw trail.*

Mrs. Patterson kept staring at Sarah with speculative eyes.

"That'll be five dollars for the baked goods, as usual," Sarah said at last, reminding the proprietress why she had come. She didn't want to think about Jesse or Ada anymore, not when she had Sunday to anticipate, when she and Nolan would go to church together and then for dinner and a buggy ride.

"And Papa would like a half pound of peppermints," Prissy piped up.

Chapter Twenty-Three

"This is indeed a day of celebration," Reverend Chadwick announced, beaming from the pulpit as he looked out over the congregation. "Our first service since the influenza epidemic has abated, thanks to the goodness and mercy of the Lord..."

There were several calls of "Amen, preacher!"

"Thanks also in no small part to our dedicated physician, Dr. Nolan Walker," Chadwick continued, gesturing to where Nolan sat in a pew close to the front, with Sarah, Milly and Nick Brookfield and Mayor Gilmore and Prissy, "and his dedicated corps of nurses, also known as the Simpson Creek Spinsters' Club. Would you stand, Doctor, and you ladies, too, that we may show our appreciation?"

They did so, to the sound of loud applause, but to Sarah's surprise, Nolan raised his hand as if he wished to speak.

"Dr. Walker, you have something to say?"

"Yes, indeed I do, Reverend. I want to add my thanks and admiration to these devoted ladies," he said, gesturing next to him, where Sarah and Prissy stood, then around the pews to indicate Faith Bennett, Bess Lassiter, Maude Harkey, Jane Jeffries and Polly Shackleford. "Doctoring is my duty, and I accept it gladly, but these ladies *volunteered* to nurse the sick, going above and beyond anything that could have been expected of them and exposing themselves to the danger of contagion—" He caught Sarah's gaze then. His eyes glistening, he seemed to have trouble going on.

"And we are very glad Miss Sarah survived her brush with death," Reverend Chadwick finished for him. "Thank you, ladies, Doctor." They sat down to more applause. "And now we should remember those who the Lord chose to call home in the epidemic," the preacher went on, "so that we may pray for their families—Mr. Parker, Mrs. Gilmore, her sister Mrs. Tyler..." As he began to speak, the steeple bell began to toll, one tinny bong for each name. "Mr. Patterson, Mr. Calhoun, Sheriff Poteet, Pete Collier—who had so lately come to live with us—Mr. and Mrs. Spencer..."

The preacher kept reading the list of the dead. But Sarah heard a muffled sob from the back of the church, and thinking it was Caroline Wallace, who'd been Pete Collier's fiancée, turned around. She was surprised to see that the weeper was Ada Spencer, garbed in deep mourning, sitting with a black handkerchief to her eyes. None other than Jesse Holt sat beside her.

Their gazes met, and Jesse smirked at her.

They must have come in late. Quickly, Sarah turned around again, glad that Nolan hadn't noticed her looking. But Milly had followed her gaze, and Milly's wide-eyed, shocked face reminded Sarah that she had much to tell her sister.

Sarah told herself it was nothing to her if Ada wanted to put on mourning only when it suited her, and have Jesse Holt console her. At least Ada was no longer claiming she was pregnant, and accusing Nolan of fathering her child. Nolan was a much better man than Jesse had ever been, and Nolan loved her.

And then she felt ashamed for allowing herself to be distracted by less than spiritual thoughts in the Lord's house, and resolved to keep her mind on the hymns and the sermon to follow.

"Let us now stand and sing the first hymn. Mr. Connell, if you will lead us? I'm sure Miss Sarah will be back at her piano next week...."

For the rest of the church service, Sarah threw herself wholeheartedly into worshipping God and being thankful for Nolan's presence beside her, thankful too that he seemed to be thoroughly enjoying the singing and listening carefully to the preaching.

"Would you and Nolan like to come out to the ranch for Sunday dinner?" Milly asked afterward, as the congregation filed out and spilled down the church steps onto the lawn. "Now that I'm feeling better, I'm finding I love to cook. I'd like to show you how accomplished I've become."

"Could we make it another Sunday?" Sarah asked. "Nick's taking me to dinner at the hotel, and then for a buggy ride."

"Of course we can!" Milly exclaimed with a pleased grin. Then, seeing Nolan had been buttonholed by Mrs.

Detwiler to discuss her grandchild's teething woes, she pulled Sarah aside out of the earshot of others.

"If you're not coming to the ranch, then you'll have to tell me now when Jesse Holt reappeared like Lazarus coming forth from the grave!" she said in a low voice. "Why didn't you warn me? I nearly swooned in surprise when I turned around and saw him. And what's he doing with that Ada Spencer, who I see is no longer 'with child'? Dear Sarah, how do you feel about all that?"

Sarah couldn't help but chuckle at the spate of dramatic questions, and told her all about her surprise encounter with Jesse and what had followed.

"Well, I think you've made the right choice," Milly said a few minutes later, just before they walked back to rejoin Nolan and Nick. "Jesse Holt will come to no good end if he doesn't change his ways."

Dinner in the hotel had been wonderful, and since the weather had cooperated to produce a sunny, mild February day, they took Nolan's buggy out to the meadow west of the creek. Nolan couldn't believe he was actually sitting in his buggy with Sarah close beside him and stealing frequent smiling glances at him. If he was dreaming, he didn't want to wake up.

A mule deer doe and twin fawns hopped away as the buggy crossed the bridge. The cottonwoods and live oaks along the creekside were bursting with pale green leaves unfurling from their stems. Birds warbled their songs from the trees or flitted from branch to branch, twigs clutched in their beaks, building their nests.

"Just wait a month, and this meadow will be carpeted in bluebonnets," Sarah promised him. "And the next month, gold and red flowers, Indian blanket, Mexican hat, primroses—Nolan, you can't believe how beautiful it is!"

"I can't believe how beautiful *you* are, Sarah," he said, cupping her cheek. "And as I said in church, how kind, how brave…"

"Brave? Me? I'm not brave at all," she protested. "Milly would tell you I've been a quiet little mouse all my life. She's been the brave one, the leader."

"I don't think she'd say that anymore, *Nurse* Sarah. In fact, I think you have all the qualities to make an excellent doctor's wife."

When his words hit her, she gaped at him. "Dr. Nolan Walker! Did you just propose to me, on our very first outing together?"

He grinned. "Ayuh," he said, in a deliberately exaggerated "Downeast" accent. "We men of Maine don't waste time. Am I going too fast, sweetheart? I promise you'll get your courtship, never fear, but you and I both know I've been courting you every time we met—as much as you'd let me, anyway—ever since Founder's Day last fall."

She considered his words. "I guess that's true. All right, as long as you don't stint on the courtship—we Texas ladies set great store by courting, I'll have you know—I agree."

"Did you just say *yes*, Miss Sarah, on our very first outing as a courting couple?"

She nodded, blushing a rosy pink that made her even lovelier still.

He couldn't wait any longer, and lowered his lips to hers.

They were still exchanging kisses interspersed with sweet words when they heard horses approaching them from eastward beyond the town.

Letting go of one another, they lifted their heads.

Sarah's first thought chilled her heart—was it another Comanche attack? They were not far from the road—there was no time to hide—they'd both be killed… She sat paralyzed, wondering if there was time for them to run and conceal themselves in the underbrush along Simpson Creek.

Then common sense asserted itself and she relaxed. No, these horsemen didn't seem to be in any hurry, and she could hear the jingling of bits and spurs and the creaking of leather saddles as well as snatches of talk and laughter. Just some ranch hands coming into town for the afternoon…

But the riders who came into view did not look like any cowboys from the outlying ranches. They were bearded and rough, and each had loaded saddlebags with rifles and bedrolls strapped to the cantles. Their hats were worn low over their foreheads. They passed by without seeming to notice the buggy sitting in a grove of trees near the road, and there was something about them that put Sarah in mind of a pack of wolves—or of Jesse.

"Wonder where they're bound for?" Nolan murmured in a low voice. "They look like trouble."

Sarah nodded, keeping her eyes on them.

Snatches of talk drifted back to Sarah as they

passed. "…Said he'd meet us east a' town. Hope he's got some whiskey—saloon's probably closed up tighter'n a drum on account of it bein' Sunday…"

"Reckon he's made up his mind by now…"

"Yeah, well, if he ain't, we ain't hangin' around while he chases some skirt…"

Sarah put a hand out to steady herself against Nolan's arm. "Nolan, I think those men are the Gray Boys—the gang Jesse spoke of being their leader."

He gazed after the cloud of dust they had left behind, then back at her. "Perhaps we'd better wait no longer to tell Prissy's father what we've seen. It's all very well to advertise for a new sheriff, but in the meantime, he's got to have a plan in place to deal with troublemakers."

By tacit agreement, they left the peaceful glade and drove back across the creek into town.

Mayor Gilmore, wakened by Prissy from his Sunday afternoon nap, listened attentively, absently stroking his full beard.

"I don't know that I'm convinced that those men have anything to do with your Jesse Holt, Sarah—"

"Papa, he's not *Sarah's* Jesse Holt anymore!" Prissy cried, her gaze apologetic as it flew from Sarah to Nolan.

The mayor blinked and cleared his throat. "Pardon me, Miss Sarah, I spoke without thinking—meant no offense—but it would probably be prudent to appoint somebody as temporary sheriff, until the right man answers our advertisement, just in case. Trouble is, I don't know who'd be up to the job. His deputy sure isn't. How about you, Dr. Walker?"

Sarah saw Nolan's jaw drop at the question.

Nolan said flatly, "Mayor, I'm a *physician*, not a lawman."

"I know, but you were in the war… I'll warrant you had to be capable with a firearm in the army, even if your weapon was more often a scalpel."

Sarah saw Nolan's jaw tighten, and sensed the turmoil churning inside him from his rigid posture.

"There are several men of the town who were actually *soldiers* in the war," Nolan argued. "Naturally, I'd be willing to assist whoever you select—"

"Yes, there are, but the job calls for judgment and common sense, and the ability to lead, and I'm convinced you have that in good measure, Dr. Walker," the mayor retorted briskly.

"Thank you for the compliment, sir," Nolan said, "but I think I can serve the town better as its doctor."

The phrase "ability to lead" sparked an idea in Sarah. "Mayor Gilmore, what about my brother-in-law, Nicholas Brookfield? He was a captain in the British army, and he certainly led the effort to have the fort built in town last fall."

The old man blinked. "Of course, of course. I think that influenza must have boiled my common sense, not to mention my memory! Do you suppose he'd accept, Miss Sarah?"

"Until a permanent sheriff could be hired, yes, sir. But we won't know till we ask, will we?"

The mayor rubbed his chin whiskers, then said with a flash of his old decisiveness, "I believe we'd better act quickly. Doctor, would you be willing to take Miss Matthews out to the ranch now and ask Brookfield if he'd do it? Of course it'd be subject to town council approval, but I think they'll follow my suggestion if he accepts."

"Of course, Mayor," Nolan said.

"Good. Prissy, would you go 'round to the councilmen's houses now and tell them I'm calling an urgent meeting at ten o'clock tomorrow?"

Sarah sprang up along with Nolan feeling relieved to be doing something to help in the crisis, but she couldn't help wondering if even Nick Brookfield would be enough to stop the trouble that was coming.

Chapter Twenty-Four

By the time they left the ranch that evening, they had not only secured Nick's agreement to serve as the temporary sheriff if the council agreed, but had been given a delicious early supper by Milly.

"Your sister and brother-in-law are delightful people, Sarah," Nolan said as they neared Simpson Creek.

Sarah smiled in the darkness as the horse trotted along. "I can tell they like you, too. And Milly's relieved that I've finally seen the error of my ways. Once she'd met you, she was so upset with me for rejecting you because you're a Yankee." She chuckled. "I wonder what she'd say if she knew you've already proposed, this very afternoon!"

Nolan favored her with a teasing sidelong glance. "Why didn't you tell her?"

Sarah rolled her eyes. "Because then she'd say I gave in too easily! She can't let go of being the big sister who knows best, you kn—"

Her voice trailed off as the saloon came into view,

all lit up. From within, the strains of tinny piano music drifted out on the chilly evening air.

"What's going on?" she murmured aloud. "The saloon's never open on Sunday, never. I've always heard George Detwiler would like to, but you know Mrs. Detwiler, his mother—she'd never stand for it." Then she spotted a handful of men striding into it, laughing and talking loudly—and one woman, around whose waist a man's arm was curled.

The buggy drew closer, and Sarah saw the woman turn to hear something the man was saying. Sarah recognized Ada Spencer. The man touching her so familiarly was Jesse Holt—which meant the men pushing open the batwing doors were the Gray Boys.

"Nolan—"

"Unfortunately, there's nothing illegal about a bunch of drifters visiting a saloon, even if it is Sunday," he said, guessing the cause of her apprehension. "And they've committed no crimes, as far as we know. We'd best get you inside out of the cold, sweetheart," he added, seeing her shiver.

That night, she was wakened by gunfire from the direction of the road, and went to her window, which looked out on the street. Pulling aside the curtain, she was in time to see horsemen galloping away. Even through the closed window, she could hear their raucous whooping and hollering and shooting into the air.

Sarah came out the next morning with a load of pies for the hotel just as Nick was mounting his horse at the Gilmores' stable.

"Nick, am I to call you Sheriff Brookfield?" she called, raising a hand in greeting.

"For the time being, yes," he confirmed as he swung his leg over the saddle. His face was grim, absent of the good humor that usually marked it. As he turned to greet her, she saw the five-pointed tin star already pinned to the collar of his coat.

A premonitory trickle of apprehension skittered down her spine. "Has something happened?"

"The ranch was hit by rustlers at sunrise," he told her in his crisp British accent. "They drove off all the cattle in the back pasture, every last head. Micah happened to be out there checking on a cow with a new calf, and they shot him."

She couldn't stifle the sound that escaped her. Micah was the youngest of the Brown brothers who were all cowhands at the ranch.

At her cry of alarm, he held up a hand. "He'll be all right, I think. He's at the doctor's right now, getting the bullet removed from his arm."

What he wasn't mentioning, Sarah knew, was what a devastating effect the loss of the cattle would be to the ranch if they were not recovered. They'd lost almost half their herd last year when the Comanches had raided. Milly and Nick had hoped to build up the herd enough to make a profit when drovers came through next year.

"I—I'll go see him," she said, feeling unfocused, "and see if there's anything I can do to help Nolan."

"You're a good woman, Sarah. I know Micah would like that. Milly's there, but she's rather shaken up, you know, what with waking up to the sound of gunfire, then seeing Micah riding in, his arm all bloody…"

Sarah could well imagine, having awoken to the sound of gunfire herself. And as stalwart as her sister was, she never could stand the sight of blood, and now she was expecting a child…

"Is Milly all right? Shouldn't you be with her?" She heard a sharp, disapproving edge in her voice, and was sorry, but this was her *sister.* "Perhaps she should stay at the cottage with Prissy and me while you're serving as sheriff."

"I tried to stay with her at the doctor's," Nick protested, "but she knew I was supposed to be at the council meeting here and chivied me out the office door. Besides, your Nolan said he'd check her to make sure all was well with the child. And I *did* already suggest she stay here with you while I'm away from the ranch, but she insists that since there's nothing left to steal, we won't be troubled again."

Milly was probably right. Reassured somewhat by the news that her sister was behaving with her characteristic feisty resolve, Sarah felt her tensed shoulders relax some, though the worry remained.

"Josh and the others have already rounded up a posse to catch the rustlers. I'm riding to join up with them now."

She didn't know if it would prove helpful, but she told Nick about seeing the group of men and Ada going into the saloon last night.

His eyes narrowed. "Your erstwhile friend Ada sounds a right foolish woman," he said. "But thanks for letting me know. Leave word at the jail, if you spot them again."

Stopping only long enough at the cottage to tell Prissy the news and ask her to deliver her pies, Sarah picked up her skirts and hurried down the street to Nolan's office, arriving out of breath and feeling her carefully pinned hair falling down her back.

Milly jumped up from her straight-backed chair in the waiting room and fell into Sarah's arms. "Oh, sister, I'm so glad you're here!"

Elijah, Micah's eldest brother, rose more slowly beside Milly, his face betraying his anxiety.

Milly's shoulders shuddered with sobs. "Your Dr. Walker says Micah'll be all right as long as gangrene doesn't set in…."

Sarah stayed with her sister and Elijah until Milly was calm again, then went through the office door to see if she could be of help.

As she entered, the sharp tang of carbolic stung her nostrils. Nolan looked up sharply from the roll of linen he was winding around the cowhand's arm, but his stare softened as he recognized her.

"I'm glad you've come," Nolan said, his gaze caressing her. "I was afraid it was your sister trying to help again. She means well, but she turned white as this bandage when she attempted to be my assistant a few minutes ago."

"Hello, Miss Sarah," Micah said from the doctor's examining table. Under his dark skin, he looked a little pale himself.

"Hello, Dr. Nolan, Micah." Their formality in front of the cowboy felt odd after what had happened between them at the creek yesterday. "Micah, how are you feeling?" She tried to avoid looking at the small, round metal container beside him in which a bloody, misshapen bullet lay.

"Better now, Miss Sarah," he said in his soft, slurred drawl. "This Dr. Nolan, he's one fine bullet remover. I barely felt it," he said. The pain shining in his eyes, and the beads of sweat shimmering on his brow, however, belied his words.

"Young Micah, you're a very polite liar," Nolan told him. "It's all right to say it hurt like h—that is, it hurt very badly. You bore up well, though."

"Thank ya, Doctor."

Nolan assisted the other man down from the exam table and into the waiting room, where Elijah and Milly waited. Sarah followed.

"You keep that bandage clean and dry, Micah. I'm going to send along enough linen that Mrs. Brookfield can change the dressing every day. Mrs. Brookfield, please have someone notify me at once, day or night, if there's any fever or a great amount of swelling, or any cloudy drainage—*any* of that, understand?"

Milly, Micah and Elijah all nodded solemnly.

"I'll send some morphine pills with you in case Micah's pain gets worse," Nolan told Milly, "though the willow bark tea may well be sufficient."

"Now don't worry about Nick, Milly," Sarah said while Elijah helped his brother into the wagon. "Prissy and I will take his supper down to him at the jail every night."

"And don't you worry about your sister, neither, Miss Sarah," Elijah assured her in return. "I'll guard her and the house like a hawk."

* * *

By the next day, word reached town that two other ranches had been struck by the rustlers, as well. At those ranches, the thieves hadn't contented themselves with only the cattle, but had raided the ranch houses, too, and had stolen the ranchers and their wives' valuables, including the heirloom pocket watch of one and the garnet earbobs from his spouse. Sarah couldn't help but wonder if Milly and Nick's valuables had been left alone at Jesse's order because of her, or if the gang had merely grown greedier as they went along.

Nick and the posse returned the second evening without having caught up with the robbers and the stolen cattle, but with the news that yet another ranch had been hit. This time, the rustlers had killed a foreman and gravely wounded one of the cowhands who had attempted to drive them off. He was brought into town to Nolan, but the man had been shot in the chest and died despite Nolan's efforts to save him.

Now that the gang had added murder to their list of crimes, the ranks of the posse swelled and the president of the Simpson Creek Bank announced the formation of a reward account for the apprehension and conviction of any or all of the Gray Boys gang. Sarah heard threats to hang Jesse highest of all since he'd been one of their own, yet was now leading the pack of outlaws who preyed on them.

She felt a pang of grief for the idealistic young Jesse Holt who had gone off to war, promising to marry her and start a family as soon as the war was over, and who had returned as a cold, ruthless criminal. Perhaps it would have been better if he *had* died in battle as a soldier, his honor intact.

As the days went on and reports reached them that the Gray Boys had struck ranches in the neighboring towns, Sarah was the recipient of decidedly odd looks from some townspeople she encountered in the street. She knew the gossips were having a field day telling anyone who would listen about the scene in the hotel restaurant between Jesse and herself, and reminding each other that the two had once been engaged to marry. She wouldn't have been surprised to hear that some of them actually *blamed* her for kindling Jesse Holt's wrath on Simpson Creek by rejecting him.

The outlaw raiding even managed to cast its shadow over Sarah and Nolan's burgeoning romance. The influenza epidemic was over, spring was fast approaching and their love was a growing, thriving thing, yet how could they plan a wedding with carefree hearts when the outlaws' reign of terror over San Saba County continued?

A very discouraged foursome—Sarah, Nolan, Nick and Prissy—had supper at the sheriff's office on the first Saturday in March to toss around ideas of how to capture the Gray Boys.

"Have you questioned Ada?" Sarah asked while she ladled the vegetable soup into bowls and handed them to Prissy to pass out. "Perhaps if she thought she might be arrested as an accomplice, be tried and go to prison if convicted, she'd give up their hideout."

Nick steepled his fingers and eyed the ham Sarah was now slicing. "She might well do so, but the problem is finding her. Have you seen her lately?"

Sarah paused and laid down the knife. "Now that you mention it, no," she admitted.

"Neither has anyone else," Nick said. "'Neither hide nor hair' of her, as they say. She seems to have gone missing, though some of her neighbors have reported seeing her coming and going from her house at odd hours. Just the other night, Nolan, Donovan and I paid a surprise visit in the middle of the night after Donovan spotted a light in one of the back windows and summoned me—"

Sarah looked up, surprised, for Nolan hadn't mentioned it.

"—but the place was deserted when we got there."

"Yes, there was a pile of dirty laundry on the bed," Nolan said. "It looked as if she'd come home to fetch more clothes, and left just as quickly."

"Apparently she's come to enjoy the outlaw life," Nick went on. "The latest reports from the victims of their attacks have mentioned that she's riding along with them and packing pistols just like the others."

Sarah and Prissy stared at one another, horrified. Had it really been less than a year ago when Ada Spencer had been as excited as any of the Simpson Creek Spinsters about meeting a beau through the newspaper advertisements?

Chapter Twenty-Five

"They're overrunning the lines, heading straight at us!" the sentry screamed, his voice a mere thready cry against the din of booming cannon and the crack of rifles and the frantic whinnying of horses and the shouts of men grappling in mortal combat.

A trio of frightened-looking boys—surely they were only boys, even if they wore corporal's insignia on their uniforms—scrambled into the medical tent and huddled in the far corner, trembling. One of them was crying; another yelled "They're after us! We gotta hide till they go past, Doc!"

Nolan wrenched up his head from the bloody operative field beneath his hands. He was in the middle of the amputation of a shattered leg of an unfortunate captain whose limb had received a glancing impact of cannon shot just an hour ago. He didn't have the time to deal with fleeing soldiers using the medical tent as sanctuary—he had time for nothing but the man bleeding and nearly insensible from blood loss and the last of the whiskey.

The Rebel Yell, the unnerving Confederate battle cry, ululated nearby—*too* nearby—as pounding feet thudded closer, closer…

"Turn them—you've got to turn them!" he shouted to the sentries crouched at the tent's entrance.

One of them ran toward Nolan, screaming, "We can't! They're too many of them! They—" And then a bullet struck him in the back with such force that he went down, arms flailing, against the side of a nearby cot, sending a rifle skidding toward Nolan as he collapsed in a welter of blood.

Wild-eyed men in threadbare, tattered remains of gray and butternut uniforms charged in, bayonets fixed.

Nolan lay down his scalpel as carefully as his shaking hands allowed. "Get out! This is a medical tent! By all the laws of war and decency, you have no right to be here, interfering while we're trying to care for the wounded!" Nolan thought the unkempt fellow at the head of the pack would surely raise his rifle and silence him with a single shot, but the latter paused only long enough to spit in contempt.

"We saw them yella belly Yanks runnin' in here, lookin' for their mamas, prob'ly!" he shouted back. "You jes' let us have them and we'll let you tend to your business!"

He couldn't let them shoot at the boys where they crouched, not only for their sake but also for the sake of the wounded men lying on pallets and on the bare ground inside and outside, awaiting their turns for surgery. Flying bullets were no respecters of canvas barriers. Grabbing for the rifle the sentry had dropped, he raised it and shot the man, but too late to prevent the invader's round from striking one of the huddled corporals. The boy screamed; the rebel fell in a heap in the aisle between the operating tables.

Sentries and Yankees whose wounds were not too disabling ran in now, and used their rifles as clubs and fired their pistols at the rebels. The yells of the combatants rose to a cacophonous din as the air grew thick with smoke and the bitter smell of gunfire.

And still the surviving rebels kept shooting, and many of the previously wounded died like lambs in a slaughterhouse.

A red mist of rage swam in front of Nolan's eyes. Not pausing to reload, he tightened his grip on the fallen rebel's rifle and with a roar of fury, charged the rest of the attackers with the bayonet, skewering one man, then yanking the blade free to go after another.

It took only moments to kill the rest of the invaders, but as Nolan trudged back to the operating table, heart pounding and hands shaking, he saw that death had claimed one more victim. The soldier would not need his leg amputated after all, for he had bled to death while the battle raged around him.

Nolan awoke from the nightmare with a jerk, his entire body bathed in the cold sweat of horror. What battle had that been—Petersburg? Spotsylvania? It didn't matter; by the time the war was nearing its end, they had all blurred together.

Another man might have conceived a deeper hatred for the enemy after this attack; in Nolan it resulted in a more fervent desire to defeat death no matter which color uniform its victims wore.

As a physician, he was still fighting death, he thought as he lay there feeling his pulse return to normal. Was his dream prophetic? Was he being warned that even though the war was over, violence committed by outlaws such as the Gray Boys still took a toll on lives?

"Let us rise and sing our closing hymn, 'A Mighty Fortress is Our God,'" Reverend Chadwick said with upraised palms, and the congregation stood as one. "And while we are singing it, let us remind ourselves that He is indeed a 'mighty Fortress,' no matter what brand of troubles are besetting us, whether it be Comanches, as it was last fall, or an epidemic, as we have just been through, or the depredations of outlaws, as we are currently experiencing. Let us pray together that God will enable our acting sheriff, Nicholas Brookfield, and his posse, who are at this very moment patrolling the countryside, to apprehend the outlaws who are endangering our peace. The army has been requested to aid us. In the end the Lord will enable us to triumph over all these trials, beloved, never doubt it."

Before opening his mouth to sing with the rest, Nolan added a silent amen to the preacher's prayer. If only he didn't feel so personally helpless in this matter. He, along with Sarah and the other "Spinster Nurses" had been instrumental in turning the tide against the influenza epidemic, but now he could only tend his patients, when they needed him, while other men rode out in pursuit of the gang.

Yes, medicine was his profession—it was up to him to help patients amid the "mortal ills prevailing" that the hymn spoke of, but in the midst of this crisis, it no longer seemed enough. His protestation to the mayor that he could not serve as the sheriff now seemed like a mere excuse to him to stay in his office, safe and secure, while other men risked their lives.

His gaze fell on Sarah as her fingers coaxed the melody of the majestic hymn from the old piano and those around him sang the age-old words of faith. Just to think that this lovely, talented lady loved him gave him a thrill each time he looked at her. He wanted to set a date for their wedding, to plan their future, yet there was no peace while these outlaws, led by one who had once been the center of Sarah's life, preyed on the people of Simpson Creek.

After church, they took a picnic lunch across Simpson Creek, and sure enough, they found the first bluebonnets peeking up in their striking blue, white-topped glory from the tender new grass in the meadow where he had so recently asked Sarah to be his wife. They reminded him of the bigger lupines he had seen in Maine, but these were more vivid, more *brave* somehow, blooming before the calendar had officially decreed spring.

"Sarah, during church I was thinking—"

Once again they were interrupted by the sounds of approaching horsemen, and both of them went still, only to relax when they recognized the returning posse. But all was not well; Nick cradled in his arms Pat Donovan, the deputy sheriff. Donovan was unconscious, his face pallid, his trousers and the lower part of his coat saturated in blood.

"We ambushed them by Barnett Springs—almost

had them, too, but they shot Pat's horse out from under him and then shot Pat in the thigh," Nick called, even as Sarah and Nolan rushed forward. "He's lost a lot of blood…passed out on the way back…"

"Get him to my office," Nolan shouted, gesturing in that direction, as he and Sarah ran for the buggy. His heart sank, for he knew the man was already doomed, but he had to try.

Thank You, Lord, for this dauntless woman. Sarah didn't have to be asked to help him. Once they ran into his office, she just rolled up the sleeves of her Sunday-best dress, threw on the heavy canvas apron he tossed her and began scrubbing her hands and arms with soap before rinsing them in carbolic.

Half an hour later, Sarah stared at Nolan from the other side of his exam table, her eyes wide with wordless grief as Nolan pulled a sheet over the deputy's face.

"He lost too much blood before he got here," Nolan muttered dully, wiping his hands on a towel. He wasn't sure if he spoke aloud or not. "If I'd been with them, maybe I could have saved him…."

"Nolan, you mustn't blame yourself," Sarah said gently, shrugging off her crimson-stained apron and coming around the table to take him in her arms, heedless of the tears that bathed her cheeks. "You did all you could…."

"I have to do more." He hugged her for a moment, then loosed her and pushed open the office door where Nick and the rest of the men waited.

"I couldn't save him," he announced. Some of the men stared at him, others dropped their gazes to their boots. "Nick, I want to take his place, till this is over. Swear me in."

"Nolan, no!" Sarah cried.

"Nolan—Dr. Walker—that's not necessary," Nick began. "The town needs a doctor, and only you can do that."

"I might have saved Donovan if I'd been along," Nolan said. "If I'd been there to staunch the bleeding, apply a tourniquet... No, my mind's made up, Brookfield," he added as Nick opened his mouth again. "You're a rancher serving as a lawman, I'm a doctor and I can help you. I can shoot. My buggy horse is trained to the saddle, too. I'll pack the medical supplies that might be useful in my saddlebags."

He walked Sarah home after that, Donovan's tin star pinned to his coat.

"Nolan, I wish you wouldn't do this." Sarah's voice was choked with unspent tears. "I don't know what I'd do if I lost you...."

"I'll be all right. Don't you see, I have to do this, sweetheart," he said, his arm around her waist as they walked toward the cottage. "Doesn't the Bible say there's a time for war and a time to heal? Right now I have to be willing to fight so I can go back to being a healer, and we can go on with our lives in peace. It's not the first time I've had to put my scalpel down and pick up a gun," he added, and told her about the day he'd done so in the medical tent.

She was wide-eyed when he finished. "Dear me. And yet the man you tried so hard to save, Jeffrey Beaumont, was a rebel."

"I had nightmares for months about the face of the

man I had to shoot," he told her, not mentioning the fact that the nightmare had come again last night. "I think that's why I was so determined to save Jeff, to atone for it, even though I'd done what was necessary to save the others."

They had reached the cottage. "You *will* be careful?" she begged, worry creasing her lovely brow.

He nodded, and pulled her into his arms again, kissing her tenderly. "Of course." Then he had another thought. "Perhaps I should teach you to shoot, as well? I'll be away some with the posse—I don't like the idea of leaving you defenseless in case Holt takes a notion of trying to 'persuade' you to come with him again."

She shook her head. "It's not necessary, Nolan. Papa made sure both of us girls learned how to shoot a pistol in case we met up with a rattlesnake or something on the ranch. I have a derringer in the cottage—Milly made sure I brought it, just in case."

"Then promise me you'll keep it handy."

Chapter Twenty-Six

Prissy flushed pink with pleasure as Major McConley, riding at the head of a score of cavalry soldiers, tipped his cap at them as he trotted past. She rewarded him with a flirtatious smile.

"I'm so glad I wore my new bonnet," she said. "The major has such a cute dimple when he smiles, doesn't he? Sarah, do you suppose he's a bachelor?" Her gaze followed the disappearing cavalry detachment. "Perhaps we should issue an invitation to him—and the others in his regiment who are unmarried too, of course—to a Simpson Creek Spinsters' Club event. I might like to be a major's wife, I think."

Sarah thought it would be a long time until they'd be able to plan any more Spinsters' Club parties, but she had to smile at her friend's obvious attempt to distract her from her anxiety about Nolan. Only this morning the bell had tolled at the church—the signal for the posse to assemble there. Nolan had ridden eastward with Nick and the rest to investigate a report that the outlaws had been sighted camping on the banks of the Colorado River.

"Prissy Gilmore, living in a stockade, miles from the nearest stores?" Sarah teased. "I can't imagine it."

"You think I'm just a frivolous flibbertigibbet, don't you? I'll have you know I would make a very good soldier's wife. I'd organize tea parties for the wives, regimental balls… And just imagine the wedding—with his men crossing swords to form an arch over us as we left the church." She sighed dreamily. "But since you'll obviously be married before I will—to your handsome, brave doctor/deputy—perhaps we should ride out to see Milly. She's probably bored to tears with Nick away. I'm sure she'd help you design a wedding dress fit for a princess, then sew it for you."

"I'd love to go see her—I don't like her being out on that ranch without her husband there, even though the hands are sticking close to the house—but you know Nolan advised us not to ride out of town without him along until they've caught Jes—I mean the rustlers." She winced inwardly as she imagined the man she had once loved dying in a hail of bullets, or being marched up a gallows to be hanged.

"Well, we can at least look at the fabrics in the mercantile, and peruse their latest copy of Godey's," Prissy said.

Sarah gave in with a nod. Maybe it would keep herself from fretting about Nolan. She needed another sack of flour and a couple pounds of sugar, anyway, or she wouldn't be able to bake tomorrow.

"My, look at the time," Prissy exclaimed as they left the mercantile, peering at the delicate gold watch pin that had been her mother's. "Four o'clock already. I had no idea it was getting so late, but didn't we have fun?"

Sarah had to admit poring over fashion designs and bolts of fabrics had been a pleasurable way to pass the afternoon. She'd found an exquisite ivory silk broche and Mrs. Patterson had agreed to put it in the back room for her until she could show it to Milly. And Prissy had gone ahead and bought a dress length of hussar blue cotton which she planned to pay Milly to sew into a party dress for when they invited the bachelors of the Fourth Cavalry to a Spinsters' party, saying, "Won't it look gorgeous against the darker blue of the major's dress uniform?"

Soon it would be time to go up to the big house for supper with Prissy's father, and with any luck Nolan might return to town in time to join her there. She hoped he would bring good news at last.

Crossing the street and entering through the massive gates to the Gilmore grounds, they walked to their cottage. Once inside, Sarah went into the kitchen with the staples she'd bought, while Prissy walked down the hall to her room to put her bonnet back in its hatbox.

Perhaps tomorrow she'd try the new recipe Caroline Wallace had given her for Washington pie. She liked to experiment with new things, and it was probably a wise idea to vary the fare she sold at the hotel and mercantile. It wasn't long before she would be able to get fresh peaches, and—

"Sarah, could you come here please? Quickly?" Prissy called from her room. Her voice sounded strained, unnatural, but Sarah only smiled, for it was the same tone she'd used before when she'd been startled by a mouse scurrying across the room to disappear into a crack in the wall.

"I'll be right there," Sarah called, wanting to finish pouring the five pounds of flour she'd bought into a canister before she went to console Prissy, who was no doubt standing on her bed. Prissy was deathly scared of mice. Maybe it would be a good idea to get a cat, she thought. It might be fun to get a kitten and teach it to chase after a length of yarn—

Sarah heard the door open, and footsteps coming down the short hallway between the two bedrooms. "Sarah..." Prissy called again, her voice quavery.

Prissy must have managed to get between the door and the mouse.

"I'll get the broom and shoo it outside," Sarah said without turning around, as the now-empty bag of flour sagged in her hand. "You know, we ought to get a cat." She was determined to convey calmness in the face of Prissy's tendency to hysteria around rodents. "Mrs. Detwiler's cat is always having kittens. What would you like, a calico one, or maybe a sweet little black one with white boots—"

"I've always been partial to gray tigers, myself." The voice was female, but it was not Prissy's.

Sarah whirled and looked into the ruthless eyes of Ada Spencer, and then into the bore of the pistol the woman had leveled at her. In front of Ada was Prissy, her blue eyes enormous in a face that was leached of all color, holding her hands in the air, and as Ada pushed her forward, Sarah could see she had the barrel of another pistol poking between her friend's shoulders.

"What are you doing here, Ada?" Sarah's voice

sounded strange in her own ears, as if it belonged to someone else, someone far calmer than she felt, someone whose knees felt more substantial than a half-baked cake. *Dear God, help us!*

"Jesse wants you taken to him, so I've come to accomplish it," she said, as if it should be perfectly obvious and logical. "I'm the only one who can do it. He and his men can hardly storm into town after you—they'd stick out like sore thumbs. That's why they let themselves be seen by some yahoos over on the Colorado River so the sheriff and his men would go riding after them—leaving you here in town alone."

If only I'd put the derringer in the reticule sitting just inches away on the table, as I'd promised Nolan that I would.

Even so, the idea of going anywhere with this madwoman was ridiculous, and ignited her ire. "I'm not going," Sarah told her. "I don't love him anymore."

"You'll go if you want Prissy to live," Ada said, a mad glint in her eyes told Sarah that she would be perfectly willing to pull the trigger of the gun pressed into Prissy's back.

"Sarah…" Prissy shook like a leaf in a gale, and Sarah thought she may faint. If she did, Sarah might be able to use the element of surprise if she acted fast—or it might give Ada an even greater advantage. She would have two pistols to aim at Sarah, and no Prissy to get in the way. *Lord, show me what to do.*

Ada was armed, and not in her right mind. Sarah realized she would have to rein in her temper, and try to reason with a deranged woman.

"Why would you want to do that, Ada? I know you

love Jesse, so I would think you wouldn't want a rival for his affections." If she could distract Ada enough, perhaps she could overpower her before Ada could get a shot off. But she'd be risking both her life and Prissy's.

The woman's laugh was brittle as the sheerest glass. "Oh, you won't be a rival. As if you could be! No, Jesse has other plans for you. And if I do this, Jesse's going to marry me. He said so. He'll buy me a beautiful ring and a fancy dress…." She recited the outlaw's promises in a strange singsong that sent chills down Sarah's back. It was like a child reciting a nursery rhyme.

"'Other plans?'" Sarah echoed. "What other plans?"

"We're taking a little trip with you, going up on the Staked Plains where we'll sell you to the Comanches, along with the cattle the boys've gathered. Some Comanche brave will pay a fine price for you, Miss Yellowhair." She laughed, a laugh that teetered on the edge of maniacal. "Or maybe you'll go to the Comancheros—maybe they could find a use for you. Meanwhile, of course, Jesse's men will…get to know you better." Again, that brittle laugh.

The idea of any of the Gray Boys touching her, then being taken north and sold as a slave to a brutal Indian or the Mexican traders that sold firearms to them paralyzed Sarah, but she couldn't give in to that fear.

For God hath not given us the spirit of fear....

"But why would he do that?" Sarah asked, if motivated by curiosity alone. "He loved me once, but now he has *you*, Ada. He doesn't need me. Why can't he leave me in peace and go off with you?"

"You have to pay, Jesse says." Again, that eerie

singsong tone. "He came back for you, and you broke his heart. I'm mending it, of course, in my own sweet way, but you have to pay. No one gets away with breaking my Jesse's heart." Her grip tightened on the pistol.

"He doesn't have a heart anymore," Sarah said. "He lost it somewhere in the war." She tried another tack. "Why would you want a man like that, Ada? What if he gets tired of you and sells *you* to the Comanches?"

"You stop talking like that!" Ada cried, her voice shrill. The pistol—the one that wasn't pressed into Prissy's back, rose again and pointed at Sarah's chest. "Jesse wouldn't do that. He *loves* me! Now stop wasting time. We have to leave. You two kept me waiting—kept Jesse waiting—too long as it is. I thought you'd never come back here, once the posse left town. We have to go."

Where was Nolan? What time was it? Was it late enough that the posse was even now riding back into town? Was there a chance Nolan would come here, looking for her, and save her from Ada? She dared not look at the clock, but she knew that if she and Prissy didn't show up at the big house for dinner, eventually Mayor Gilmore would send Flora or Antonio to check on them.

Could she stare over Ada's shoulder and convincingly say, "Hello, Nolan, I'm so glad you're here," as if Nolan had returned and sneaked silently into the cottage? Would Ada turn around, and would she be able to overcome the crazed woman before Ada could fire either of the pistols?

It would be taking a chance with Prissy's life. And

she couldn't do that. She couldn't live with the idea that she had gotten Prissy killed.

"If you want your silly friend to live, you better come with me right now," Ada said, waving the pistol aimed at Sarah. "I'll shoot her—it doesn't matter to me."

"But the sound of the shot will make the Gilmore servants come running, Ada," Sarah said reasonably. "You don't want that."

"But she'd still be dead. Maybe you, too."

There was no help for it. She had to walk out of the cottage with Ada, and hope Nolan would intervene before she was in Jesse's clutches.

"All right, Ada, I'll walk out of here with you, and Prissy won't tell anyone, will you, Prissy?"

Clearly mindless with fear, Prissy shook her head.

"But someone will see us," Sarah went on. "It's getting late, and the posse's due back in town any minute now. Even if I leave with you, and Prissy does nothing to stop you, someone will see us walking out of here together. The whole town knows you've been riding with the outlaws, Ada. They're not going to stand by and let you take me anywhere."

"The posse isn't coming back," Ada said. "The boys set up an ambush, and they're probably all dead. Your precious Yankee doctor isn't coming to save you."

Nolan, dead? No, it couldn't be. Surely she'd know it, in her heart, if he'd been killed. But even if the outlaws hadn't succeeded in murdering Nolan, Nick and the others, she couldn't count on them coming back in time to keep Ada from taking her from Simpson Creek, taking her to Jesse.

"All right, then, Ada, what's your plan?" Sarah said, determined not to give in to panic and grief. Even if she left with Ada, Prissy would be left to tell Nolan and the others that Ada had kidnapped her at gunpoint, with the intention of taking her to Jesse and the Gray Boys, to be transported north to the Staked Plains, the Comanche stronghold.

As if she had been able to read minds, Ada killed that hope by raising the pistol she'd held against Prissy's back and striking Prissy viciously over the top of her head—all the while keeping the other pistol trained on Sarah.

Prissy went down without a cry, as limply as the sack of flour Sarah had emptied only a few minutes before. Sarah stared in horror as a red stain spread through Prissy's strawberry-blond hair.

"You've killed her!"

"Shut up. I just knocked out the silly fool, that's all."

"But she's bleeding—"

Ada shrugged. "If she dies, what do I care? She's nothing but a spoiled, pampered daughter of a rich man. She's always had everything she ever wanted—what did I have? Her mother even gave me some of her cast-off clothes, did you know that?"

Sarah shook her head numbly.

"But we're wasting time," Ada snapped. "I'm going to put on her bonnet and coat—and you're not going to do anything or I'll shoot her and make double sure she's dead, understand? No one will look twice at Sarah and Prissy, strolling down the road that runs south of town right between the Gilmore land and the saloon. Jesse's waiting for us just outside of town."

Chapter Twenty-Seven

Ada donned Prissy's coat, keeping the pistol within easy reach.

Sarah's gaze went back and forth from Ada to Prissy's motionless, sprawled body on the floor. If only she would move! After a few moments, Sarah finally detected the slight rise and fall of breathing in Prissy's slender shoulders. So she wasn't dead, Sarah thought, trying to take hope from that slight encouragement. While there was life, there was hope, wasn't there?

But Prissy could be dying, a pessimistic voice within her whispered. There was so much blood seeping from Prissy's scalp and pooling onto the wooden floor, staining it. Beneath Prissy's skull, she could be bleeding to death. Would Nolan arrive in time to save Prissy, at least?

"I'm ready," Ada said, settling Prissy's bonnet over her hair.

Why had she never noticed before how similar Ada's hair was to Prissy's? Prissy's was more vibrantly curly and shiny, but in the fading light, and with Ada's hair mostly covered under the bonnet, no one would notice the difference. The two women were of a similar height. People were so used to seeing Sarah and Prissy together, and they would see what they expected to see.

"Let's go," Ada said. Now that Prissy was no longer a threat to her, she had shoved one of the pistols into the waistband of her skirt. She waved the other one at Sarah. "How convenient that your precious Prissy's arms are longer than mine. It'll make it easy to conceal the pistol—but it'll be aimed at you the whole time, Sarah, never doubt it. If we meet anyone on the way out of town, and you try to tell them anything, I'll shoot you *and* them, I promise you."

"A-All right." Sarah stopped to take one last look at Prissy.

"She won't wake up for hours, if she ever wakes up at all," Ada said with a cruel chuckle. "So don't imagine her telling them where you've gone. Now *move*."

Sarah sighed. *Please save Prissy, Lord. Let her live.* She started for the door, praying with every step.

Maybe Antonio would be lingering outside the stable, as he often did in the late afternoon after feeding the horses, before he went in to help Flora serve supper. He'd see them, realize it was nearly suppertime and remind Prissy that her father hated her to be late to the table. Then Ada would react in an un-Prissy-like way that would betray her true identity. Antonio would get suspicious, approach them, then challenge her. Ada would take fright and flee, despite her threats, for Antonio was tall and as solid as an old live oak.

Or maybe Nolan would arrive, just as they reached the gate. Nolan would never be fooled by Ada, who'd been his patient, after all. He'd recognize her immediately.

But Antonio was not lounging at the barn door, nor did Nolan happen to be entering the grounds.

"You know, Ada, your outlaws would've been smarter to circle around and rob the bank after they lured the posse toward the Colorado," Sarah remarked as they walked out through the gates, her gaze darting all around her for someone—*anyone*—who might be able to help her. But there was no one exiting the hotel or the saloon. "There's a lot of money in the bank and valuables in its safe. That's what I'd have done, if I'd been an outlaw. It sure would have been a larger prize than me. So maybe they aren't so clever, after all."

"Shut your mouth," Ada hissed. "My Jesse's smart as a fox. He's not just any outlaw."

"But maybe he doesn't know how to rob banks," Sarah suggested. "That's all right. Not every outlaw's daring enough to rob a bank." Maybe if she could spark Ada's temper, the other girl would lunge at her and Sarah could wrestle the gun away.

"I said shut up." Ada's voice was definitely a snarl now. "Jesse knows what he wants, that's all. You. Teaching you a lesson is more important to him than robbing banks. He can do that any ol' time, after he's handed you over to some savage.

"This way," Ada said, indicating the road that led south out of town, which didn't make sense if the outlaws were headed north for the Staked Plains. Sarah was about to point this out when she spotted Mrs. Patterson exiting the mercantile. The recent widow was locking the door of the shop, but then she turned around and saw them.

"Good evening, Sarah, Prissy! Where are you headed? Warm for this early in March, isn't it? I suppose that means we'll have a hot summer… Oh, were you headed to the store for something? I could unlock again if that's the case."

Sarah pondered the wisdom of claiming the need for sugar or some other item. Mrs. Patterson would become suspicious if Ada remained where she was standing, but Ada would never dare follow her into the mercantile.

Once again, Ada seemed to have the uncanny ability to read Sarah's mind. Sarah felt the unmistakable nudge of the gun barrel in her side, hid by the long sleeve of Prissy's coat. "Don't try it," Ada said in a low, menacing tone.

"No, no thank you, Mrs. Patterson," Sarah called back. "We…uh…we were headed to Mrs. Detwiler's," she said, pointing down the road which would lead past Mrs. Detwiler's large house. "For supper. She invited us for supper. Wasn't that nice? She knew we'd be bored, especially me, what with Nolan riding with the posse and all…" If she accomplished nothing else, she wanted to imprint on Mrs. Patterson's mind which way they had gone, in case Nolan questioned her about seeing Sarah leaving. Maybe, if Sarah was very lucky, the widow would decide it was strange that Sarah was talkative to the point of babbling, a trait that had never been characteristic of her.

"That *is* nice. Mrs. Detwiler's always been an excellent cook," Mrs. Patterson called back agreeably. "All right, if you don't need anything, I'll just go home and have my supper then. You girls have a good evening."

Sarah felt an ache of regret as the woman waved, then turned and walked away down the side street that ran between the hotel and the mercantile.

Maybe Mrs. Detwiler would be out in her front yard, admiring the tulips coming up in her flower beds, and Sarah could make another attempt to free herself of Ada. Mrs. Detwiler's eagle eye missed nothing, but she would have to be very careful not to endanger the old woman, too.

"A wild-goose chase," Nolan grumbled as they rode westward back toward Simpson Creek in the chilly March air. "They wanted us to catch glimpses of them, but not get close enough to capture them."

"Indeed," Nick agreed, as the two men rode at the head of the posse. Earlier, they'd catch sight of one of the outlaws, who'd gallop off, then disappear—only to be replaced by another of them springing up nearby seemingly out of the blue and running off in a different direction, over and over again. A wild-goose chase, all right—a well-orchestrated one.

"I wonder what that game was about?" Nick mused aloud. "Why not keep out of sight until they struck again, instead of leading us on a merry chase?"

"Unless they were decoying us…." Suddenly Nolan was sure that was exactly what it had been. "Nick, they *wanted* to keep us out here, trying to catch each of them in turn. *They wanted us out of town.*"

"But why? Was part of the gang going to rob the bank? Of course, that must be it. What a fool I've been to be lured by such an obvious trick!" Nick cried. "We've got to get back to Simpson Creek!" He set his spurs to his mount's flanks as Nolan and the others did likewise.

Nolan wasn't convinced the bank had been the target, however. All at once a soul-deep dread had entered his heart, and he was certain within himself that the trickery somehow involved Sarah. *Sarah!* He'd gone haring off with the posse, trying to prove he was just as brave as any other man, *and left Sarah unprotected.*

"Jesse?"

At first, all Sarah saw in the gathering darkness was what appeared to be an extra thick trunk of a live oak tree. Then the long, lean frame of Jesse Holt detached himself from the trunk he'd been leaning against, spitting out the unlit cheroot he'd been chewing.

"Where have you been, woman? You dillydallied so long it's dark now," he grumbled at Ada. "Gettin' mighty cold, too."

Now Sarah could see the shadowy forms of the horses tied to the back of the grove of trees, and heard them stamping and jingling their bits.

"I didn't know this stupid female was going to spend all afternoon in the mercantile with that Prissy Gilmore ninny, did I?" Ada whined, pointing at Sarah. "But I got her here to you. I even had to knock Prissy out with the gun. I think I killed her, but I don't care. I did it for you." Her tone was suddenly servile, and her supplicant posture reminded Sarah of a cringing dog wagging its tail in hopes of not being kicked. *Hmm....* So Ada wasn't quite Jesse's darling as she had boasted—perhaps Sarah could use that to her advantage.

Sarah saw Jesse's eyes narrow and sensed he hadn't liked Ada calling her stupid, or perhaps it was her whiny tone that had set his teeth on edge.

"She didn't hurt you, did she, Sarah?" Jesse asked, coming forward to peer at her.

"No, of course I didn't hurt her!" Ada snapped. "What kind of idiot do you take me for? You said not to, and I didn't. Though I surely wanted to slap her smug face," she muttered.

"She didn't hurt me," Sarah confirmed in the calmest tone she could manage. "But I don't want to go with you." She had little hope that she'd change his mind now after he'd gone this far, but she had to try. "Jesse, we loved each other once, but we've each changed. For the sake of what we had, let me go. I'll walk back into town and tell them you went the opposite direction of whichever way you go. I promise I will."

"Sweetheart, I'm not gonna do that," he said, his tone soothing, his hand rough as he stepped closer and caressed her face. "I'm right pleased you're here, and I'm not about to let you go now."

Sarah hadn't expected him to agree, but she couldn't help backing away from his touch.

"No, you aren't, 'cause you've got big plans for Sarah, isn't that right, Jesse, darling?" cooed Ada. "I've been telling her how you're gonna trade her to some dirty redskin up on the Staked Plains, or maybe some half-breed Mexican Comanchero. I can hardly wait to see that."

"Be quiet, woman, or I'll give *you* to 'em for nothing," Jesse snapped. "Me and Miss Sarah, here, are gonna get reacquainted-like, on the way up to the Llano Estacado, aren't we? That long a ride, I reckon there'll be plenty a' time to remember why we were once so sweet on one 'nother," he drawled, keeping a hard grasp on Sarah's chin so she couldn't look away.

His breath smelled of stale whiskey, and now, out of the corner of her eye, she caught sight of an empty bottle propped up against the tree trunk.

"Yes sir, if you're friendly enough, Sarah Matthews, I might forget all about tradin' you and just trade the cattle instead," Jesse continued.

"Jesse Holt, you stop talking that way!" Ada cried. "*I'm* your woman, not her! We're gettin' married after you trade her off, you said so! And I don't share with nobody!"

"Is that a fact?" Jesse inquired, lifting an eyebrow. He sounded as if he didn't mind very much one way or the other, but a prudent person would have detected the cold menace in his gaze as he shifted it from Sarah to Ada.

"Yes, it is. You said you were a one-woman man, and I'm going to take you at your word," Ada said, but her tone had changed to wheedling again.

"I am," Jesse agreed. "Only you ain't the one." As soon as the words left his mouth, he whipped his pistol from his holster and shot Ada.

Chapter Twenty-Eight

"C'mon. The boys'll be waiting for us at the hide-out," Jesse said, yanking on Sarah's arm as she stood frozen in horror, staring at the fallen form of Ada Spencer. "We're gonna settle in for the night, snug an' cozy, and then head north at first light."

"You killed her!" Sarah cried, for the second time in an hour, but this time she was very, very sure it was true. She'd seen the bullet strike Ada's chest. "How could you do that, Jesse Holt? Ada *loved* you. She thought you loved her. She said you were going to marry her."

Jesse gave a harsh bark of laughter. "From what I've heard in the short time I've been back to town, ol' Ada believed quite a few things lately—she thought that Englishman was going to marry her, too, didn't she, and that she was with child by your precious Yankee doctor. Some women'll believe anything you tell 'em, 'long as it's somethin' they want to hear. Now get on that horse—we've got some hard ridin' to do, Sarah-girl."

Sarah tried to yank her arm out of his iron grasp. "But you can't just leave her there, lying in the dirt," she protested. "It isn't right, Jesse!"

He stared down at her and gave her a sardonic smile. "Do you think I'm gonna take the time to bury her? I ain't done much lately you could call *right*, so there's no use startin' now. The critters'll take care of her carcass. Get on the horse now, Sarah Matthews, or I'll shoot you, too."

Just as Nolan had thought, the Simpson Creek bank had been undisturbed. It was closed now for the day, and the bank president assured them that he'd seen nothing of the Gray Boys.

Nolan then gave voice to his fears about Sarah, and the posse had headed for the cottage. Filled with foreboding, Nolan jumped off his horse.

"We'll wait here till you make sure everything's all right," Nick called after him as he pounded on the door of the cottage.

"Sarah! Sarah! Are you in there?"

Had his ears caught some faint sound within, or was he hearing things? He pushed at the door, found it unlocked and ran in, then nearly stumbled on Prissy sitting propped up against the stove, a blood-stained dish towel to her head.

He dropped to his knees. "Prissy! What happened to you? Where's Sarah? Nick! I've found Prissy! She's injured!" he called over his shoulder.

Prissy winced at his shout and favored him with a swollen-eyed gaze. "She hit me over the head. With a gun."

"Sarah hit you with a gun?" Could he be hearing her right?

Prissy shook her head weakly, then moaned at the obvious pain the motion caused. "No. *Ada* hit me. She surprised us here and forced Sarah to go with her at gunpoint."

"Go? Go where?"

"She was taking her to Jesse Holt and the outlaws—said they were going to take her and the stolen cattle up on the Staked Plains and sell her to the Comanches, or the Comancheros."

Her words struck Nolan like a blow, rocking him back on his haunches.

"Why would he do that?" he demanded, as Nick ran in.

Prissy lifted one shoulder and winced again. "Revenge. Nolan, you've got to stop them! Hurry! You can't let them take her!"

By this time, Antonio had heard the commotion and come running into the cottage, as well.

"What has happened? The senorita, she is injured?"

Nolan jumped to his feet, overwhelmed for the moment with conflicting responsibilities. A dangerously insane Ada was taking Sarah to the outlaws, and they intended to sell her to the savages, or renegade Mexicans—but as a doctor, he had a responsibility to tend Prissy, too. A blow from a heavy object like a gun could fracture a skull.

"Nick, you've got to ride after them!" he told the Englishman. "Prissy, do you know if you were knocked unconscious?" He pulled the dish towel gently from Prissy's hands and probed Prissy's scalp with gentle fingers, seeking and finding the swelling beneath, but no disruption of the bone.

"Just d-dazed for a moment, I think… After that, I pretended to be unconscious," she said, and a tear trickled down her pale cheek. "I'm so sorry, Nolan! I was scared out of my wits, but I should have fought her…kept that madwoman from taking Sarah…"

"No, you could have been killed for your pains, my girl," Nick soothed in his sensible British voice, "and then we'd have *no* idea what had happened to her. You did the right thing."

"How bad is your head hurting? Can you see straight? How many fingers am I holding up?" Nolan asked.

Prissy blinked at the barrage of questions. "Three. Yes, I've got a headache, but if Antonio will bring me some ice from the springhouse, I'll be fine. *Go with the posse, Nolan,* don't stay here with me. Go! Every minute, they're getting farther away!"

Nolan nodded. "All right, Prissy, I will. Antonio, can you carry your mistress up to the big house, then get her some ice?"

"*Sí,* senor, I will do this," the other man said, scooping up Prissy as if she weighed nothing. "Flora will stay with her. But it grows dark, and there will only be a half moon tonight. There are lanterns in the stable. Take them."

Nolan locked gazes with Nick. "You know the area better—what way would they go, if they're headed northward? The road between the mayor's house and the saloon is handy—Ada wouldn't have to risk them being seen going through town—but it runs south, not north."

"But only a little way out of town, there's a fork that bends north," Nick told him. "It's the only way north that's close."

"That's likely the way, then. We'd better get those lanterns."

Both men ran out of the cottage. As Nolan headed for the stable, he heard Nick tell the posse what they'd learned.

His brain seethed with rage and fear at the thought of the fate Holt had in mind for Sarah. How could any man contemplate selling a woman—any woman, but especially the one he'd once professed to love—to a savage? And crazy Ada—he should have had her locked in an asylum when he'd had the chance. He'd let compassion blind him, he thought angrily. If he'd done the responsible thing as a physician, realizing she was dangerous and beyond his help, they would not now be riding after the outlaws in the dark, hoping they could find them before they went very far.

How terrified Sarah must be in the hands of the insane woman, much less Jesse Holt and the pack of wolves he ran with! If Holt touched so much as one golden hair on Sarah's head, he promised himself, he'd make the outlaw wish he'd never been born.

If she had lain where she had first fallen, they would never have seen her as they thundered past. But after Jesse had left with Sarah, Ada had crawled with the last of her strength out of the grove of trees, collapsing at last by the side of the road. Even so they might have missed the slight, crumpled form if the wind hadn't picked up as the posse approached and caught the edge of her petticoat, fluttering it in the breeze like a signal flag.

"Look yonder! Somethin'—somebody's layin' by the road!" one of the men in the posse yelled, raising his lantern high and pointing ahead. "I think it's a woman!"

Nolan spotted what the man had seen. His heart rose to his throat and threatened to choke him. Had they killed his Sarah here and left her body for the coyotes to find? He spurred his horse toward the body, vowing retribution against every last one of the Gray Boys gang. He'd make sure Jesse Holt strangled at the end of a rope, if he didn't succeed in shooting him himself.

He jumped off his horse, who shied at the fluttering petticoat, ran to the fallen woman and turned her, his mind going numb at the sight of the dark red stain drenching the front of her coat and bodice.

It's Ada, not Sarah. For a moment he could hardly speak for the relief that flooded through him. Ada was dead. As long as the body he was cradling wasn't Sarah's, there was hope, wasn't there?

And then the woman's eyes flickered, and she took a shuddering breath, opened them, then blinked as she tried to focus on Nolan's face.

"Dr. Walker…f-fancy meeting y-you here," Ada whispered. She tried to smile, but the effort resulted in a grotesquely lopsided grimace instead.

Even in the wavering light of the lantern one of the other men held high above them, Nolan could see the ashy, waxen quality of the woman's face. Her lips were bloodless, her eyes dilated, and a trickle of blood had dried at the side of her chin.

"Ada, where's Sarah? Where have they taken her? Tell me," he pleaded, knowing that he might have only seconds to worm the truth out of her. "I'll do everything I can to save your life, if you'll just tell me."

Ada's slender shoulders heaved with the effort to speak. "E-everything you…can? Isn't…very much… anyone could do, is there? E-easy t' say…"

"Please, Ada," he begged as the woman's eyelids drifted shut. Any second now she would take her last breath, and they'd know nothing more than they had before. *Please, God, give her strength to tell me, and forgive her...*

"Wouldn't have…told you…till that s-snake betrayed me…chose her…instead… He shot me…"

"Holt shot you?" Nick demanded, standing beside Nolan.

Ada shifted her gaze to include the Englishman, tried to nod. "Sh-should-should've known…couldn't trust him. Not any man… Now listen, not much time…"

Nolan had to put his ear almost next to Ada's mouth to hear words that weren't so much whispered as breathed. A minute later, he closed her eyes and laid her body down again.

At Nick's direction, they sent the oldest man in the posse, the mill owner, back to Simpson Creek with Ada's body, while the rest of them rode northward into the night.

Jesse tied her hands together in front, then held a gun on Sarah while she mounted one of the two horses in the grove. This horse was saddled, but bridleless, with a rope around its neck so he could lead it, but she could not direct it. The fact that there were only two horses in the grove told Sarah that Jesse had probably never intended to take Ada with them.

And he'd had to know that if he'd merely left Ada standing there and deserted her, that she'd tell others out of sheer spite where they were headed. So it was likely he'd planned all along to murder poor, foolish Ada. The thought sent icicles shooting through her veins, but she said nothing. What was the point of hearing him deny it, or worse, admit it?

Jesse struck a match against the rock and lit the lantern that had been hanging over his saddle horn, and they headed back onto the road at a lope. They rode steadily in silence until they reached the Colorado River, where Jesse stopped to water the horses. He whistled "Tenting on the Old Campground" as the horses lowered their heads into the water.

"They'll come after you, you know," Sarah said. She didn't know if it was possible, but she had to try to chip away at Jesse's confidence. It was all she could think of. Besides, his answer would tell her whether Ada's assertion that the outlaws had killed the posse was true or not. "Nolan and the rest of the posse won't just let you take me without doing anything about it. You could still let me go, you know, and save your skin."

"Goldilocks, by the time they figure out which way we've gone, it'll be too late."

Then Nolan is alive. Thank You, Lord.

"Who's gonna tell 'em? Ada left Prissy with her head split open, didn't she? She's likely as dead as

Ada by now. You tryin' to make me believe there was anyone else there? You're lying."

"There was no one else," Sarah admitted, "but Prissy wasn't dead. I saw her breathing." She prayed it was still true. "They'll find her—in fact, they probably have already because it was nearly suppertime. We're expected at her father's house. And when she comes to, she'll tell them you're headed north, because Ada bragged about the whole plan before she knocked Prissy out."

Jesse's jaw hardened and he spat in irritation. "Why do women have to talk so much? Oh, well, it don't matter, even if she does wake up. We've got a long head start, and once we reach the hideout, they'll never find us."

"And what if Ada didn't die, either?" Sarah needled. "They'll find her, too, and she'll tell the posse exactly where the hideout is, won't she? I'm sure you've taken her there. After what you did to her, she'll be delighted to testify about you and see you hang."

Jesse's hoot of laughter sent a couple of bullfrogs plopping into the water in alarm.

"Oh, crazy Ada's dead all right. You saw where that bullet hit her. She won't be telling anyone anything. I will admit I shouldn't have wasted my time with her, though, if it makes you feel any better. I should've tried harder to sweet talk you into coming with me, Sarah-girl. You could still change your mind and be agreeable about it, you know, and if you're smart, you will."

Sarah's laugh was mirthless. "'If it makes me *feel* any better'? You can talk till the end of time and I wouldn't change my mind."

He tipped her chin up and stared down at her, and Sarah froze. He could do anything with her right now, anything—even throw her tied up and helpless into the chill waters of the Colorado. She was helpless and alone.

No, you're not alone, Sarah Matthews. The Bible promises God is with me always.

"Yeah, you'd best be reconsiderin' your position before we get up to the Staked Plains. You try spoutin' off to some Comanche buck like that, and he'll decide that yellow hair would look mighty nice decoratin' his teepee. Or he'll let the squaws have you, and I hear that's worse. Either way, I hear captive white women don't live too long among the Comanches, and by the time they die, they're beggin' for someone to put them outa their misery. And if by some miracle you got back to civilization, what decent man would have you?"

His words left Sarah speechless with horror.

Please, Lord, let Nolan save me!

Chapter Twenty-Nine

Sarah awakened from a fitful, miserable doze when the horses halted.

"Took you long enough," the outlaw standing sentry duty grumbled as he opened the gate and let them ride inside.

"Things involving women always take longer than you'd think," Jesse muttered, "'specially when one of 'em's loco."

"Yeah, where *is* crazy Ada?" the other asked, peering at Sarah and beyond her. "You promised she could be mine once you got Goldilocks."

"'You promised,'" Jesse mimicked. "You sound like some little kid. Shut up, Jones. Go find your bedroll and get some shut-eye. We leave at dawn."

"Hope she's worth it," Jones muttered, and stalked away.

"Where are we?" Sarah asked, peering around them in the dim light cast by a campfire, around which lay sleeping men. She made out the dark mass of a barn, with an irregularly shaped corral filled with the cattle lowing, some lying down, some milling slowly around. She'd lost track of time as they'd followed the snake-like path of the Colorado northwest, finally crossing it at a shallow ford. The water had drenched her skirts nearly to the waist, and now, in the cool March air, she was wretchedly cold.

"Far from home, Sarah-girl," Jesse said with smirk. "This here's the farm of a loyal Confederate colonel, one who hasn't bowed his head to the blasted Blue Bellies, though he pretends to enough to get along. It's far off the main road and other farms that no one pays him any mind. He's been real happy to hide us, re-brand the cattle as we bring them to him, and all he asks is a share of the money when we sell them, to start the new treasury."

"Treasury? Treasury of what?"

"The treasury of the New Confederate States of America," Jesse said proudly, puffing out his chest. "We're gonna help him overthrow the Federals one a' these fine days and he'll be the president of our new republic."

Sarah could only stare at him and fight the urge to laugh hysterically.

The lanterns had run out of fuel and the half moon had gone behind a cloud.

"We've got to stop till first light," Nick said, after Nolan's horse had put a hoof into a gopher hole along the dark road and gone down, throwing him off. Fortunately, the beast hadn't broken its leg, and only Nolan's pride was injured, but now the horse was limping and couldn't be ridden. They'd have to leave him at the first ranch they came to, and return for him later.

Nolan, walking toward the spare mount that had been brought along for Sarah, stopped and turned around. "Not on your life. It won't be dawn for hours yet, and who knows what might be happening to Sarah?"

"Walker, we can't help Sarah if our horses break their legs and have to be shot," Nick pointed out.

"And it'll be tricky finding the right ford in the dark, too," said Amos Wallace, the postmaster. "You risk running into quicksand if you try to cross in the wrong place. Anyway, like as not Holt's stopped, too, Doc."

Wallace was probably correct that Holt and Sarah had stopped, Nolan knew, but what Holt was doing while stopped didn't bear thinking about.

"The horses will be fresher if we rest them now, Nolan," Nick continued. "I promise, soon as it's light, we'll make good time and catch up."

"Holt's horses will be fresh, too," Nolan countered stubbornly. The idea of stopping even for a minute filled him with furious frustration, even though he knew they were right.

"But he won't know we're coming," Nick reminded him. "He'll figure poor Miss Ada died without having the chance to tell us where the hideout is. As far as he knows, we have no idea where he's taken her. If we hadn't known they were headed for the Staked Plains, I'd have figured them to go south, heading for the Rio Grande, to sell those cattle to the Mexicans."

And Sarah.

"I dunno what makes Holt think them Comanches are gonna just tamely trade them rifles or whatever for them cattle," observed another man. "What's t'stop them from scalpin' all them outlaws and takin' the cattle, too?"

And Sarah.

Nolan glared at him, and the fellow realized what he'd unwittingly implied. "Sorry, Doc. Guess I spoke when I shoulda kept my trap shut. Don't you worry, we'll catch them outlaws tomorrow, and get Miss Sarah back safe and sound."

Colonel Robert Throckmorton, late of the Confederate Army, waved a hand in welcome when the posse galloped up the muddy road to his farmhouse the next morning.

"Gentlemen, what can I do for you this fine mornin'?" he called out with bluff heartiness, his lips curving into a genial smile under a heavy silver mustache. "I'd offer you breakfast, but you look like y'all are in too much of a hurry. And surely it's not necessary for all y'all to have your firearms aimed at me. I've offered you no harm."

Nolan studied the man, who looked like the epitome of the defeated but unreconstructed Southern officer. There was something shifty about his gaze, something that hinted to Nolan he'd much prefer shooting them in the back as they left to merely sending them on their way peaceably.

"I'm Sheriff Nicholas Brookfield of Simpson Creek, San Saba County," Nick said. "We need you to tell us which way the Gray Boys are heading."

"'Gray Boys?' I've got no idea who you're talkin' about," the man said.

Nolan cocked his pistol. "Stop your nonsense, or I'll shoot you where you stand, Throckmorton. We know they've been hiding out here, them and the cattle they've stolen. So you'd better tell us what we need to know right quick."

"First a foreigner, now a Yankee," the man sneered.

"But the rest of us are good Texans who believe in doin' what's right," Amos Wallace said, and cocked his weapon.

Throckmorton visibly flinched at the metallic *click* and turned back to Nick. "Sheriff, honest, I don't rightly know what you're talkin' about," the man protested, palms up. He studiously avoided Nolan's glare. "You see there's no cattle here," he said, pointing at the empty corral and pastures. "I sold my cattle to a drover just last week, as a matter of fact. Got a good price for 'em, too," he said smugly.

Out of the corner of his eye, Nolan saw Amos Wallace loosen a coil of rope that had been tied to his saddle. He calmly began to knot a hangman's noose at the end of it. "I reckon that cottonwood over yonder would serve right well for a hanging, Sheriff."

The florid-face colonel blanched. "Hanging? Me? You can't do that! On what charge?" He turned back to Nick. "You're a foreigner! Are you even familiar with the laws in this country? You can't lynch an innocent man!" he bellowed, his eyes bulging over fat cheeks.

"Oh, can't we? Who's to stop us?" Nick said, looking around him. "I'd think a farmer would have at least a hand or two around, but your place looks fairly deserted. I'd say you sent your men along to help control the herd—and to make sure the Gray Boys don't double-cross you out of your share of the money."

"Throckmorton, the men you've been hiding have a kidnapped woman with them," Nolan said, keeping a rein on his temper with difficulty. "Surely a chivalrous Southern gentleman such as you can't possibly approve of selling her to the savages along with the cattle," Nolan said, giving the man one more chance to redeem himself.

"Of course not!" the colonel said, trying to assume a shocked expression and failing deplorably. "I told you, I've seen no outlaws, and no woman, either. You have to believe me." He pulled at his shirt collar as if it was suddenly too tight.

Nick nodded to Wallace, who trotted his horse over to the cottonwood and threw the noose over it. It bounced obscenely in the breeze.

Throckmorton couldn't take his eyes off of it. He swallowed with difficulty, as if the noose was already tightening around his neck.

"Now, just a minute, gentlemen, surely we can come to some agreement," he said quickly.

"What's it going to be, Throckmorton?" Nick asked. "Are we to hang you or are you going to take us to them?"

"Take you to them?" the man said, his Southern colonel dignity suddenly vanished, his tone now wheedling. "Surely it would be enough to just tell you which road they've taken, Sheriff. They can't be far ahead of you—they left just an hour ago, and they're driving cattle. But please don't make me go—y-you can't imagine how ruthless these men are! Why, they'd shoot me on sight if they saw me riding with you. Please… I'll give you all the information you need…"

"All the more reason for you to go," Nolan growled. "Getting yourself shot is one way you could atone."

"Nolan, Amos, take him into the barn and make him saddle a horse," Nick ordered. "Keep your pistols on him at all times. If he gets up to any mischief, shoot him—but make sure it's only painful, not fatal. We'll need him for directions—I'm told there are at least three roads leading north near here, and we need to take the right one."

Fifteen minutes later, they were galloping up the road again, heading north, with the colonel riding alongside Nick. Behind him, Nolan rode, keeping his pistol aimed at Throckmorton's back.

"So much for your gallant rescuer," Jesse mocked, as both of them watched from the vantage point of an upper window in the old farmhouse as the posse departed. "He an' that Englishman took the bait like a pair a' hungry perch. The colonel will lead them down the wrong road, and meanwhile, you an' I'll be on our way to the rendezvous point with the boys."

Sarah, her hands still tied, a gag in her mouth, watched with a sinking heart until Nolan rode out of sight. She had never felt a despair as complete as the one that swept over her now like icy water, so much colder than the river they'd forded last night. Nolan had come to rescue her, but had ridden off believing she and her captor were with the rest of the gang when she had been only a few yards away from him. If the posse had just searched the house!

As for me, I shall call upon God, and the Lord will save me. The verse from the Psalms came to her out of nowhere.

All right, Lord, I'm calling. Save me, and please protect Nolan, too.

"We might as well make ourselves comfortable," Jesse said, "since we can't leave for a spell. We need to let them get a few miles on the way before we go."

He laughed at the Sarah's quick step backward. "Don't worry, I didn't mean what you're thinkin'," he said. "I meant we might as well grab ourselves some grub—some a' that ham I spotted hangin' in Throckmorton's smokehouse that he didn't see fit to share. You know, I can't abide selfishness." He stepped forward and untied the gag around Sarah's mouth, letting it fall to the floor.

She swallowed, wishing she could wash away the nasty taste it had left.

"Why don't we mosey out an' get that ham," he said, gesturing with the gun, "and stop by the henhouse and get us some eggs, too. I remember you're a fine cook, Goldilocks. You cook us a good breakfast, one that'll last us till we stop at nightfall."

He untied her hands, and gestured for her to lead the way to the smokehouse. She found the ham hanging inside, just as Jesse had said it would be, and pulled it down. It must have weighed at least ten pounds, but he didn't offer to carry it for her.

"Now the eggs," he said, waving the gun toward the henhouse.

"How am I 'sposed to gather eggs while I'm holding this ham?" she asked.

"Put it down on this," he said, upending a bucket that was lying on its side near the door to the henhouse. "Carry the eggs in your skirt."

Once her eyes adjusted to the gloom inside, she looked for something she could use against Jesse as a weapon. A pitchfork—anything! She could not tamely get on a horse and ride with him into the Comanche stronghold like a sacrificial lamb. But there was nothing.

Sighing in resignation, she pushed away the hens which tried to peck at her hands, searched until she had collected nearly a dozen eggs, then trudged back outside. Jesse had managed to pick up the ham, while still keeping hold of the pistol with the other.

"C'mon, Sarah-girl, shake a leg, we don't have all day," he snarled. "I'm hungry. You don't think that redskin brave you're gonna belong to is gonna let you dillydally like that, do you?"

She gave him a look, but said nothing. Instead, she went inside, cut slices off the ham and set them frying in a skillet, then cracked one egg after another into another skillet.

"That was mighty fine," he said, a few minutes later, pushing away from the table and shoving the plate over toward her. He'd left her about a fourth of it, not enough to fully satisfy her growling stomach, but it was better than nothing, and probably better than what she would get on the journey. Fare on the trail most likely consisted of tinned beans and coffee.

"You know, it really would be a shame to trade you to the savages," he murmured, watching her eat.

Something in her, something she'd kept buried during the long night of terror, snapped. "You keep saying that, Jesse. Since it *would* be a shame, why don't you stop saying it and take me home?"

He snickered. "Temper, temper, Sarah-girl. You know I can't do that. All I meant was you'd make a great cook for us, if you'd just decide to stop bein' so unfriendly. I'm just sayin' I could get used to cookin' like this—"

"But I doubt they have cooks like Sarah where you're going," said a voice that was familiar and beloved to Sarah.

Sarah jumped, and looked up to see Nolan in the doorway between the kitchen and the front hall. He had a rifle aimed right at Jesse's head.

"Don't move, Holt," said another voice, an English voice, from the steps to the upstairs. A rifle barrel protruded into the kitchen from that direction. Nolan and Nick must have circled back and hidden in the house while she and Jesse were getting the ham and eggs.

Despite the warning, Jesse jumped to his feet, grabbing the pistol he'd laid on the table when he had started to eat.

Instinctively, Sarah threw herself under the table, and gunfire erupted over her head.

It stopped in less than a minute. Jesse's bullet, fired after he'd been struck from both sides, buried itself harmlessly in the ceiling, and he lay dead on the floor. Sarah scrambled to her feet and ran into Nolan's arms amid the haze of gun smoke and floating plaster dust.

She promised herself she would never leave those arms again.

"Thank God, thank God," Nolan murmured, in between kisses.

"Take Sarah home," Nick said after a few moments, during which Nolan kissed Sarah thoroughly and assured himself she hadn't been hit by any flying lead. "I'll catch up with the others."

Sarah saw warring impulses in Nolan's eyes—the desire to stay with her and take her home, and the need to offer his help to the posse, to finish the duty he had taken on.

"I could ride with you," she offered gamely, though in truth it was the last thing she wanted to do. "I'll keep to the rear when you catch up with the outlaws, I promise."

Nick shook his head. "We can manage, Sarah. Even if I wanted to take you up on your gallant offer, I have your sister to answer to, you know. Go home, the two of you. The posse's probably already caught up to the rustlers by now. I'm sure I'll meet them coming back, driving the rustlers before them, with the cattle bringing up the rear. We'll see to Holt's body on the way back, as well."

"All right, then," Nolan said. "There was at least another horse in the barn. Sarah, let's go home. You have a friend with a sore head waiting for you there."

"Prissy? She's all right? Oh, thank God!" she said, then turned into Nolan's embrace again. "Home," she murmured. "With you. What a wonderful sound that has."

Epilogue

A week later, Sarah and Nolan sat in the meadow across Simpson Creek from the church, enjoying a picnic lunch among the bluebonnets and Indian paint-brushes that carpeted the ground. Peace had reclaimed Simpson Creek now the rustlers had been captured, due to Colonel Throckmorton's attempt to save his own hide by leading the posse straight to them.

"Where was Prissy off to so quickly after church?" Nolan asked, lounging on his side amid the lush green spring grass and gnawing on a chicken leg. Behind him, mockingbirds called to each other from the cot-tonwoods. Simpson Creek burbled on its way to join-ing the San Saba River.

"Oh, she's taken over as chairwoman of the Spin-sters' Club, and she's hosting Sunday dinner up at the big house for them. They're planning a big party for bachelors and spinsters in late May, you see, and she thought the ladies should get together and discuss the plans."

"She's perfect for the job," Nolan agreed. "Our Prissy is quite the planner."

Sarah sighed. "I hope she meets someone this time. She had planned to invite Major McConley, you know—she'd been flirting with him outrageously at every opportunity—but then someone told her that he had a wife and four children back east. She was devastated for at least half an hour."

Nolan chuckled. "Never say die, that's Prissy. Don't worry, Sarah, she'll find someone when the time is right."

Sarah sighed. "I'd just like to see her as happy as I am," she admitted. "I know she's happy for us, but she knows she'll have to make a change when I move out and get married. She can hardly stay in that cottage by herself, it'd be too lonely. But she can't quite make up her mind whether she wants to invite one of the other spinsters to live there or move back in the big house with her father."

"That's my Sarah," he said, extending an arm to tickle her nose with a vivid red Indian paintbrush blossom. "Always more concerned for others than herself. It's one of the things I love about you."

She swatted playfully at the flower, capturing it, and tickling him back. That led to kissing, naturally, but after a while she drew back again and studied him.

"I think we should discuss setting a wedding date," Sarah said suddenly.

Nolan laid aside the battered flower. "You do?" he said, clearly pleased. A slow grin spread over his face. "I'm ready to marry you at any moment, you know that, sweetheart. But I thought you wanted to wait a while, to be courted."

Sarah smiled back. "I do. But I think some time in June would be perfect, and between now and then, my 'Man of Maine' could do quite a bit of courting, don't you think?"

"Oh, Sarah," he said, taking her in his arms again. "I don't plan to ever stop courting you, even when we're married. It's too enjoyable."

* * * * *

Pamela Nissen started writing her first book in 2000 and since then hasn't looked back. Pamela lives in the woods in Iowa with her husband, daughter, two sons, a Newfoundland dog and cats. She enjoys scrapbooking weekends with her sister, coffee with friends and running in the rain. Having glimpsed the dark and light of life, she is passionate about writing "real" people with "real" issues and "real" responses.

Books by Pamela Nissen

Love Inspired Historical

Rocky Mountain Match
Rocky Mountain Redemption
Rocky Mountain Proposal
Rocky Mountain Homecoming

Visit the Author Profile page
at Harlequin.com for more titles.

ROCKY MOUNTAIN REDEMPTION

Pamela Nissen

And we know that for those who love God
all things work together for good,
for those who are called according to his purpose.
—*Romans* 8:28

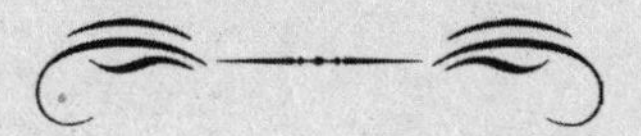

In loving memory of Mom

Your laughter delighted
Your generous love deeply motivated
And your courage…your courage inspired

Chapter One

Help Wanted...

Callie blinked against the wind-whipped snow that swirled in curling waves onto the small porch where she huddled. She fastened her weary gaze to the simple black and white placard, staring at those two words: *Help Wanted.*

She'd gladly snatch up the job her brother-in-law, Doctor Ben Drake, advertised in the front window of his office. He certainly wouldn't mistake her sudden appearance here for some heartwarming family connection.

Clamping her teeth against their chattering, she scanned down the road to the heart of Boulder. Only a few horses stood tethered to hitching posts, their broad, saddled backs flocked with fluffy, white snow. Apart from the welcome lantern's glow spilling from a few windows into the dark of night on this early October evening, the town seemed as if caught in a dreamy, blissful slumber.

So where in the world was Doctor Ben Drake?

She'd never even met the man and already had a mountain of bias against him. The two long days she'd spent journeying from Denver to Boulder on foot, she'd recoiled at the thought of asking Ben Drake for charity like some beggar.

The idea of another debt hanging over her head sent repulsion snaking through her veins. If she could offer her services and get paid…now that was far more appealing.

Perhaps there existed a slim thread of hope in her frayed life. A second chance. An opportunity to start over and find some peace.

Callie gave a solid knock on the door, her icy cold hand throbbing as she waited for him to answer. She gave another determined knock then, with frozen-to-numb feet, hobbled left a few paces to the long window. Cupping trembling hands around her eyes, she peered inside. But there was no sign of life, just like the hollow, dark look in her husband's eyes when he'd died in her arms six months ago.

Images she'd just as soon lay to rest swirled into her mind. Max, wracked with pain and delirium from a gunslinger's fatal shot. His inconsolable groan for help, when it was clear he was beyond help. On a ragged whisper and dying breath, he'd said, "Find my brothers. Find Ben. He'll see to you."

Even then, in the midst of Callie's frantic fight to keep Max alive, those words had stunned her as much as they did now. He'd wanted nothing to do with his brothers, so why would he drive her to their doorstep with his last breath?

Battling back the haunting memories, she peered

inside the office again. No oil lamp flickered to life. Not even the weighted sound of hurried footsteps advanced this way.

Shaking and frustrated, she drew her lightweight wool cloak snug around her shoulders in a vain attempt to shield herself from the storm that barreled through the quaint mountain valley. The small, covered porch gave no protection from the sting of icy snow. The cast-off satin dress she wore from the brothel did precious little to insulate her from even the whisper of a breeze.

Even so, this didn't seem half as bad as the uncontrollable hardships of the last seven years. At least now she had some control over her future, and if she froze to death, it would be because she decided to do so.

When a harsh cough tore through her lungs, she braced her pounding head against the siding. Irritation mounted with each frosty breath in winter's threat.

"Where are you, Ben Drake?" Her words sputtered between chattering teeth.

Maybe he'd landed in some saloon, drinking and gambling away the night, just like his brother, Max.

Shivering, weak and exhausted, Callie slid down the thick clapboard. She tugged her cloak tighter and pulled in a deep, steadying breath to calm her irritation. When the bitter air hit her lungs, a spasm of wrenching coughs doubled her over, threatening to cave in her resolve.

Still, she closed her eyes and pictured herself snuggled before a warm, crackling fire. A soft groan escaped her lips as she imagined her hands cradling a steaming mug of cider—or cocoa, maybe. Nestling deeper beneath the thick luxury of a cozy quilt and sleeping till she could sleep no more.

A mean gust of wind whipped across the porch, slapping reality in her face once again. She didn't have the job yet, and until she rectified the situation that loomed like some noose before her, she was a prisoner to her past, a slave to her present and a hostage to her future.

With a stuttering sigh, she closed her eyes. She should probably be angry that Max had left her standing alone down one of life's dark dead ends, but really, she just felt numb. The irony of that sunk deep as she shivered, slipping slowly into sleep. Yes, she was definitely numb—she could barely feel her arms, her legs, or her heart.

"Ma'am?" A deep, mellow voice stirred her senses. "Are you all right?"

"Ma'am?" Ben Drake tried again, keeping his voice low.

The woman raised her head, sending a wave of relief washing over him as a stark curtain of snow lashed across the porch.

She was alive—that much was good.

When he'd arrived home just moments ago and had spotted a dark form huddled here on his office porch next door, a sick sense of dread had roiled in the pit of his stomach. The thought of someone seeking him out for help, only to die waiting for his return, would likely haunt him for the rest of his days.

"Come on...let's get you out of the cold." He scooped up her rail-thin frame.

With a grunt, she stiffened arrow straight, squirming out of his arms. When her feet met the floor with a dull thud, she sliced a sharp breath through her teeth. “Oww…”

“What’s the matter?” He hunkered over to get a look at her as she sagged against the building. “Are you hurt?”

From beneath a tattered hood, the young woman peeked up at him. “My feet. They’re cold as ice.” The woman’s unfamiliar, raspy voice hit him square in the heart.

“Well, then, let’s get you inside.” He made quick work of unlocking the door. “I’m sorry I wasn’t here sooner.”

“Are you Doc—Doctor Drake?” Her teeth chattered.

“Yes, I’m Ben Drake.” When he braced an arm at her back, she dodged it as though he meant to hog-tie her. “Have you been waiting long for me?”

“Long enough,” she muttered, shuffling inside, each shivering, wobbly step piercing his heart more than the last.

She pulled her cloak tighter, but the way it puddled on the floor, hanging like a big, old drape, he wasn’t quite sure how she’d managed to maneuver ten feet in such a garment.

The lingering feel of her thin, quivering frame and her wariness to his touch sent compassion thrumming through his veins, especially when she produced a harsh cough.

“That cough of yours sure doesn’t sound good.”

"It's nothing," she answered, her teeth chattering. "Just an everyday kind of cough, that's all."

"Well, it sounds like more than that to me. Good thing you came when you did. Follow me," he said, leading the way through the dark waiting area into the exam room where he lit a lamp. "I'll get a fire going so we can get you warmed up."

When he wrapped two warm quilts around her quivering frame, he had to hold his confusion in check when she shrugged them off as though they were some disease-ridden rags. She possessively clutched her arms around something as though he might snatch it away, and he tried not to react. This woman was mistrustful and guarded and set against a little help. She eyed him as though she'd seen his face plastered on some Wanted poster.

"Why don't you sit down here by the woodstove so you'll be close to the heat?" Gesturing to a chair, he barely contained a wince when she avoided his outstretched hand as though he meant her harm. "It shouldn't take long for the place to warm up."

She sat on the edge of the chair. Bunching her shoulders up tight, she made a valiant effort to stop shivering, but as long as she kept that thin and wet cloak on, she'd likely never warm up.

While he banked the coals and loaded fresh kindling in the stove, he stole furtive glances at her shadowed, pale face, looking for signs of bleeding. Or broken bones.

She coughed then grabbed her side, and Ben's blood ran cold through his veins. His hair prickled at the back of his neck. That she might be another unfortunate bride of some no-good excuse for a husband, who treated his wife worse than his livestock, made him push back a ready curse.

When her whole body heaved with a sudden cough, he hunkered down next to her. "Easy, now. That sure doesn't sound like an everyday kind of cough. How long have you had it?"

At her dismissive shrug, he gently laid the back of his hand against her forehead, concern mounting at the heat that met his touch. "You're fevered, too. That's not good. I hope you'll forgive me for not coming sooner."

She flicked her gaze to him, cagey as a mouse in a barren field. Edging away, she angled her focus downward, intent on unknotting tattered ties that held her cloak together by mere threads.

His heart squeezed. He had to bite back a groan of sympathy at the sight of her shabby, wet shoes that poked out from her cloak. When she tipped her head back, nudging her hood off a mat of auburn waves, his throat grew tight.

And when she glanced up at him with the most beautiful almond-shaped blue eyes he'd ever seen, he struggled to gather his wits. She looked like an ethereal waif who'd been to the depths of darkness and back.

The glassy-eyed look veiling her gaze quickly snuffed out his fascination.

He struggled to find his voice. "I think you could use some hot tea about now."

Her focus skidded to a halt at him, her lips lifting at one corner with the faintest look of pleasure.

Ben swallowed hard, then set to work measuring out

a dose of sassafras tea he kept with his medical supplies. When he set the kettle on to boil he was thankful to find heat already radiating from the woodstove.

"So, what's your name, ma'am?" Straddling a chair directly across from her, he silently tallied her respirations, unable to miss the way she breathed in shallow, raspy rhythms.

"Callie."

"Callie..." he prompted.

"Just Callie."

"I'm Ben Drake. I'm the doctor here, but then I think we already covered that." He offered her a reassuring look. It was nearly killing him to take up precious time with niceties, but as skittish as she was, he didn't want to risk having her walk out the door. "Are you from around here, *just* Callie?"

She shook her head. "No, I'm not."

"Well, how can I be of help to you? You must've come about that cough, am I right?" He dipped his head in an unsuccessful attempt to catch her attention. "How long have you had it?"

"Not long." Callie slowly rose from the chair, the dingy flour sack grasped firmly in her hand. A wince, so slight he almost missed it, crossed her face as she stood ramrod straight, her chin held high, a heart-rending contrast in vulnerable fatigue and determined strength.

"So, you must be in need of a doctor?" he attempted again, inward alarm mounting at the unhealthy flush of her sunken cheeks. "You came to the right place. I'll do whatever I can to help."

Her perfectly shaped brows creased in a stern look

over red-rimmed eyes. "I'm not here for medical attention. I—I want to speak with you about something of *pressing* importance."

Smoothing a hand over the day's growth of stubble on his chin, Ben bit back the sympathetic look that was close to surfacing. There was just something about her show of strength, about the way she wore bravery like a suit of armor five sizes too big that tugged at his heart.

"Well, whatever it is must be important for you to seek me out in a snowstorm like this." He resisted the urge to stand when she stared at him as though he was some wily predator. "So tell me, how can I help you?"

She coughed, and a definite wheeze threaded through the harsh sound. Turning, she shrugged her cloak off and laid it on the chair along with her sack, then faced him once again. "I'm here to offer my services to you."

Ben slammed his gaze down to the floor. Fumbled to cover his shock, but the sight of her standing before him…it was nothing short of shocking.

He braved a glance up again to see a ruby-red satin dress hanging on her thin frame, the gaudy ruffles and lace worn almost beyond repair in places. And the scoop neckline—he swallowed hard—plunged way too far down to be considered appropriate.

Ben averted his attention to the floor again. Frowned in confusion. What could this woman possibly offer him?

When he sneaked another glimpse and took in her tattered but risqué appearance, he had to steady himself as a ghastly glimmer of understanding enlightened him.

Did she mean to sell herself?

Gritting his teeth, he prepared to set her straight right here and right now. He may be a twenty-nine-year-old bachelor, but he hadn't ever, nor would he ever, resort to using a woman like that.

"I'm sorry. But I'm not interested in that kind of thing, Miss… Miss Callie." He forced himself to meet her cautious gaze as she clutched something at her neck. "If it's money you need, I'm glad to give you some. But I would never think of paying for female companionship."

Her red-rimmed eyes widened as though she'd been scandalized. "Doctor Drake, you misunderstand me." She squared her shoulders. Grasped the front of her dress, yanking it up in an awkward, unnatural angle for such a garment. "I'm here to inquire about the job. You do have a sign at your window advertising for such, am I right?"

Her bravado ended on a fit of coughing that sent him bolting to her side.

"I do." He forced his hands to remain at his sides when she instantly sidestepped. "But for the life of me, I'm trying to figure out why you'd inquire about the job this late at night. In a blizzard. And in such poor health. I am looking for help, but I think that before we discuss anything like that, we should *first* get you well."

On a wheezing breath, she slapped him with a reproving glower.

She was proud—that was for sure.

He inwardly kicked himself for saying what he had. But she'd dressed the part—though now that he thought about it, her skittish behavior and repulsion to his touch didn't correspond with a woman of that line of work.

But her dress…

"I'm here about the sign you have in your window, Doctor Drake." She nervously toyed with some trinket at her neck. "I can start working immediately, if that suits you."

"First of all," Ben began, glancing at her neck. He expected to see some worthless bit of whatnot hanging there, but when his tired gaze settled on a small silver locket, an icy chill doused his weariness. His heart ground to a stuttering stop. His breath caught.

He'd recognize that locket anywhere.

It was one of a kind. Handmade for his mother by his father who'd dabbled in jeweling throughout the years. The locket had been a priceless treasure. A gift deeded to Ben by his mother shortly before she'd passed twelve years ago.

Memories surfaced with breakneck speed, shooting up from a miry depth he'd tried to ignore all these years.

The constant run-ins he'd had with his brother, Max. The way Max would milk Ben's compassion for his own ill-reputed gain. The way Max would venture off for weeks at a time, returning with tales of some young harlot. And then that night seven years ago, when Max had come home thoroughly drunk. It had been a final, awful conflict. Max had destroyed anything he could get his hands on, furniture, dishes, relationships…

After Max had forced a lewd, unwanted kiss on Aaron's sweetheart, Max and Aaron, the fourth in a line of five Drake brothers, had gotten into a terrible fight. By morning, some of the money Ben had set aside for medical school had come up missing. Along with the heirloom locket. And Max.

A sharp stab of betrayal cut deep as he stared in disbelief. Max had stolen the locket and now here it was, hanging on the neck of some woman who was dressed for more than just baking bread.

Was this the young harlot Max had told them about? The one who'd likely lured him away for good, leading him into a sordid lifestyle of gambling and drinking?

Callie lifted her chin a notch, her slender fingers clamping around the silver locket. "The job, Doctor Drake… What about the job? I can assure you that I would be a good—"

"Where did you get that?" He took one step closer, craning his neck to get a better look. The fine, detailed filigree and etched scrolling shone even in the dim light, a testament to his father's talent.

She slid back a step. "Get what?"

"The locket." He nodded toward the object, forcing himself to remain calm.

"This locket is no concern of yours." She flattened both hands over the locket, her dress slipping down to a brazenly improper draping.

He clenched his jaw tight, furious that his dear mother's locket hung from this woman's neck.

"And it certainly has nothing to do with my being here. Like I said, I'm here about the job."

"Oh, it doesn't?" He gave a sarcastic laugh, infuriated at her bold censorship. "Funny thing, that locket. It looks just like one I once had."

"I'm afraid you're mistaken. This was a gift given to me. There's no way it could belong to you." She coughed again, glancing over her shoulder toward the door. "Now, about the Help Wanted sign."

He shifted his focus to the door, suspicion creeping up his spine, and setting his hair on end. What if Max lurked out there? Waiting for her? Maybe this was all just some ploy to make off with more money.

That possibility had Ben's blood boiling red-hot.

Resisting the urge to open the door and see for himself, Ben stepped closer to Callie. "Forget about the job for now, ma'am. *Where* did you get that locket?"

She balled her fist around the locket, inching away. "I told you, it was a gift."

He pinned her with an intense stare. "Who gave it to you?"

When her sunken eyes widened with the smallest hint of fear, a subtle sting of remorse pricked his conscience. He'd never spoken like this to a woman—ever. Even if she was a conniving thief sent by Max, she was a thin, sickly, delicately beautiful one, and he could've gone a little easier on her.

She drew her lips into a silent, grim line.

"My mother gave me that locket twelve years ago," he said evenly, determined to remain controlled. "On her deathbed."

Her fine features creased in a frown.

"The last time I saw it was just before my brother Max took off with some harlot over seven years ago. Do you know Max? Is he out there now?" he probed with a brisk nod toward the door.

Callie opened her hands. Slammed her gaze down to the silver locket, and for a split second he thought he saw her perfectly shaped lips quiver.

That worked the slightest bit of unwanted softening in his heart. He'd rather disregard the vulnerability he saw there, but try as he might, he couldn't banish the pathetic image of this woman huddled on his porch. Clad in nothing more than dirty rags. Doomed to freeze to death had he not come along.

"Let me put it this way." He took a step back and held his hand out. "That rightfully belongs to me."

Panic shuttered her eyes. "But I—"

She blinked with deliberate concentration, once, twice, her face paling as white as the stark snow whipping through the valley. She sidestepped. Teetered like some piece of fine china hanging over the edge of a high shelf.

When her eyes began a slow roll back, Ben lunged forward, catching up her light frame just before she hit the floor.

Callie draped limp in his arms, her hand slowly slipping from the locket and flopping down toward the floor. From the way her body burned with fever, she'd be here for a while. And despite her interest in the Help Wanted sign, he was positive that she hadn't come here for a job.

Chapter Two

Callie struggled to force open her heavy eyelids. She stared through a fuzzy haze up at the ceiling. Pain pounded her head. Her eyes burned, but still she inched her gaze around the room, trying to remember where she was.

Bits and pieces came to her… Trudging through the snowstorm, huddled and waiting on a porch. Strong, capable arms holding her…

A strangely familiar man, tall and dark-haired, came into focus next to her.

She shot up in bed. Regretted it instantly when her head spun and her stomach roiled.

"Whoa there, miss." Ben eased her shoulders back to the feather mattress. "Not so fast."

"I need to get up." She weakly wriggled from his unsettling touch.

Sighing, he crossed his arms at his chest. "I would strongly advise against doing anything of the sort. You're in no condition."

When she looked up at him, the world spun out of

control. She closed her eyes and hoped he wasn't observant enough to notice her condition, because the absolute *last* thing she wanted was to look feeble and needy in front of this man.

"Seeing as how I'm not your patient, I believe that I'm more than capable of making my own decisions." She pulled her chin up a notch, wincing at the thin, raspy sound of her voice.

"Like it or not, you're my patient now."

Averting her focus from his steel-blue gaze, she recalled fainting. And just before that, she'd been arguing with this man over—

"My locket! Where is it?" Dragging herself up to her elbows, she scanned the room. "And my box! Where did you put my things?"

When she spotted her box snuggled in the old flour sack atop the bureau, she tried to quell the frantic beat of her heart. But the idea that this man could've taken the few possessions she had left in this world seized her heart with utter, unexplainable panic.

At the cool touch of silver against her chest, she discovered the locket was where it had always been and dropped back to the pillow.

"You see." Ben drew his mouth into a grim line. "The locket's still there. Around your neck."

Peering down at her chest just to make sure, she screeched. "My dress!" She jerked the quilt clear up to her chin, being clad in nothing more than her paper-thin chemise and threadbare drawers. "Did you—"

A violent cough had her bracing herself, but she still managed to glower at him. "You undressed me without my consent? How dare you!"

His steady gaze didn't flicker an ounce. "Your dress was soaking wet, ma'am, and the weather prohibited me from summoning my sister-in-law's help as I usually would have."

"But still, I—"

"You're not the first woman I've tended to and you won't be the last. It was in your best interest that I get you as warm and dry as possible. And I can assure you that I honored your modesty in every possible way." He emphasized the last three words, his low, rich voice reverberating right through the layered quilts and chemise, to her bare skin.

Huddling tight beneath the covers, Callie turned and stared at the fresh cream-colored wall. A wash of shame spread through her like some dread disease. She hated reducing herself to this kind of ungrateful behavior, but she didn't even know this man.

Max, though no saint himself, had never spoken one kind thing about his family—especially Ben. Callie didn't have a single reason to like him. After all, Max's bitter edge surely didn't exist simply because of some innocent family sparring. He'd had a long list of reasons that fed his loathing.

She grasped the locket, recalling Ben's adamant claim that it belonged to him. Apparently this was one of those situations that Max had referred to… when his brothers would edge him out of something for their own gain. She'd like to give Ben a dressing-down about that, but since she had nowhere else to turn, and desperately needed the job, she decided to go for a more mild-mannered approach.

Plastering on an awkward smile, Callie attempted

a pleasant look. But it felt so odd and she was pretty sure her expression didn't come off pleasant at all.

The sting of his words—that Max had married some harlot—came racing back, barging into her mind and producing instant outrage.

A harlot?

The very reason she'd come crawling to Boulder had been to avoid becoming just that—a harlot. She'd had nothing else to wear, but the cast-off dress Lyle Whiteside had thrown in her direction six months ago when she'd started working as a housekeeper at the brothel. He'd burned her other dress, saying that he didn't want some lowly-looking scullery maid walking his halls, scaring off the paying customers.

Callie could almost feel her eyes darken with indignation. "It seems there's some confusion about this locket," she tried to say sweetly, but failed miserably.

He quirked one dark eyebrow. "There's no confusion as far as I'm concerned."

She stifled a ragged cough, her ire kicked up a notch at the sight of his steady, grating calm. Regardless of the fact that she needed this job, she nailed him with the most threatening glare she could muster. Held his penetrating gaze for a lengthy moment.

The man was wily, of that she had no doubt. Probably as clever and intimidating as the oldest, meanest wolf living in the Flatirons.

"Look, let me make this easy for you." He crossed his arms at his broad chest. "I can prove the locket belongs to me."

"How?"

"There's an engraving on the inside."

Prickly heat crept up her neck. Her pulse slammed in her ears as she grasped frantically for some argument. "How do I know you didn't inspect the locket while you were—while I was unconscious and you *undressed* me?"

"You don't, I guess," he managed with an insignificant shrug.

"Exactly." She swiped at a wayward, fever-induced tear rolling from the corner of her eye. "How do I know what went on then, Doctor Drake? I mean, having been dead to the world as I was, I would've been none the wiser had you sniffed and pawed through my things."

She grappled for control, but, horrifically, felt it slipping through her hands.

"The engraving says *All for Love*." The oddly tight and low sound of his voice arrested her attention. "It was something my father used to say to my mother."

Swerving her focus to the ceiling, a memory staggered into her mind. Shortly after she'd met Max, he'd given her the locket as a pledge of his love. She remembered the gloriously heady feeling she'd had as she'd stared at the romantic engraving.

She'd loved Max.

Even in the darkest hours of their seven-year marriage, she'd loved him. She'd held out hope that he'd change, and return to the wonderfully adventurous Maxwell Drake she'd fallen in love with. Before bitterness ruled his moods. Before he'd taken to gambling, drinking and the other things that followed.

Hot tears pooled in her eyes. She could only hope

that they would pass off for a fevered symptom instead of betrayal's bitter sting.

She'd been deceived. Again.

She could stubbornly stand her ground regarding the locket, but even as a lame argument began forming in her mind, she felt her feeble case sinking beneath unsteady footing. She'd love to believe that this was all just some innocent mistake, but she knew she'd stumbled onto another one of Max's lies, and for some reason the discovery wasn't any easier than the last time.

Or the time before that.

Or before that.

Disgust knotted her stomach tight. Just moments ago the locket had hung as a precious symbol of first love. Now it burned with dishonesty's harsh reality against her skin. It took every bit of poise she possessed to resist the unrefined urge to rip it off.

The sound of Ben dragging a chair across the room jerked her from her thoughts.

He sat beside her bed, looking almost as tired as she felt. On a yawn, he dragged a hand over his face. "We can talk about this another time, Callie. You need to rest."

The concern-filled way he responded tugged at her heart. It could easily be her undoing if she let it. But she wouldn't. Couldn't.

He definitely was not safe. He had a way of getting to her that was nothing short of a threat to her strong resolve.

When a deep cough tore through her throat, she winced at the merciless pain. Squeezing her eyes shut, she drew quivering hands to her neck, scrambling for a foothold with this bothersome sickness.

And this man.

Before she knew it, Ben had his strong arm wedged behind her shoulders as he held a glass to her parched lips. "Here, try to drink some water."

As much as she didn't want his help, she just didn't have the strength to spurn his gesture. Especially as the cool moisture touched her lips and slid down her throat.

"There you go. That's the way," he soothed, settling her against the pillow again. "Better?"

She nodded, feeling a small bit of relief. Blinking hard, she avoided Ben's penetrating gaze and instead lugged her focus to the gleaming dark hair that dangled loosely over his brow.

He scooped up her wrist and monitored her pulse. Though his eyes were watchful, his touch was gentle and respectful, even kind.

Uncomfortable with his attention, she struggled to push herself up again. If she set her mind to it, she could make herself get out of this bed.

With a slow shake of his head, Ben eased her back to the mattress. "Would you *please* just lie still? You have no business getting out of bed."

He smoothed a lock of hair from her face, the simple gesture bringing her a foreign sense of comfort.

Sighing, he gently tucked her arm beneath the thick layer of quilts. "It's three in the morning and the snow's coming down harder than ever. And you are very, very sick. If you have plans to move on in the middle of this blizzard, you might as well walk out there and dig your grave in the nearest snowbank," he added, biting off a yawn. "Though, frankly, I think you're too stubborn to die."

"I can't be sick." Squeezing her eyes shut, she felt stuck. Trapped. Dratted sickness! Why'd she have to fall ill now, of all times? "I have to work. The job. Is the job filled yet?"

He gave a tired chuckle. "If you mean, has someone else ventured over here tonight in the middle of a heavy snowfall to interview for this job…" He furrowed his brow as if trying to recall. "No."

"So does that mean you're hiring me?"

"Tell you what, Callie…" The tired droop of his eyes almost made her feel sorry for him. "We'll talk about the job when you're feeling better. All right?"

"I'm feeling fine now. Really," she rasped, her voice catching on a cough that wrenched her entire body.

The calming weight of his hand on her arm sent a small, soothing rush through her.

"I'm not sick," she argued, noticing the rugged, masculine scruff of dark beard growth on his face. "It's nothing. Just a bad cough."

After a long, unreadable look, he stood and walked over to the window. He parted the lace curtains that bracketed the cloudy, paned glass and leaned his arms against the frame. "A bad cough *and* a fever that'll be the death of you, if you don't get adequate rest. I'll repeat it again…you're in no condition to get out of bed."

Callie stared at his broad, strong back, then she sliced a glance to her dress on the bureau, an unwanted prickle of sensitivity working through her. In spite of the way he felt about her dress, he'd folded it. Neatly.

She tried to brush the feeling aside. Within a year of marrying Max she'd learned that she was better off not expecting anything in the way of care or loving concern. She'd buried her needs and feelings right along with her dreams. Couldn't allow things, good or bad, to affect her. She would've never managed the past seven years, otherwise.

She blinked hard. She had to get better soon or Ben might hire someone else, since he certainly hadn't made any move to hire her. Yet.

Had she any other option when she was back in Denver, she would've taken it, but given Max's history, she had little chance of getting a decent, wage-earning job. When she'd married Max, any bridge to her father's good graces had been burned. Even the church had turned away from her when she'd inquired about a position in the orphanage. Though she'd never once partaken in Max's sordid hobbies, she supposed that in their eyes she was guilty by association. She was the shunned widow of a *sinner.*

And for all she knew, God must look at her that way, too. Because since she'd disobeyed her father and married Max seven years ago, her life had been one hardship after another.

Coming to Boulder had been out of necessity alone. Without a job, she'd have no money and no hope to escape what awaited her back in Denver if she didn't pay up.

Max had barely been cold in the ground when Lyle Whiteside had come knocking on Callie's door, hanging the significant gambling debt like a noose before her. Since then she'd been working feverishly to pay it off by cleaning his saloon and brothel, but the payback hadn't been fast enough to suit him. Three days ago he'd stared her down with those snapping black eyes of his, demanding that she pay off the rest upstairs on her back.

He'd vowed to be her first customer.

She could not—*would not*—slide her neck into that rope and drop to that low a level, no matter how desperate the situation. No matter how risky it was to run out on such a powerful man.

"I'll be up and moving by tomorrow." Her hoarse voice barely sounded. "I'll make sure to compensate you for your doctoring. And room and board."

He came to stand next to the bed, peering down at her with a certain compassion that had her averting her gaze. "If it's money that has you concerned, don't worry about that right now. It'll all work out. I won't charge you a thing."

No matter how destitute she and Max had been over the years, she'd never taken charity.

Callie gripped the bedsheets when another deep, brutal cough commanded her strength. Maybe she was flirting with death to even think about getting out of this bed. The way her head and body ached, she couldn't imagine walking twenty feet.

"I have nothing to pay you with." She set her jaw. "But I don't—won't—take charity. You can just subtract what I owe you from my wages."

"Your wages?" he echoed on a bemused chuckle.

"Yes, my wages."

When she absently set a hand to the locket, she

caught herself, suddenly wishing that she'd never been given the gift.

She lifted her head from the pillow and fumbled for the clasp. If it belonged to Ben Drake, then she'd promptly return it because the lovely piece of jewelry had obviously never belonged to her. Or Max.

His brow furrowed. "What are you doing?"

"I'm giving this back." She steadied her fingers enough to undo the clasp. "Like you said, it belongs to you."

His hands lightly grasped hers, stilling them, his face a mask of confusion. "No. Please, don't take it off, Callie."

She couldn't move, couldn't look at him. Inside she was in an all-out war for control. She was deeply hurt, betrayed by Max, though he was six months gone. And Ben wore self-assured confidence like some fine evening coat fitted to a T. Yet he showed concern and compassion.

"It's not mine," she declared, weeding out any sign of self-pity from her voice. "It never was and I—"

Her words died on another violent fit of coughing that paled all others. It wrenched her chest, her shoulders, her head. Every muscle convulsed.

She was barely aware as Ben slipped an arm behind her shoulders. She felt his strong arms cradle her as he whispered soothing words while she fought to gain her breath. When he pulled her closer to himself and wedged another pillow behind her head, his warmth seeped into her. And much needed relief slowly settled over her as he lowered her to the pillow.

"That really didn't sound good." Ben hunkered

down to eye level with her. "At all. I'm very concerned."

"I'll be fine," she rasped, with painful effort.

She wasn't sure if her throat felt like it was closing up because of her cough and sore throat or the emotion his tender care evoked. For the first time in a long time, she might be experiencing what it was like to have someone care about what happened to her. To care for her.

But how could that be? Max had done nothing but speak ill of his brothers—especially Ben.

She pushed away from Ben, thinking about how Max must've been wronged and how things could've been so different if only…

The bitter sense of betrayal and pain and unfulfilled dreams stripped her bare. There was no way to change the past, but she could be unwavering in her quest to carve out a future of her own making.

After she'd paid off the debt.

Her eyelids drooped heavily, blatant fatigue demanding every bit of her attention. She could barely hold a coherent thought, but as she drifted closer to the blessed brink of sleep, Ben's face flashed in her mind.

He deserved the truth about his brother. Especially if she was going to be working for him. It was only right.

Forcing her eyes open, she yawned. Coughed. "I need to tell you something if I'm going to be working for you," she managed, her words sounding far away, though Ben's presence felt almost as near as her next, ragged breath.

He leaned in just a bit closer.

"That woman Max ran off with…that was me. I'm your brother's wife." She gripped the sheet as she worked down another painful swallow. "I was married to Max."

Ben's strikingly handsome features creased in a disturbing wash of pain and anger. "Was? What do you mean, *was?*"

She quickly stuffed down the raw emotion. "Max was shot in an alley for double-dealing. He died six months ago."

Chapter Three

The news of Max's death echoed in Ben's head like a gunshot in a deep mountain canyon. He'd not heard one thing. Not one thing.

When Callie had uttered the words a few hours ago, his emotions had warred between deep anger and grief. The death was an utter waste of a life so young.

And a mark of shame for Ben.

If he'd been able to turn his brother around, Max might still be here.

Ben let out a stuttering, remorse-filled sigh. He hadn't realized he'd been holding his breath, and tried to relax his tight muscles, calm his beating heart, but it seemed useless. His entire being had been drawn into a knot of unrest and regret in hearing the news.

He would've questioned her further had she not drifted off to sleep. He wanted some proof of marriage or of Max's death, but the longer he sat here staring at her—his brother's widow, a young woman whose brow even now furrowed in pain—the more he questioned his need for evidence.

He didn't know one thing about Callie. Had no reason to trust her. Still, she didn't strike him as someone who'd lie about something so severe.

Ben had a volume full of unanswered questions regarding his wayward sibling. Twice as many misgivings. If he could learn even a little about what had transpired in the past seven years, then maybe, just maybe, Ben could put to rest the painful remorse.

He doubted he'd ever find peace about certain things, though. With Max dead, there were some bitter words Ben had said that could never be taken back: that Max was good-for-nothing, a stain to the Drake family name and the worst of scoundrels. Sitting on this solitary side of things, he had no idea what kind of damage the last words he'd said to Max could've done.

The shameful memory pierced Ben like buckshot, shredding his already shaky confidence. In the past six months his assurance in his work as a doctor, and his trust in God, had been dealt some rough blows.

First, he'd been unable to help his brother Joseph after an accident that left him blind. Ben had doctored him to the point that Joseph demanded to be left alone. The sleepless nights Ben had spent worrying, praying, and reading anything that might be a key to Joseph regaining his sight had been to no end.

He swallowed a thick knot of guilt. The inability to produce a winning outcome did something to a man who was supposed to be an instrument of healing in God's hands.

Then his brother Aaron had been dealt a double blow when his newborn baby and his wife died within a day of each other. Complications of childbirth. Ben had done everything he knew to change the course, but it hadn't been enough.

And now this.

Surely, had he done things differently with Max, spoken some sense into him, things would've turned out differently.

He blinked hard as he stared at Callie, asleep and burrowed in a thick cloud of blankets and pillows. The frown that had creased her brow had smoothed out to reveal a feminine softness. And the stern, unrelenting purse of her lips had relaxed to render a full pout that made his mouth tip in an unprovoked, tired grin.

For a petite little thing, no more than five feet, two inches tall, she'd put up quite a fight. The bold determination he'd seen in her eyes and stubborn set to her jaw belied her small stature.

She'd felt alarmingly thin in his arms when he'd cradled her limp body and settled her in bed last night. He'd removed her cold, damp dress, its tattered hem caked with snow, to make her more comfortable. But her lightweight undergarments did nothing to conceal the fact that this woman probably hadn't seen a decent meal in a very long time. And they did nothing to hide her undeniable, womanly curves.

Forcing his thoughts elsewhere, he snapped open his pocket watch, flicking a glance at the hour. It was already nine o'clock in the morning, and though he'd dozed a time or two in the chair beside her bed, Callie's ragged breathing and rattled cough had kept him on the alert.

While he switched out the warm oil of camphor–soaked compress at her chest, he realized that as much as he didn't trust her, he felt drawn to this young woman. Wanted to make sure she received the best care he could provide.

Bracing his forearms on his legs, he monitored her breathing, watching her chest rise and fall in small breaths. All the while wondering what he was going to do with her once she was well. If he didn't give her the job would she hightail it out of Boulder?

It was painfully apparent that she needed help.

And it was no secret that he desperately needed an assistant. But was he willing to hire a young woman he had a deep interwoven history with, yet, until a few hours ago, had never even met?

Ben quietly crossed to the bedroom's lace-draped window and peered outside through the cloudy panes. The snow had finally tapered off to a light dusting of flurries that glistened like tiny diamond chips in the morning sun. He squinted against the stark brightness, his eyelids drooping over his eyes, weighted by fatigue and by the bright glare spilling into the room.

Kneading his forehead, his thoughts strayed to the past seven years. They'd tracked Max down several times, finding him in saloons, slouched at gaming tables like some permanent fixture. Though Ben had never met Callie—didn't even know her name—Max had lamented about how he'd needed to play the tables to keep his demanding little woman clothed in finery and frills.

Turning to glimpse the bleak condition of her ragged dress and threadbare cloak, he couldn't imagine that anything of the sort had been true.

Remorse regarding Max hovered over him like a

coffin lid suspended, just inches from closing. He'd done his best to set Max's feet on the straight and narrow, but Max had given the term *maverick* a whole new meaning, dodging responsibility at every turn, thumbing his nose at right living and common sense, and bucking hard against anyone who tried to bridle him. He was nothing like the rest of the Drake boys, and for that Ben felt a guilt-laden weight of responsibility.

Ben had promised his folks before they passed on that he'd see to his brothers. Make sure they turned out to be the fine, upstanding men his parents had intended.

Moving over to the bed, he refreshed the compress at Callie's chest, praying that it would ease her deep cough.

When she stirred then dragged in a ragged breath in her sleep, he was grateful to see that it didn't catch on another cough. With attentive medical care, she might just be all right. The idea of any other outcome made his throat go instantly tight. There was something vulnerable hidden behind the inflexible front she'd worn that begged for release, and he couldn't ignore the strange desire he felt to be her liberator.

"You're going to do what?" Aaron protested, his voice likely cutting through the closed door to where he'd just peeked in at Callie.

"Keep your voice down." Ben shot his brother a glower of warning then tugged him farther into the waiting area. "I said, I'm thinking about giving her a job as a cook and housekeeper."

He glanced at the second-oldest brother, Joseph,

whose brow creased in an unmistakable, disagreeing frown over his sightless eyes.

His brothers' forthright responses contrasted dramatically with the quiet, solemn grief they'd shown an hour ago when'd he'd broken the news of Max's death. There were plenty of regrets to be had regarding Max. The tension-filled years preceding his disappearance. The betrayal prompting his leaving. And the futile times when Ben and Joseph had tried to coax Max home.

All the years growing up hadn't been that way, however. There'd been good times, when all five of them had roamed the backyard on stick horses, as though the ground yawned like some wide-open range. When they'd worked together with their father to build houses for the steady stream of settlers moving West. When they'd hunkered down in eager anticipation of Christmas morning.

Those fond memories made it almost impossible to imagine Max dead. With nothing of his brother's life left to redeem, Ben was left feeling helpless.

"A cook and housekeeper?" Aaron's eyes widened.

"You want me to throw her out?" Ben queried, irritated.

Aaron splayed his hands in an it's-not-my-problem kind of gesture. "It's your call, but the whole thing sounds fishy to me. I mean, her showing up here in the middle of the worst October snowstorm I can remember, and then asking for a job? There's gotta be a good reason for that kind of behavior. If that's not fishy, I don't know what is."

"What other information did you get out of her, anyway?" Joseph inquired.

"Not much. She isn't very talkative." Ben's admission rankled a little, especially as he remembered how stubborn and evasive she'd been. "She's pretty sick. In fact, we need to make this brief so I can get back in there to see to her."

"If it were me, I wouldn't trust her as far as I could throw her." Aaron's sure look altered to an instant frown. "Well, maybe not, seeing as how she's such a tiny thing." He nudged Joseph's arm and whispered conspiratorially. "As small as she is, Joe-boy, a fella could fit her into his coat pocket."

Relishing descriptions, however lame, Joseph grinned at Aaron's remark.

"You're all talk, Aaron," Ben dismissed. "You couldn't turn your back on her either, and you know it."

"So, what if you're wrong about her?" Aaron folded his arms at his chest. "If I were you, I'd get that locket from her before she takes off with it."

"She already tried to give it back to me."

"Well, then..." Aaron held out his hand. "Why don't you have it?"

Ben met his disbelieving gaze. "I didn't have the heart."

"Oh, for the love of—"

"Go easy, Aaron," Joseph cautioned. "You never know how hard something is until you walk it yourself."

"I'm not arguing that. It's just that Max pulled the wool over Ben's eyes more than once," Aaron responded then turned to Ben. "And I think we all know that he left because of this woman."

With a tentative shake of his head, Ben raked a hand through his hair. "That might be what he said, but how do we know it's true? How can you judge her, if you haven't met her?"

"Facts are facts, Ben. And it was as clear as a mountain stream that Max got in with the wrong crowd," Aaron bit off, his jaw tensing. "He always was wild on the vine. I just never thought he'd go so far as to steal from his own kin then walk away without ever looking back. If you ask me, I'd say that little lady in there had to have played a part."

Ben peered down at the box Callie had brought. He hadn't wanted to take it from her room, and sure wasn't about to look inside at the contents, but he had to know if it was the box Joseph had made for Max years ago. That would be just another point of proof in her favor. "I know it doesn't make sense. And I can't say as I trust her, but—"

"I'd be disappointed if you did." Aaron snorted. "I wouldn't put it past some young, sickly thing sent by Max, to try and con you out of money."

Joseph shifted his long cane from one hand to the other. "Knowing how hard it was for you to come to grips with the way Max took advantage of you, I'm not sure why you'd want to take that risk again."

"I'll admit, I've been wrong a time or two." Aaron took the box from Ben. "But the lady came here with this one box and the locket. Lord knows she could be lying through her teeth about being married to Max—even about him dying."

"Why would she lie about something like that?" Ben asked.

"I don't know. Why would Max steal from his own brothers? And, when he was sloppy drunk and barely able to stand, kiss my girl?" Aaron's jaw ticked. "People with no conscience do the unthinkable."

"Just take some time to think this over." Joseph grasped Ben's shoulder. "Don't make any rash decisions."

"Why you'd want her workin' for you, I'll never know." Aaron scuffed over to a rounded-back chair and plopped down.

"Believe me, I wondered the same thing, too—when I saw the locket, anyway." Ben sank into a chair next to Aaron. "I don't have a single, solid reason why I'd say this, but I think she's telling the truth."

"And *I* think you're gettin' all thick in the head." Aaron placed the box in Joseph's hand after Joseph sat down.

"You're a bleeding heart, Ben. Always have been." Securing his cane on the floor next to the chair, Joseph traced his fingertips over the walnut box. "It's been ten years since I made this for Max, and it's just as I remember."

"It's beautiful," Ben commented, impressed by his brother's talent. Even now, with his sight gone, he did flawless work. "You were good back then, and you're even better now."

"Taught him everything he knows." Aaron gave a self-satisfied wink.

Half grinning, Joseph shook his head and sighed. "That joke is getting old, Aaron. We've heard it… I don't know…what would you say, Ben, *hundreds* of times?"

"At least," he answered with a chuckle.

"Maybe try it out on someone new next time." Joseph's eyes grew wide with exasperation.

"You know I only say it to convince myself."

"That's better. Best to remember your place." With a wink, Joseph took in the detailed carving with his fingertips.

"It looks to be in good condition." Ben angled his head to examine the box again.

Aaron rose and scuffed over to the doorway leading from the front waiting area. He peered down the hallway to where Callie slept. "You better make sure you keep a close eye on her. You never know what she might steal."

The words stuck like a prickly burr, and had Ben narrowing his gaze at his brother, yet again. No matter that the callous comment could be true, it didn't diminish the sudden, unexplained need to come to Callie's defense.

Joseph set the box on the end table. "You're compassionate to a fault. Whether it's a stray animal or someone down on their luck, you'll take most anything in and not think a thing about it if you get bit in the process."

Ben couldn't deny Joseph's words. Puffing out his cheeks on a sigh, he pictured the most recent strays that now shared his home.

"Yeah," Aaron agreed. "Take those two starving kittens that showed up in your barn last summer. I sure wouldn't have wanted to get my hands close to them when they ate. The way they protected their food with those little, needlelike claws…" He demonstrated with an amusing amount of drama that had Ben chuckling. "And remember those pathetic, warning growls they'd make even while they chewed?"

"How could I forget? But now they're a good, healthy weight." With gleaming black and white fur, full bellies and a lackadaisical demeanor that made Ben wonder if he'd spoiled them to the point of incompetence.

"I realize I'm taking a chance here, but I'm not going to take the locket from Callie. I just can't do that to her." Somewhere deep inside his heart, his words rang true. "And, as far as the job goes, she's not going to take no for an answer. She obviously needs the money."

Goaded by the lackluster vote of confidence in the stoic expressions on their faces, he raked his fingers through his hair, trying to see their side of things. They'd all four been betrayed by Max. Even so, there'd been a hope that existed among Joseph, Aaron, Zach and Ben that Max would come to his senses someday. That he'd return home to the family.

The idea that Max lay cold in some unmarked grave made Ben's chest tighten with ready sorrow. How had he failed so miserably? It should've been different. He should've been able to turn Max around and get him to see reason.

When he thought of his brother's widow lying in the other room, her weakened body racked with fever and sickness, his heart wobbled off-beat. There had to be more to her than met the eye. And he wanted to be the one to uncover it.

"I think if you had the opportunity to talk to Callie, you'd see why I couldn't just turn her out in the storm."

"Maybe," Aaron conceded. "But why you feel like you have to go and give her a job, room and board, when it's pretty obvious she's trying to pull a fast one, is beyond me."

"Keep your voice down." Ben sliced another reproving look to Aaron and moved to stand next to him. "She won't take a handout. She insists on paying me back for her care, and I'm inclined to believe that she means it. You both know that I could use help around here. One good look at this place proves that."

"I don't know…it all looks fine to me." Joseph quipped good-naturedly, stepping toward them. He turned his head as though taking in the full measure of the place.

"This from a blind man." Aaron rolled his eyes, clapping Joseph's arm. "Inspect things with those sensitive fingertips of yours, and I think you will change your tune."

Ben chuckled softly. "I'm not arguing. We all know that I didn't inherit the 'neat and tidy' ways in the family like you, Joseph."

"At least you're right on that account." Aaron quirked an eyebrow.

"Listen, I know how much guilt you carry over Max leaving the way he did." Joseph sighed, setting his focus dead center on Ben. "We all feel responsible in one way or the other, but we tried to get him to come back. Even doled out more money for him when it was obvious he'd been a fool and spent all of his inheritance."

Aaron slid his hands into his pockets. "Pulling this little lady into things when we don't know her from a stranger could be barkin' up the wrong tree."

Ben glanced over to the front window where the town slowly dug out from the foot and a half of snow that had fallen last night. In spite of the impeding snow that made movement outside difficult, at best, his brothers had been on his doorstep at ten o'clock this morning, checking to make sure he'd returned safely from his calls last night. The youngest, Zach, likely would've been here, too, but he was probably buried knee-deep in chores on the cattle ranch where he worked as foreman.

Ben valued the close relationship he had with his brothers. They looked out for each other, picked up slack when one was down. And they all felt a profound hole where Max had been.

His jaw ticked with edginess. "Max aside, Callie is obviously in need of a little help, and I'm going to do what I can for her."

He remembered, with a sense of shame, the panic in her eyes last night when he had as much as accused her of stealing the locket. "You're right, though. She could easily be some fast-talking thief who knows an easy target when she sees one. And if that's the case, I'll do my best not to get taken, but until I find out more, she's staying right here."

Chapter Four

"That is the *longest* uninterrupted stretch of sleep I've ever seen," came the soothing, cellolike timbre of Ben Drake's voice.

"What time is it, anyway?" Indulging herself in the heady, restful feeling, she stretched beneath the warm covers. She edged a sleep-fuzzed gaze over to see him leaning against the wall, one booted foot draped over the other and his arms crossed in a relaxed fashion at his chest.

The merest whisper of awareness quivered down her spine.

"Eight o'clock."

When he moved over to the bed, she focused on the way the sunlight danced about the room. "Hmm…the way I feel, I would've thought—"

"Friday. You've been asleep for over a day, straight."

Horrified, Callie slammed her eyes shut.

"Catching up, are you?"

She'd had no intention of languishing for so long. This would only delay her in getting the job. Ben could've hired someone else, for all she knew. She had to have this job so she could pay off the rest of Max's debt—before Whiteside came looking for her.

She glanced up at Ben, trying not to notice his fresh-shaven, squared jaw and the half grin tipping his lips.

And the rebellious trip of her heart.

She gave her head a hearty shake. "I apologize that I've taken up—"

"No apologies are necessary." He settled a warm hand against her brow. "How are you feeling? You look much improved from the night before last when you showed up here."

"I feel fine." Folding back the covers, she hauled her legs over the edge of the bed and sat up.

"Hold on, there. Not so fast." He braced a hand at her back and hunkered down, eye level. "You may feel better, but you're probably weaker than a new-born colt."

"I'm just fine. And I don't need your help." The sound of her own pulse surged like breaking waves through her head. Dizzy, she clutched the quilt to her chest and feebly pushed herself up to standing. She teetered, struggling for balance. "Better than ever."

Her knees buckled and she started to fall, but his strong arms caught behind her with disarming comfort.

"Well, I'll give you this much, your stubbornness hasn't weakened one bit." He lifted her into bed, his muscle-roped arms searing straight through her thin undergarments like a warm, mesmerizing flame.

She drew in a slow, pulse-calming breath.

"You must've grown up with a passel of brothers to stand your ground with, right?"

"Wrong."

"Then what?" His eyes sparkled. "Let me guess, the middle child in a houseful of girls?"

"Wrong again," she shot back, noticing, for the first time, a picture hanging on the wall next to the bed. Her gaze moved slowly over the photograph.

The image captured five boys, all neatly tucked in and trimmed for a moment in time. She stared at the hopeful faces. She recognized Ben, standing like some sturdy pillar, his dark hair dangling over his brow even as it did now.

"That's a picture of me and my brothers. I was thirteen, there." He pointed to the middle boy in the frame, his long arms draped around his brothers.

She shifted her gaze from the image to Ben then back again, remembering how Max used to say that Ben had been so controlling. That he'd been harsh and demanding, squashing fun and taking his role as the oldest way too seriously.

"And this is Joseph, Aaron, Zach…" He pointed to each face then stopped at the boy to the far right. "And here's Max. He was nine at the time."

She swallowed hard, seeing a much younger and far more innocent Max. "That spark of adventure was in his eyes even at that age."

"That's for sure. He was always off doing something or other. It was hard to keep tabs on him," he said, his voice low and tight.

She found it hard to disagree. Max would often be gone for days at a time, never disclosing his whereabouts when he left or returned.

Studying his image again, she noted the way he stood straight and tall, almost out of Ben's reach. He leaned away from his brothers, his arms folded stubbornly at his chest, while the other boys seemed to take comfort in Ben's arms.

Tucking the covers under her chin, Ben sat down on the chair next to the bed and sighed. "So, did you have siblings?"

She picked at an errant thread on the quilt. "I was the only child born to my parents."

"Spoiled, then, huh?"

She met his lighthearted gaze. "My upbringing was one of privilege, but little freedom to enjoy it. My mother died when I was five, and after that my father changed. Dramatically so," she admitted, even still missing the happy, carefree way of life before Mama had died and her father exacted a strict existence for her.

Ben gave a slight nod. "I'm sorry to hear that, Callie. That must've been difficult."

Swallowing back the familiar grief, she remembered just how difficult it'd been. To once delight in her father's love and care, only to have it replaced with a gruff demeanor and emotional distance. Her father's heart had been broken, of that she was certain. She'd often wondered if he'd been so fearful of losing her, too, that he'd hemmed her in so tight with his principles and rules that nothing ill could befall her.

Only she'd been desperate to escape the confines of her father's grief and frustration, and found ways around his stringent demands.

That's when she'd met Max and had fallen in love.

The man had fairly swept her off her feet from the moment their gazes connected. He was handsome, witty and—glancing at the picture again—had a spirit of adventure that had been like honey to a bee for her. With the elegant brushstroke of words, Max had painted pictures of places that had her yearning to break free from the colorless canvas defining her life.

The moment her father had discovered she'd been stealing away to be with Max, he forbade her to see Max, drawing a hard, dark line of demarcation.

She'd dared to cross it.

It didn't take long after they'd married for her to learn that Max's charm and wit went as far as the door to their house. Inside their private life there had lived a man who seemed as different as night was to day.

The guilt she carried from the way she'd left home had been nearly unbearable at times. It was as if her choices had set into motion a lifetime of sorrow.

Ben cupped her chin and urged her focus toward him with a tenderness that loosed a shiver of comfort straight through her. "Do you think you feel up to a hot meal?"

Her stomach growled as if on cue.

"Say no more." On a pulse-skittering wink, he crossed to a small table where he poured a glass of water. "You need to get your strength back so you'll be ready for what's ahead."

She frowned in confusion. "What do you mean?"

"The job…" He stood over her.

She gave an almost imperceptible nod, her heart thudding against her ribs. He was giving her the job? As thrilled as she felt, she masked the excitement. "So you finally came to your senses?"

His low chuckle warmed the room. "Let's see…

that wasn't exactly how I was looking at it, but yes. I finally came to my senses."

Callie eyed him as he leaned down next to her. He supported her shoulders with one arm as he helped her to drink. When he gently laid her against the pillow again, she savored the residue of cool moisture by licking her lips.

His gaze fell to her mouth and lingered for a long, tenuous moment before he turned away as though embarrassed.

She barely noticed, though, since she was already calculating how long she'd have to work to pay him back for her care. "I'll work off my bill first. For the doctor services you've rendered."

"Consider it a benefit that comes with the job."

"Absolutely not. I told you before that I wouldn't take charity. And I mean it."

"Hmm… I don't remember saying anything about charity. I need a cook and a housekeeper, if you haven't already noticed." He swiped his index finger over the glass window panes, leaving a telltale mark. "Maybe even help with some medical calls. So, when you're well, I'll be expecting you to work for me. That is, if you think you can handle that kind of labor." He pivoted to face her, his challenging yet enticing gaze advancing on her.

She tried not to fidget at the sight of him, but it was nearly impossible. The honest expression he wore and the hopefulness in his gaze seeped into the very pores of her skin.

She fingered the edge of the quilt. "I— Of course I can *handle* this. It should pose no problem at all."

"You *can* cook, can't you?" He arched one dark eyebrow.

Callie stuck him with a prickly look.

"Apparently so." His mouth tipped in a distinctly male, self-satisfied grin. "Then it's settled. For now, I just want you to relax and take it easy. As badly as I need help, I can't have you sick, can I?"

She shook her head in outward agreement. But inside, doubt filled her mind. Why was he being so kind? So unlike Max's description? It just didn't make sense.

Callie's heart twisted with bitter irony, remembering the last words that had passed through Max's lips before he died.

Find my brothers. Find Ben. He'll see to your needs.

Max had died then, leaving Callie confused, angry and laden with sorrow.

Certain that his words must've been delirium-driven, she'd ignored his dying sentiment. She'd grieved for her husband, for the life he could've had and for the unfulfilled dreams she'd never know with him. She'd grieved his untimely death.

And that of their newborn baby girl he'd buried almost nine months to the day they'd married.

But instead of wallowing in the insurmountable grief that permeated every thought and every breath, she'd had to begin working immediately, to make right on his debt.

She wouldn't be here now, except that she'd had nowhere else to turn. At the moment she felt too weak to even drag herself out of bed. *And* she was in debt to a man Max had said was controlling, a cheat and a liar.

Just as soon as she could, she was going to make

right on what she owed Ben by cooking mouthwatering meals and cleaning till his office and house gleamed. Once she'd paid back Whiteside, she'd leave, thereby ridding herself of the confusion of it all.

"I'll bring over something for you to eat while we wait for Katie to arrive."

At the mere thought of food, Callie's mouth began watering like a leaky pail. "Who's Katie?"

"She's my brother's wife. I thought maybe I'd have her help you with a bath. As long as you don't spike a fever before then, you can soak in hot, soapy water to your heart's content."

She gave a contented sigh. "It's been so long—" She cut her words off. Ben certainly wasn't interested in the details of her bleak, almost nonexistent, bathing schedule.

"It'll probably go a long way to making you feel better," he added with a brisk nod.

She barely hid her profound delight, finding it impossible to recall the last time she'd taken a full-fledged bath with hot water. Most of the time she'd made do with the invigorating yet harsh cold of a mountain stream or sponging herself from a pail of used dishwater. Twice, at the saloon, she'd managed an early morning soak after the customers had all gone home to their poor, unsuspecting wives and children. Even though she'd hated utilizing Lyle Whiteside's *girls'* amenities, it had been a memorable bit of pure luxury.

"That is, if you want to?"

"Oh, yes." She touched her matted hair. "That would be wonderful."

"Katie will help you. You'll like her."

Instant humiliation ricocheted through her veins as she lowered her hand to her side. Her stomach clenched. She fingered the rough seam of a haphazard, angry-looking scar that blazed like a streak of lightning around to her back, a result of one of Max's liquor-induced tirades and a lasting symbol of betrayal that had embedded deep into their marriage.

Oh, he'd been somewhat remorseful for the way he'd treated her, but not enough to get her proper medical attention. Drunk, he'd awkwardly stitched the gaping wound then stormed out the door, leaving for days while she struggled to fight off a wicked infection, alone. That had been a year ago, and though the gash had finally healed, the pain inflicted by his total disregard for her well-being stung, still.

"Callie?" Ben's voice cut through the dismal memory.

She jerked her attention back to the present. "I—I'm sure I can bathe myself."

His eyes shrouded with doctorly concern. "Tell you what, when you're stronger and well out of the woods, I won't argue."

"There's no need to bother her," she shot back. "I can manage just fine on my own."

"I'll rest easier if you have a little help." Moving toward the doorway, he turned to her as he cleared his throat. "And by the way, room and board is part of the job. That is, if this bedroom here suits you well enough." He gestured to her surroundings almost apologetically. "You can take your meals with me next door. Or bring them here and eat alone, if you'd rather," he added as he stepped out of the room.

Callie gulped against the thick emotion clogging her

throat. She hadn't slept in a bed so comfortable, had a room so cheery, or had the delicious promise of consistent meals for seven years. The accommodations were modest by her father's standards. But to a woman who'd spent the past years moving from shack to shack, sharing a bed with rodents and contenting herself with whatever food she managed to purchase, this was a castle. And for a short while, anyway, she was the queen.

Ben peered down at where he'd absentmindedly heaped a plate full of shepherd's pie for Callie. The way her stomach had audibly growled at the mention of food, he felt confident that she finally had an appetite—just probably not enough to eat half a roasting pan of the tasty dish.

He dropped the wooden spoon in the pan and braced his hands against the counter, attempting yet again to convince himself that he was merely concerned for her as a patient.

Hauling in a deep, stabilizing breath, he glanced down as Molly and Smudge meowed sweetly at his feet, curling their thick tails in feline affection around his legs.

Who was he trying to kid?

He felt an unrelenting draw to her that plagued his every thought, making him wonder if he might well be getting himself in too deep.

The empty sadness he'd seen waft like some dark wraith across her face when she'd spoken of her upbringing tugged at his heart. What secrets did her past hold?

She'd grown up with privilege. And she was clearly uncomfortable with any action that could be viewed as charity. He couldn't miss the way she'd flinched at his touch. Nor had he missed the way her eyes had lit with awe then instant shame when he'd mentioned both the meal and bath. It was as if she didn't want to make herself vulnerable enough to receive help...so much like the strays he'd taken in. Often times he'd have to coax them to eat, even when their ribs protruded in glaring proof of starvation.

Ben recalled the way he'd found Callie that first night. In spite of her tangled hair, tattered appearance and puzzling background, he'd felt pulled by some unseen force to help her.

To save her.

Just like the scrawny kittens that had shown up.

He gave a short laugh and loosened his fists, reflecting on how this little lady had loosened his ordered world a few notches, turning his life upside down in less than two days.

Maybe he was the one who needed saving.

When he peered down at his feline companions, Smudge gave him one of those I'm-as-cute-as-a-button squinty-eyed looks while Molly stared wide-eyed up at him, as though he owned a pond full of tasty fish for the eating. He hunkered down and stroked their fur, tracing the ragged scar on Molly's neck that had been a festering wound when she'd come to him. He looked at the irregular kink crooking Smudge's front leg, saddened to think of what these two had suffered.

He couldn't help but open his heart to them when they'd shown up. And they seemed to know it, too, because like most all the animals that came his way, these kittens had somehow known they could trust him.

He peered through the kitchen window toward his office, and his chest tightened. Was Callie one of those strays? Had she scraped her way through life and, by providential design, landed on his doorstep?

Callie's pride prickled from head to toe. "I could never take these garments from you, Katie."

Katie sat on the bed behind her, gliding a brush through Callie's freshly washed hair. "Sure you can. Besides, I really want you to have them."

She ran a hand over the sturdy, attractive fabrics. "They're far too nice to give away."

"Ben said something about you being stubborn," Katie remarked, threading her fingers through Callie's hair. "He just didn't say *how* stubborn."

Having figured out long ago that her existence hinged on a firm resolve to keep moving forward, no matter what, she'd gladly embraced stubbornness like some lifeline.

When she slid her gaze from the lavender day dress to the emerald-green dress and then to the soft, white eyelet undergarments, she knew each item would be perfect. She hadn't seen clothing like this for seven years. And she sure hadn't felt cared for like this in almost as long.

But she already owed Ben—even though he'd said it was part of the job. She didn't want to take charity. Didn't want to be in debt to someone else. Not for a single cent. Not even for a single stitch of much needed clothing.

"Barring some unforeseen fortune splashing at my feet, it'd be a month's worth of paydays before I could afford a new dress, let alone nice undergarments," she admitted reluctantly. Even when she'd paid off Max's gambling debt, she wasn't about to spend her earnings frivolously on new garments. She had her future to think of.

Katie smiled. "Then you can look at this as a timely provision. But with the way you swim in this nightdress," she responded, plucking at the cream-colored flannel material, "I'm worried if the other items will even fit, you're so slight."

The simple nightdress whispered against Callie's skin like luxurious silk. "This is very comfortable, Katie, and I'm sure the other items will be absolutely fine. But I—"

"I've already shortened things a few inches since Ben said you weren't much over five feet. If they're still too big, then I'll help you alter them."

Her chest grew tight and her eyes stung with ready shame. In all the years of living on the edge of destitution with Max, she'd avoided charity, while Max would seek it out.

"I want to tell you something." Katie drew the covers back, gesturing for Callie to lie down. "I don't know how long you'll be here working for Ben—"

"I'm not sure either," Callie noted with a sniff as she scooted down into the fresh linens.

"Well, however long it is, the Drake family is first in line when it comes to helping others. Believe me… I'm blessed to have married into such a wonderful family. And you are fortunate to be employed by such a fine man as Ben Drake."

Everything she'd ever heard from Max would lead

her to suppose the exact opposite. She'd already made one severe, life-altering error in judgment regarding Max's character. She wasn't about to be fooled like that ever again.

But three days with Ben, and already she had inarguable reservations as to Max's sordid opinion.

Not just because of the tender way Ben had cared for her or the gesture of kindness he'd shown by not taking the locket, but it was the unsettling look of gentleness she'd seen deep in his eyes that stood in direct contrast to what she'd believed.

She sighed. She couldn't deny Ben's sincerity. And certainly couldn't seem to escape his earnest gestures of compassion and care, though she'd tried.

Maybe she could enjoy just a few days of refreshing. Time to collect herself, heal and firm up her determination to make the best of what lay ahead. To find out who Callie Drake really was after years of being first under her father's strict hand, then Max's harsh one.

Though until she left Boulder, she'd just have to stay alert, keep a watchful eye. If she let her guard down completely, she could well walk out of this town with nothing, not even the scrap of dignity she clung to like some shredded lifeline.

"I guess what I'm trying to say is…" Katie's voice slipped through Callie's thoughts. "That if for some reason you oppose the idea of others looking out for you and treating you well, you might as well let that go right now, because it's bound to happen more often than not with the Drake family."

Callie nibbled at her lower lip, unsettled by how emotionally raw she'd felt the last couple of days.

"Believe me when I say that Ben has needed help around here for quite a while. He's talked about hiring someone for months, but has never gotten around to it." Katie moved to the knotty pine chest at the foot of the bed then began laying the garments she'd brought inside it. When she closed the chest with a quiet click, Callie felt utterly helpless to summon an argument. "That man keeps so busy that it would take an enormous weight off him to know that things here and at his home are being tended to as they should."

At those words, an instant swell of compassion-driven duty rose within Callie. After all, she owed Ben. Not just because he'd cared for her while she was sick, but also because he'd taken her in. A total stranger. And he'd tended her with a gentleness that had her broaching tears more than once. If the truth be told, he'd probably even saved her life.

Pulling her damp hair to the side to dry across her pillow, she decided that just as soon as she was the slightest bit stronger, she'd get to work cleaning and cooking. She'd steer clear of him. Fade into the background, as she had the past six months at the brothel. Hopefully he'd forget that she was even here. No one would give her a second thought.

"You know, Callie," Katie began, perching her hands on her hips. A wistful smile stole across her face as she eyed Callie in a way that had her squirming. "I think that you may have arrived just in time for Ben."

Chapter Five

"I was about to send the cavalry after you." Ben left Joseph in his wake, meeting Katie as she entered the front door of his house. "What happened? Did you lose Callie in the tub?"

She gave an innocent smile and edged around him. "She's a slight thing, but no, I didn't lose her. You know how girls can be." Waving a slender hand in the air, she moved toward Joseph. "Talk, talk, talk."

Ben pivoted, peering out a side window to his doctor's office next door where Callie was now. He turned and followed Katie to the dining table. "I was beginning to worry."

"Beginning?" Joseph focused his sightless gaze at his wife then arched an eyebrow Ben's way. "You started worrying the minute you left her side and came over here to wait. You're a dead giveaway when you're nervous, you know. Pacing and clearing your throat the way you do."

Ben produced a half-hearted frown. "And *you* are too observant for your own good."

With a self-satisfied grin, Joseph lifted Katie's cloak from her shoulders and draped it over the chair. "I can't help it that my other senses are so sharp. I come by it naturally."

Ben sighed. "Katie, maybe you ought to give him a lesson in humility. Seems like he's a little weak in that area."

"Believe me, I don't need her to do that. All I have to do is make an embarrassing mess of things, like last Sunday at church, and my feet are firmly planted on the ground." Joseph raked a hand through his chestnut hair.

"What happened this time?"

"Do you really want to know?"

"Well, sure I do."

On a heavy sigh, Joseph shook his head. "I was introducing myself to a newcomer and I reached out to shake her hand, but it wasn't her hand I touched."

Ben grimaced. "You didn't."

"I did." Joseph pinched the bridge of his nose. "I touched her—her bosom," he ground out. "That's not even polite to say in mixed company. Sorry, darlin'," he added with absolute sincerity to Katie.

The way she looked up at Joseph with undeniable adoration was something to see. And snagged at Ben's own yearning for the same.

At twenty-nine, he could've married several times over, but after a difficult end to a relationship while he was away at school, he'd decided to bypass that aisle. And with as much as his practice had grown, he could easily distract himself from the loneliness he felt at times, by throwing himself into his work and his patients.

Unfortunately a certain five-foot-two-inch, auburn-haired, blue-eyed patient residing in the living quarters of his office next door presented a bit of a problem. He was distracted completely by Callie's presence.

"I could've crawled out of the church," Joseph finished.

Grabbing the two empty mugs from the table, Ben couldn't help chuckling. "So, what did you do?"

"Apologized. What do you think? Then held my head high and made some small talk as if nothing had happened."

"If it's any consolation, I don't think she realized you were blind until…well, until that," Katie offered, stacking the plates and bowls and setting them in the basin, too. "She looked as shocked as you did."

"There's the silver lining." Ben clapped his brother on the arm. "You've been working hard at gauging where to aim your focus. Sounds like you're doing a great job—at least where your eyes are concerned, anyway."

"Very funny." Shoving his hands in his pockets, Joseph shook his head. "Next time I'll remember to hold my hand out and let the other person do the grabbing."

Inwardly, Ben was thankful to see the ease with which Joseph was handling his blindness. He was adjusting well. Though he could see some dim shadows, he was pretty much dependent on his other senses. And with the help of his wife, who'd come to him as a teacher of the blind, he'd made huge strides toward independence.

"So, Callie is back in bed, right?" He swung his focus back to the conversation.

"I gave her a fresh glass of water and tucked her in. Satisfied, Doctor Drake?" Katie teased.

Ben gave one swift nod. "As weak as she is, I want to make sure she doesn't overdo it."

"She didn't. We were just getting to know each other, that's all. She seems very nice, but you were right. She's a proud young woman." Katie tucked strands of blond waves into where she'd swept it up at the back of her head. "She almost refused to take the clothes I brought over. And she's determined to pay you for everything. Once she's on her feet again, I'm guessing she'll be a tough one to corner long enough to get her to open up."

He frowned. "That's what has me worried."

"I thought so," Joseph gibed with one raised brow. "You're taken by her, aren't you?"

Ben shrugged off the brotherly taunt. "Well, something about her has snagged my attention, that's for sure."

"Like I've said before," Joseph measured out, patting his chest. "You're a bleeding heart."

Ben dropped his gaze to the floor. "I'm just worried about her, that's all. It's obvious she doesn't have anywhere to go from here. As much as this area has been built up with the railroad coming through and all, a young woman trying to find her way alone is as good as a death sentence. It's clear that she needs a leg up in life."

"You're right to be concerned." Katie threaded her arm through Joseph's.

"What do you mean?" Ben's pulse prickled through him at the way her features pinched with concern.

"I have a feeling that if you want her to stay safe, then you're going to have to find enough things to keep her busy right here. But most importantly, you need to treat her with great care." Her voice grew suddenly soft and strained as Joseph wrapped her protectively in the crook of his arm. "Even though she tried to hide them, the awful scars I glimpsed on her body are a horrid indication that her past is something she'd like to forget."

The thought of Callie enduring a cruel beating, even once, touched every part of his mind and heart, stirring up anger so hot his blood still thrummed with furious force through his veins. Images of her being mistreated thundered through his mind, unearthing fierce rage and the innate need to protect her.

"Callie? Are you awake?" Ben spoke low as he gently knocked on the bedroom door and awaited her reply.

After several silent moments, alarm barged into his head, dominating all reasonable thought. He opened the door, peeking inside.

He hoped he hadn't seemed rude when just moments ago, he'd eagerly ushered Joseph and Katie out of his house. But from the second Katie had returned from helping Callie with her bath, he'd been chomping at the bit to get back over here to his patient.

Especially after Katie had mentioned the scars.

A few old scars. Some newer ones. The bold signs of chronic abuse that had been hidden beneath her tattered undergarments. He'd been fortunate enough to get her out of her wet and dirty dress after she'd arrived. But since then, every time he'd attempt to examine her, she'd flat-out refused, wrapping the covers so tightly around her, he thought she might cocoon herself in them permanently.

Completely missing the glorious opportunity to break free as a beautiful butterfly.

He gulped hard, sliding a trembling hand over his mouth. That thought had come out of nowhere. The delicate image of Callie emerging and spreading her wings to fly had his insides drawing up taut.

Every step from his house to his office, he'd kept telling himself that his was just a doctorly kind of concern, making sure she hadn't taxed herself too much or spiked another fever. But the way his heart thudded inside his chest as he quietly slipped into her room, he knew he was fool—

He stopped cold in his tracks when he glimpsed her nestled safe in a fluff of quilts and pillows. His throat constricted. His pulse skidded to a halt, staring at her as though he'd never seen her before. He was so taken by her innocent beauty that he couldn't seem to tear his gaze away, even if he tried.

He advanced one step closer, growing increasingly uncomfortable at the way his thoughts were so caught up with this patient and the intense need he felt to protect her.

And wholly compelled by the way her auburn hair fanned across her pillow like rich strands of fine satin, gleaming in the sunlight. The late-afternoon glow poured through the windows in warm, comforting streams, lighting on her face to reveal a freshly scrubbed, pink tint there. Revealing also a small, ragged scar at her hairline. He'd missed it before with her matted hair, but now in the soft glow, he could see it. And the sight fixed a tight cinch around his stomach.

He gritted his teeth. Fisted his hands as images of this delicate woman being mistreated whipped through his mind once again. Any man who'd do that to a woman wasn't worth his weight in gold, and must've been raised by the devil's minions. Had it been an employer? Her father?

An appalling suspicion brought him up short.

Surely not Max. Max may have come by lying and cheating and drinking and gambling easily enough, but surely he couldn't have found it so easy to physically harm his own wife.

Or could he?

Ben seethed with fury that Callie had been treated with such abject disregard.

When she stirred slightly and gave a small, distressed moan, he stepped nearer, instantly troubled by the way her brows creased in a frown. The way her mouth turned down at the corners in a distinctive look of fear.

Hunkering down next to the bed, he gently braced a hand on her shoulder. Instead of easing her distress, she jerked hard. Gasped in fear as her eyes flew open. She scrambled to the other side of the bed. Heaved a pillow over her head as if she meant to defend herself.

"Callie?" he spoke low, noticing how the covers quivered with the force of her heartrending trepidation. "Callie, it's me. Ben."

Her fingers blanched white with force. Her breath came now in short pants as she inched the pillow down. She slid a terror-filled gaze to him and blinked hard, once, then again as if bringing him into focus. He saw the light of awareness dawn in her eyes.

"What's wrong?" he asked as she swung her gaze aside, fastening it to the wall as though holding the structure in place. "Are you all right?"

"What are you doing sneaking up on me like that?" Heaving a big sigh, she shot up to her elbows and glared at him. "Do you always do that to your patients?"

"I didn't sneak up on you." He kept his voice low and even. If she'd suffered abuse, then it would certainly account for her skittishness around him. He'd have to tread lightly when it came to touching her. "I came in to check on you. Just like I would any other patient. You've been sick, remember?"

The way she studied him out of the corner of her eyes as he raised his hand to her forehead to feel for a fever, one would think he had a gleaming scalpel poised, ready to make a deep incision. But the way she jutted her chin out in obstinate refusal to show weakness pierced his heart straight through.

"Well, next time knock, if you would, please." She summoned her rose-colored lips into a headstrong pucker that brought to mind dainty rosebuds.

"I did knock." He wrangled up his patience and his good sense, even as unsolicited images of those perfect lips touching against his drifted through his mind. He was pretty sure she hadn't meant to convey that, but darn if his thoughts didn't find their way there. "You must've been having a bad dream."

"I was not," she retorted.

He tried to hide his dismay at her stubbornness. "You feel cool to the touch. I'm glad for that."

When he withdrew his hand, silky strands of hair whispered against his fingertips, kicking his pulse up a notch. He busied himself, pouring her a fresh glass of water as he forced himself to focus on her needs as a patient.

"I hope you didn't overdo it with the bath." He offered her the glass, his errant gaze locking on her lips as she took several generous sips. "I probably should've waited to make that suggestion."

"Don't worry about me. I'm just fine." She fell back to the pillow. "In fact, I can't believe how much better I feel. I'll be up and working probably by tomor—" Her proclamation was interrupted by an unceremonious, lingering yawn.

"No, ma'am. Not tomorrow, you won't." Ben shook his head, trying hard not to grin at her strength of will, and the small glimpse of innocence he saw right then in her cute frown. "Not the next day either. I'll let you know when you're well enough to begin work."

When she knit her brows together even tighter, he had the distinct feeling that he'd probably just stepped on her pride. He'd do it again, since he was a stickler for enforcing ample recovery time. And in her case, much needed rest.

"Thank you all the same, but I am fully capable of judging that for myself." She crossed her arms at her chest. "And I feel *more* than ready to tackle the tasks that need to be done."

"You are stubborn enough that you would, too." He gently grasped her wrist to feel her pulse. "But I'm a doctor. And, honestly, I question whether you're in the habit of making sound decisions regarding your health."

With a protesting huff, she jerked her hand back.

"And before you go thinking that I just insulted you, let me assure you that it wasn't meant as such," he cut in, distracted by the way her soft skin remained imprinted on his. "Given the way you showed up here, I'd say mine is a fair assessment, don't you think? No one in their right mind would have braved that kind of weather in the condition you were in at the time."

Crossing to the dresser, he eyed the locket lying atop her worn garment. "Nothing is worth that."

An uncomfortable silence filled the space between them and since he'd given her his back, he could only guess what her reaction was. But the one thing he'd learned about Callie, thus far, was that even though she'd make gallant efforts to hide her emotions, the uncertainty that churned inside her pretty little head was evident on her face.

"Your brother told me to find you." The words fell from her lips, stiff and measured and loaded with things unsaid.

He faced her. "What do you mean? Max sent you here?"

Suspicion, thick as mud, overpowered the compassion that had just moments ago pervaded his mind. Joseph's and Aaron's strong words of caution echoed through his mind. Maybe they were right—that he was too trusting at times. That he was too much of a soft heart. That he opened himself up to get taken.

But when he peered into Callie's distressed gaze, he couldn't bring himself to make that kind of outright conclusion. Not without direct proof, unshaded by doubt.

"That was his last sentiment." The words sounded as if forced from her lips.

"His last words were about me?" Rubbing his temples, he dragged in a deep breath.

The nod she gave was slow and painfully measured. And seemed meant to sever any further inquiry he might have, promptly pricking his irritation.

"Tell me what this is all about, Callie. Why are you here, anyway?" His voice had raised a good notch. "Because, had I not come along when I did, you likely would've frozen to death on my doorstep. Why would you put your life at risk like that?"

Hauling her chin up a notch, she glared at him as he advanced on her. Flinched as if he might haul out to strike her. Then gave him a hollow kind of look.

And that had him inwardly kicking himself.

When she slowly rolled away from him, he knew he'd pushed too far, too fast.

"Listen, I didn't mean to sound so—" He braced a hand at the back of his neck, feeling every bit worthy to play the evil part of the nightmare he'd found her in when he'd entered the room just minutes ago. He gently adjusted the quilt at her back, tucking it in so that she wouldn't catch a draft. "I'm sorry. I'm just glad that you turned to me."

When he pivoted to leave the room, he could've sworn he heard her whisper, "You were my last resort."

Chapter Six

For the past hours those words, *You were my last resort,* had marched through Callie's mind like dark shadows marking out her future. She'd hoped to eliminate Ben and the disturbing effects of his concern from her thoughts, but his subtle, piney and masculine scent lingering in the room infused her every sense with his memory.

She'd lost track of time as she'd crawled out of bed and slowly made her way around the room. She grasped the satin-smooth furniture to steady herself, studying the few other framed photographs hanging about the room. Raw emotion squeezed her heart seeing the way a much younger Max seemed bent on puffing his chest out in some kind of stubborn refusal. As she inched her gaze over a picture of Max, looking close to the age she'd first met him, she trailed a fingertip over his charming yet devilish grin. That smile had once drawn her, like some forbidden fruit.

But one taste of his empty promises confirmed the

grave mistake she'd made in succumbing to his tempting charm.

The image of Ben's half-cocked grin and earnest gaze barged into her mind as she made her way back to bed. This job was her only hope to earn the money she needed, but the way Ben seemed focused on probing into her life and her heart…well, she was walking in very dangerous territory.

Ben was nowhere near safe.

His caring touch, the tender way he looked at her, the kindness in his gentle ministrations, all of those things worked against her, wearing down a very hard-won safeguard she'd erected. His thoughtfulness threatened to destroy her resolve. Threatened to uncover the vulnerability she'd vowed to protect. She'd never again find herself stuck in a defenseless and vulnerable relationship.

Especially with a man like Ben Drake.

The heavy weight of her desperation pressed in hard, making her feel horribly frail and even weak as she crawled under the covers.

Max had always hated it when she'd cried. Rarely would she weaken, seeing as how he'd grow instantly angry. Out of mere survival she'd learned how to stop up the sorrow, though sometimes there was no helping it. Like an overgrown vine in dire need of tending, grief would smother the light of hope.

Especially after she'd lost her newborn baby girl at birth, six agonizing years ago.

Setting her trembling fingers to her lips, Callie tried to ward off the memory's bitter sting. But Max hadn't allowed her even the opportunity to see her little girl, kiss her, hold her. Callie had been left with an aching emptiness that hurt, even today. And sometimes, out of nowhere, that familiar, painful lump would swell in her throat, her stomach would grow queasy, and hot, unshed tears would threaten.

Would the anguish ever go away? Would she ever rise above regret's relentless storm, enough to see the possible hope of what lay ahead?

Or maybe, for Callie, hope was dead.

"No," she whispered, thrusting the miserable thought away. If she didn't, she'd fall into the hands of a fate worse than death. A fate that threatened to crush her spirit.

Determined to remain strong, she dragged in a steadying breath. She'd need to be firm with Ben, especially after he'd decided that it was his place to tell her what was best for her.

Ha! As if he knew.

He had no idea.

She clenched her teeth, riled in an instant at the memory of his pushy, self-important ways. Twisting a corner of the quilt between her fingers, she remembered how her father had played that role. He'd been like one large, prickling burr to her side at social functions, scaring off any and all suitors with his gruff, unfriendly exterior.

Max had been much the same in his control, only he'd used force when she tried to exert her will. A hard backhand to her face, a rough shove into the wall, or his hands clasped like iron shackles around her wrists.

But his cutting words…they'd been the worst.

Apart from a few short seasons of seeming sanity, he'd remained the antithesis of the man she'd married.

Trembling now, she tried to shut out the bitter memories. Having seen her father take up residence in a stronghold of bitterness and resentment after her mama had died, Callie knew she could never stomach herself if she grew to be the same.

There had to be hope. Even if she couldn't see it, and everything around her looked hopeless, there had to be hope.

There were times throughout the past years when she'd felt a quiet wooing, a gentle calling, to pray. To climb above the darkness that seemed to surround her.

But then the clear and dismal message she'd gotten about God, growing up, would haul her back down with ruthless force. Her father had jammed Scriptures down her throat and demanded she quote them to ensure her standing with God. The minister at their church had beaten his meaty fist against the thick, wooden pulpit weekly, decrying God's fiery wrath and judgment. And then Max, he'd barely given God a second thought unless he'd lost his shirt in a poker game, then he'd railed at God to the point that Callie would cover her ears and hide, fearing retribution.

Was God fickle? Was He liable to punish her at the hint of wrongdoing, as the minister back home often said? Had God sent all the heartache she'd gone through the past seven years as payment for her mistakes?

The very thought made Callie's heart pitch with deep sorrow. Just as she began to feel nearly overwhelmed by it all, she heard a rustling sound behind her back.

Rolling over, she rose to an elbow and found a boy staring back at her. Blinking hard, she took him in.

He was probably eleven years old or so. His dirt-smudged face and thick mop of dusty blond hair that hung almost to his eyes made her think of a sheepdog pup. The image lifted her heavy heart a bit.

"How did you get in here?" she asked when he made no move. She swiped at the moisture rimming her eyes.

His hazel gaze grew wide as he took a step toward the door.

"Is there something you need?"

"I—I was jest—" His focus cut from one thing to another in the room, finally landing on her face. "Lookin'. That's all. Who are you?" He gave an audible swallow then anchored his lips off to the side.

Pushing up to sitting, she leaned against the walnut headboard. "My name is Callie. And you are..."

"Luke. Luke Ortmeier."

"It's a pleasure to meet you, Luke Ortmeier." Nodding, she smiled, hoping to coax one from him, as well.

Instead, his eyebrows crept like small golden caterpillars into a suspicious scowl as he settled his fists on his waist. "Does Ben—Doc Drake know you're here?"

"Yes, he does. Does he know *you're* here?"

"Doc Drake's my friend." He folded his arms at his chest, revealing threadbare holes in the elbows of his muslin shirt. "Fact is...we're best friends, him and me. He lets me come to his office here and have a look at his things. All the time."

For some reason, that bit of knowledge settled on her like a soothing touch. That Ben had entrusted this young boy in that way cut off a few suspicions regarding the doctor's character.

"Oh. I see," she finally said.

"Yep," he confirmed with a single nod. Threading his fingers together, he turned them outward and cracked his knuckles in slow succession, making her wince. "I'm gonna be a doctor jest like him someday. Gonna git me a black bag and some of those whatnots he carries 'round with him."

"Really now?" Callie pulled her legs beneath her as she turned to face him. "Will you attend school somewhere?"

"You betcha. I figure it won't be for long, though, seein' as how I'm learnin' so much already." Snuffling, he wiped his nose with the sleeve of his shirt. The innocent determination that cloaked Luke's unwavering gaze prompted a smile she struggled to bridle. He jutted his chin out and moved closer. "Right now I go to the schoolhouse down the way, but only sometimes, cuz my ma don' like it when I'm gone all day long."

"She doesn't? Why not?"

"She needs me to work," he responded in an offhand sort of way as he eyed the chair next to the bed.

"Here, have a seat." She patted the edge of the bed, wondering if he lived on a large ranch that needed many hands to turn a profit. "So, you must live on a farm?"

Luke edged over to the bed and sat down with hesitant care. And when he trailed his fingers almost reverently over the stitches on the quilt, she felt certain he wasn't used to a well-built, hand-carved bed or lovely quilt.

"Naw…we don' farm. Ma's mostly busy at nights. That's why she needs me 'round durin' the day to do the cookin' and such." Luke peered at her, his gaze drifting to her hair. "I leave now and again when Ma's sleepin' to visit Ben. Make sure he don' need my help or nothin' with his calls."

She smiled, her heart squeezing at his earnest loyalty. For some reason, she found herself easily imagining Ben taking this boy under his wing. Treating him like a son, even.

"I found me some kittens the other day," Luke offered.

"You did? Where did you find them?"

"In the alley behind Gold-Digger's."

"Gold-Digger's?" she queried.

"You know, the saloon. Anyways, the kittens musta' been 'bandoned by their ma cuz they was real hungry."

"Aww…the poor things." She felt equally sad thinking about this young boy scouting around in an alley behind a saloon.

"Don' you worry none." He gave his head an adamant shake. "I'm raisin' 'em now. Ben's helpin' me."

Turning toward her, Luke's face was alight as he looped his left knee up on the bed. "Did Ben ever tell you 'bout me goin' with him that one time?"

"Umm, no. He hasn't mentioned that."

"Well, I did. It was flat-out nasty, too." His hazel eyes transformed from round orbs to narrow slits.

"What happened?"

"A broke leg pinned under a wagon." He pointed

to his midthigh with fingers that bore the red and raw signs of a recent blister that had her wondering what had happened. "We got 'im out jest in time. And Ben, he got the wound all patched up good as new. Took a spell for the feller to walk right again, but he did, jest like Ben said he would."

"That's wonderful. I'm sure the man is grateful."

"Yep. Lucky we was both there seein' to him." He shoved his thick hair out of his eyes then pulled in an exaggerated breath. "Otherwise, no tellin' what would'a happened."

Pride beamed like the noonday sun from Luke—Callie could feel it. "Well, I'm sure your parents had to be very proud of you that day, Luke. Very proud indeed."

He gave a quick shrug. "Don' know my pa. And Ma…well, she don' take kindly to me bein' 'round here none. Says that I'm a big ol' bother. I asked Ben, though, and he said my bein' here is fine by him."

Ready compassion welled up inside her. She set her hand on his arm and gave a light squeeze.

"You're welcome anytime. You know that, Luke." Ben's low voice startled her, sending a tiny shiver of pleasure straight down her spine.

She glanced up to see him leaning against the doorjamb, his arms draped in casual ease at his chest, his legs crossed at the ankles. His steady, discerning gaze seemed to peer straight through to her soul.

She scrambled to cover the bitter scars grooved in her heart from years of regret and shame, but felt like her attempts fell short and that he could see everything.

"Were you sleeping, Callie?" He pushed away from the doorway, his intense gaze shifting not one inch from hers. A tender, thawing kind of smile tipped his lips, warming her from the inside out, even though she wasn't the least bit cold.

"No, no. I was wide-awake." She fumbled with the quilt.

"Cross my heart," Luke added, shooting up from the bed as he drew an invisible X over his heart. "I didn't wake her. She kinda looked like she'd been gushin' some, but she wasn't mad or nothin' when I came in here."

Without even touching her, Ben grabbed her attention, compelling her to look into his eyes. "I didn't think she'd be mad, Luke," he finally said. "I just don't want her rest being disturbed, that's all."

Callie glanced up to see Luke hook his thumbs in his pockets then gesture back at her with his head. "She yer girl? I figured she was, seein' as how she was layin' here and all."

When Callie's cheeks grew hot with an instant blush, she berated herself for acting like a ridiculous schoolgirl. This man had taken her in as his patient, then as an employee. He was her deceased husband's brother. And a low-down thief, spending Max's inheritance before Max could even get his hands on it—by all Max had ever said.

Or was he so bad?

The less-than-exemplary titles she'd tacked on Ben were beginning to hang on threads.

"No. She's not my girl." His crystal-blue gaze sent her heart fluttering inside her rib cage. "Right now,

Miss… Callie is a patient here. Someday when you're a doctor, you'll need to make sure that your patients get plenty of rest, too—so that they recover fully. That's why Callie is here."

Luke angled a perplexed look her way. "She looks fine to me."

Smiling, she glanced from the boy to Ben. "You're a very smart young man, Luke. Very perceptive, indeed."

"Appearances can be deceiving," Ben argued. "She may look better and feel better, but if she gets up and resumes activity too quickly it could cause her to relapse."

"Relapse?" Luke's brow creased.

"It means that she'd get sick all over again." Ben peered down at the boy with steady patience. "We don't want that, now, do we?"

"No, sirree." Luke stuck his face in Callie's line of vision. "Miss Callie, I think you should be lyin' down. When yer sick, ya gotta make sure you get rest. Jest like Ben said."

"You're going to make a good doctor someday," Ben remarked with a satisfied grin.

"Ya got any stitchin' that needs to be done on 'er, cuz I can hold 'er down for ya. T'ain't nothin' for me to do seein' as how small she is," he noted, pointing at Callie as though she wasn't even in the room.

"I'm sure you'd do a fine job, but I don't need to perform any stitch work today." Ben passed an all-innocence glance her way, prompting an unavoidable grin.

"It's a comfort to know that you would help me,

Luke," Callie added, despite being ganged up on. "Really. Thank you for the offer."

"It's almost suppertime, so if you're hungry, Callie, I'll bring you a plate of food." Ben raised his brows in question.

She nodded, suddenly famished.

"You're welcome to stay for supper, too, Luke."

"Awww! I gotta git home 'fore Ma wakes and finds that I ain't made supper yet. She'll wring my neck."

"I'm glad you stopped by. Don't forget your coat and the sweater I fished out of my drawer for you. You might need it. It's cold out there."

"I won't. Thanks for the food. It was real good."

"Come again just as soon as you can. Promise?" Ben held out his hand.

"Promise." Luke clasped Ben's hand in an exuberant handshake then headed toward the door. "Good meetin' ya, Miss Callie."

"Nice to meet you, too, Luke." Callie smiled and waved.

Luke came to a sliding halt then suddenly backtracked. He stood on his toes and crooked a finger, motioning Ben down, ear level. "She's a perty lady," the boy whispered, his words reaching her ears as Ben slowly stood, sliding his pulse-pounding gaze and heart-seizing half smile to Callie. "Real perty."

Chapter Seven

Ben had barely gotten a wink of sleep. His thoughts had been consumed with Callie. Her health. The way she'd been so kindhearted and engaging with Luke. The quick, intelligent responses she'd given. The delicate, lovely features etched with artistic perfection on her face.

In three short days, she'd acquired his attention, and he was pretty sure she hadn't the foggiest idea she'd done so, either. He'd been nothing but professional in his care of her, but it had taken uncommon restraint.

When he'd happened upon her conversation with Luke yesterday, he'd stood mesmerized by her tender ways and warm smile—he'd never seen her smile. It had forced his heart all the way up to his throat, and he'd been thankful they hadn't seen him standing there, if for no other reason than that he'd had time enough to find his voice again.

He stepped up to the porch, waving to Sven Olsson, the lumber mill owner, as the man drove his wagon through the sloppy streets. The foot and a half of snow that had covered Boulder in a thick white blanket the night Callie had arrived was now a sludgy mess of mud and slush. With the mild temperature that bathed the valley this morning, the snow would probably be a memory by tomorrow.

He unlocked the door to his office, his mind settled, as it had nearly every waking moment for the past three days, on Callie. This whole thing was as complicated as it could possibly be. When he stopped to consider the tangled mess, his head spun in outright confusion, leaving him feeling strangely out of sorts.

Striding into the front room with the basket containing her breakfast, he caught sight of the *Help Wanted* sign that was still propped against the window. He grabbed it, reminding himself as he shoved it under a pile of papers that there were several reasons why he should rethink his decision to hire her. And at least a dozen reasons why he should tug his heart away from the direction it seemed committed to traveling in.

He'd been silently naming those reasons off all morning long.

Callie had been married to Max. He sighed—that was a huge reason. And Max had betrayed Ben and his brothers, storming out of their lives with their money and anything else of value—another big reason. Also, Callie seemed set on remaining closed off, and as far as Ben was concerned, openness and honesty were nonnegotiable elements in any relationship.

And both Joseph and Aaron had expressed reservations about her presence here. Most often he trusted their judgment, but he wasn't so sure this time. This morning when Aaron had swung by for a cup of coffee before work, he'd urged Ben again to reconsider his dealings with Callie. Although Ben had come to her defense, he couldn't ignore the tiny niggling of doubt eating at him.

Walking down the hallway to her bedroom, he started when he glimpsed Callie dressed and sitting on the edge of her freshly made bed. He instantly furrowed his brow and gave his head a frustrated shake.

"What do you think you're doing?" He came to a sudden stop just inside the doorway. "It's way too soon to be up, Callie. You're not ready yet."

"I'm fit as a fiddle," she responded with honey-dripping innocence. Clearly avoiding his admonishing gaze, she painstakingly smoothed a hand over her dress.

Though she was still pale, she looked beautiful. The soft lavender print got along so well with her fair complexion and the auburn hair she'd plaited loosely down her back. The color gave her still-too-pale skin some semblance of life—though the pink tint coloring her cheeks made him instantly suspicious that she'd been pinching them for effect.

"I brought your breakfast." He placed the heavily laden basket on the table, bracing his hands at his hips as he tried his best to look stern. "And yes. I absolutely think you're up too soon."

"Nonsense." Callie stood then quickly grasped the bedpost with a trembling hand. The forced look of confidence etched in her features didn't fool him one bit. "If I spend one more hour in bed—I'll be impossible to be around."

Crossing his arms at his chest, he moved a step closer. Then another. "Hmmm…that would be interesting."

She flicked her attention to him. "Believe me, you wouldn't want to see it."

"It'd be nothing new, seeing as how you're being impossible right this very minute." He snapped open the basket and unloaded the contents, the unmistakable look of awe as she peered at the food tugging at his heart.

When she hugged her arms around her middle, it accentuated how thin she was, a small detail which he was determined to remedy. Starting now. She needed to put on weight, and if he had to sit with her at every meal and make sure that she ate, then he would. Gladly.

"Have a seat." He gestured to one chair as he pulled another one up to the table.

He watched her closely, and though his hands itched to steady her, he willed them to remain fixed at his side. He was fully prepared to catch Callie again if she weakened—which was highly likely given the way perspiration beaded her lip.

Once seated, she unwrapped the large hunk of cheese as he poured her a glass of milk. "So, what task would you like me to start with this morning?"

"I'd like you to start by crawling back in bed after you've finished eating," he urged. "That would be the best and *only* start as far as I'm concerned."

She broke off a piece of cheese and popped it in her mouth. "That's not likely to happen, so unless you make another suggestion, I'll find things to do myself." She slid her gaze around the room before she lifted the lid off the four eggs, three biscuits, generous portion of gravy and five thick slices of smoked bacon. "Oh my, this smells delicious. Did you make all of this?"

"Wish I could take the credit, but this morning Katie brought over enough to feed a small army," he answered, watching as she dug in to the cast-iron crock.

Almost as an afterthought, she pulled a napkin out of the basket and laid it over her lap, one-handed, since she kept her other hand clamped tightly around the fork. The way she closed her eyes as she chewed and savored each bite pierced his heart. She was so much like the strays he'd taken in, eating their food as though they might not live to see another meal.

"Taste good?" he asked, smiling.

Nodding vigorously, Callie covered her mouth with her napkin. After she swallowed she said, "This is wonderful. Just wonderful."

"I'm glad you like it."

"Oh, I love breakfast." She speared another chunk of gravy-covered biscuit then shot him an after-thought kind of gaze. "Would you like some?"

"No, thanks. I already ate." He couldn't help but grin at the way she seemed almost relieved.

Bite after bite after bite, she made quick work of the large meal. And he decided, somewhat unexpectedly, that he rather enjoyed a woman with a healthy appetite, instead of the usual picking at food and moving it around on a plate.

She chased down a mouthful of eggs with several swallows of milk. "Can't you think of a task you'd like me to do? Surely there's plenty of work to be done."

"First day up and you're already complaining about the living conditions?" he asked, grinning.

"I'm terribly sorry, but have you looked at these

windows?" She nodded toward the glass panes directly in front of her as she bit down on the last hunk of cheese.

He glanced at the windows. "I know, it's a hazy view, isn't it? I like to think that it creates a sort of blissful mood with the sun shining in."

When she ignored his sarcasm, forking the last of the scrambled eggs into her mouth, he added, "I've never claimed to be a stellar housekeeper."

With a light elegance that contrasted sharply with the hearty way she'd just eaten, she dabbed her napkin to her mouth. "*Stellar* would undoubtedly stretch the truth."

Sliding a fingertip down a glass pane, he affirmed her claim as he shifted his gaze back to her. "*Stubborn* for you, however, wouldn't stretch the truth one bit."

When she turned to look at him, he couldn't tear his gaze from the lovely blue of her eyes, like an early spring sky. He looked deep, but found it disconcerting when he couldn't seem to see past the protective barrier she'd erected. It was as if she'd firmly locked away any deep emotion or poignant memory, and the empty look he found there made his heart ache for Callie.

"I believe you've made note of my stubbornness more than once," she breathed, laying her fork down into the empty cast-iron crock. She dabbed at her mouth again. "Please, tell Katie thank you. That was—it was delicious."

"I will."

Her hand drifted to her neck as she fingered the locket with the lightest touch, peering out the window for a long while.

Ben lifted the crock back into the basket then rested his arms on the table, watching the way her face shadowed ever so slightly, as though some memory haunted her. "You must've been quite a match for Max, seeing as how he had a willful streak in him a mile wide and equally deep."

Callie clutched the napkin on the tabletop, her knuckles whitening with force. "My life with Max is not your concern."

Ben furrowed his brow. "Really?"

"Really."

He tapped the table with one solitary finger. "Callie…if you were married to Max then you're my concern."

"I've done fine on my own, this far. I don't want to be your concern."

"You're his widow." He crooked a finger under her chin and gently turned her head to face him. "Of course you're my concern. You don't have a choice."

The fleeting look of distress that passed over her fine features made him want to sweep her off her feet and carry her through every difficult thing she faced.

"I want to help, Callie. God knows I've been praying for you, but unless you're willing to open up, I can only take care of the outward things you need." He held her gaze. "I can make sure you have a warm comfortable dwelling, good food and a decent wage. And I can protect you from the elements. But I can't protect you from whatever it is that makes you so wary and guarded with me."

Callie pushed up from the table and walked slowly toward the doorway. When she sidestepped then grabbed the thick wood trim as if to steady herself, Ben trained an eye on her every move, her every breath.

She had undeniably captured his attention. She was beautiful, delightfully stubborn, and she was his only connection to Max.

The times he'd tracked Max down with Joseph, they'd found him at a gambling table. There'd been no warm greeting or farewell hug. The last time, Max had barely spared them a glance for a good ten minutes then he'd followed them outside, carrying on about how broke he was, how he needed their help. After he'd lamented about how hard he had it, they'd handed over a fistful of money, and he'd proceeded to thank them with a series of sarcastic, scathing remarks.

The whole thing had finally gotten to Ben. He'd been used one too many times. Infuriated by Max's total disregard for family and the way he was raised, something in Ben finally snapped. The quiet patience that usually was his guiding force was long gone and instead, years of frustration and anger he didn't even know existed had boiled to the surface. To this day he couldn't believe the words that had spewed from his mouth. At the time it had felt like a huge relief, a weight off his soul.

It hadn't taken more than a few hours for him to realize that his remarks were nothing but vengeful and caustic.

And as it turned out, they were the last words he'd ever said to his brother.

The blatant reality of that stung with burning, debilitating force.

Max had died.

And Ben couldn't make amends.

He felt himself slipping further and further into regret. Guilt ate at him, even more so now that he couldn't take back the last, awful words he'd said to his own flesh and blood.

When he heard Callie's feet shift on the hardwood floor, he was instantly jerked from his haunting thoughts. He watched to see if she was steady as he crossed to her.

"I don't know the first thing about what happened with Max," he finally said, stopping just behind her. "But I can imagine there was plenty. And if ever you want to talk about it, I want you to know that I'm a good listener."

On a muffled cough, she hugged her arms to her chest.

"You were married to my brother. Do you know what that means?"

"Apparently not," she breathed. Then did a slow turn to face him, sliding her arms down to her sides and pulling her shoulders back. The look she gave him—as if she were facing a firing squad—well, that nearly broke his heart. "But it appears you're going to tell me, Doctor Drake. So go ahead."

Ben gently grasped her thin shoulders and looked deep into her eyes. "It means that we're family. I don't know what that means in your book, but in mine it means that we take care of one another."

She barely breathed, confusion momentarily flitting across her face, leaving behind a very empty gaze that pierced his heart.

"My brother Joseph and I came after him a few times," he continued, gauging her response as he slid his hands from her shoulders. "Did you know that?"

Her brow furrowed. "You did?"

He nodded.

"I wonder why he never told me that."

"Maybe it wasn't memorable for him. I don't know," Ben offered with a frustrated shrug. "It was memorable enough for me. That's for sure."

A faint tremble stirred her rosebud lips. "Why wouldn't he tell me about that?"

"I'm sure he didn't just forget to tell you. It doesn't surprise me that he'd leave out information like that." Seeing the desperate edge to her gaze, he braced a hand against the doorway and leaned in a little closer, wishing he could just fold her into a comforting embrace. But like the strays he'd taken in, she'd probably run off, or at the very least, close herself up even tighter.

"We found him each time at a saloon," he measured out. "I wish I could say that he was glad to see us."

Her gaze drifted to the floor as if she were looking for some kind of answer there. "Were you trying to get something from him?" she almost accused, as if trying to convince herself even as she asked the question. "Is that why you tracked him down?"

Ben's ire-tainted chuckle died on a sobering sigh. "Not exactly. We were there because we wanted him to know that we still cared. That he was part of the family. And that no matter what had happened in the past we wanted him to come home."

The long moment of silence that followed had Ben

wondering what exactly Max had shared with her about his family. She'd been married to him for seven years. The fact that she was so mistrusting didn't surprise him in the least if Max had filled her head with his bitter, blame-others-for-your-mistakes view on life.

She blinked hard as if forcing back tears. "He never said anything. And—and I wish I had known."

"I wish you had known, too." He threaded his hands together at the back of his neck in an effort to keep himself from reaching out to her.

"Listen, Callie…it has to be hard on you, this whole thing. Since you arrived a little over three days ago, you've made some difficult discoveries. You'd have to be dead not to have it affect you." And Ben was sure that she had too much fight in her for that. "It would've been helpful to meet you at that time. Instead of this way."

Ben recalled the stories Max had told about his wife. That she was demanding. Insisted on having the finest, most up-to-date clothing. Turned her nose up at anything less than the best… Having never met this high-need wife, they could only assume there must be some truth woven in amongst the words.

Looking at Callie now, and remembering the way she'd shown up in such overt need, his heart clenched with painful regret. Max had lied. About his own wife. Of that Ben was certain. She may have been tight-lipped about her past, but he could tell she'd suffered.

For that reason, Ben didn't know whether to grieve for the loss of his brother—or be glad for the fact that he was dead.

Chapter Eight

Water-wrinkled, red and chapped hands were a small price to pay if having them meant avoiding Ben Drake for the day.

He was a dangerous, dangerous man.

Oh, he seemed nice, all right. Probably was everybody's best friend. The town confidant. And though Callie couldn't imagine him lifting a hand to harm another living soul, he was an enemy to her resolve, and definitely a threat to her vow to never make herself vulnerable to another man again.

She'd gladly work her hands raw every day if that meant diverting her attention from him.

Heaving a bucket of cleaning water up to the sink, she dumped the filthy contents out, determined to just as easily get rid of her unruly thoughts regarding that man.

His face suddenly jumped into her mind and she could've sworn she heard his deep, mellow voice right along with it, saying, *"Callie, it's me again and I'm not leaving."*

She hissed a breath through gritted teeth, nearly losing her grip on the bucket handle as she forced the image from her thoughts.

Getting him out of her mind wasn't going to be as easy as she thought. Not when he had such a—a *way* about him.

He was disarming. Charming. And downright pushy, too. The way he looked at her, with that silvery-blue gaze of his that seemed to travel deep inside her heart. His smile…well, that was another risk altogether. The effect of his half-cocked grin wriggled inside her like a sneaky snake, wrapping around her determination and nearly constricting the strength right out of it.

And the way he showed such concern… She'd tried to convince herself that the compassion was all just a wonderfully crafted act. A show. But she was horribly, horribly afraid that that wasn't the case.

Every time he'd get close to her, she'd feel her willpower crumbling like a poorly constructed barricade. She'd catch herself staring at his arms, wondering what it would be like to be swallowed in his steady and comforting embrace. She'd find her focus riveted to his eyes, craving one of his deep, hopeful glances that made her want to believe in 'good' again.

Callie picked up a towel and swiped at the perspiration beading her forehead. She felt near to collapsing, she was so worn-out, but she'd made it through the entire day. And if she put her mind to it, she could last a little longer, before she dropped, half-dead, into bed.

After the conversation she'd had with Ben this morning, she wasn't so sure she'd be any use at all.

To find out that Max had never said a thing to her about their visits had stirred instant anger. He'd always—*always* made her believe that when he'd left home, they'd gladly pushed him out into the world and slammed the proverbial door.

Callie sank into a chair, resting her elbows on her knees. Betrayal had cut deep, lancing all the way to her heart. It'd been her stubborn pride that had seen her through without letting loose the deep cry that begged for release.

She couldn't take Ben's words at face value if she wished to remain exempt from getting *taken* again. The fact that he was Max's flesh-and-blood brother should give her pause, for sure. No matter what she felt when he'd do all of those…well, *nice* things, she had to keep him at arm's length.

Just thinking about warding off his niceness made her weary, though. How long could she keep this up?

Drawing in a deep breath, she wiped her face with her apron, determined not to give in to the raw emotion waiting in the shadows. No man was worth that.

"Callie? Have you seen my stethoscope?" From down the hall came that rich warm voice she couldn't seem to exterminate from her mind.

She raised her head just in time to see Ben walk in the room, his long legs eating up the space between them. The starched, ecru shirt he wore had been rolled up to reveal muscle-roped strength.

"Your stethoscope?" She rubbed a hand over her eyes as she made to stand.

"No. Please, stay seated." He hunkered down next

to her, setting the back of his hand to her forehead. "You overdid it, didn't you?"

"Not at all."

"I don't believe you." Quirking his mouth to one side, he moved his hand down to her arm. "You look completely worn-out. You're pale and your eyes are red and watery again."

She gave a weak, sardonic chuckle. "Oh, Doctor Drake, you do have quite a way with words, don't you? Do you say that to all of the ladies?"

"Only the ones that don't listen to good, common sense." He brushed a tendril of hair from her forehead, sending a quiver through her.

"I listened. I just didn't line up and salute."

When he set his fingers to her neck, palpating her glands, she tried not to squirm under his warm, gentle, spine-tingling ministrations. Scrutinizing him out of the corner of her eye, she wished he'd just keep his doctoring hands to himself.

But something in the way his fingers felt against her skin awakened a hunger that rumbled deep inside her for a comforting touch—*his* comforting touch. It'd been years since she'd really felt cared for.

"Your glands aren't as swollen. That's good news." Standing, he braced his hands on his hips. "By the way, do you mind calling me Ben? Most everyone does, apart from an occasional few, and since we'll be working together it'd make things a little more relaxed."

She nodded, having silently referred to him as such from day one. "Yes, if that's what you want."

"That's definitely what I want. Would you prefer

Miss Callie, Mrs. Drake, or...*just* Callie," he said on a wink.

Oh, she hated it when he winked. Who'd guess that a simple little gesture like that could inflict such massive damage to her resolve?

Averting her gaze to the dainty lilac flowers splashed across her dress, she touched her fingers to the locket at her neck. "Callie is fine," she finally said, pushing herself up from the chair.

"Good, that's settled. Now, about the stethoscope," he continued, clapping his hands together as he walked toward the examination room. "I'm sure I left it in here. Have you seen it?"

She slowly followed him, trying to recall. "I don't remember seeing it and I've cleaned that room from top to bottom."

"I noticed. You've been busy." He scanned the room, a satisfied smile growing on his lips. The day's growth of his dark beard shadowing his face gave him a rugged look that kicked up her pulse a notch. "I'll say it again... I wish you'd take it easy for a few more days, but I do appreciate your hard work. The room looks better than it has since I built the place five years ago." He turned to her, his ice-melting gaze making her stomach turn to mush. "Thank you."

She swallowed hard. "You're welcome."

While Ben began searching around the room, Callie inwardly berated herself for falling so easily for his charm. How in the world was she going to be able to continue working for him? If she had another choice, *any other choice,* she'd jump at it. But she had to have this job.

As it was, with every passing day, she risked having Whiteside find her and drag her back to his nest to settle up. Having spent months walking down the hallways, cleaning his girls' rooms and getting to know them in the process, she'd much rather be here in Ben's care.

For the most part, Whiteside's girls didn't seem to be much different than herself. Harder maybe, but then, she'd gradually seen the same hardness start to develop in herself, too. Though their backgrounds were varied, one thing had seemed a common thread among them: they'd all been down on their luck and had grabbed at the promise of food, clothing and shelter.

But surely they'd never been loved in a place like that. They'd sold their souls for basic needs. Callie would rather go hungry and wear rags under the shelter of a pine bough than do that.

She noticed the perplexed look on Ben's face as he searched in vain. "Maybe you weren't thinking and stuck the stethoscope somewhere else."

He angled his head in challenge.

"What?" Callie said with a defensive shrug. "You might have forgotten what you did with it." She sank to her hands and knees to peer under the examination table again. "I moved every last piece of furniture in this room and scrubbed the floor, so I seriously doubt it's here. Are you sure you didn't put it in your bag?"

When she reached to pull herself up, a warm rush traveled straight through her as he gently grasped her arm to help her. His touch did something to her. It had an effect that was destabilizing, yet completely alluring.

When Max had touched her, it had always been to take. But when Ben touched her…well, his touch just seemed so different, as if he meant not to take, but to give.

"I suppose anything's possible." Ben's jaw tensed. "But I usually leave it in this room since this is where I see to my patients. Wouldn't that make sense to you?"

"I'll keep looking." Callie moved out of his grasp in an effort to calm her pulse. "It must be around here somewhere."

He gave a resigned sigh. "I'm sure it'll show up. But if you happen to remember where it is, I'd be much obliged."

She walked over to the medicine cabinet in the corner of the room and knelt down, ducking her head to look under the large cupboard.

A rattling knock sounded at the door. "Doc, ya in?" A thin, male voice straggled into the room.

"In here," Ben poked his head into the hallway. "What can I do for you, Pete? Is that leg giving you trouble again?"

Out of the corner of her eye, Callie caught sight of a lanky man trailing Ben into the room. "I been tryin' to do what you told me with that salve and them bandages, but—"

"But maybe you missed a time or two?"

Pete hung his head. "Well, maybe."

"You're becoming a regular fixture here, Pete—not that I mind your company, but I'm sure you have better things to do."

When she glanced up to see the man's reaction, she found herself under his close scrutiny.

"I'd like to introduce my assistant, Miss Callie." Ben stepped over to lend her a hand up. "This is her first day working with me."

Callie gained her feet then adjusted the bodice of her dress.

"Ma'am." The man tipped his wide, dusty Stetson to her.

"Callie, this is Pete O'Leary."

"It's nice to meet you, Mr. O'Leary." She held out her hand to the man, trying to hide her surprise when his slender, sweaty hand shook hers so vigorously that she had to tug her hand free. She made her best attempt to smile.

"Ben's gonna be mighty glad fer yer help, to be sure, ma'am. He's been needin' it for a while now."

"When my patients make comments like that, I guess you know that the *Help Wanted* sign was long overdue," Ben commented.

She had to smile at that. If he was half as glad to have the position filled as she was to have this job, then hopefully it'd benefit both of them.

"You look mighty familiar, ma'am." Pete tugged at his collar, but even buttoned clear to the top, it gaped open, revealing his razor-sharp Adam's apple bobbing with a swallow. "Do I know you from somewhere's?"

"I don't think so." Uncomfortable with his direct perusal, Callie dodged his gaze. "I can't imagine where you might have seen me."

"I jest swear I seen ya before. Not too long ago, neither." He took a step closer, narrowing his already small eyes as if to bring her into better focus. "You from around here?"

Callie swallowed hard. She didn't want to cause any embarrassment for Ben and his family, and therefore didn't plan on going into detail.

"No," she finally responded. "No, I'm not."

"Hmm…it's bound to come to me. I'd never forget a perty face like yours."

"So what seems to be the problem today, Pete?" Ben cut in, stepping between her and Mr. O'Leary.

She squeezed her eyes shut, knowing that she would have to field questions. She just didn't want to divulge any more information than necessary, and Ben had obviously been astute enough, good enough to rescue her at the moment.

She tried to counter the warmhearted feeling that little fact gave her with the reasons why he was not safe. But for the life of her, she had a hard time scrounging up even one.

"That shifty little good-for-nuthin' ferret I bought off that travelin' salesman is gonna be the death'a me. I swear to ya, Conroy went and drug that tin'a salve off somewhere and now I can't find it. That varmint steals pert near everything—specially if'n it shines."

"You haven't seen a stethoscope lying around your place, have you?" Turning, he slid a wink to Callie then faced his patient again.

There it was. That wink again.

She buoyed herself against the effects.

"Huh?" Pete pulled his head back.

"Oh, I just can't find my stethoscope. Wish I could

blame Conroy, but that wouldn't be very fair to him since he's not stepped his little paws in here."

"I'm near ready to throw that varmint's wily behind out the door. He's a rascal, I tell ya." The man sliced a breath through gritted teeth. "But sure as shootin', I'd probably miss the little feller."

Ben chuckled, the low, comforting sound like gentle, lapping waves against her soul. He patted his hand on the exam table. "Why don't you take a seat up on the table, Pete, and we'll take a look at your leg."

Jamming his cowboy hat down on his head, the man lifted his chin a notch. "No need fer that, Doc."

"Now, Pete, you know me better than that. I'm just going to check you over, and if the wound looks decent then I'll send you on your way with a new tin of salve."

The lanky man managed an inordinate display of grumbling under his breath while he scuffed over to the table.

She could barely hold back her grin. It was clear as the sun shining through the sparkling clean windows that Mr. O'Leary knew what he was in for when he'd stepped into this office.

She had a feeling that Ben probably always conducted things in that way—making sure his patients were well cared for. He'd done the same for her.

"Get on up there." Ben laughed as he made his way to the doorway. "I've got to run next door for the new shipment of gauze I just picked up. Don't you go anywhere." Turning to Callie, he added, "Would you mind fetching me a fresh basin of water?"

"Not at all," she answered before the front door shut.

Retrieving the basin off the small table, she carried it into the kitchen, cleaned and rinsed it well then filled it with fresh water. She tried to ignore the weary fatigue in her arms as she carried it back to the exam room and set it down.

"I know where I seen ya." Mr. O'Leary gave a thin chuckle. "Denver."

Her stomach did a slow churn as she turned to face him. The smug smile he wore did nothing to calm her as she tried to place him.

She forced her feet to stay planted right where they were even though she wanted to run from the room. Tucking a wayward strand of hair behind her ear, she comforted herself with the idea that he might well have her mixed up with some other woman. How could he remember someone like her, anyway? She'd certainly never tried to draw attention to herself. And the jobs she'd worked most often kept her busy behind the scenes.

"Yep." He nodded slowly. "Took me a while, but I finally figured it out."

"Really?" she asked, silently scolding herself for the strangled sound in her voice.

"Must say, it threw me, with you bein' here, workin' fer Doc Drake. He's a good man, Ben is." He slid his suddenly not-so-friendly, leering gaze up the length of her in a slow, rude manner. "He don' strike me as the kind, but then—"

"The kind?" Callie backed up a step. She wished Ben would return. "The kind to what?"

"Oh, now don't you start with that. You take me fer a fool, missy?" Pulling his hat from a slicked-down mat of bright red hair, he gave it a hearty slap against his leg, sending a cloud of dust into the freshly cleaned room.

Refusing to be intimidated, she braced her hands at her waist as she watched the dust settle. "I'm sorry, sir, I have no idea what you're talking about."

He turned his hat in his hands, a poor showing of teeth centered in his unsettling grin. "That sly dog, Ben. He must be gittin' his money's worth outa ya, huh?"

The coarse chuckle that erupted from his mouth made her cringe. She didn't want to cower like a rabbit frozen in fear, but the way he looked at her… She'd been stared at with that greedy, predatory look before, when she'd been cleaning the saloon and brothel, and it had made her feel dirty.

Then it dawned on her…his meaning. She drew her hands into balls. Tried to still her quaking knees. Fought to calm her raging pulse as he gave her a slow nod.

"You for hire by others, too?" He quirked his eyebrows at odd angles over his beady little eyes. "'Cause it's been too long since I had me a good-lookin' woman like you."

If what Ben had always believed was true, that children and animals were a good judge of character, then Callie surely passed with flying colors.

He watched as Luke angled a buoyant glance at Callie from beneath a mop of sandy hair, seemingly oblivious to the fact that Ben sat with them in front of the woodstove.

Ben braced his elbows on his knees, watching as

Callie met Luke's admiring gaze. The way she smiled at the boy, giving him her undivided, honest attention, made Ben's throat grow thick. Luke might've been ten feet tall for the look of sheer pride on the boy's dirt-smudged face.

It was good to see Callie smile. For the past two days she'd been more withdrawn. When Pete O'Leary had visited two days ago, he remembered walking into the room, finding her eyes wide and wary and her flushed, as if she'd just run a mile.

She'd shrugged off his show of concern afterward, chalking it up to being tired, though that did nothing to minimize the reservations tumbling through his mind and heart. If somehow he'd pushed too fast, and in doing so shoved her away, then he wanted to make things right.

Seeing her now, looking so relaxed and at ease, he dismissed the lingering uncertainty.

The boy had lugged his heavy crate of six-week-old kittens all the way over here—the third time this week—just to show them to Callie since she'd not met the little felines yet. The look of pride on the boy's face as he slowly scooped up a slumbering kitten from the box was enough to make a grown man cry. And the sensitive way Callie responded to Luke made his heart surge with admiration. She was a natural with children.

Taking extreme care, Luke held up the black-and-white short-haired kitten. "I named this one here Mittens."

"Oh, that's a perfect name for her," she cooed, trailing a fingertip down to the kitten's tiny paws. "The white markings on her feet look just like mittens."

"Yeah. She'll be ready this winter." With an endearing giggle, he carefully laid the kitten down into the bed of straw Ben had replenished just moments ago.

"How did you come up with the names for your kittens?" she asked.

"Easy." He fluffed some of the straw around the sleeping kittens. "I 'membered hearin' Ben prayin' once for one'a his animals, and I got ta' thinkin'...if'n God answered his prayers 'bout that, maybe He'd answer me if'n I asked Him 'bout names."

Ben squeezed his eyes shut for a moment, sobered by the simple and complete trust Luke placed in him. Even when he felt like his faith in God was challenged, this young boy found enough faith to grab on to, to spur him toward believing.

"And this one's named Fluffy." Luke reached down into the crate and carefully lifted out a puff of gray fur as he glanced up hesitantly at Ben. "I know it sounds kinda girly and all, but with how puffy he is, that's what fits 'im. Don'cha think?"

"Absolutely." Ben gave a brisk nod. "You couldn't have chosen a better name."

"It's a perfect name." Callie cradled the ball of fur then nuzzled the downy softness. "He's so soft, isn't he?"

Wide-eyed, Luke observed Callie as if he'd never seen a woman fawn over an animal before. It didn't surprise Ben one bit that Callie would be kindhearted toward animals. Watching her now with the kittens, the way she quietly cooed to them and gently pet them, he could see that she was likely as much of a soft heart as himself when it came to animals.

"I had a cat named Fluffy once." Ben omitted the small fact that the cat had been a female.

"Really?" Luke's eyes widened further.

"I sure did." Ben slid one finger gently down the kitten's head, inspecting his eyes and nose as he did. "This little guy's eye infection seems to be healing up just fine. What do you think?"

Luke instantly scrambled to his knees, leaning over and peering at the kitten. "Yeah. I'm thinkin' so, too. There ain't no more stuff in his eyes."

"You're doing a good job caring for them, Luke." Callie smiled at the boy then briefly swung her gaze up to Ben, making his mouth go suddenly dry.

When she looked away, he focused his attention down at the crate of felines again and drew out the biggest kitten in the box. "What about this little guy? His fur is almost like a panther, but with how fat his little belly is, he reminds me more of a black bear cub. What's his name?"

Luke pulled his mouth to the side, staring at the kitten in Ben's hands with a look of pure affection and pride. "That's Benjamin."

Ben's heart tightened in his chest. A lump formed in his throat. When he stroked the tubby little guy, he realized that for some reason, Luke naming this kitten after him meant more than if an entire state had been named in his honor.

"And why did you call him that?" Callie asked softly.

Luke hitched his shoulders up. "Oh, I don' know.

I just wanted to, that's all. Seemed like a good name for a little cat like him."

The boy's bashful response had Ben swallowing hard.

"Well, Benjamin's certainly a nice-looking kitten." Callie touched the kitten's thick paws.

"You must be feeding them plenty. This little guy is as round as he can be." Ben handed the kitten back to Luke.

"Yeah. I feed 'em four times a day, jest like ya said." He lowered his head and touched his nose to the kitten's. Then he shot his bright gaze up to Callie. "Ya know what?"

"What?"

"He's really strong. He can almost climb out'a this here box already."

"That's quite an accomplishment for such a little one."

With an adamant nod, Luke pulled the kitten to his chest, cradling it in a most tender way. "He's prolly gonna be a real good hunter, too. And the way he's always snugglin' with the other kittens, I'll jest bet he's gonna make a good daddy cat. Don'cha think?"

"Yes, I'm sure he will." Callie slid her gaze to Ben, the subtle look of appreciation he saw there taking him aback. "What about this little girl?" she finally asked, averting her attention to the last kitten.

"Oh, I named 'er Beauty." Luke lifted the long-haired black-and-white kitten out of the crate and delicately handed her to Callie. "After you, Miss Callie."

She gave an almost inaudible gasp as she cradled the kitten in the crook of her arm. "Aww…that's so sweet, Luke." She blinked hard, giving Luke's hand a squeeze. "So very sweet."

"Thanks." He cracked his knuckles, emitting tiny popping sounds into the quiet room.

The tender warmth that stole over Ben as he stared down at Luke and Callie took him by surprise. Never had he felt quite this way. It was almost as if he could picture himself as a father and a husband.

He'd been hard-pressed to get this young woman out of his mind. Found himself daydreaming about her when he had several reasons not to.

He couldn't help himself. She unknowingly commanded his thoughts, even when she'd made a habit of avoiding his presence.

The tender gleam in her eye gave him pause.

"She's the prettiest one in the bunch," Ben agreed quietly.

Silently, he hoped that he could keep his head enough to notice if she decided to turn on him. But seeing her now, the genuine way she had with Luke, he couldn't imagine her being so callous.

Chapter Nine

Callie…

The sight of her stole the breath from Ben's lungs.

Securing the reins, he stepped up to his office porch, all the while reminding himself to breathe. He had to will his pulse to stop pounding through his veins as he took her in.

The color of her dress was so perfect for her that Ben was pretty sure God must've had Callie in mind when He created the emerald-green shade.

He gave a long, approving sigh. "You look very nice."

"Thank you." She met his gaze with a wobbly smile. Then fastened the last button of the heavy wool cloak he'd purchased for her yesterday. "And thank you again for the cloak. It's very warm and more than suitable. I'll pay—"

"Shh…" Ben gave his head a slow, steady shake. "You agreed you wouldn't argue with me about this. Remember?"

She dropped her focus to the small reticule she held—compliments of Katie. "I must've been delirious."

"I don't think so." Ben chuckled low. "You seemed perfectly in control of your actions and speech."

When he prepared to help her up into the wagon, she pulled away. "I can make it just fine by myself."

"I know you can, but you're a lady and I'd like to help. All right?" He circled her waist with his hands and lifted, noticing that she didn't feel quite as fragile as she had the night she'd come to him, almost a week ago. Once she was settled on the seat, he spread a thick wool blanket over her lap, silently thanking God for the progress she'd made.

It had been a whirlwind six days. Since she'd been up, she'd been as diligent and hardworking as anyone he'd ever known. And though he was getting her to open up a little, he had a feeling it'd be a long time before she'd trust him.

He'd promised himself that he'd not push her to open up too hard too fast, but the more time that ticked by, the harder it was to live up to his promise.

Situating himself next to her, he clucked his tongue to urge his horse along, waving to the bundle of folks in a passing wagon.

"I'm glad you decided to come with me today," he said, glancing down at her. "It'll mean a great deal to Katie to have you join us for dinner after church."

"Are you sure it'll be all right if I attend with you?" Her knuckles grew white as she clutched her reticule.

"Of course."

She avoided his questioning gaze, her throat visibly contracting.

"Are you worried that you won't be welcomed? Is that it?"

She traced a fingertip the length of the braided, drawstring cord closing her bag. “Not exactly.”

“Then what?”

She turned those beautiful eyes of hers on him. The depths of which made him seriously question his long-ago decision to remain a bachelor.

“It’s just that, well, a while ago I inquired after a job at an orphanage that was run by a church. They made it clear that they didn’t want me working with the children.” The faintest of winces contorted her delicate features.

“Why would they say something like that?” He swept his gaze over each of her lovely, sweet features. “I can’t imagine anyone turning you down.”

He hadn’t been able to turn her down. She had that certain look about her that pierced the heart. It wasn’t a piteous look, but he imagined it was a David-against-Goliath sort of look. He’d seen it in her from the get-go…a certain strength and courage to face the unknown.

“Did Max have anything to do with the minister’s perception of you?”

Her focus shifted downward. “He wasn’t looked upon very favorably. Wherever we ended up living,” she added discreetly.

“And being his wife, neither were you, right?”

Determined silence was his answer. The way she’d skirted the truth, as if she’d somehow dishonor Max, made Ben’s heart ache. He wondered if she felt like she had to protect Max’s memory by protecting his name.

“Ahh, Callie. I’m sorry.” Knowing how hard it must’ve been to be shunned because of Max, his heart broke for her. "I've seen the patient and loving way you interact with Luke. You would've been their best and brightest asset."

He had to battle back the instant irritation that her words had triggered inside him. He was furious at Max, yet again, for not taking into account how his actions might affect others.

And he was furious at the way some people, in the name of God, could set up ridiculous standards that had nothing to do with God, and everything to do with their selfish desire to have a respectable club of sorts, instead of a family.

He struggled to tamp down his ire as he reined his horse to a halt in the wagon-packed churchyard.

"I didn't tell you that for your sympathy. The last thing I want is your sympathy." Brushing a hand over the wool blanket's thick weave, her fingers trembled. "I just don't want to cause any embarrassment for you or your family. That's all. If you'd rather that I not attend with you, I'll completely understand."

Ben set the brake and faced her. Draping an arm on the seat behind her, he gave a brief nod to a lone straggler entering the church building.

"Listen to me, Callie…" He covered her hand with his, pleased that for once, she didn't startle or pull away at his touch. "First of all, no one here knows that you were Max's wife. They'll find out sooner or later, but even if the whole town was privy to the information, it wouldn't matter."

At the faint strain of some hymn seeping through the thick, tall doors, Callie moved to get down from the wagon, but he pulled her back to the seat.

"You'll be late." A slight quaver undermined her usual calm reserve.

"It's all right. I'm sure that God is every bit as much here with us as He is inside with the other folks." He gave her hand a gentle squeeze and continued. "I'm sorry about what happened in the past, Callie. It was wrong, plain and simple. I can assure you that you'll be welcomed here." He nodded toward the church building.

Staring down at where his large hand covered hers, he felt an overwhelming desire to protect her like this and more. He wanted to help her trust again. To break through her protective barrier, allow her to spread her wings and fly.

But what if she refused his help?

And what if the niggling suspicion that had taken up residence in his mind was warranted? In the past two days he'd discovered that both his stethoscope and then some tweezers had come up missing. In five years of doctoring, he'd never, ever misplaced those things. He might lack for administrative and housekeeping skills, but he'd never been careless about the tools of his trade.

Though she might be tight-lipped about her past, there was nothing about her demeanor that would point to her being a thief. She was caring, patient and hard-working, just to name a few noteworthy attributes.

So what was he thinking?

He fought back the doubts and suspicions, ashamed that he could've made such judgments. He'd thought himself to be above such actions, but this whole situation with Callie had so far served to reveal a side of himself he didn't much like to see.

"You have to know that when that kind of judging and blame-casting happens, it has nothing to do with God." At the faraway look in her eyes, he crooked a finger under her chin. Drew her half-shuttered gaze to his. "People can be cruel. But God… He's never cruel."

"I want to believe that," she whispered, nibbling her bottom lip.

He wanted to believe it again, too. At one time he'd never questioned that. In spite of his mounting failings and regrets, he wanted to trust God. But could he ever forgive himself for the way he'd made a mess of things with Max? For the way he'd let his brothers down in their greatest time of need?

Had God brought Callie into his life as a way to make up for his failings with Max? Something about that idea didn't quite sit right, deep down, but he couldn't deny that the thought had crossed his mind more than once.

After a long moment, he instinctively reached out to pull a fallen leaf from where it had floated down to land in her hair. The backs of his fingers touched feather-light and ever so briefly against her cheek.

She slid an expectant gaze to him, the whisper of space between them resonating and humming from the simple touch.

When he held the bright yellow aspen leaf out to her, she took it from his hands, staring down at it and tracing the brown spots marring the brilliant yellow hue. "It's always so sad, isn't it? That things have to die?"

"It is. But if they didn't, new life could never come

forth." Trailing a finger over the edge of the half-dried leaf, he smoothed his hand over hers. "It's God's way," he said as much to himself as to her.

He relished the feel of her silky-smooth skin. Cherished the tender glimpse of vulnerability. It was small, but real.

The heated, searing sensations, as true and as warm as if he sat before a blazing fire, seeped from her fingers all the way up to his heart, belying the freezing temperature outside.

Its power affected him in ways that undermined his common sense. Tugged at his self-restraint. And upended his moral convictions.

Pulling his hand back, he hauled in a thick, steadying breath. Willed his heart to slow to a normal beat. It took every bit of summoned restraint to resist the urge to pull her into an embrace. His arms ached to hold her and drive away the shadows of her past. But she wasn't ready for that.

He didn't know if he was ready for that, either.

While she tucked the leaf into her reticule, Ben jumped down from the wagon and crossed to her side, lifting her down. "It's only fair to warn you..."

"Warn me about what?" She burrowed a hand in the pocket of her cloak.

"Some of the busybodies in the congregation will probably beeline for you just as soon as the pastor says his last *Amen.*" Winking, he crooked an arm and held it out for her then led her up the steps of the white clapboard church. "Don't mind them if it happens, though. They're fairly harmless. Besides, they'll love you."

Upon opening the door, he stepped into the harmonious sound of his favorite hymn. He wasn't sure he'd ever felt as proud as he did now, walking into church with a lovely young woman beside him.

He had to remind himself that Callie was Max's widow.

And his employee.

But he sure did have a hard time remembering that.

While the congregation sang the last strain, he noticed heads turning, staring at him as though he'd brought the Queen of England into their midst. Ben was certain that his appearance here with Callie would be an all-out shock. Over the years, the townsfolk had finally gathered that he wasn't in the market for a wife and, for the most part, had ceased trying to set him up with every eligible young woman this side of the Rocky Mountains.

That had been a relief of epic proportions.

He wasn't sure he was in the market now, but he couldn't deny the attraction and growing feelings he felt for Callie. And he sure couldn't ignore them since they seemed to consume his every thought.

With a hand placed lightly at her back, he ushered her into a pew toward the back where Joseph and Katie stood singing. The eager way Katie greeted Callie, and the way Callie seemed to glow from that warm acceptance, made his heart swell with an odd sense of satisfaction.

When the song ended and the people turned in the pews to greet each other, Joseph leaned toward Ben. "You're putting the fear of God into some of these women." He shot Ben a playful grin.

"What?" Ben asked, confused.

"Katie tells me that Callie's liable to make a stir among the single men, with how pretty she looks." He leaned back in the pew then, all casual and carefree, as if he'd just made some benign comment on the weather.

Katie answered with a shake of her head and bridled grin.

Out of the corner of his eye, Ben could see a pink blush touching Callie's cheeks.

Throughout the service, he found himself inarguably distracted. First…by the simple fact that Callie, beautiful and extraordinarily resilient, was seated here beside him. And second…by the guarded reactions he witnessed from her. Her tightly balled fists. The rigid posture she'd maintained throughout the service. She closed her eyes and tensed several times, as if bracing herself for a regular old fire-and-brimstone, pulpit-pounding message. Hugged her arms in unyielding protection of herself—a stark contrast to the single-minded strength she normally displayed.

But it was the visible sigh she gave at the benediction that made his heart fall hard. It was as if she was inordinately grateful to have made it through the church service without some scathing rebuke aimed her way.

The image still weighed him down when they arrived at Joseph and Katie's house to join his family for dinner. The way she seemed to trudge on in the face of her apparent fears made him want to pry away all of the demons of her past.

Though right now it seemed she was facing a new demon.

Aaron.

From the moment they'd stepped foot in the house, Ben could see and feel the heated stare coming from his brother. For some reason, Aaron's mistrust and dislike of Callie had swelled like some infected wound in the past two days. Though he had no intention of making a scene about it, Ben was bound and determined to wrangle Aaron aside and pin him with a few pointed questions.

"Callie, I want you to meet my family. Of course, you already know Katie," he said.

Katie threw her arms around Callie in a huge hug. "This is my husband, Joseph," she said, stepping back. "He's the second Drake brother."

When Callie reached for Joseph's hand, Ben noted that the usual awkwardness that new folks felt with Joseph's blindness didn't seem to be present. At all. "It's nice to meet you."

"Good to meet you, too," Joseph greeted congenially. "Sorry if I embarrassed you with the comment in church."

Her carefree chuckle made Ben proud. "That's all right."

"Katie's told me a lot about you."

Callie shifted a surprised look to Katie.

"All good, Callie," Katie affirmed.

"This is Zach," Ben continued. "He's the baby of the bunch."

The past months that Zach had spent working on a cattle ranch just north of town had done him a world of good. At twenty-two, he seemed comfortable in his own skin. Even sported a manner of contentment about him that had been refreshing to see. And he looked healthy, had packed on hard work-induced muscle. Though he was a good three inches shorter than Ben's six feet three inches, Zach made up for it in his sturdy build and quick speed.

Zach held out his hand to Callie. "It's nice to meet you, Callie. Good to have you join us today."

"I'm glad to be here."

"I hear you've been spending time reading classic literature," Ben aimed at Zach, chuckling when his brother rolled his eyes in mock annoyance. "Shakespeare and the like… Maybe you can do a little recitation for us today?"

"Yeah, what do you say?" Joseph added.

"What is this? Pick on your little brother day?" Sighing, Zach angled an exasperated gaze down at Callie. "They love to do that to me. They think it makes them all big and powerful. Honestly, I doubt they could even understand the stuff."

"Really," she braved, sliding a hand to her mouth.

"Well, that's insulting enough," Ben parried.

Zach stuck Ben with a good-natured glare. "Ya know, you'll rue the day you decided to pick on me."

"You're all talk," Ben retorted in dismissal. "Powerful as a charging bull, but harmless as a nursing pup."

"Rue the day?" Joseph cracked with an ire-provoking smirk. "You've definitely had your nose in Shakespeare again, haven't you?"

"So what if I had?"

"Nothing." Joseph crossed his arms at his chest, shaking his head in innocence. "Not a thing."

Zach sighed. “Don’t think that just because you can’t see, Joseph, I won’t take you.”

Joseph pulled his shoulders back, his deep amber eyes sparkling as he rubbed his hands together. “I’ll be waiting for you. Listening for your every move.”

“And this is Aaron,” he said, gesturing to where Aaron leaned into the corner of the room.

Callie stepped forward and held her hand out to Aaron.

When Aaron merely looked from her hand to her face as if determining whether he could stand touching her, Ben almost decked him. Right then. Right there. Scene or no scene. No matter what bias Aaron had against her because of Max, it didn’t warrant that kind of rude behavior.

At Ben’s scathing, dart-throwing gaze, Aaron finally came to his senses and stepped up to shake her hand, but the look in his eyes bordered on sheer malice as he peered down at Callie.

“Callie, would you be so kind as to help me in the kitchen?” said Katie in a rescuing request.

“Of course.” Callie slid her hand from Aaron’s grasp. When she turned to follow Katie, she avoided Ben’s searching gaze and whisked right past him.

Not a second later, Ben jerked a thumb toward the door, fully expecting Aaron to follow, and if he didn’t...well, then Ben would drag him out. When the door closed, Aaron, Joseph and Zach were all standing on the porch with Ben.

“*What* was that all about?” He balled his fists at his sides. Glared at Aaron.

Aaron managed a disbelieving snort. "What are you doin' bringing her to church? And then here?"

"We invited her for dinner, Aaron." Joseph raked a hand through his hair. "Katie wouldn't have it any other way. Neither would I."

With a rough shake of his head, Aaron narrowed his eyes. "I don't care if the president of the United States invited her. She has no business being here."

Ben jammed his hands to his waist, his blood nearing the boiling point. "She has just as much business being here or at church as you or I do."

"Well, if she's fooled you that bad, then you're twice as blind as Joseph here," he spat out, slapping the back of his hand against Joseph's broad chest.

"Keep my eyes out of this." Joseph raised his hands.

"Sorry."

"What is the matter with you, Aaron?" Ben challenged.

The loathing that had cloaked Aaron's words hung in such an awkward fashion for him—as if wearing an overcoat four sizes too big. He'd gone through a difficult time in the past months, but even that didn't account for the bitter edge with which he spoke.

Ben attempted to tamp down his ire. "I mean, I know that you and Max weren't exactly on the best of terms when he left, but why do you have to hold that over Callie's head?"

Aaron's jaw muscle visibly pulsed. "It's not right that Max could plant an unwanted kiss on Ellie-girl without so much as a thought. He did it just to spite me, even though he knew good and well that her lips were for me, and me alone."

"I'm sorr—" Ben began.

"Then he added insult to injury and blistered me in a fight," Aaron added, his jaw so tense, Ben thought his tendons might snap. "It's something I'll never forget."

Ben remembered well how enraged Aaron had been that night. Drunk, Max had stumbled in one evening shortly before he took off for good, and had helped himself to a kiss with poor unsuspecting Ellie. She'd tried to push him away and wriggle from his grasp, but he was too strong and too drunk.

Settling his hands at his waist, Ben commanded Aaron's attention. "It was wrong what he did to Ellie and to you."

"It was wrong what he did to me. To Ellie. To you. To all of us," Aaron hissed, throwing his hands up. "But for some reason, you had to go after him to try to make amends. Not once, but several times."

"I'd hoped to reason with him." Ben felt the old, familiar clamping in his gut at the memory of each failed endeavor. "To talk some sense into him."

"He was weak. Weak willed." Aaron pulled his mouth into a rigid line and gave his head a stiff shake. "And it seems to me that if you have to talk someone into doing what's right, then it'd be just as easy for them to be talked out of it. They've gotta *want* to do what's right. And Max, he never did."

Ben's whole body tensed, ready to retaliate with some kind of excuse, but Aaron made sense. "You're probably right. As many times as we'd try to convince Max that he was heading down the wrong path, he never would turn around for good."

Aaron jammed a finger into Ben's chest. "Exactly. And if he did it for a short season, then it wouldn't take more than a gentle breeze to blow him into the wrong path again."

"I had to try," he finally said. "I promised Ma I'd raise him to walk the right path." And he'd failed. Miserably.

"I don't think Ma or Pa, either one, expected you to raise the dead." Aaron jammed his hands into his pockets. "And as far as I'm concerned, that would've been an easier task."

Joseph gave a frustrated sigh. "Ben carried more responsibility with Max than you may realize, Aaron. It wasn't easy being the oldest and having to look after all of us."

"I'm not questioning that. What I am questioning is why, with the way Max betrayed us time and again, he feels the need to look after that girl in there." Aaron cast a glance over his shoulder to the front door. "She just can't be trusted. Max said himself that he'd shacked up with some harlot."

"You watch your mouth," Ben warned, his voice low as he glared at his brother.

Aaron met his icy, angry stare. "That woman in there helping Katie is one-and-the-same. Do you know that?"

"You know how easily Max lied." Joseph's jaw pulsed.

"I just met her, but I sure can't imagine Callie playing the harlot." Zach's eyes grew wide. "Come on, Aaron…lighten up. Does she look like one to you?"

Aaron narrowed his scorn-filled gaze.

Ben stood firm, the ready contempt Aaron exhibited raining down upon him. Images of the dress Callie had shown up in flashed like streaks of lightning through his mind, the tattered and worn ruby-red dress, cut so low in front that the word *decent* would come nowhere near describing the garment.

But nothing about her—not her actions, the way she walked, the way she handled herself around other men—would come close to measuring up to her being a harlot.

"She just doesn't have it in her," he finally said.

Aaron raised his eyebrows in a way that had Ben ready to haul off and hit him. "She's a harlot, Ben, and she's going to rob you blind, just like Max did. Mark my words. Even from the grave Max is trying to tear us apart. And he's using his widow—his *harlot*—to do it."

Ben jammed his brother against the side of the house, doing everything in his power to contain the fierce anger rushing through his veins. "I'm warning you now, if you don't shut your mouth about this, I'll shut it for you," Ben ground out. But even as the words crossed his lips he wondered why he felt the need to so vehemently defend Callie. Something about this sprightly young woman had snagged every single protective bone in his body. Maybe his heart, too.

Chapter Ten

Callie had never felt quite so wanted. Or unwanted, where Ben's brother Aaron was concerned.

She glanced around the kitchen in the doctor's office, searching for the thick pad she needed to lift the steaming teakettle of water from the stove.

Aaron was nothing if not surly. Proud. Arrogant, really. She hadn't shrunk back from his unfriendly, cold greeting that—she recalled with a generous amount of indignation—had come as hard as tack from him. If not for dear Katie saving the day and suggesting Callie keep her company in the kitchen, Callie might still be standing there, five days later, toe-to-toe and nose to chest with Aaron.

His reaction only confirmed Max's descriptions of his brothers, and had irritated her almost as bad as a rock in her shoe. As far as she was concerned, she'd spent far too much time and mental energy trying to reason his response. Maybe he harbored more ill will toward Max than could be overcome. Or maybe he simply had a strong aversion to auburn hair.

With a dismissive shrug and sigh, she headed toward the exam room where Ben waited with a twitchy Mrs. Duncan. Whatever had caused him to be so aloof, she wasn't about to let it waylay her.

Things were finally starting to look up.

Callie hadn't ever felt so useful. Between cooking hearty meals for Ben, cleaning his office and home, and assisting him with patients, her days were full. And very rewarding.

On the way home from knitting with Katie one day, she'd even gotten an offhand chance to talk with one of the girls from down at the Golden Slipper. Callie had beelined to strike up a conversation with the woman.

Someday, after she had the debt paid off and a little nest egg for herself, she wanted to maybe try to help some of the ladies. Where others looked on them with a derisive snort, Callie had seen another side to the women in her months of cleaning for Whiteside. She had to believe that those women yearned for something more than what they had settled for. That somewhere hidden beneath their hard exteriors were vulnerable young women in need of a friend and a fresh start. And Callie wanted to be that for them.

She entered the exam room, feeling bolstered by the fact that she was making a difference. The wages she'd received so far had been generous. In fact, if things continued as they had been the past ten days, she could well deliver the remainder of the balance to Lyle Whiteside by Christmas. Though this would be her first Christmas without Max and she was sure to feel that loss, being freed from his gambling debt, and from a mean-spirited bully who stood for everything she detested, would be an enormous weight off her shoulders.

Feeling a wonderfully foreign sense of control over the direction of her life, she set the kettle next to the basin and smiled. "Here's the hot water you asked for."

"Thank you." Ben glanced her way as he stood in front of Mrs. Duncan.

Callie turned and took in the plump woman who sat perched on the examination table, her full skirts draped around her in a fluff of light gray-and-peach print fabric. Like a hen refusing to leave her nest, she folded her hands in her lap all prim and proper, while fiery-red wisps of hair frayed from her chignon in an unruly contrast.

"So, you're Miss Callie…" A sedate, almost deflated smile contorted Mrs. Duncan's thin lips.

"Just Callie," she responded, unable to miss Ben's quick wink. "How do you do?"

"I saw you at church a few days back. But land's sakes, I can't seem to go far without some soul or t'other stopping to speak at me," she muttered, somewhat self-importantly. The way the woman worked her hands and leaned forward slightly conjured up unpleasant images of a spindly spider preparing to cocoon its prey.

Callie bit back an amused grin. At least it was glaringly apparent what this lady was here for. Information.

Callie hated to disappoint her.

"By the time I'd made my way clear to the back of the church, why, you were up and gone already." Her haphazard eyebrows rose in awkward arches over her eyes. "Seems that you made an awful fast escape."

"Actually, I lingered for several minutes." Callie stepped over to the cupboard and retrieved a tray of clean and readied medical tools for Ben. She took shamefully morbid satisfaction in lifting a sharp, gleaming scalpel from the metal tray, as though inspecting it. "I had the pleasure of meeting some of the church members. Very nice people you have here in Boulder."

"Course, the welcome wagon sets the tone there. If a body makes folks feel welcome as they join our town, those folks'll turn around and do the same." She gave a swift, confident nod then added, "At least that's what I'm always preachin', bein' the Chairwoman of the Boulder Welcome Wagon, as I am."

"You must be making quite an impact." Callie nibbled her lower lip.

"My friends certainly tell me I do." Mrs. Duncan's full face creased in a pleased-with-herself kind of grin. "So, what brings you to Boulder?"

Ben cleared his throat as he took the tray from Callie's hands. "Callie's my assistant. She's here working for me."

As if struck by a sudden case of dropsy, the woman's face fell. "Well, now, I can see that just as clear as a church bell, Ben Drake," she scolded, her beady-eyed gaze not leaving Callie for an instant. "What I'm meanin' is—"

"Mrs. Duncan, I believe you came here about your toe. Am I right?" He gently tapped the lady's brown-booted feet poking out from under her skirts.

"My toe?"

"You said that it'd been giving you some trouble. You thought you might have an infection?" he added as if to jog her memory.

"I did?" The woman's face pinched in squeamish distaste. Peering down her nose, she stared at her feet as if unsure whether they belonged to her.

When Ben turned and gave Callie another wink, her stomach launched into a flurry of activity. His playfulness, and the ready, warm smile he always seemed to have for her, constantly caught her off guard.

"We would hate for you to go walking around town with an infection." Pushing his sleeves up, he scanned the display of medical instruments. "That wouldn't do at all. Would it, Callie?"

"Not at all. In fact—"

"So, girl…do you have a husband? Family?" Mrs. Duncan's loud voice interrupted. "Setting a good example as Boulder's welcoming committee, I surely wouldn't want to miss them on my rounds. I make it my *personal* business to get to know the new folks in town."

Callie ventured a guess that there was more to her work than met the eye. Mrs. Duncan struck her as a woman who definitely made it her business to not only meet folks, but to get to know every little thing about them, as well.

"No family," she answered carefully.

"She's part of our family," Ben added.

"Well, now, that's not unusual for you Drakes," she dismissed. "Especially you, Ben Drake. You'd take in most any wretched thing."

Callie clamped her jaw tight, wondering if she'd actually heard the woman say something so tactless.

"I hear tell from Mr. Peter O'Leary that he's seen you before?" A distinct element of accusation threaded through the woman's words, sending dread snaking through Callie's veins.

Swallowing hard, she suddenly craved fresh, cool air. Maybe from some mountain over on the next range. A heated blush crept slowly up her neck. She'd do most anything to keep it from advancing all the way to her cheeks, but it was no use. Her cheeks started burning even as the thought popped into her head.

She chided herself for responding as if she'd been caught red-handed in a crime. She had nothing to hide. Sure, she'd not been forthcoming with Ben about the details of her life with Max, or about some of Max's activities, or about the fact that she'd carried Max's baby. But knowing how difficult it must be for Ben and his brothers to learn of their estranged brother's death, she hadn't wanted to add to their misery and grief. If his brothers had composed their own pile of bad memories with Max, then she wouldn't want to add to it with her own unpleasant recollections.

In the strange, misplaced sort of way that had ruled her actions for seven years, she felt as if she had to protect Max. Or at least Max's memory.

"I have no idea where Mr. O'Leary would've seen me, ma'am," Callie finally said, her voice steady.

With a dirty sense of shame, she remembered the way the man had looked her up and down as though she was one of Whiteside's 'girls.' The leering gaze he'd given her had made her stomach convulse with instant dread.

"Really, now?" the woman uttered slowly. "No idea?"

Ben cleared his throat, the muscle at his cheek pulsing. "Could you slip your boot off for me, Mrs. Duncan? More than likely, you've got one of those sore spots again, and I'll probably want to do some cutting around the nail. What do you say? We might as well get at it." He picked up the same scalpel Callie had held. "Callie, could you please get me a clean towel. Maybe some thread for stitching while you're at it."

Mrs. Duncan shoved her thick frame off the table, landing with a heavy thud on the floor. "Actually, my toe is feeling better already." She stomped her foot. "You see. It don't give me a lick of pain. I'm sorry to take up your time like this, Doctor, but I do believe I'm feeling much improved."

"Callie? Are you awake?" Ben's voice sounded from across the room, followed by a knock on the door.

"Ben?" She turned over in bed, forcing her heavy, sleep-laden eyes open.

"I'm sorry to wake you at such an hour." Urgency permeated his words. "May I come in?"

She tugged the blanket up to her chin. "Yes, of course." Blinking against the dim lantern light penetrating the dark room, she brought him into focus. "What time is it, anyway?"

"Just past two o'clock."

Callie rose to her elbows. "Is everything all right?"

"That's why I'm here." He knelt down next to her.

His nearness, the warmth of it and the way his breath fanned feather-light over her skin, sent every nerve ending humming to life. "I was hoping that you could help me with a delivery. Mrs. Nolte's oldest boy, Travis, showed up at my place a few minutes ago. His mama's laboring."

"She's having a baby?"

"Yes. And I'd feel better if I had extra help on this one since her husband's out on the range. She had a hard time with the last baby."

Sitting up, Callie rubbed her eyes and stared at Ben's whisker-shadowed features. The flickering lantern light played across the strong, masculine angles of his face, knocking her heartbeat off-kilter. Had the night's nipping chill not sent a quiver of reality down her spine, she might've thought she was in some wonderful, breathtaking dream.

She gathered her wits about her. "Yes, of course. Just give me a couple of minutes. I—I'll be right there."

Callie made fast work of getting ready. But with each inch the wagon traveled from town, her stomach knotted tighter and tighter. She'd never attended a birth except when she'd been an active participant in the delivery of her very own baby girl. The wee hours of that night had been a blur of pain and suffering. One that had left a deep chasm in her heart she feared might never heal.

She'd barely spoken of the baby girl in the past six years. Max hadn't tolerated her tears or any of her nostalgic musings. Not even when anguish and sorrow threatened to consume her. She'd had to pull herself up from the trauma and move on. But, silently, she'd grieved plenty.

There were no guarantees with pregnancy. But never in a million years would she understand why it had been her baby girl who had been taken.

Had God punished her for defying her father? Had He made the past seven years one continuous, humiliating consequence born from one hasty decision? If so, there might never be a second chance for Callie. A second, life-changing chance to find the peace she longed for.

Perhaps Mrs. Nolte also had done something that was grounds for punishment. Would this woman lose her baby, too?

Hoping to allay her growing fears, she grasped her cloak tight around her and asked Ben for a detailed description of what she could expect. She found great comfort in the methodical, calm way he explained the process. His knowledge of the situation went a long way to quelling the insecurity and apprehension creeping around her heart.

Ben pulled the buggy into a small ranch yard where the full moon's gentle, pearly light illuminated a generous-size house that sat amidst two large barns.

He set the brake. "If you can gather the items we'll need, I'll check her over to see how close she is to delivering."

"All right," she responded, mentally going over the list of things he'd told her to prepare.

"Travis should've made it back by now, and Dillon will be here," he said, grabbing his bag from the floorboards and helping her down. "But since they're just eight and four, it'd be best if you could coax them back to bed."

Callie agreed, her heart going out to the little boys. Before they were even at the door of the clapboard house, she could already hear a woman's anguished cry coming from inside.

Her heart sank rock hard and fast. Her stomach lurched while brisk, northerly winds whipped mercilessly across the front yard.

When the door opened, a young boy, his eyes wide with fear, stood before them. "Ma's hurtin' real bad, Doc."

"It's a good thing you came for me, then, Travis," Ben answered, hunkering down to eye level with the youngster. "Your pa will be proud of you."

"I sent our ranch hand out lookin' for him."

"Good thinking." Ben gave the lad's shoulder a squeeze.

"Thee'th thith way," came a soft voice from the shadows. The younger of the two boys stepped forward in his nightclothes, his chest stuck out proudly even as he clutched a blanket in his chubby little hand.

"Thank you, Dillon." Ben gave the boy a gentle pat on the head then passed a sobering glance Callie's way before he disappeared behind the door.

"Why don't you boys come with me?" She bent over to catch their attention. "My name's Callie."

Almost in unison, the two boys turned and peered at the door behind them. The staid and brave way they held their ground, like two little soldiers guarding a sacred monument or a beloved patriot, had her struggling to keep her composure.

From the bedroom their mother cried out in pain once again. Callie motioned for the boys to follow her as she made her way to the kitchen to boil water. While she located clean rags and other linens Ben had requested, she tried to distract the boys by asking questions. She also found herself praying for the woman as pain-filled moans filled the dwelling.

After she tucked the children into bed, she loaded up her arms and carried the hot kettle and rags into the bedroom, closing the door behind her.

"Just pour the water into the basin there, Callie," Ben instructed, his hand bracing the pale woman's shoulder as she toiled for each short panting breath. Perspiration had plastered the poor woman's light brown hair against her head. Tiny rivulets streamed down her face. "I'll need your help on the other side."

Willing her heart to slow its frantic pace, Callie did as she was told, each step toward the bed a silent victory.

"Mrs. Nolte, this is Callie, my new assistant." Ben felt the woman's pulse at her wrist. "She's going to be helping us tonight."

"Hello," Callie offered.

The woman's eyes fluttered open and she braved a smile. But her face almost instantly contorted with the arresting pain of another contraction. She stared up at Ben, pleading with a fearful gaze for him to help.

"It's all right. Just take deep breaths," he uttered, his voice like a gentle, calming touch.

Callie sat on the bed opposite Ben, patting the woman's face and neck with a cool, damp cloth.

"Good, Callie." He nodded her way. "Just keep her as comfortable as you can."

As the moments ticked by she felt her control slipping from her desperate grasp. She silently berated herself. If she couldn't maintain her composure in this situation, she could well risk losing her job. Ben needed her to keep her head.

And this poor woman…she needed her, too. Callie had only to focus on the pleading, fear-filled look etched in Mrs. Nolte's kind face to testify to that.

Ben glanced up at Callie every now and then, offering her an encouraging look. She found that if she kept her eyes on him, watching the way he worked with quiet direction and confidence, she was able to maintain her focus.

Just seeing how tender Ben was with the poor woman as she battled through each contraction made Callie's heart swell with gratitude. He handled Mrs. Nolte with a gentle strength and wisdom, challenging every last, lingering question as to Ben's character.

The tenderness she witnessed called up a heartbreaking contrast of bad memories. When her own nightmare barged into her mind, Callie's tender world jerked off its axis.

Six years ago this had been her. She'd labored for a day and a half. There'd been no doctor, not even a midwife. Max had refused. And she'd struggled alone through every pain and contraction. She'd been exhausted at the end, much like this woman. And it had been with the final push that she'd lost consciousness.

The woman gasped, jerking Callie from the agonizing memories. "Oh, dear… Please. Help me. I can't—"

Mrs. Nolte clutched Callie's arm with such force, as if a pack of ravenous wolves were nipping at her flesh. She cried out in pain, but this time it merged into an almost animal-like grunt as she bore down, pushing.

"Lift her shoulders, Callie. Prop another pillow behind her." Ben moved to the foot of the bed.

"You're doing fine, Mrs. Nolte," he spoke above another gasping cry. "Just make the most of each contraction, all right? You're almost there."

Callie looked up and found herself pinned by Ben's concerned look. In spite of her best attempt to keep every emotion shuttered deep inside, he must have sensed her unease and raw emotion. He was like that, and where it had strongly irritated her just a few days ago, now it almost gave her a strange sense of comfort.

"Are you all right?" he mouthed while Mrs. Nolte sank with relief, albeit brief, into the feather bed as that contraction subsided.

Callie nodded, probably a little too vigorously since Ben cocked his head as if to say *Are you sure?*

She had to be all right.

Ben needed her.

Mrs. Nolte needed her.

When the woman began growing restless again, Ben braced a hand at one of her knees. She clawed at then gripped the bedsheets, her perspiration-beaded brow furrowed in pain and concentration with the onslaught of another labor pain.

"Garrett is going to be proud of you when he gets off the range, ma'am. Just keep up the good work and the little one will be here before you know it."

Callie heard Ben's encouraging words to the

woman, but all she could seem to see was her own worst nightmare playing out in her mind. The helpless moans. The intensity of each tormenting contraction. The fear that permeated the room. The evening was wrought with stark reminders of six years ago.

She could face anything. Blood. Gaping wounds. Protruding bones. She just didn't know if she could face the most natural and beautiful moment, when a newborn child entered the world.

It loomed as a horrifying reminder, a shameful testament to the fact that she'd been unable to last out the labor to see her child born safely. Maybe if she could've held on for a few more minutes—even seconds—she might've given birth to a healthy baby girl. Maybe if she'd taken matters into her own hands and insisted on help. Maybe if she'd never made the decision to marry Max in the first place…

But then—then she'd never have known the intimate honor of carrying her baby for nine blessed months.

With the wound still gaping in her heart, she had to wonder if nine months in the womb was better than nothing at all.

When she peered down and saw Mrs. Nolte sinking into the bed as though she was unable to last through another second of labor, Callie felt overcome with desperation.

"Mrs. Nolte… Don't—don't give up now, ma'am," she managed through clenched teeth and a thick throat. "We're right here with you. Just make it through this one. That's all you need to think about right now."

Ben's head snapped up. He stared at Callie for a

lengthy moment then gave her a single nod of appreciation. “That’s right. Just this one contraction,” he echoed.

The next minutes seemed to blur by for Callie. Mrs. Nolte made it through the last few pushes with one encouraging word after another from Ben and Callie. And when her newborn boy finally emerged, Callie felt a shared sense of enormous relief.

But the relief was swallowed whole in the next few moments. Her blood ran cold. Dread and raw fear pulled down all hope like a lead weight.

The baby was bluish in color. He wasn’t moving. Wasn’t breathing. Wasn’t making a sound.

While Ben focused completely on tending to the newborn, Callie’s hands trembled uncontrollably. She tried to calm Sarah Nolte’s growing panic. Tried to stuff down her own seizing panic. But she couldn’t seem to tear her gaze from the little baby, wondering if this was what it’d been like when her little girl had been born.

When the newborn finally let out a small whimper what seemed like minutes later, Callie’s stomach surged. The cry of relief that came from Mrs. Nolte, and the quaver Callie heard in Ben’s voice as he assured the woman that all was well, brought ready tears to Callie’s eyes.

She might’ve cried a river then, but she couldn’t. Wouldn’t. If she let herself break down now, she might never, ever stop up the deep well of tears that capped off all of these long and anguished years.

Chapter Eleven

Ben was still shaken inside.

Though it'd been three hours since Sarah Nolte had given birth to her baby boy, and the little guy was doing just fine, the tenuous moments when it seemed the baby wasn't going to breathe still tromped over Ben's weakening confidence.

This baby, the third boy in the Nolte family, had been bigger than the first two. Probably close to nine pounds. And he'd come face up and with the cord wrapped around his chubby little neck. Sarah had been courageous throughout, and by the look on Garrett's face when he flew through the door an hour ago, he wholeheartedly agreed.

Ben remembered breathing a heartfelt prayer of thanks when the strapping newborn had finally taken his first breath, after a good minute outside of the womb. Within half an hour, the little one's coloring was nearing perfect, and his cry hearty. A very good sign, indeed. The baby was healthy. Doing well. And even suckling at his mama's breast as Ben ushered Callie out to the wagon to return home.

So why didn't those things comfort Ben deep down? It seemed that one tragedy after another stacked up against him, challenging his ability and skill as a doctor. Ben had failed to turn Max around and bring him back into the fold. He'd failed to save Aaron's sweet baby and dear wife. And he'd failed to restore Joseph's vision.

Over the past hours, it'd been all he could manage to hide the lack of confidence that plagued him without mercy.

The look in Sarah's eyes—that pleading, unquestioning look that bequeathed Ben far too much faith in his expertise—troubled Ben to the core. And then the way Callie had peered at him, with a vulnerability and trust as tender and fragile as a tiny seedling. He swallowed hard, remembering the way it shook him deep—made him wish he could be found worthy.

But the fleeting look of terror he'd seen cross Callie's face had almost brought his heart to a sudden, sobering stop. Plain as day, he'd seen it. Her fear had tugged at his compassion with relentless force.

As the pale glow of morning's earliest light climbed over the horizon, Ben urged the horses down the frost-covered, grassy path. He contemplated the sense of helplessness he felt, finding an odd sense of quietude as he watched the way the horses' warm breath made rhythmic puffs of steam into the cool and crisp late October air.

When Ben glanced over at Callie hugging her arms to her chest, his uncertainty faded some. She was a mystery, just Callie. A deep and exquisite and beautiful mystery. A gift to him the last two weeks…tonight. Perhaps forever?

His nerve endings hummed to life. Grew louder as he saw the wisps of hair that had fallen in loose waves from her braid. He had to clench his fist tight to keep from touching the rich strands. The radiant, almost ethereal way her fair skin reflected the first inkling of breaking light entranced him completely.

"Are you cold?" he finally asked, his throat gone tight.

"A little." She breathed into her hands.

Ben grabbed the lap robe from behind the seat and settled the blanket over her shoulders. "Here, this should help."

The fact that she didn't flinch at his touch or his nearness was heartening. "Were you all right in there?" On a sigh, Ben threaded a hand through his hair. "Did I throw too much at you?"

He focused down the road, realizing that maybe he'd assumed too much from her. But for several days now, she'd been remarkably adept as she assisted him with patients. Never once had she balked or seemed uneasy. She'd handled situations as naturally as if she'd had training. In fact, he couldn't quite get over just how perfectly she complemented him.

"I guess I thought with how well you've handled other patients this past week, you'd do fine."

She turned toward him. "It's not that."

"Then what is it?" He met her gaze, and even in the pale light he could see the way her eyes took on that faraway, pain-filled shadowing. "The way you looked, I thought I was going to have another patient on my hands."

Callie lifted her chin in that familiar and stubborn I-don't-need-your-help kind of way. "It won't happen again."

Ben gave his head a slow shake. "Callie, I—"

"I promise," she added, laying a hand on his right forearm. "I won't let you down again, Ben. I don't know what came over me, but I promise I won't let it happen again."

He dropped his gaze to where she held his arm, saddened that she could think him so demanding and unforgiving.

And moved by the way her touch soaked right through his heavy sheepskin coat and wool shirt, to his skin. Then to his heart. Her touch, her lingering gaze, the way she seemed torn between maintaining her distance and reaching out to him, brought his breath up short.

He covered her hands with one of his. "You didn't let me down, Callie. You were wonderful back there." He gave her hands a gentle squeeze, hoping this glimpse of vulnerability heralded, even as the morning's first light, a new day. "The encouragement you gave Mrs. Nolte couldn't have been more perfect. It kept her with us."

She swallowed visibly. Sitting so close to her, he could feel her tense as she averted her attention to where the horses plodded steadily toward home. He hadn't really been privy to this fragile side of Callie before, and seeing it now made him wish that he could take her in his arms, sheltering her from her silent storm.

Right now it didn't seem to matter that she'd once been married to Max. Or that her past was still shady, at best. Or that a hint of suspicion hung over her.

"What matters to me isn't *that* it happened, but *why* it happened. You looked like you'd seen a ghost." Pulling on the reins, he brought the horses to a halt in the middle of the path. "Please. Tell me what's bothering you."

She pulled her hands into her lap. "I can't."

"Can't? Or won't?" Ben closed his eyes momentarily and sighed, wondering if he was pushing too much. But at the moment, it didn't really seem to matter. He opened his eyes and looked at her, pointedly. "Do you trust me, Callie? Have I ever given you a reason not to trust me?"

Callie studied him as though trying to dig deep into who he really was. It evoked a strange discomfort when she looked at him like that.

Was she seeing Max?

Or comparing him to Max?

The thought of being compared to his wayward, immoral brother stung deep.

"The way you're looking at me now, I'd think you were trying to find some reason to mistrust me," he choked out. "Some piece of evidence that would justify your determination to keep your distance. For whatever reason, you're committed to staying at arm's length."

"No. It's not like—"

"Do you think I'm like Max? Is that it?"

"I thought—I thought she was going to lose the baby," she finally said, her rosebud mouth drawn down at the corners as though she might cry. "She almost did."

"But she didn't." Toning down his ire, Ben cautiously reached up and smoothed wayward strands of hair from her face even as he battled back his own taunting failures and silent accusations.

"She was in such pain." Her voice quavered. "And having such a hard time."

He cupped his hand at the side of her head, struggling to remind himself that ultimately life wasn't his to give or take away. That ultimately, God was in charge of the outcome.

Seeing the remnant of torment in her eyes, he searched for words that would ease her. "It was a difficult labor, but she made it through—and you were part of that."

She almost leaned into his touch, but not quite. "I feared for her, Ben."

He swallowed past a lump that had been there since the time they'd arrived, three hours ago. "I did, too."

Her breath caught. "You did?"

"I did. It was touch-and-go. But we made it through. God saw us through," he added, remembering how desperate he'd been to find God's presence there guiding him.

Ready emotion seized his throat as he recalled the overwhelming expression of gratitude and relief he'd seen on Sarah's face when her baby gave his first, small cry.

And the look of trauma and fear he'd witnessed

marring Callie's lovely features. There had to be something more to the unveiled look of horror. Yes, she'd feared for Sarah Nolte and her baby, but was there something beyond the sympathetic, compassionate concern? Some dark and daunting image from Callie's past that had come back to haunt her?

Callie might as well have aged ten years in four days.

With an unnerving sense of irony, she peered at her image in the mirror hanging above the bureau. The woman staring back at her, all done up and ready to attend Boulder's annual Harvest Dinner and Town Hall Dance, appeared far younger than the way she really felt.

Ever since Sarah's baby was born, Callie's struggle with the haunting memories of her own tragic delivery had been nearly insurmountable. The incident had dredged up the familiar pain and deep ache far more than she'd experienced in the past.

But comfort seemed out of her reach. Like the rippling cascade of a waterfall echoing through mountains, she was almost sure she could hear comfort's alluring, peaceful call, but she couldn't seem to find it.

She'd longed, yearned for someone to talk to these past days. Callie found herself craving a real peace to subdue her very real fears and hurts, but nothing she did seemed to satisfy. Not throwing herself into her job, helping Luke with the kittens, befriending one of the girls at the Golden Slipper, or even knitting mittens for the orphanage with Katie.

Perhaps she was missing something. Something

bigger than herself. Bigger than the things she did to feel useful. Bigger than the stubborn strength she'd strapped on these past years. Bigger than even Ben Drake.

In a moment of utterly shameful weakness, she'd almost spilled everything to him. About her pregnancy, the labor, the delivery. But she just couldn't tell him about all of that. Doing so would only add to the shadows already cast over Max's memory. Besides, there was certainly no guarantee that he'd believe her.

With a heavy sigh and determination to climb above the grief, she adjusted the lace collar on her emerald-green dress as images of Sarah's chubby little boy flitted through her mind.

Jared Benjamin Nolte…

He was such a sweet baby, so content and peaceful. She'd gone along with Ben to check on the little one the day following the birth, and when Mr. Nolte had told Ben that they'd named their new boy after him, Ben had become disconcertingly quiet.

A heartwarming smile coaxed up the corner of Callie's mouth.

First a kitten. Now a baby.

Ben should be honored—at least that's what she thought. But for some reason he seemed agitated by the whole thing. As if he didn't think he deserved the tribute.

Callie hadn't met anyone who deserved such an honor more than Ben Drake. He was caring. Kind. Compassionate.

He was everything that Max was not.

For the past three weeks she'd seen Ben tend to

one patient after another, his steady demeanor never altering from his usual calm and gentle way. Even in the face of one patient's rude behavior, he seemed to walk above the unseen realm of discourtesy, treating the person with respect and consideration and patience.

At times, he seemed almost larger than life.

That very attribute had been the quality that had drawn her to Max seven years ago. It was the trait that had dramatically changed after they'd married, too. But for some reason, with Ben things seemed different, as though the person she saw day in, day out was the real, genuine Ben.

When she heard the front door open, she felt her heart skip a beat. He was here. Ben had come for her.

And she was going to be attending the dinner and dance with him. It'd been a last-minute request on his part, and though she was fairly certain he was just making an attempt to include her in community happenings, she'd been glad for the invitation. For as long as she could remember, she'd wanted to attend a function like this. But first her father had deemed dancing a sin, and then after she'd married, Max hadn't wanted anything to do with an occasion like this.

He'd preferred a more raucous crowd to fulfill his desire for pleasure. And thankfully, he'd never once forced Callie to accompany him.

Regardless of the fact that she considered herself to be fairly naive, it wasn't hard to guess what he did when he was out. He'd drag himself home in the wee hours of the morning with red lip paint on his neck and face. And the overwhelming smell of perfumed powder and booze wafting around him in a noxious cloud.

Having no intention of dwelling on those unpleasant memories, she swept her gaze down her dress one last time then emerged from her room.

She glanced up just in time to see Ben come to a sudden stop in the hallway. He stood there all still and straight, staring at her, almost as if he were seeing her for the first time. His gray-blue eyes darkened with an intensity that sent a quiver of contentment all the way down her spine to where her toes curled in her new, buttoned boots.

"You look lovely, Callie." His voice was low and husky as he advanced a step closer.

She slid a hand up and touched the locket at her neck, taking in his appearance, as well. Indulging herself—if truth be told—in his striking good looks. "You're looking very nice, yourself, Ben," she breathed, swallowing hard as she noticed how handsome he looked in his dark gray trousers, crisp white shirt and navy blue vest and coat.

Feeling a warm blush coloring her cheeks, she worked frantically to stuff those thoughts back down.

After Max had died, she'd vowed never to make herself vulnerable to a man again, and now here she was, practically throwing herself at Ben. As good as Ben Drake seemed, there had to be a flaw to him. And if she knew what was best for her, she'd figure out his weakness just as soon as possible.

If not for the fact that she felt her resolve fade away whenever she was around him, she might be able to do just that.

Though a good three feet still remained between them, they may as well have been nose to nose. Her heart fluttered madly inside her chest. The distance between them seemed charged with a force she was sure she could touch, its command so real and powerful that she had a difficult time breathing.

A sudden shyness crept over her. She glanced down at her dress, fingering the fine fabric between her thumb and forefinger. "I've worn this before," she mumbled. If she'd been any more ridiculously inane right then, she might have won some kind of award for it.

"I know." He nodded, one side of his mouth curving up in one of those devastating sideways grins of his that made her knees all weak and stomach all aflutter. "You look beautiful."

Max had said that kind of thing to her early on in their relationship.

But never—*never* had his words matched the look in his eyes, like Ben's did now.

Pulling in a steadying breath, she grasped at her wilting resolve before it fell completely away from her. She made a mad dash, groping for a way out from the strangely consuming emotions he induced inside her.

"I must say, you're getting better with your compliments, Doctor Drake," she managed, her voice trembling. "From—how did you put it—'You look completely worn out, pale, and your eyes are red,' to this," she blurted, trying desperately to douse the mind-numbing, heated intensity that seemed to build whenever they were in close proximity.

"That's not fair." He slid one breathtaking step closer. "When I said those things, I was making a medical statement of fact. Trying to get through that stubborn head of yours that you had no business being up when you were so sick."

She willed her hands to grow still. "And I thank you for your concern. But I'm none the worse for the wear. Am I?"

He shook his head. "You give *stubborn* a whole new meaning." Dragging in a breath, he moved to grab her cloak and hold it out for her. The soft edge of a grin tugged at his mouth. "Are you ready to go?"

"Absolutely," she answered sweetly with a smile, as he covered her with the warm wool. "Will Katie be there?"

"Oh, yes. She loves to dance. So does Joseph."

Before she even knew it, he was securing the ties of her cloak at her neck, the errant, featherlight brush of his fingers against her skin sending heated sparks straight through her again.

She willed her mind to stay clear of the emotions she felt at the moment. "Really? Without his sight?"

He held the door open for her as he picked up the basket of food and followed her out. "Without his sight."

"Well, that's remarkable. The first time I met Joseph, it was a few moments before I even realized he was blind." Peering at Ben, she couldn't miss the sudden, far-off look that had half shuttered his gaze.

"He has a remarkable ability to look you in the eye, doesn't he?" His voice had grown tight and strained.

"Ben? Is there something wrong?"

"No." His quick retort was far from convincing.

Something had altered the fine mood he'd been

in just moments ago, and Ben wasn't given to being moody.

"What's bothering you?" she tried again. "You can tell me."

"It's nothing," he ground out through tightly clenched teeth as he stepped down from the porch.

"Are you sure?"

"Yes. Let's get going." He turned around and gave her an are-you-coming kind of look.

Callie threaded her arms at her chest and planted her feet. She nailed him with the most serious look she could muster. "Is this how this works? You can pry and prod to try and get me to spill my heart, but the same rules don't apply to you?"

"It's not that, Callie. And I certainly haven't pried or prodded." He raked a hand through his dark hair. "I've been very *careful* with you."

"I'm choosing to ignore that you've been *careful* with me." Failing miserably, she stalked to the front of the porch. "I don't want to be treated as though I'm fragile."

His wide-eyed look made her cringe. "Can you honestly say that you wouldn't have taken off if I had been pushy?"

"Maybe," she forced through clenched teeth.

He tilted his head, quirking one dark eyebrow.

"All right. So I would have." She jammed her hands on her hips. "But what about you, Ben? Here you are, obviously bothered by something all of a sudden, and I… Well, I just wanted to help. That's all."

Ben unceremoniously set the basket down on the ground and clenched his fists. "You want to know?"

"I wouldn't have asked otherwise."

He gave a shuddering sigh. "Every single time I see Joseph, whether it's at church, in his home, in his wood shop, or out and about on the streets of Boulder," he added, fanning an arm in one giant, sweeping gesture toward the heart of town, "I feel responsible for the fact that he can't see more than the dull gray shadows he does."

"Responsible? Why?"

Ben dragged a hand over his squared jaw. "Isn't it obvious? There must've been *something* that I missed. *Something* I could've done for him that would've made a difference." Even in the fading light she could see his jaw clench, his hands fist at his sides. "If only I'd had more training. Or done something differently."

"Does he blame you?" she asked in stunned disbelief.

She didn't know Joseph Drake well at all, but she couldn't imagine him casting even the slightest bit of blame Ben's way.

"No. He's never said so." He shook his head slowly then added, "But, then, Joseph's a big enough man that he wouldn't admit to it even if he did feel that way."

An odd sense of anger built inside her. Not at Joseph. Not at Ben. But at the very idea that Ben had been on the losing end of a lie.

"Then why are you blaming yourself?" She stepped down and came to stand in front of him. Made bold by her resolve, she reached out and grasped his hand. "I've seen you work, Ben. You're so thorough and attentive with all of your patients. Boulder is lucky to have you around." Her chest tightened with emotion as she gave his hand a warm squeeze. "You're a wonderful physician. You have to believe that."

His mouth formed a harsh, unforgiving line as he stared down at where she held his hand. "But I couldn't save my own brother from a life of groping around in the darkness. I couldn't protect him from the life he now faces."

"But you did all you knew to do. And from what Katie's said, you brought her into Joseph's life," she added, desperate to ease his guilt. She swallowed hard. "You gave him a gift. Love. That's more than some people will ever hope to know."

Was it more than she could ever hope for?

Chapter Twelve

Ben had never told another soul about the guilt he carried. Not Aaron, not Zach, and certainly not Joseph. There wasn't an ounce of self-pity attached to his struggle, but with each additional failure he met, the sense of responsibility and regret he carried haunted him with greater ferocity.

No matter how successful he was at his profession, no matter what praise others had given him, he'd let his family down. He was desperate for a way out of the shame and regret that had him trapped.

He hadn't felt inclined to offer another word of explanation as they walked, side by side, to the town hall. But for the distance between them, he may as well have been on the other side of the Flatirons. When they'd arrived at the already crowded town hall, Ben had to force his bad mood aside. For Callie. He was pretty sure, from the excitement lighting her face when he'd first arrived to pick her up, that she'd been looking forward to this evening.

He'd been looking forward to this, as well. It'd been

three weeks since Callie had first come into his life. And in that short amount of time he'd grown very fond of her. The spirited way she met a challenge, like when Mrs. Duncan had come to the office to steep information from her. The brave way she faced an uncomfortable circumstance, as she had with the birth of the Nolte baby. The deep, almost childlike need she had for friendship, yet refused to acknowledge.

And then there was the way her eyes, recently, had begun to light up whenever she caught sight of him. He could tell that she'd try to snuff out the telling glow. Had cleverly found ways to busy herself in order to avoid him. But he'd be willing to wager the house, the farm and the whole town of Boulder that she felt the same innate, powerful attraction as he did.

He remembered that first night she'd shown up, the way his heart had been pierced by one look in her blue eyes. For all the stubbornness, strength and willful tilt of her chin, she had gripped his heart and mind without even trying.

Ben had spent a good amount of time praying about what purpose God had for him in all of this. Would God defy all of Ben's reason and lead Max's widow straight into his arms? Could he trust God with the outcome of all of this? Ben was committed to finding a way through this and had to trust that God was committed to the very same thing.

Even last night when he'd prayed about his relationship with Callie, he'd felt like God reminded him of the Old Testament Scripture addressing the issue of widowhood. Where God charged the husband's brother to take the widow for his own wife. To see after her. To protect her.

Ben would never presume to know God's plan, but he couldn't help but wonder if he was living out that Scripture.

He didn't consider himself a hero. A martyr. Or even a strict religious man. Just a man who knew God. A man with compassion. And, as they entered the newly built structure, a man with a growing amount of love for a certain young woman who'd shown up on his doorstep like some lost and lonely stray.

If only he could put to rest the lingering question as to her honesty. He'd tried to ignore the missing stethoscope here, the vial of medicine there and the other things that had gone missing over the past three weeks, but he couldn't deny the uncanny, oddly coincidental timing of it all.

"I been wonderin' if you was comin'," Luke exclaimed, his booted feet clomping over the wood floor as he rushed up to meet them.

"You were, huh?" Ben smiled down at the boy.

Seeing Mrs. Duncan just ahead, he nodded in greeting as she stood gaping at him and Callie as if she were preparing to paint a portrait of them. In some ways, Ben figured with a wry grin, she probably was. It was common knowledge that the woman was the hub, self-proclaimed and generally recognized, for gossip in this town. With her colorful descriptions and deep-hued intrigue, she'd painted plenty a portrait. Most of which he didn't pay any attention to.

"How are those kittens coming along?" He reached down to give the boy's shoulder a squeeze, relieved to notice that the hearty meals Callie had set in front of the lad were starting to pay off.

"Jest fine. They're growin' up real fast. Had to get a bigger box to put 'em in and everything."

"Really?" Ben replied.

"Yep or they'd be jumpin' out everywhere. Then they'd prolly go and get theirselves lost."

"They're definitely growing fast," Callie remarked.

"I wonder jest how heavy they are..." When the boy grabbed his shapeless, threadbare hat from his head to scratch his blond mop, Ben made a silent note to purchase a warm hat, mittens and a scarf for Luke tomorrow. "You'd be real proud, Ben. I been doctorin' 'em some, and they're doin' jest fine."

"I am proud of you, Luke." Ben looked him in the eye, man-to-man, wishing that Luke's mother could see what a treasure she had in Luke. "Very proud."

"You want me to bring 'em by again so you can see 'em, Miss Callie?" he asked, stuffing his hands into his pockets.

"Of course."

"Bring them with you anytime," Ben added then slid a subtle glance around the room, hoping that maybe his ma had shown up for Luke's sake. "Is your ma here with you, Luke?"

His ma had never been one for attending church functions, town functions, or any other function Boulder might have. She kept late, active hours, mostly with men-folk from out of town. She was usually too hung over during the day to do much socializing. Or housekeeping. Or parenting.

Ben's jaw bunched at the thought. His pulse fired

a rapid, ugly rhythm in his veins. He had a great deal of sympathy for the poor folks who struggled to provide enough food, yet still found plenty of love to go around. He'd just never understand how a mother could disregard her own child so thoughtlessly.

"Naw…she's sleepin'. Been sleepin' all day, so I decided to come down myself."

"Why don't you join us for dinner, then?" Ben suggested.

"Can we sit over there with Mr. Joseph and Miss Katie?" Luke pointed to the far end of a long line of tables, where Joseph and Katie were sitting. "He said he was gonna teach me to write my name usin' them funny dots he's gone and learnt."

"Sure we can." Ben felt a small tugging at his heart as he ushered Callie and Luke around the gathering crowd. After a chorus of greetings and hugs, they'd barely gotten seated when Luke shifted a shade closer to Joseph and tapped him on the shoulder.

"Hey there, partner." Joseph draped an arm on the bench behind Luke.

"I'm ready." Luke sat stock straight on the long bench, his hands fastened around the hole-riddled hat in his lap.

Ben glanced to his left to see Callie holding a hand over her mouth, her beautiful eyes dancing with amusement.

"Ready?" Joseph furrowed his brow and angled his head as if trying to gather Luke's meaning. "For what?"

Ben had to chuckle when Luke slid him a wide-eyed, what-do-I-do-now expression.

"Seems that Luke's eager to learn how to write his name in Braille," Ben explained, giving the lad a how'd-I-do nod.

"Well, sure. But you've got to promise not to show anyone." Joseph set his hand on Luke's mop of hair. "It'll be our secret little code."

When the first dance began after dinner, Ben turned to find Callie watching him, her eyes so full of hope and joy that he had to swallow hard. Had there been no lanterns, the unrestrained smile lighting her face could've illuminated the room.

With his gaze firmly locked on hers, he strode over to where she stood with Katie, wanting nothing more than to have the valid, acceptable excuse of a dance to hold Callie in his arms. "Would you care to dance?"

For a brief moment, as her attention drifted to the edge of the crowd where Aaron stood rock still and staring right at them, he thought she was going to refuse him. He wouldn't blame her if she had. Aaron was being as rude as he could be to her, and Ben was determined to put a swift end to the silent protest and discourteous behavior just as soon as he had a chance.

"Yes, thank you."

He led her onto the table-cleared dance floor, joining the others who'd already begun a lilting waltz.

"You dance very well, Ben." Her alluring glance was cloaked in a shyness she seemed completely unaware of. She displayed no coyness, no predictable batting of her eyelashes or demure side glances to tempt.

No. This beautiful woman in his arms was without pretense or pomp. She was just Callie.

"Thank you. As do you." Ben gave her a slow, easy grin, loving the way her mouth and cheeks suddenly went all tight. "Where did you learn how to dance so well?"

She focused on where he clasped her hand. "Max taught me."

He chuckled as long ago memories trickled into his thoughts. "Max always did enjoy going to town dances. As long as I can remember, he enjoyed them." He gave her hand a tender squeeze. "I suppose he dragged you to every dance there was to attend?"

She slowly met his gaze, the rosy color in her cheeks fading some. "Before we were married, yes. And we always had so much fun." Swallowing, she lifted her chin ever so slightly. "But once we married he wouldn't go anymore."

"I can't imagine Max passing up a dance." He furrowed his brow, grasping her hand a little tighter. "I'm sorry, Callie."

On a sigh, she smiled, though it didn't quite reach her eyes like it had only moments ago. "There's nothing for you to be sorry about. Max just found other things he thought were more enjoyable."

Ben gradually swept her to the fringe of dancers. He pulled her a shade closer, just on the edge of being considered inappropriate, though right now, he didn't much care. Not when all he wanted to do was to bring Callie a small bit of comfort.

"Callie, remember…we're talking about my brother here," he acknowledged, slowing to a stop. He settled his gaze firmly on hers so that she wouldn't look away. "If you wanted to go…well, then, Max should've whisked you off to every dance there was to be found. But he didn't—for some selfish reason—and for that I am very sorry."

"Thank you," she finally managed after a long and

weighty silence. "But let's not talk about all of that to-night. It's too wonderful in here to darken it with those silly old memories," she added, the warm glow from the room flickering in her deep blue eyes.

His chest tightened at the way she was making such a valiant effort to dismiss history's sting.

How much had Callie missed out on over the years because of Max? Town dinners? Church functions? Special nights out? Romantic dances? Just how little had Max cherished Callie and seen to her desires and needs? Had he merely cloistered her within the four walls of their home, giving her no opportunity to socialize with others?

A life like that would be torment for a woman like Callie. She was strong and smart. Given the time to trust and the courage to spread her wings, she would pale other women with her ready wit, intelligent responses and her resourceful approach to life. And the simple yet striking beauty that indelibly marked her outward appearance would be hard to match. Anywhere.

Pulling in a breath, he cleared his throat of the thick wad of emotion. "All right. For you, Miss Callie, the night has just begun. And if you want to dance every single dance I will gladly oblige."

She blinked hard, a softness stealing over the remnant of bitter memories etched on her face. "It's a perfect evening, Ben. Thank you."

He slid his gaze down to her neck where her creamy white skin colored to a tempting shade of pink. Folding her hand in his, he felt the slightest, almost undetectable tremble there, and a lingering feeling of satisfaction stole completely over him.

He loved the way she responded to him. The tiny shudders. The trembling. The shy glances filled with longing.

He'd completely broken his own standard. Where he'd once decided that he rather liked being single, he now felt a strange sense of being unfulfilled—as if he needed Callie to be complete. He wasn't thinking with his head, but with his heart, and though he'd cheered both Joseph and Aaron on when they'd done the same and found their brides, he now wondered if it was a safe path to follow.

He peered down at Callie again as another song began, maneuvering her between the other couples. The slow and steady way she seemed to relax in his arms, as if she found a long-awaited security there as the night wore on, made his heart lurch. He wanted her to find security and trust in his arms. And love.

He—Ben Drake—wanted Callie to find love in the center of his embrace.

At that startling revelation, his mind spun. The music seemed to fade into the background, the other dancers and people, too.

Except for Aaron.

When Ben had turned Callie around in a graceful sweep just seconds ago, he'd come face-to-face with his brother. The pointed, unrelenting look on Aaron's face could've frozen spring's first sprigs of grass on the spot. It was all Ben could do not to react. For the remainder of the evening he avoided Aaron's attention, setting his focus completely on Callie. He wasn't about to let his brother's morose mood ruin her night.

When the last dance of the evening came to an end, he set his hand to the small of Callie's back and ushered her protectively over to where Katie and Joseph stood with Luke. Excusing himself, he stalked to where Aaron stood alone as some silent sentry.

"Who nominated you to head up the cheerful committee?" Ben forced through clenched teeth.

Aaron snorted, rolling his eyes in disgust.

Ben stood directly in front of him so as to block out the unpleasant view from curious others who milled about as if they wished the night had only just begun. "So, what's with the glowering mood tonight? Care to tell me? Or not? Either way, I'm not leaving you alone till you do."

Aaron narrowed his eyes. "I'm pretty sure it's nothin' you'd want to know about."

"Really?" Folding his arms at his chest, Ben was grateful that most everyone had taken to the dance floor as the musicians announced one more dance…the Virginia reel. "Maybe you should let me make that judgment."

"Do you know who you're dancing with?"

"Callie. My brother's widow. My very capable employee," he said, clipping off each word.

Glancing over his shoulder, his heart swelled at the sight of Callie and Luke walking out onto the dance floor. When the music began, he watched the way the two of them smiled and laughed as she instructed Luke in what to do. Ben's throat tightened with instant and very real emotion. And he knew…he *knew* that she was everything he'd ever wanted in a woman.

Turning back, he found Aaron's face contorting in disgust as he shifted a glance to Callie. "You're fallin' for this woman even though we all warned you not to."

Ben's hands formed fists. "Listen, I'm sorry for

how you're hurting over Ellie," he said, figuring that Aaron was having a hard time dealing with his wife's death with all of the festivities around him to remind him of the empty loss he felt. "I know that it must be hard seeing other couples enjoying themselves. If there was a way I could go back and change—"

"Keep Ellie out of this," he hissed. "This isn't about her. It's about that woman out there."

Ben flexed his fingers. "Since you haven't taken the time to get to know Callie, what is so important that you feel it needs to be said?"

Aaron averted his gaze for a brief moment. "You know Pete O'Leary?"

Ben sighed. "Of course I know Pete. What about him?"

"He told me he recognized Callie."

"Yes, I know. He said so the day he came to the office about his leg and I introduced him to her. So, what about it?"

Aaron shifted his boots nervously on the wood floor, the stamping feet of dancers drowning out the scuffing noise. "I'm telling you this for your own good, Ben." Aaron raised his chin a notch. "Callie's fooling you and everyone else around her. Leading us to believe she's our poor, widowed sister-in-law."

"You doubt that she was married to Max?"

"I never said that."

Ben jammed his fists at his waist. "Well, she's sure not bemoaning her past circumstance. And from what Katie saw, Callie has the scars to prove that her situation was undesirable, at best."

"Oh, it was undesirable, all right."

He could've throttled his brother from here to tomorrow for the caustic way he referred to Callie. "You and I both know that life married to Max must've been horrible, yet she's never uttered one single, bitter word."

"Did you ever think that maybe life married to *her* had been horrible, too?" Aaron challenged, meeting Ben's severe gaze.

"Not only have I not thought that, I can't imagine it, either." He glanced over his shoulder at her again, the way she lit up the room as she danced with Luke, likely making the boy feel like a king. She brought immeasurable joy to Luke's life. And to Ben's.

"Pete saw her plain as day in Denver." Aaron's features creased in a frown. "She was walkin' the halls of a brothel, dressed in one of those low cut, silky getups that no decent woman would wear."

Ben's stomach clenched at those words. His pulse slammed steady and loud in his ears as he remembered the dress she'd shown up in. The tattered, ruby-red satin dress with a dangerously low neckline and a wilting flounce of gaudy ruffles. His blood ran cold as he recalled how sick he'd felt seeing the way his mother's locket had hung in the midst of all of that.

"Pete saw her talking to one of those harlots down at the Golden Slipper the other day, too." Aaron's voice was low, apologetic. "Callie…she's nothin' but a harlot."

The night hadn't ended soon enough for Ben. After Aaron's disturbing news, he'd walked her home, doing his best not to spoil her perfect evening.

With a groan, he sank down lower into the stuffed chair in front of his fireplace. Stretching his feet out on the ottoman, he tried to keep his head above the battering, heartbreaking accusation. Much as he didn't want to admit it, it all made sense. Her showing up here unannounced. In a harlot's dress. Desperate for a job. Unwilling to parcel out anything but the most general information about her past.

He swallowed hard, fisting his hands, wishing he could waylay something with his pent-up fury. But what good would that do? It wouldn't change a thing. Not her situation. Not his situation, either.

A strong northwestern wind howled outside, emitting an eerie, lonely whistle down the stone chimney, adding to his already dreary mood. He stared into the fireplace, watching the flames leap and flicker, and he wondered how Callie could do such a thing. How could she cheapen herself, selling an act that was designed as a God-given gift for a man and wife?

He'd tried to act as normal as he could around her when he'd walked her home, but it'd been next to impossible. And sadly, she had to know that something was amiss.

Until he could corroborate the claim, she wouldn't know, either. Pete O'Leary certainly wasn't a man given to gossip or to the telling of tales—he shot straight. Though the fact that he'd walked the halls of some brothel didn't exactly boost Ben's opinion of Pete's character. But regardless of all that, Ben wouldn't be able to sleep sound until he'd validated the information for himself. If he had to locate the brothel Pete had seen her at and make his own inquiry, then that's what he'd do.

He remembered the stories he'd heard told of

women who'd been caught up in that lifestyle. When they'd tried to escape they'd been dragged back, beaten or worse, then thrown back into bed to pleasure the next patron as soon as the bruises faded some.

"What am I going to do?" he forced through a weighted sigh and thick throat.

He could find out the truth for himself, but would it change anything?

No.

Yes.

Maybe...

Tension ticked at his jaw. It might well change everything. It would raise all kinds of questions about her life with Max, and why he'd been driven to drink and gamble as he had.

When Smudge hopped up on his lap, turned a circle then plopped down, purring loudly, Ben smoothed his hand over the soft fur. The cat peered up and gave Ben one of those trusting kind of looks, and Ben couldn't help but remember how long it'd been before the cat had been this comfortable around him.

Trust hadn't come fast. And it hadn't come easy. In fact, it'd taken several weeks of proving that he was worthy before Smudge obliged. So why should it be different with Callie? He'd gone slow with her, working hard to get her to trust him. He'd opened his heart for the taking, and...he'd been taken.

"When will I learn?" he choked out.

His compassion was like some disease, at least sometimes. In spite of the red flags that had whipped around wildly for any sensible person to see, he'd forged on in his growing admiration of Callie.

Yet she'd omitted a very large and questionable detail of her past. One that challenged the very standards he lived by. And Ben didn't know if he could ever look past that omission. Or that she'd falsely represented herself.

Just Callie…

She'd been light in his day, humor in his evenings, and a decidedly uncomplicated outlook at the morning's first break.

Until now, he had discounted any thought of her as some harlot. Remembering how shy and hesitant she'd felt in his arms when they'd danced that first dance tonight, how she'd glowed when she'd taught Luke to dance, Ben didn't know if he could imagine her as a harlot now, either.

Bone weary and emotionally spent, he bunched down deeper in the chair and gave a slow, exhausted yawn. Closing his eyes, he leaned his head against the winged side of the chair. Just hours ago, he'd entertained thoughts of marrying this woman. And now? Now he had to admit that thinking with his heart had definitely not been safe at all. It'd set him up for a long, painful fall.

But if he was led by his own understanding, then he was bound to find himself lacking. And if he trusted enough to open his heart and follow God's leading, there were no guarantees. None.

Fatigued, he gave himself over to sleep's coaxing call. His last thought was, if he followed his heart, he would get hurt.

Again. And again. And again.

Chapter Thirteen

Ben woke with a start, his body protesting the awkward way he'd slept, slumped in the chair all night long. The flames had long since died in the fireplace, giving way to the invigorating chill of the morning. When he shoved himself out of the chair, both Smudge and Molly slid down his legs and plopped unceremoniously on the floor in a furry heap. They gave him one of those what'd-you-do-that-for kind of looks as he hunkered down to pet them.

"Sorry, little ones." Ben gave them both a scratch behind the ears. "I didn't realize you were still there," he said to Smudge then looked at Molly. "And you joined him sometime in the night, didn't you? You two kept me warm."

Standing, he rolled his head on his neck in a vain attempt to work the kinks out. It'd been a night of unrest. And in the midst of the flurry of dreams, and God-breathed truths that had floated through his mind as he'd slept, one thing had been made startlingly clear…

when it came to Callie, he needed to listen to his heart, trust God with the outcome.

Problem was…he didn't know if he could. Could he just look the other way?

Raking his hands through his mussed hair, he noted that he'd never been one to let unresolved conflict fester long. If there was a way to bring resolution, then that's what he'd do…even though he felt a small reservation in his heart. There was nothing bad, and everything honorable in being open about the claim, getting the truth out on the table. Right? All he needed to do was talk to Callie.

After he washed up and pulled on clean clothes, he walked next door, grappling for the right words. Words that would bring life into the situation.

While he slowly moved down the hall to Callie's door, his heart slammed hard against his chest. His hands grew damp.

He wiped them down his britches as he peered in her room and saw her standing at the bureau, holding the wood box she'd brought with her—the one Joseph had made. Though she looked like the same Callie from last night, he couldn't seem to see past the startling image of her as some harlot. He fought to push away images of her flaunting herself in front of a man, a commodity for the purchasing.

He tried to remind himself of what God had spoken to his heart…that he needed to trust God and follow his heart.

He pulled in a slow breath and watched her as she stared intently at the contents inside the box, as if she were caught up in some faraway memory. Was it a good memory? Bad?

"Callie," he said, his voice low.

She started, dropping the box to the floor with a crash and clatter. "Oh, I didn't see you there." She pressed a hand to her forehead.

It took one glimpse into her eyes to realize that the light he'd seen there recently had dimmed some, and that stirred up a sadness he really had no business feeling right now. Not if he was going to keep his head about this whole thing. She'd lied. She'd falsely represented herself. *And*…more than likely, she was guilty of stealing the medical things that had come up missing over the past three weeks.

He didn't know what she planned on doing with the items she'd taken. Maybe sell them. The money she might make from the objects certainly wouldn't be the equivalent of her ship coming in. Not even a small boat.

"I'm sorry. I didn't intend to sneak up on you." He moved into the room to help her gather the few paper items that were strewn about the floor. Then realized that the box had broken into several pieces.

"Oh, no." She crouched down and fingered the pieces.

"It's my fault," he breathed.

"No." She neatly tucked away any vulnerability. "I dropped it."

The sight of her tenderly gathering the few photographs, along with a small square of fabric apparently taken from some cherished garment or blanket, tugged at his heartstrings. This attempt to clear the air wasn't getting off to a very good start. Already, moments into seeing her, he was losing focus.

She began picking at the wood pieces, her breath catching as she fingered a folded paper. “What’s this?” She picked up the yellowed and stained paper. “This wasn’t in the box before. It must’ve been hidden.”

He noticed how one wood piece was thin, square and made of a different kind of wood than the rest, as though it’d been added at another time. “Hmm…looks like there might have been a false bottom to the box.”

He collected the remaining pieces and set them on the bureau in a neat pile then gave her a hand up.

Callie lent him a strained smile as she swept a trembling hand down her lavender print dress then carefully unfolded the paper.

She stared down at it. Her brow furrowed. Face contorted in a look of utter horror. Her hand shot to her mouth, but not before a small, unforgettable and haunting whimper escaped her quivering lips.

Dread rooted firmly in the core of his being. He rested a hand on her shoulder. “Callie?”

“Oh, dear,” she cried, sagging to the point that he caught her against his chest. “No. It can’t be. It can’t be.”

His heart surged to his throat as he wrapped her in his embrace. “What? What is it, Callie?”

It was several moments before she responded, and with each second that ticked away, the sense of dread building in Ben cut a path, deep and wide, straight through his heart. Since she’d never allowed herself to give over to emotion, he had no idea what the paper in her hand could say that would induce such a strong response. He braced for the worst.

She pushed away enough to slide the paper out. With hands that quivered almost unnaturally, she held it up to Ben, her tortured gaze locked on the yellowed parchment. He took it from her and folded her into the crook of one arm. Read the words to the heartrending backdrop of her anguished, muffled cries.

> I, Maxwell Henry Drake, deed my infant daughter, born August 22, 1884, to Thomas Blanchard, as payment in full for the said amount of one hundred eighty dollars in gambling debt.
>
> Maxwell Henry Drake

The hair at Ben's neck stood on end. His pulse pounded through his veins.

No. There was no way…

Surely he'd read it wrong.

He blinked hard, wondering if maybe his gaze was still sleep-fuzzed. Ben held the paper up, read the words again and examined the signature. Bile rose and burned in his throat as he peered at Max's unmistakable, looped scrawl that had been scratched across the bottom, sealing the deal.

His brother, his flesh and blood, had sold a child, a baby girl, to pay some gambling debt?

He swallowed hard, nauseated.

How?

What would cause Max to stoop so low?

His hands seemed to burn from holding the contract. He set the paper, a validating, sickening stamp of his brother's legacy, on the bureau.

Flexing his hand, he crooked a finger beneath Callie's chin. Lifted her focus to him. "Whose baby, Callie?"

His heart came to a grinding, arresting halt. His jaw bunched and his blood ran red hot with anger at Max for deeming a young life, an innocent baby, so invaluable.

"My baby," she squeaked through a muffled cry. Her whole body shook. "My baby girl."

He folded her in his arms. Held her. When she glanced up at him again, pasty-white with tears streaming down her face and pooling in her eyes, his concern grew tenfold.

As did the pure fury that was directed completely at a man who could no longer answer for his actions. A man who'd taken his pitiful reasons for doing such a heinous thing with him to his grave.

Ben held her for some time, stroking her silky hair, tightening his arms around her to give warmth to her quivering, shuddering form.

Through a pool of his own tears, he glanced at the window, to see the sun spilling inside in cheerful rays, a direct contrast to the grief-stricken pallor that filled the room. "I'm so sorry, Callie. So sorry."

She pulled in a fractured breath. "I thought my baby had died. Max told me she'd been stillborn."

He gave his head a slow shake. "Why would he..."

"He'd never want—never wanted the baby," she braved on a fractured breath. Even in the light of this kind of revelation it seemed she still felt the need to protect Max's honor.

"Callie, listen to me." He grasped her arms and set her back a few inches so she could see him. Dipped his head to catch her eerily blank gaze. "You don't need to protect him. Not from me or anyone else. I want you to tell me everything. Do you hear me?"

She finally gave a hesitant nod and slid her focus to the note on the bureau. Her face contorted in a pain that went way beyond the physical. "He didn't want the baby. Not from the time I'd gotten pregnant."

"Why?" Seeing her shuddering with such force, Ben pulled her into his arms again. "Why wouldn't he want the baby?"

Then Ben remembered the reason he'd come here this morning. To question Callie as to her past. If she'd sullied herself, if she'd become pregnant from some long-gone patron, then Ben might be able to half reason why Max would've had a hard time accepting the baby. But he'd never even begin to reason the fact that Max had sold off the baby.

The child wasn't at fault.

"I don't know. Once, when I was six months along," she continued, clasping her hands beneath her chin, "he pushed me down some stairs. He said it was an accident, and I wanted to believe him, but it had seemed so deliberate," she choked out, her entire body heaving on a sob.

If Ben had thought he was angered before, it was nothing like what he felt now. Whether or not the child was Max's was irrelevant. In Ben's book, any man who'd lay a hand on his own wife or child, born or unborn, to bring harm wasn't worth the air he breathed.

"Then when my time came, he—he didn't want to help." Her voice pinched off like the heartrending sound of a child, terrified and alone. "I asked him to bring someone to help if he couldn't, but he ignored me."

"No woman should have to go through that alone." He pressed a silent kiss to her head. "I'm sorry, Callie."

Callie's breathing came in short, labored gasps, as if she'd run the length of town and back. "I'd been laboring for over thirty-six hours. I was so tired, Ben," she whispered against his chest. She burrowed deeper into his arms, as if trying to hide from the memories. "So tired. I could barely hold my head up."

"I'm sure you were. Anyone would be tired."

"When it came time to push, I couldn't seem to get enough breath. I was so worried about my baby. Would the little one be all right? I hadn't felt any movement for some time."

She peered up at him; the frantic look in her eyes sent an alarming chill straight down his spine. He raised a hand, and with the pad of his thumb caught a tear that poised just above her lips. "He shouldn't have done that to you, Callie—or your baby. It wasn't right."

In a roundabout way he felt responsible for all of this. If he'd been able to turn Max around then the man wouldn't have turned out like some minion of darkness.

"It didn't seem like the labor should be so hard. And Max wouldn't help. I was scared, Ben." She gave a strangled cry.

After a few moments, she sniffed raggedly and raised her chin a notch, that same look of bravery she'd shown the night she'd arrived here right there on her face.

Ben thought he might break down himself, for the sight of it.

She wiped her eyes then pulled in a steadying breath. "I barely remember Max coming in at the end. And right before the baby came I lost consciousness. I ha-had no idea of anything until probably two hours later."

"You could've died," he breathed, his insides seething with anger so deep he could've killed Max in cold blood—if the hopeless excuse for a man wasn't already stiff in his grave.

He'd seen women go through far less and lose their lives because of it. But Callie was a fighter. She would have never made it through such an ordeal, otherwise.

"It might've been be-better if I'd died," she sobbed, her breath broken by uncontrollable emotion. "At least that's what I thought for a while, anyway."

Ben swallowed hard and hugged her close, aching to take away her pain and anguish.

At the moment it didn't matter what Pete O'Leary saw in Denver. It could all be true, that she was a harlot. The stealing…that could all be true, too. But at this moment, it just didn't matter. Not when he held a woman who'd endured a cruel betrayal that had wounded so deep, he wondered if she'd ever trust again.

"Then he told me," she continued, struggling to hold

her tears at bay. "He told me that the baby had been stillborn. And that he'd *done the right thing*."

She peered up at him, her chin quivering, her mouth all tight. "I wanted to hold my baby. I wanted to see her. Even if she wasn't alive, I wanted to kiss her tiny head. She was my baby, Ben. My little girl," she whispered, piercing him straight through with her frantic, imploring gaze.

"But Max wouldn't hear it. He refused to show me where he'd buried her, too." She swallowed hard, her throat convulsing. "Finally, he did. But apparently it wasn't a grave," she added, her voice the faintest of whispers. "I cried countless tears over an empty grave."

"I don't know what to say, Callie." Ben's voice was rough with emotion. "It was so wrong. Max did the unthinkable, and he let you believe it."

"All of these years I've grieved alone because he didn't want to hear it." She pulled away from Ben then, her hands fisted and her body quaking so that the floorboards shook beneath her small frame. Deep anger flitted across her face as she looked past him, her mouth pulled into a grim line. "It probably reminded him of how he'd betrayed me."

"He was a coward. He always was."

"It hurt so bad. He knew it wasn't true and never ever said one thing to lift my sorrow." Untold fury turned her pupils to deep, dark holes that took over her beautiful eyes. "He lied to me, in spite of my grief."

She hugged her arms to herself and shook, her shock-filled gaze planted on the floor as if seeing it all play out again. "And God…" she said, glancing up briefly. "He allowed all of it to happen."

Ben pulled her to himself, wishing that he could take the grief and pain barraging her body and heart, but only God could heal a wound that deep and that wide. Ben could say and do all the right things, but he'd miss the mark. He smoothed a hand down her back as she gave in to the overwhelming emotion again, her deep sobs coming harder and louder this time.

With her fists bunched and pressing into Ben's chest, she cried, "How could God allow my own husband to do that?"

Callie had been cleaning nearly nonstop since she'd learned the truth about her baby two days ago. Ben had insisted she take as much time off as she needed, but if she didn't keep her mind and hands occupied, she'd lose herself to the bitter rage that snapped at her mind and heart.

Having just finished reorganizing the vials of medicine for the third time today, wiping each glass bottle till it gleamed in the lantern's glow, she ceased cleaning for a moment. Reaching into her apron pocket, she withdrew the small square of flannel fabric she'd kept in the wood box all of these years. Brushing her fingers over the soft pile, she remembered how she'd cut the small snippet from the blanket she'd made for her baby, since Max refused to have the blanket lying around. She'd kept the flannel all of this time, every so often holding it while struggling to reconcile the loss of her baby.

Struggling to reconcile something that never happened.

Anger, hot and ready, boiled up inside her at the thought.

Had it ever touched the soft pink of her baby's skin? Or had Max just fled into the cool night with barely a stitch of clothing on their little one, delivering the baby as though she was some crude package?

"Was that from your little girl?" Ben's low voice broke into her helpless thoughts as he stepped up next to her.

She nodded, pulling in a quivering breath. "Do you think she's all right?"

"I don't know, Callie. But I have to believe that whoever received your baby could only love her." He turned her to face him, his comforting touch remaining on her shoulders. "Is there anything I can do to help?"

She paused, wishing she could release the heavy, dark burden weighing down her heart into his hands, but that wouldn't be fair to him. Her sorrow, grief and anger were hers alone. She'd been without help this far.

Slipping the flannel back into her pocket, she knew that she'd continue to stand and face this alone, just like the past seven years. "There's nothing."

He slid his hand down her arm and scooped her hand into his. "Are you sure you can't remember who Thomas Blanchard is?"

"The name sounds vaguely familiar, but I can't recall."

Warmth from his hands moved up her arm to her heart. She longed to make her way into his embrace again—like she had when she'd found the note. Had it not been for his arms holding her then, she surely would've collapsed under the horrific discovery. But if she did give in to her need for his comfort now, she'd question if he bestowed his compassion upon her because of guilt. Guilt for Max's sins.

She shook her head, hugging her arms to her chest. "It's been six years. Besides, I've thought about this, Ben. What if something happened to her?" Her hands trembled as she tucked wayward wisps of hair back into her chignon. "I don't know if I could bear the idea of learning that now."

He gave a heavy sigh. "I understand."

"And if she's with a loving family, then to try and get her back would be no better than Max taking her from me in the first place. It wouldn't be fair to her. It would be just as wrong," she admitted, her voice tight with emotion. "I'd give anything to know that she's safe, though. And healthy."

She would, too. But until she fulfilled her obligations here, she'd have no opportunity for searching. And no money.

Ben threaded his hands through hers. "Callie, I'll never understand how Max could do something so awful. I wish I could somehow make it up to you."

Exactly as she thought. He wanted to make up for Max's mistakes. Well, he couldn't. They weren't his to resolve.

Eager to turn the attention elsewhere, Callie gently tugged her hands from his grasp as she crossed to the exam table to wipe its already gleaming surface once again. "I forgot to tell you… I found this, too." She pulled a small piece of paper from her pocket and held it out to him. "I didn't see it at first when I found the other—the other paper. But apparently he'd hid this, too."

"What is it?" he asked, taking it from her.

"It's a wire from my father. The date is hard to decipher, but from what I can tell he'd sent it about eight months after I left home."

Ben stared down at the tattered paper as Callie silently recited the words while he read them.

Callie. Please come home. We'll work things out. I miss you. Dad.

He turned his focus to her again, a shadow of sorrow crossing his face. "You didn't leave on good terms, then?"

"No. He didn't think much of Max. He'd forbidden me to see Max after he found out we'd been meeting secretly." She took it from him and slipped it back into her apron beside the flannel and the contract. "Until two days ago, I had no idea he'd tried to contact me."

Ben shoved a hand through his hair. "Why would Max keep this from you?"

"I keep asking myself the same question." She fingered the two life-altering pieces of paper in her apron, wishing she could find a reasonable excuse, even a small one.

Ben came to stand across the exam table from her. "Are you going to contact your father?"

"Eventually, maybe," she answered, staring down at the small scars in the exam table, remembering how bad things had been when she'd left home. She'd never imagined her father could seethe with such rage and hatred. "But as much time as has gone by, he may have already burned the olive branch."

"Oh, I'm sure he'll still want to see you, Callie. More than likely, he'll gladly open his arms to you again." Bracing his hands on the table, he leaned heavily over it. "I know that if Max had come home, I would've opened up my arms. No matter how much water had streamed under the bridge."

That, she'd learned over the past three weeks, was the exact antithesis of what Max had ever told her. And now she knew enough to grasp how much Max had lied. About most everything. She should've never trusted him.

But could she put her trust in Ben?

And could she put her trust in God when it seemed He'd looked the other way?

Would all of this have been easier had she not discovered the notes? There were so many unanswered questions that swirled through her thoughts.

"Ben? Why do you suppose Max kept the notes?" Staring out the window to where the sun eased down to meet the horizon, she felt where she'd worn the edges of the papers down to a soft, buttery feel. "It seems like it would've been easier for him to just burn them."

With weighted steps, Ben moved over and parted the lace curtains to look outside. "Maybe he figured that someday he'd have the courage to admit his failures—though I can't imagine Max doing that. He never could seem to apologize for things. He was always bent on blaming someone or something else, instead of himself."

That much was true. He'd blamed Callie plenty…for everything bad that had happened. It'd taken a while for her to see it for herself, and from that point on she'd silently refused his blame when it wasn't hers to take.

Now, if only she could face her own blame.

Chapter Fourteen

Three days had never lasted so long. From the moment he'd learned about Callie's baby, he'd been compelled to do all he could. He'd had the sheriff working with him; even Aaron had lent a hand.

Though Ben had almost refused his offer, something kept him from doing so. Maybe Aaron was having a change of heart or maybe this was his way of getting back at Max…either way, Ben was grateful for the help.

Ben rode out as the break of day began a slow and steady creep over the eastern horizon. He prayed his trip would produce something hopeful. He had to allow God to work out the details. As much as Ben wanted to take matters into his own hands, he had to trust God. He couldn't jeopardize the life of Callie's daughter.

It was a long shot, and nothing short of a miracle that he'd managed to locate Thomas Blanchard. Six long years had passed since Callie's baby had been born, but with the sheriff's help, and the help of Brodie Lockhart, a U.S. marshal living in the area, they'd discovered the man's whereabouts to be in the Golden area, a few miles from where Callie had given birth.

That's exactly where Ben was headed now.

The trapper by trade was no stranger to the law, and no stranger to gambling tables around the area, either. He'd even spent some time in jail.

That small detail strummed a chord of urgency deep in Ben's heart.

He touched his hand to the wad of money in his heavy, deerskin coat pocket. Yesterday at the wide-eyed, disapproving inspection of Thurman Franklin, the bank teller, Ben had made the hefty withdrawal. He figured that maybe with a little coaxing, a man like Blanchard could be paid off and relinquish what he'd purchased six years ago.

Pulling his coat a little tighter to ward off the wind that stormed through the canyon, a small niggling of guilt ate at him thinking of Callie back home. He could've brought her along, but had chosen not to. He didn't want to get her hopes up only to have them crash down again if they arrived to find out that something had happened to the child. She'd said herself that she didn't think she could bear such news.

He wanted to protect her…any way he could.

Rounding a narrow bend a few miles south of Golden, his watchful gaze landed on a small, run-down cabin with a rickety front porch hanging on the house like a frail old woman on her way to her grave. After leading the horse into the yard, he tethered the gentle, trusty mare to a post, giving her a pat before he strode up to the house.

Spotting a ruffle of hen feathers beside the house,

he was surprised that a mangy dog or two wasn't skulking around the edge of the scrub brush like ravenous wolves circling their prey.

He scanned the property, his attentive gaze snagging on a makeshift lean-to hidden in a thick grove of trees, where the sound of a few nickering horses met his ears. Brodie had mentioned that Blanchard was suspected of horse thieving.

With a shake of his head Ben decided that he'd gladly tip off the U.S. Marshals. But only if he had the girl in the safety of his arms and far from this place first.

"You got yerself exactly ten seconds to git yer hide off'a my property." The gruff voice came from the deeply shadowed porch.

This wasn't getting off to a good start.

Setting a hand to his brow, Ben shielded his eyes from the sun and peered straight ahead to see a grizzly mountain of a man prowling at the edge of the porch, his britches hooked low beneath a rounded belly. A shotgun lodged in the crook of his arm.

Ben ignored good sense and moved closer so that the sorry looking structure with its crumbling rooftop created a block for the sun. "I'm a doctor from up north. Are you Thomas Blanchard?"

He narrowed his black eyes on Ben. "I am. What're you wantin' with me?" The man's voice reverberated, thick and liquor-slurred.

Blanchard shifted his feet awkwardly against the decaying porch floor. Made several clumsy grabs at a suspender hanging down his back, invoking images of Joseph's Newfoundland, Boone, halfheartedly chasing his own tail. Finally he pulled it forward and hooked it to his pants.

He looked just as Ben had imagined…like a filthy, gambling drunk who'd heartlessly agree to forgive a debt with the procurement of an innocent baby.

"I'd like to talk with you about—"

The rickety front door creaked open and a small face appeared. A little girl with lily-white skin, smudged with dirt, her clothes in need of a wash, and her thick, auburn hair awkwardly tied up in a tattered, pink bow, squeezed through the door. She stood there, timid as a church mouse yet brave as any orphaned kitten.

And he knew right then that this little girl, the spitting image of his stubborn, brave assistant back home, had to be Callie's little girl. She had the same courageous tilt to her chin.

It was all Ben could do to keep a steady front.

"Didja git yer chorin' done, girl?" The abrasive sound of the man's voice sent a whole flock of birds fluttering madly away, their wings beating the air as though their very lives depended on it.

She gave a quick nod, glancing longingly at the birds for a brief moment before she locked her wary gaze on Blanchard's hands. "Yes, sir. I did it all, just like you said." The slight quiver in her voice raised the hair at the back of Ben's neck.

"Then git yerself back in there." He gestured the little girl away with a brisk nod. "I got me some business out here."

With a certain dignity that defied her age, the girl slowly turned then scampered back inside. But not before she passed one last glance Ben's way, her large, innocent eyes sadly shuttered, just like Callie's had been.

Ben advanced to the bottom step, throwing off any plans of easing through this confrontation with diplomacy. "I'll not beat around the bush. Is the girl yours?"

Blanchard cocked the hammer on the shotgun, holding the gun with both hands now. "You insultin' me, son? Cuz iffin' you are, you better hope that horse'a yers can cut and run fast."

He held his ground, his jaw tensing. "Is she yours? Because I heard otherwise."

Blanchard spat a brown wad of tobacco, just missing Ben's boot by a few inches. "Course she's mine. I won 'er fair and square."

At that thick-skinned response, Ben could've knocked the drunk to kingdom come, if not for the fact that the life of Callie's child—his niece—was at stake.

"Won her?" He set his back teeth and stepped up to the porch. Resisted the urge to ball his fists. "How's that?"

"The wife never could seem to grow herself a young'un. She was always belly-achin' 'bout needin' a baby to put things right," he slurred, liquor's loose lips on Ben's side. "Yessiree, Lady Luck smiled on me when some fella over his head in a game'a cards made me an offer I couldn't refuse." He tapped his thick fingers against the gun's steel barrel. "Didn't have to listen to the wife's wailin' and carryin' on no more. No sirree, she shut right up, sure shootin', soon as she had the baby in her arms."

Setting his focus over the man's shoulder to the door, Ben's heart dropped a notch. Any woman who'd ache like that had to love this little girl. “Your wife… is she here?”

“She gone and died. Four months back.”

Ben cleared his throat. “I’m sorry for the loss,” he managed, not because Blanchard seemed overly wrought with grief, but because the little girl had been in this man’s sole care for so long.

“That’s the way of it,” Blanchard dismissed as though referring to the loss of one of the poor laying hens Ben had spotted. “Bein’ a doctor and all, you should know that.”

“It must be hard…raising her on your own.” Ben jammed his hands into his pockets. “Without a woman around.”

“I’m doin’ fine.” He snorted. “Just don’t know what I’m gonna do with ’er come winter.”

“Hate to be the one to break the news to you, but winter is here,” Ben added, rubbing his gloved hands together.

“That’s what I mean,” the man retorted, impatiently. “Trappin’. All over them hills.” He peered with a half-lidded gaze at the mountains surrounding him, as if they were his very own pot of gold. Then with a sneer said, “Ain’t no place for a sissy girl like her. The wife spoilt her somethin’ awful.”

Having seen the girl and the surroundings with his own two eyes, Ben found that impossible to believe. He didn’t doubt the woman had loved her, he just didn’t think Blanchard cared much about providing. And was repulsed by the fact that the man considered Callie’s daughter so lightly.

“She ain’t nothin’ but a bow-decorated, ruffle-clad

girl who don' like to get dirty. It's jest like I told the wife. Tess, I says, she gonna be nothin' but trouble."

Ben swallowed back the bile burning his throat. Perhaps Max had felt the same way…that this little girl was going to be too much trouble. The thought made his blood boil hot with rage and regret for how Max had gone so astray.

"I believe I told you that I'm a doctor…"

"What of it? I'm fit as a fiddle." He stood up a little straighter then sagged a moment later. "Don' need no doctor pokin' on me."

Ben pulled his shoulders back. "You're in a predicament, Mr. Blanchard," he stated boldly. "With the missus gone and winter setting in, you won't be doing much trapping with that young lady in there."

"I'm not stickin' round just cuz'a her. If'n I don' git my lines out in them hills, some other greedy son will," he guaranteed, confirming that his trapping territory was of more importance than a little girl.

"Well, you can't exactly leave her here to fend for herself. She's hardly old enough."

Blanchard aimed the gun at Ben and spat again. "T'ain't none of yer business. 'Sides, I got me some other prospects that'a way. She's nearin' the marryin' age."

"Well, it's my business now. Now that I know." He stared hard at the sorry excuse for a man. "And she's nowhere near the marrying age."

Decayed, yellowed teeth showed through Blanchard's sneer.

"The law will have to know, too," he added. The

last thing Blanchard would want if he possessed stolen horses was the law sniffing around. "It's only right."

Blanchard's gaze slithered the length of Ben, as though sizing him up to see if he'd fit into a boiling pot. "The wife's the one who wanted her. I had nothin' to do with 'er till Tess up and died."

"Exactly." Grasping at his fading self-control, Ben bit back the vicious litany of names he could let fly at the man. "Tell you what… I know of a young woman who lost a baby girl some time back. She'd love this little girl as her own." With the most authoritative air he could muster, he added, "I'd be glad to take this young charge off your hands."

After tenuous moments of deliberation, where Blanchard's knuckles turned white around the barrel of the shotgun, Ben wondered if he'd gone about this all wrong. He'd tethered a small handgun to his saddle, but that would do him little good now. The man had done jail time for attempted murder. Ben didn't want to give him a reason to pour out his rage on an innocent little girl.

He nailed the man with a steady, unwavering stare.

Blanchard met his gaze with a hungry grin. "For a price."

Callie hugged her arms to her chest and grasped for some silvery thread of hope, her heart barely thudding inside her chest.

On her way down to Golden, her optimism had surged to new levels, thinking that she might be able to see her little girl—just once. But when she'd asked around town and finally located the Blanchard homestead just minutes ago, she'd made the agonizing discovery that Thomas Blanchard was gone.

The weathered door hung open, dangling by a single rusty hinge as it creaked with eerie sadness in the brisk wind. The run-down house had been ransacked, and every last item in the sparsely furnished dwelling had been turned upside down.

Much like her life.

For six years, she'd lived in turmoil, had thought that God had punished her for the way she'd disobeyed her father and run off with Max. That had been a horrific and shameful reality to come to terms with. Learning that her baby had been born alive, and that Max had given the little girl—*his little girl*—as payment for a gambling debt, had been devastating. How could God allow such a horribly unjust thing to occur?

And now this?

A chill worked down Callie's spine as she slid her gaze over the small, two-room cabin. She could barely breathe. Had there been some kind of attack? Some kind of ambush that sent her little girl fleeing for her life?

Aided by the wide-open door and the daylight that streamed through cracks in the walls where chinking had long since fallen away, she gave the cramped cabin a thorough, bone-chilling perusal. There were no signs of blood—at least that much was good.

She pulled in a steadying breath, wishing that Ben was here with her. She'd feel safe then.

He'd been a refuge in those moments after the discovery. Her saving grace…the way he'd held her and listened as she'd spilled more information than she ever should have. At the time, she hadn't been able to stop herself. The words had tumbled out so hard and so fast that if she'd tried to put a lid on them she might well have exploded.

Her head and heart still swirled with unanswered questions. She longed for peace…any kind of peace she could find.

She wanted to find peace with God. It wasn't good standing on the other side of a powerful and wrath-filled God.

Before her mama had died, Callie remembered watching Mama sing the hymns at church. Where the other adults had seemed so stoic and somber as they'd sung, Callie had often wondered if her mama was singing the songs to God Himself. She'd looked so beautiful. Had sung beautifully, too.

But it was her father's fear-invoking, anger-filled words that had haunted her time and again, marking her steps. He'd always said that until she straightened herself up and lived by the Lord's word and commands, the Almighty wanted nothing to do with her.

Even now, knowing that he'd tried to contact her didn't seem to remove the rut his words had formed in her soul.

"I've been trying, God," she whispered, stepping over the trash littering the floor. It just seemed like every time she was getting her footing, feeling like maybe she could approach God without fear of punishment, something came in to knock her off her feet.

A shaky sigh escaped her lips. She cushioned the crumbling anticipation of seeing her daughter with the idea that maybe the place had been empty for some time and had fallen prey to passing thieves.

She could only hope, could only pray that her daughter was safe. But when she spotted a little girl's dress, tattered, filthy and heaped near a straw-filled mattress, dread crept like a whole host of spiders down her spine.

Ghastly images infiltrated her thoughts. When she spied a small rag doll in the corner, her hopes faded to a deathly pallor. She knelt and picked up the doll, held it to her chest, trembling with the thought that perhaps her daughter had held this very doll. She pulled it to her face. Breathed in the distinct scent woven in the fibers. The doll hung limp in her hands. It was worn, almost to shreds, really. Probably well-loved by her little girl.

Carefully, almost reverently, she tucked the doll inside her cloak, her heart quaking with ready emotion. But when she felt the makeshift contract in her pocket and recalled how Max had boldly signed his name, her heart churned with revulsion. The deep, cavernous hole those emotions created threatened to consume her.

If she allowed that to happen, she'd go to the grave knowing that she'd been no better than Max. Or her father, who'd become so bitter and angry after her mama had died.

Callie refused to let that happen.

She'd faced plenty of bad things before and she'd made it through. She could do it again.

It's just that she'd so wanted to see her daughter. Just one glimpse to ensure that her little girl was healthy and happy and content…then maybe that huge hole in Callie's heart would begin to heal.

At the distant pounding of horses' hooves, she hurried to the door, eager to leave before someone discovered her here and accused her of pilfering. On the way to the door she caught sight of a silver filigree frame lying on the floor, the glass broken, photograph torn, and the frame bent. She picked it up.

Her breath hitched as she peered at the image. A woman, her hair dark and her smile timid, cradled a baby, her arms wrapped around the little bundle in motherly protection. The woman looked happy, Callie decided, blinking back tears as she raised a hand to her mouth. Very happy.

While the pounding hooves grew closer, she glanced at the man in the photograph. A chill set her hair on end. Her heart came to a grinding halt.

She'd never, ever forget that face.

It was him.

The man who had shown up at their small home. Nearly breaking down the door to get at Max.

Being well into the ninth month of pregnancy, Callie had been hard-pressed to find a hiding place when the man barged in, drunk and mean as a cornered badger, insisting on Max paying up. Max had put him off with a partial payment. But not before the brutish man knocked him across the room with his meaty fist.

Callie had thrown herself at the man's mercy, begging him to stop, but he'd thoughtlessly pushed her to the side then jammed a boot firmly on Max's heaving chest. Threatening far more than that if he didn't pay the rest by week's end.

Max had paid up, all right. With his very own baby girl.

A small moan escaped her lips. A quiver ran down her spine as she stumbled out the door. To know that her husband had given their precious baby into the hands of a man like that weighted her heart with such sorrow she couldn't help but release a strangled cry.

At the same time, anger, deep and penetrating, sprang to life within her like a choking weed as she made her way to the horse she'd tethered near the tree line. Her entire body shook. It scared her, the feelings that kind of rage invoked, because, had Max not been dead already, and had he been standing here with her, she would've killed him.

And she'd hate herself for it, too.

She could write a book of regrets and give it to Max, signed and sealed just for him, but even that wouldn't release the anger and regret that barraged her soul.

She could fight. Fight to get her child back, wherever the little girl was. But what did she have to fight with? Her daughter had been signed away with a contract, however malevolent and unfair. The fact that Callie hadn't given her consent would mean nothing in a court of law. She could do nothing. At least not now. Maybe when she was back on her feet again, after she'd paid back the debt to Whiteside.

Callie untied her mount and swung up into the saddle just as two riders made their way around the bend. She edged her horse into the cover of trees, watching as two men with badges dismounted and stalked toward the cabin.

Glancing down at the photograph again, she realized that God might exact punishment on her for her mistakes, but she'd never understand how He could allow an innocent child to fall into the hands of a man like Thomas Blanchard.

She struggled to hold back the emotions that tore through her like some hungry tornado raking across the plains. Her fingers quivered as she worked the photograph free from the frame and tucked it inside her cloak, tossing the broken frame aside. In spite of the fact that that horrible man was in the picture, looking as mean as she remembered him being, she wanted to keep the photograph. If this was the one and only visual memory she had of her baby then she'd treasure it. Until the day she died. Though it was tattered and she couldn't see her baby's face for the bundle of blankets, Callie just knew that the little baby, cradled in another mother's arms, was her little girl.

Chapter Fifteen

Callie barely remembered the ride back to Boulder. It was probably close to ten o'clock when she trotted the horse into town and returned him to the livery.

When she walked the few blocks home from the livery, she stared up at the stars that studded the dark night sky. How could a God who lavished such brilliance and glory in His creation seem to be so finicky and vengeful with His children?

As low as she felt right now, she was desperate to believe something more pleasant and hopeful, but she was afraid. Afraid that if she opened her heart and soul enough to see if God was more than that, she'd be sorely disappointed. She just didn't think she could take that kind of disappointment, again.

Arriving home, she was surprised to find the lamps burning in the office. Ben must've gotten home from his trip already and was probably tending to a patient, since he wasn't normally at the office this time of night. Likely, he wondered where she'd gone off to.

He did say that she was free to do whatever she pleased while he was away, but still…

She quietly unlatched the door and moved inside. When her gaze collided with Ben's, her heart faltered for a moment at the tender, gleaming look in his eyes. He sat before the fireplace in a rocking chair, holding a child in his lap.

He motioned her closer with a crooked finger. "Callie, you have to see her." His comforting voice was almost a whisper.

Callie shed her cloak, fingering the doll again, then stepped closer, concern mounting for the young child in Ben's arms. "What can I do?" she whispered so as not to disturb the patient. "Is the child fevered? Would you like me to get a cool compress?"

"She's fine." He grasped Callie's hand. "She's yours, Callie."

Her gaze darted to the child in his lap.

Then to Ben.

Her stomach surged to her throat. Her brow beaded with perspiration. And her pulse swished through her head with bright clarity. Smoothing her free hand down her dress, she grappled for her bearings as the words echoed through her soul.

Had she heard him right? Did he just say—

"Yes. I said she's yours." The warm smile tipping his lips made her heart skip several urgent beats. "This is your little girl."

"Wh-what?" Her vision narrowed as she pulled in a thin gasp of air. When her legs grew watery beneath her, she sank to her knees at Ben's feet.

He snuggled the little girl closer and scooted to

the edge of the chair, his hand still firmly locked on Callie's.

"Just look at her." Ben's voice quavered as he crooked a finger beneath her chin and raised her gaze. His eyes shone through a glimmer of tears, and she was certain she'd never seen such visible, magnificent, powerful pride before. As if the little girl in his arms was his very own.

"She's beautiful." When he trailed the back of his fingers down Callie's face, a warm rushing sensation cascaded all the way down to her toes. "She looks just like you."

Disbelieving, she studied him for a long moment, searching his face for any hint that this was some sick and horribly cruel joke. But she knew, even as the thought crossed her mind, that he would never, ever do something like that. He was just too good. Too honorable. Too noble.

He was Ben.

A far cry from the man Max had been.

Time skidded to a halt as she inched forward. She leaned over the little girl in his arms, her lungs craving just one full breath of air. With a trembling hand, she edged the thick quilt away from the little girl's face. Peered at the child—her child. She could barely see the cherublike face through the hot, wet tears clouding her vision.

Choking back a sob, she pulled her hand from Ben's grasp. Set it to her mouth as she watched the little girl's pink lips pucker. Her breath catch. Her petite brow furrow then smooth out in a distinct expression of…

Peace.

Security.

And of comfort.

For six years her arms had ached—a real, tangible ache—to hold her little girl. She'd longed for the feel of her little girl's soft skin against her cheek. Longed for the fresh baby scent and sweet voice to hang in the air around her, like some eternal and blessed tribute to motherhood.

But now that her child was here within her reach, she felt clumsy, awkward. As if she had no idea what to do.

She'd faced an angry father with grief and suspicions that ran deep.

She'd faced a husband who drank, gambled and had fallen into long months where his personality changed so dramatically, Callie wondered if he was the same man she'd married.

She'd faced a man like Lyle Whiteside, who'd seemed to delight in holding the threat of her wicked demise over her head like some noose.

But she'd never felt as afraid as she did right now. Facing her daughter. Knowing that this little girl was dependent upon her now for food, care, love. And for hope.

Callie trailed a finger, featherlight, over her child's brow, scared to death that she might fail her daughter. What if the mistakes of her past trickled down to her little girl, bestowing a legacy of pain and hardship?

"How?" she finally asked, the word buried in a ragged whisper. She willed her hand to stop trembling. "How? I just came from there and the place was in shambles."

"You were there?" He peered at her, his brows creased in a look that had her feeling suddenly ashamed.

Callie dipped her head to the side. "I'm sorry. I just wanted to see her. That's all. I shouldn't have left, and I—"

"Don't be sorry." Ben smoothed her hair from her face. "It doesn't surprise me that you tried to find her—you're determined like that, Callie. I'm just glad you're home, safe and sound."

Was this her home?

Deep inside, she wanted to be able to call someplace home. Her daughter needed a place to call home. But if Callie allowed her heart to get too attached to this place and this man, she might lose herself once again. She might end up right where she'd been seven years ago, with a man who'd stood before her as a valiant hero, when in reality he'd been more like a shameless villain.

Ben related the events of the day to her, his voice like some quiet, serene lullaby echoing in the room.

And all the while, Callie kept her frantic gaze clasped to the little girl in his arms, frightened that she wouldn't be able to make up for the significant years she'd lost with her daughter. And desperately afraid that if she looked away, even for a moment, her child would be gone. Again.

Ben had saved lives. He'd been an instrument of healing in God's hands for many townsfolk. He'd been a source of comfort for those who passed on to their eternal reward.

But he didn't know if he'd ever felt quite as good as he did right now, holding Callie's daughter—Max's daughter.

Just hours ago he'd ridden away from Thomas Blanchard's farm, his pocketbook empty and his arms full of a precious little girl.

He couldn't help but smile down at the child as she slept. Her breathing even and deep as she dreamed, her sweet face passing from an expression of peace to stubbornness to moments of apprehension that made his heart surge with protectiveness.

Ben saw Callie, through and through.

Callie…a welcome breath of fresh air in his stale life. Callie…a beautiful young woman with courage that made his heart hurt. Callie…an uncharted treasure with walls so thick he wondered if he'd ever get through.

If ever he thought he might be falling in love with Callie, it was now. He glanced at the woman who'd shown up on his doorstep just four short weeks ago. Her big blue eyes were suspended in pools of unshed tears as she peered almost reverently at her daughter.

Her face contorted with emotion, real and raw. As if she didn't know what to feel. How to feel. Or whether to trust that this little girl was really hers.

Ben had thought Callie would've scooped the child up in her arms and hugged her till she could hug no more. But instead, she threaded her hands nervously at her waist, as if holding her own child would break some kind of magical spell.

It'd been no small task getting her child back, and

over the past hours Ben had thanked God plenty for blanketing him with favor and protection.

It was another matter altogether to break through the mistrust and reserve ruling Callie's every move. That loomed before him as an even bigger undertaking. He had to trust that God was big enough to handle a slight young woman like her, because Ben didn't know if he could gain control over the way his heart beat a sure and steady rhythm for Callie.

But finding just the right moment when he could confront her about the truth of her past, the truth of her present and her plans for her future seemed a difficult undertaking. There was the child now…little Libby. And Ben had no intention of letting the auburn-haired, delicate-boned, flesh-and-blood remnant of Max go.

A few days ago, when Callie had discovered the paper, signing the child over to Blanchard, Ben had wondered if Max hadn't wanted the child because the baby had been a product of some other man's lust. But once Ben had the little one safe in his arms and several hundred feet away from Blanchard's stingy grasp, he'd looked at the little girl closely. The moment she'd flashed him even a hint of a smile, he knew that this child belonged to Max.

Along with all of the perfect and utterly feminine physical attributes that clearly pointed to Callie as her mother, the child had the distinct, telltale dimples bracketing her rosebud lips. Just like Max.

"Who's the girl?" Luke furrowed his brow, his questioning gaze nearly lost behind a thick sweep of blond hair. He folded his arms against his chest in such an adult manner that Ben fought to hide his grin.

"Her name is Libby," Ben answered when he heard Luke shift his boots impatiently against the wood floor.

The little girl sat in front of the crackling fireplace, her attention fixed on the picture book in her lap. She'd been in Boulder for almost two days now, and had taken to following him around whenever he wasn't out on a call, chattering on and on, just as Luke often did.

She'd won his heart, just like her mama had won his heart.

But Ben couldn't ignore the awkwardness that seemed apparent whenever Callie was with her daughter. She'd watch her mama with a keen, studying gaze, the warmth and openness she readily showed with Ben turning up missing with her mama, as if she hadn't decided whether to trust her as she had Ben.

Both Callie and Ben had talked with Libby the morning after she'd arrived. The little girl had planted herself on Ben's lap, clinging to his neck as they told her that this was her new home now. That Ben was her uncle. Callie, her mama.

He'd been hard-pressed not to tear up when she'd flashed him a bright grin and hugged him so tight, he thought she might never let him go. But the pained vulnerability apparent on Callie's face when her daughter draped her arms around her neck in a loose-fitting and hesitant hug was hard to ignore.

Luke gave a curt snort. "So…where's *she* from?"

"She came from down around Golden. She's Miss Callie's daughter." Hunkering down a bit, he settled a hand on Luke's shoulder. "And she's come to live with her."

The boy's eyes grew wide with surprise as he slid his gaze to where Callie walked into the room. He'd fallen over himself to please her, and suddenly his surly expression turned congenial. Just like that. "Yer daughter?"

Callie gave Luke a quick hug. "Yes."

"Maybe I could bring my kittens by to show yer girl. You know how girls like them kinda things."

Before Ben or Callie could get out one word of response, Luke marched over to Libby and plunked down beside her.

"Hi." He stuck out his hand. "Name's Luke."

The shy smile Libby gave him brightened the room, just like Callie's did when she smiled. "Hello."

Luke roped his lanky arms around his raised knees. "I got me some kittens."

Shrugging, the little girl glanced back at Ben. "Uncle Ben's got kitties, too."

"Molly and Smudge? I know them cats." With a sorry shake of his head, Luke acted as though the felines that he'd painstakingly helped Ben care for were suddenly old news. "My cats…they're kittens. They're babies," he added, dragging out the word *babies,* as if Libby was ignorant of the English language.

Ben turned and caught a forlorn smile pass momentarily across Callie's face. She fingered the locket at her neck.

"Oh, I love little kitties," Libby cooed, as if he'd opened a treasure box of brilliant baubles. "Are they fluffy? What color are they? Can I see them?"

Luke rolled his eyes. "You can see 'em. But ya gotta promise me somethin' first."

Libby scrambled to her knees, clapping her hands together. "I promise. I promise."

Inching away, Luke's brow furrowed in an exaggerated look of alarm, but beneath the apprehension Ben felt sure a tender smile lay in wait. "Ya cain't make a promise when ya don' know what yer promisin'." He threw a determined gaze over to Ben. "Can she, Ben?"

He chuckled, pulling his hand over his freshly shaved jaw. "Well, I—"

"Ya hafta' be real careful with my kittens, cuz they're still young'uns." Fumbling with the new leather strings Ben had laced through his boots the other day, Luke set his focus on his new charge, drawing his chin up a notch. "But they're gonna grow up to be real good hunters. Prolly the best in town, I'm thinkin'. I'll be a doctor jest like Ben, *and* I might even be a cat trainer, too."

Libby's mouth dropped open. "Are *you* teachin' 'em how to hunt?"

"Not yet, silly." He gave a long, loud sigh. "They're still babies. Won't be long 'fore I start learnin' 'em, though."

"Teaching them," Ben corrected with a chuckle.

"Yep. Teachin' 'em." With one slim finger, he tapped the correction into his head. "I been figurin' it all out, how I'm gonna do that."

"Oh, maybe I can help." Libby wriggled her dainty fingers beneath her chin. "I'd be real good at it. I just know."

Ben turned to Callie, fully expecting to see her face

beaming with pride. But the troubled expression marring her beautiful features took him aback. When she caught him staring at her, he tried for a half grin and nodded to the children. "I'd say they're doing just fine together, wouldn't you?" he whispered.

"It looks that way." The too-quick, bleak smile plastered on her face hit him like a heavy weight against his chest. "I'm glad she'll have a friend like Luke."

He would've thought she'd be beside herself with joy. Her daughter was alive—very much so—and back with Callie where she belonged. Libby seemed to be adjusting so well, as if coming here to live had been a wonderful gift.

There were so many reasons to smile. To rejoice.

So why the long face?

Luke shoved himself up from the floor, jammed one stray tail of his shirt back into his britches. "Well, I'm not sayin' one way or t'other yet. Gotta see how ya fair with 'em. If'n they take to ya, then maybe."

Libby sprang up and grabbed his arm on a muffled shriek.

"Maybe," he reiterated with direct firmness.

Libby clamped her hands down to her sides, bunching her fists around the new pink dress Ben had bought for her yesterday. "My mama always told me I was good at everything."

"Miss Callie?" Luke cocked his head.

"No." She shook her head. "My mama back at my old home. She died right b'fore summertime."

Luke shoved a hand in his coat pocket. He raised his eyebrows and peered at her in the most honest and earnest expression Ben had ever seen on the boy. And

Ben was proud. Darn proud of the way Luke seemed to consider a six-year-old little girl's feelings.

"You still sad 'bout that?"

"Yes. 'Specially when I go to bed." She turned and met Ben's gaze, and when she gave him a shy smile, he was sure his heart would swell right through his rib cage. "But Uncle Ben came and got me. And he's real nice."

Ben's throat suddenly burned with a thick, raw lump. Seeing the adoring smile on Libby's face, he'd do it all again—paying the thick wad of money he had to bring the little girl home. She was worth every last cent.

So was Callie. He'd gone after the girl for Callie.

How could he not? When he'd heard the torture in Callie's cry? Seen the anguish in her crumpled features? Felt the agony in her rigid form?

The wrenching emotions had seemed to pour from some deep well that she'd stopped up for a long time—and they'd been there because of Max. Had Max not done something so cruel in the first place, Callie wouldn't have had to endure the past six years of grief.

As much as he hated to see her hurt like that, it was a relief knowing that she'd been freed of some of the secrets of her past. But looking at her now, the way her eyes were shuttered, and the way she couldn't seem to manage much more than a wane expression, he wondered what had happened. Just a week ago, she'd been much softer toward him. But she'd closed herself off almost as firmly as before.

What secrets did she still hold?

Ben eased from his contemplation when he heard Luke clomping over to stand beside him.

"You better believe Ben's nice. Ben and me, we been friends fer a while." Luke nudged Ben's arm like a puppy begging for attention. Folding his arms at his chest, he peered down his slightly crooked nose at Libby and added, "Actually, a long, *long* time. Prolly longer than you can even count."

Ben laughed and set his hand on Luke's shoulder. "You're definitely my helper, aren't you, Luke?"

"Yep." He worked his way into the crook of Ben's arm. "I'm his helper."

Holding his free hand out to the little girl, Ben added, "And Libby can be my helper, too. A fella can never have enough helpers, now can he?"

With wary optimism, Luke peered at the girl. "S'pose not."

She promptly took her place at Ben's other side, seemingly oblivious to the fact that her mama stood there, too.

Ben tried not to take notice, but the way Callie wrapped herself in a strangled hug, and the way she slid anxious glances to her daughter, she appeared as nervous as a cat in a room full of stomping boots. He didn't know how to help her. Didn't know what to do to ease her discomfort.

After Ben sent Luke and Libby off to traipse around outside in the barn, he walked into the exam room where Callie was busily organizing an already perfectly ordered supply shelf.

"Is there something wrong?" He came to a halt behind her.

Her fingers stilled on the small tins she'd been moving. "No. I'm fine."

Resting a hand on her shoulder, he released a sigh. "I can't claim to know you all that well, but if you don't mind me saying so, you look nowhere near fine." Grasping her upper arms, he turned her around to face him. "Are things not going well with you and Libby?"

"We'll be just fine." She shrugged, as if to remove his touch.

He refused to let her spurn his concern. He caught her gaze, wanting to find the same softness he'd seen there when they'd danced. When she'd softened to his gentleness. Melted to his touch. She'd felt so right in his arms, as if she'd been created just for him, and he for her. At that very moment he'd all but convinced himself that God had been masterful in the way He'd turned a very tragic, traumatic and tricky situation for good.

"Callie, what happened in the last few days?" He angled a concerned look down at her. "I mean, I know you've faced some big changes, but something is different."

She set her focus just past him. "I don't know what you mean."

"You were softening. I was hoping that maybe you were starting to trust me." He ducked his head to meet her blank stare. "What happened to that vulnerability?"

What could he have possibly done to push her away? He'd gone to great lengths to make her happy.

But why was he so determined to earn her trust when he was still a long way from trusting her?

Just yesterday he'd discovered his small weight scale missing. A large item like that certainly wasn't something he'd just misplace. The stethoscope, the tweezers, the roll of gauze and even the bottle of iodine were items he could misplace. But a scale?

He wouldn't have drawn his conclusion to Callie taking them, if not for the fact that these things hadn't started disappearing until days after her arrival.

And then there hung the constant question about her past. Aaron had made enough crude remarks as to her morality. Then there was Pete's testimony. And she had shown up wearing a dress not fit for any kind of upstanding company. She hadn't even seemed ashamed, or embarrassed. As though the dress was part of her… just Callie.

But every time he allowed his thoughts to wander to that precarious edge of suspicion, he'd turn tail and flee the other direction. Nothing—*nothing* about Callie would point to that being some murky part of her history. She didn't flaunt herself as a harlot would. She didn't hold herself with that self-protection-dripping arrogance. She didn't look at men with that sultry, half-lidded gaze meant to reel in prey.

She was just Callie.

And regardless of the way things looked with the dress and the missing items and the eyewitness testimony, he wanted to believe she was innocent.

When he looked down at Callie again and saw the way she hiked her chin up a notch, in that sweet way he'd marveled at from the beginning, he felt his heart snagged again. The desire to take care of her overwhelmed him. He wanted to see her free—really free from the pain and anguish of her past. To see her dream again. Because she'd likely not done any dreaming from the day she'd married Max.

"I don't know what's wrong with me, Ben." Closing her eyes, she gave a slow, disheartened sigh. "I'm trying. Really I am."

When he attempted to pull her close, his heart sank at the way she stiffened. "It's going to take some time for Libby to adjust. This is a big change for her, Callie. For you, too."

She shook her head. "I'm so afraid I won't be enough for Libby."

"You'll be more than enough," he said, smoothing a hand down her arm. "You'll be a wonderful mother for her."

"I don't know..." When Callie nibbled on her lower lip, Ben had to force his gaze elsewhere. "She doesn't seem to notice I'm around—not like she notices you, or Luke, or even Katie and Joseph."

"I'm the one who brought her here, so she probably does feel that way, at least for now."

She threaded her fingers at her chest. "I know that she loved her mother, Blanchard's wife..."

"She might be struggling with feeling disloyal if she gets too close to you." He wished he had the words that would take away all of her apprehension. Especially when her brow furrowed even more, and she stepped away from his touch. "Just you watch, Callie. She'll be drawn to you soon enough. She'll be at your elbow wanting to bake bread with you or help you make supper."

For a long time she stood there, close enough to

reach out and touch, yet hundreds of miles away. She hugged her arms to her chest as she turned her head and stared at the freshly cleaned exam table.

"She said something yesterday when she was playing with her doll." Wary indecision shadowed her fair, delicate features. "She didn't realize I was there listening, but I heard her."

Ben pictured the doll that Callie had brought with her when she'd returned from Blanchard's place. He'd almost suggested discarding it. But Callie had gone to great lengths to repair the ragged doll that first night, when, instead of turning Libby in to an unfamiliar bed with another unfamiliar face, Ben had held the little girl for the entire night in the rocking chair by the woodstove, while Callie cleaned and repaired the doll. She'd painstakingly added stuffing by the dim lamp's glow, and had even replaced two of the doll's tattered limbs.

Her instant resolve to take care of her child in some way had been a wonder to watch, had warmed his heart from the inside out. When Libby had spotted the rag doll resting in the crook of her arm the next morning, her eyes had lit with wonder and amazement.

"What did you hear her say?"

Callie touched the dainty lace trimming the neckline of her dress. "Apparently—apparently he told her that her real mama and papa didn't want a girl like her." The strangled sound in Callie's voice broke his heart. "She said that's why she had to live with him and her other mama…because her real mama didn't want her."

Chapter Sixteen

Callie swiped a solitary tear from her eye. It seemed that in the past few days she couldn't help herself from tearing up now and then. Watching the tender way Ben tucked Libby into bed even now, the way he'd read to her from the Bible...the story of David and Goliath just minutes ago. These things made Callie's heart and throat swell with ready emotion.

Truly, Max had missed out.

She'd missed out, too.

And she might continue to miss out if she stayed here. But every bit of her wanted to stay put in Boulder. In the safety of a family who'd been good to her. A man who'd been so very good to her.

"She's all tucked in." Ben winked, setting her pulse off-kilter.

He shut the door behind him, his nearness commissioning a flurry of activity in her stomach.

She tried for a relaxed smile, but the expression felt forced. "Good."

"Care to join me on the back stoop before I go home

for the night?" The brush of Ben's arm as he edged past her in the hallway's close proximity sent a shiver of delight inching through her veins.

She knotted her hands in front of her. "For what?"

He gave a long, lingering glance into the exam room, the way he usually did each night, in his silent and perceptive way, making sure all was as it should be. "Oh, just because it's a beautiful night." He turned to settle his half-shuttered gaze upon her. "A little chilly, but beautiful, nonetheless."

"Sure, let me get my cloak."

After Callie secured the front door lock and grabbed her cloak from the wood peg, she peeked in on Libby one last time. Struck again by the sweet way her little girl slept, her arm cradled around her doll.

Prying herself away from the peaceful scene, she made her way out the back door and sat down next to Ben. Though she'd left a good foot between them, she could feel his body heat permeating her in an unseen wave of glorious comfort.

She was so aware of his presence—whenever he was around. She'd even go so far as to say she craved it.

Without a doubt, she'd become far too comfortable around him.

Sighing at her irrational, wandering thoughts, she watched her breath puff into the cool night air in tiny clouds. "I've never really appreciated the cold months."

"Why's that?"

"I suppose because there was never enough wood for burning. I was always cold." Always uncomfortable. Always seemed to be a breath away from freezing.

"Max should've taken better care of you. The way you deserve," he breathed, his voice thick.

"It's not your fault." She wished Max, even once, would've taken responsibility, but for some reason he always blamed her for everything. For their lack of money, comfort, and general peace and solitude.

Ben's gaze lingered with hers, his eyes searching, looking deep into that part of her that she'd tried so hard to protect. Then he shifted his focus and stared up at the sky, his silken eyes shimmering in the moon's pearly light. "It always amazes me how much more stunning the sky seems on a cold, clear night."

She tipped her head back to witness the breathtaking way radiant stars soaked the midnight-blue sky. "It is spectacular, isn't it?"

He settled a hand at her back. "Things are as clear as they've ever been." The husky timber of his voice infused the placid night air with tangible intensity.

For some reason, she didn't think he was referring to the night sky. When he turned and settled that deep, searching look on her, she felt it every bit as much as if he'd pulled her into his embrace. Her pulse raced. Her cheeks warmed with an unwelcome blush. She averted her gaze, but not for long.

With tender affection, he set a hand to her chin and coaxed her focus back to him, her control rapidly—she swallowed hard—slipping away.

Desperate for a way out of this spiral of innate emotion, she jerked her attention back to the door. "Is that Libby I hear?"

She made to rise.

He set a hand on her shoulder, keeping her beside

him. The low chuckle he gave swirled her nerve endings into a reverberating hum. "Either you're more innocent than I thought, I'm really bad at dropping subtle hints, or you're downright nervous about now."

"What?" She gulped.

"Callie..." He cradled her cold hands in his. Hands that had gentled newborn babies, eased the passing of a patient and brightened the face of a cold and needy child with readily bestowed gifts. The warm, work-worn strength of his hands had been healing medicine to her. "You don't have to be afraid."

He imprisoned her total attention. In fact, she felt as if some unseen force held her firmly, right there, a breath away from the man she'd tried so desperately to avoid.

Yet felt such a compelling draw to know.

"When you showed up here," he began, rubbing the pad of his thumbs gently over her hand as if to still her wild, racing heart.

It didn't work.

"I didn't know what I was getting into, taking you in like I did."

"Probably more than you bargained for," she sputtered nervously.

"Oh, *definitely* more than I bargained for. But you were worth it." Setting his hand under her chin, he drew her nearer. His gaze fixed on her lips, sending a quiver straight through her that had nothing to do with the cool night. "You *are* worth it."

"Ben, I—"

"For the first time in a long time I'm seeing things

clearly." Like a whispered word of care, he brushed a finger across her lower lip. "I want to kiss you, Callie."

She struggled to take in the thick air caught between them.

He inched closer, a half breath away. "So if you have any objections, you better let me know now."

Her breath hitched. Held. Her pulse whooshed like steady waves through her head in an innate and age-old rhythm.

He settled his mouth against hers, a warm and tender claim.

Closing her eyes, she reveled in the moment. In the heady, cherished feeling.

His breath passed through her parted lips as if to infuse her vulnerable heart with hope and promise and whatever else he had to give her. His trembling hands rose to frame her face. She heard the breath catch at the back of his throat. Felt the rapid beat of his heart as he pressed his lips to hers in a soft kiss that threatened to be her undoing.

"I think I'm falling in love with you, Callie." His words filtered through her like warm fire.

Her eyes snapped open. "Ben…"

He drew just slightly away from her and stared down into her eyes with a deep, poignant look that had her quaking from the inside out. "I never thought I'd hear myself say that. I was content being a bachelor."

Bracing an arm around her shoulders, he pulled her close to his side. "I want to take care of you."

The mellow, soothing cadence of his voice and his inspiring presence roused her long-forgotten dreams. Dreams of a shared love that could boldly withstand the winds of change, the storms of life and the drought that could strip a life bare. Love that could convey a thousand heartfelt sentiments without uttering a word.

He pressed a slow, warm kiss to her head. "I want to make sure you don't ever lack for anything, ever again, Callie."

It was too much to withstand.

When he brushed his cheek against her forehead, her heart slammed against her chest. "I want your daughter to be raised in a good, solid home."

And would be way too much for her daughter or for Callie to ignore.

She hugged her arms tight to her chest, trying desperately to maintain control, but it was nearly impossible. His loving words, his gentle touch and his passion called to some long-ago, buried desire deep within her heart.

He was so good. Too good.

Too nice.

Too gentle.

Too strong.

Too willing to love Callie and her little girl. Too willing to promise things she'd dreamed of, but never had.

"I want to give you the world." His whispered words against her head set her hair on end.

Max—he'd said that… *I want to give you the world.*

She could barely breathe as she remembered how he'd waxed eloquent with all of his talk of adventure and love and lifelong devotion, and at the first hint of challenge a few months after they'd married, he'd abandoned every pledge.

And now Ben, Max's flesh and blood, made the exact same pledge.

She'd vowed never to make herself vulnerable again, and here she was, lapping up Ben's nurturing words as if she were some hungry kitten lapping up a bowl of rich cream.

Before she lost any more of her heart and resolve, she sprang up from the step and darted back inside. Closing the door, she locked it, wishing she could just as easily lock out the wholly consuming feelings that rocked her entire being.

Making her way to where her daughter slept soundly, she tiptoed across the room, berating herself that she'd so easily fallen prey to Ben's intoxicating presence, just as she had with Max. While she stared down at the peaceful, content way Libby slept she felt desperate to escape the compelling draw before he so completely won over Libby that the girl would never want to leave. Before he snatched away Callie's freedom—just like Max had done.

"Looky what we have here." The sound of Lyle Whiteside's low, gravelly voice coming from the alleyway brought Callie to a faltering stop.

And immediately blocked out the sun's warmth.

"You're looking real nice, Callie. All gussied up. You didn't go working for somebody else, did you?"

She made a slow turn, bracing herself for the man's snapping black eyes to land on her like a vulture's sharp talons to prey. She'd never met anyone who could wound so with a mere look. It was his way—with the girls back at the brothel and with any other poor soul who dared cross him or owe him.

"But I'm disappointed." He lunged out of the shadows. Crowded her close. "You walked out on our agreement."

Callie willed her hands to stop trembling, her stomach churning at the scent of his stale breath. "No. Of course I didn't."

She wished now that she hadn't parted ways with Ben and Libby a block back. While Libby had shadowed Ben into the mercantile, Callie strolled down the street to the milliner's shop. After what had happened last night, when Ben had kissed her and made the declaration he had, she'd jumped at any chance to be as far away from him as possible.

Whiteside drew a hand up to her face and snagged a lock of her freshly washed hair between his thumb and forefinger. He rubbed it as if inspecting it for some clue.

She half expected him to sniff it.

His thin lips tipped in a sardonic smile. "Sure you made an agreement. Remember?"

She refused to let him intimidate her. "I didn't agree to anything more than paying back the debt. And I intend on doing that."

"But we agreed that you could get that done faster on your back." He trailed his meaty hand down her cheek to her arm. "And then I come to find out that you up and left."

Callie clutched her reticule tight to her chest, mentally tallying the amount she'd saved so far. She could give him what she had, but the amount was still not enough. And if she was going to leave Boulder as she'd decided last night, then she'd have nothing with which to make her way.

She slid back a step. "I left you a note."

"I didn't find a note." He nailed her with one of his deceptively nice, understanding kind of looks.

Callie struggled to stay composed instead of flinching as she often had in his presence. She forced herself not to run. "I wrote you a note explaining everything."

"Notes aren't my way, Callie. You should know that I perform most of my business with my mouth." He laughed at his own sick sense of humor while she fought off the urge to vomit all over his shiny shoes.

She'd never do what he asked. Even if a girl stooped to that low a level and paid him back by sacrificing herself, she'd never find her way back to freedom. And Callie would never, ever allow that. She had Libby now, and would do whatever it took to keep her daughter safe from the likes of Lyle Whiteside.

She forced her gaze to meet his. "I'll have the rest for you by the beginning of December."

Shaking his head, his large jowls jiggled.

"I will." She grabbed the sleeve of his expensive coat before she thought better of it. "I'll have the whole debt paid off by then. I promise."

He looked down at where she held his coat then seized her hand and squeezed so hard that Callie stumbled forward against him. "Why would I want to wait when I could be getting my money's worth by having you pay on your back now? You'd have that debt paid off in no time, Callie. Just think, you'd be free to do whatever you wanted."

"Please." She pried his fingers loose from her hand, trying to hide her discomfort from an older couple passing by. Not wanting to be any kind of embarrassment for Ben, she smiled as though she was enjoying the present conversation. "You'll have the rest soon."

"The men might even front a good sum for you, the way you're looking." He raised his bushy brows. His beady eyes sank into his thick, red-blotched face as he held her hands out to the side, looking her up and down in a leering perusal. "If you do well, I might even throw in a bonus. Maybe a fancy new dress or two, instead of this awful get-up you're wearing."

"I like the dress I have on just fine."

"Come now." With stealthy precision, his hands slithered up to part the cloak Ben had purchased. "You can't be serious."

"Of course I am. This dress is lovely. And appropriate." Forcing the bile back down her throat, she met his gaze. "And I won't do what you're asking. I'll have your money for you, but not like that."

The way he shoved her away from him, as if he were done playing with a toy, almost sent her into a wild frenzy. He'd do that to his *girls,* toying with them then leaving them unsure of their status with him. It was his way.

But Callie refused to let him see that, deep down, her insides churned with raw fear. Not for herself, but for Ben and for her daughter.

"You have two days."

"Two days? But I'll never be able to—"

The smile he gave her stopped her midsentence, and sent an ominous chill down her back.

Would God allow another tragedy to befall her? Did He even hear her when she called to Him?

Would she ever truly be free from the stain of her husband's past?

Two days? There'd be no way she'd have the rest of the money for Whiteside by then. And she couldn't—wouldn't—ask Ben for an advance on her salary. She couldn't imagine staying in Boulder after the proclamations Ben had made. Doing so could risk repeating history, and she didn't know if she could withstand the trauma of that again.

In spite of her vow never to make herself vulnerable to another man again, her feelings for Ben were so strong and real. Whiteside's appearance today only secured her future for her, leaving her with no choice. Either she could flee with her daughter in tow and her integrity intact, or she could stay and risk losing everything she'd struggled so hard to gain.

Tipping his hat to her, Whiteside pinned her with a grave and biting glare. "I'll see you in two days. If you don't have the rest by then, you'll be doing far more than just talking."

Seeing is believing.

Only this was one thing Ben hadn't wanted to believe.

Was she turning a trick right here under his nose? Or was this some nefarious brute from her past trying to bag her now? She certainly hadn't seemed as if she'd minded the interchange.

His heart sank low. His stomach dipped to meet it.

Furious, he turned and stalked back toward the mercantile to retrieve his packages and little Libby, whom he'd left in the care of Mrs. Heath, trying to decide which flavor of candy stick she wanted.

Five minutes ago he'd felt about as confident as he could about the future. Sure Callie had run inside last night after the kiss, but he could understand her wariness, and was determined to give her plenty of understanding. But now he had serious reservations about the next few minutes, let alone the upcoming day.

Moments ago, he'd stepped outside to make sure Callie didn't need anything from the mercantile, when he'd been brought to a heartbreaking halt in his tracks.

The way his blood still pulsed with hot energy through his veins made it clear that he'd seen enough, all right. He'd stared in stunned disbelief at where Callie had stood near an alleyway a good block away, in front of some man Ben didn't recognize.

All of this time Ben hadn't wanted to believe that she had a sordid, secret past.

Striding up the stairs to the mercantile platform, he clenched his jaw in a silent admission…he'd been fooling himself. That had been made painfully apparent to him when the man had reached out to touch Callie, and she didn't move away. Didn't even seem to flinch when he'd stroked her face and arm in a very forthright manner, as if they'd shared some kind of longstanding, intimate past.

As soon as Ben had spotted the two of them clustered together as if they were lovers, the hair on the back of his neck had stood on end. He'd been close enough to notice she didn't rebuff the well-dressed man's touch.

As she had Ben's.

His gut churned with outrage and sadness.

Aaron was right. His brother had tried to warn him, several times in fact, but Ben had refused to believe Callie capable of living that kind of life. Pure and simple, Ben was just too trusting. And now, it seemed, he'd been burned.

Just last night, he'd embraced her. He'd relished the feel of her petite frame protected in the shelter of his arms. He'd kissed her, cherishing the way her soft lips melted to his. And he'd fallen over himself, declaring the things he had. Thank goodness she'd run back inside before he could ask her to marry him.

She had secrets, all right. Secrets that he'd be darned if she'd keep from him even one more day. Her little girl deserved more. Callie deserved more. But as long as she consorted with her secretive past, she'd never know how it could feel to step boldly into the future.

He forced down the thick lump searing his throat, trying to calm himself before he stepped foot in the mercantile. Libby didn't need to find him on the edge of rage. She was a sweet child with a past that begged for stability and security.

Just like her mama.

That sobering little fact sliced straight through to the very center of his heart. He had to figure out what he was going to do. He still wanted to take care of Callie and her daughter. But he'd find out about Callie's past, all right. Everything. Because if he ever meant to build a solid future with her, then he'd have to lay some kind of groundwork for trust in the present.

Right now, the whole thing lay in sinking sand.

* * *

Callie had to leave Boulder. Between Whiteside's threat and Ben's promises, she had no choice.

She touched the wrinkled and yellowed telegram in her pocket, silently reciting the words her father had conveyed some time ago. That he wanted her to come home.

She could only hope that he still felt the same way now as he did when he'd sent this to her. Had Max not hidden it from her, would she have gone to her father before?

It was useless to guess. The important thing was what she had to do now. Gathering the ends of an old sheet, she secured it with a knot, mentally recounting the items she'd packed into the roll. She didn't feel right taking the new things Ben had gotten for her daughter, but Libby had nothing else. And just as soon as she could, Callie would send money to pay Ben back.

She might never get her head above the swirl of debts that threatened to eat her alive, but at least she'd be in control of what happened to her and to those she loved.

Love… Did she love Ben?

She hadn't even considered it until now. Or maybe she had chosen to ignore the glaring facts. How could it be that she could find love with a man like Ben Drake? Max's flesh and blood?

She couldn't ruminate on such things now. It was useless.

Thankfully, he'd been out for most of the day and

evening on calls, so she'd been able to get her things together to leave as soon as night fell.

Stepping over to the bureau, she picked up the letter she'd written earlier and skimmed her heavy gaze over it one last time. The paper still felt faintly damp from her tears as she'd penned the words. The note wasn't long, but it conveyed her sincere appreciation. That would have to be enough for Ben because if she let on as to what her plans were, he'd locate her whereabouts. She didn't want to put him in jeopardy. Herself in jeopardy. Or her child in jeopardy.

Whiteside was not one to mince words. When he said something, he meant it. And if Ben was privy to what the man intended to do, she had a very real and grave sense that in order to thwart Whiteside's plans, Ben would risk his own safety.

It was like some lavish gift, thinking that someone was looking out for her like that. She'd surely never experienced something so wonderful with Max. It was within her grasp now, but she'd never be able to know the warm and tender embrace of that kind of security. Her past…her husband's past had come back to haunt her and until she rectified the situation she'd never truly be free.

But she feared that if freedom hinged on everything being all ordered in her life, she might never be free.

Chapter Seventeen

"She's gone." Ben choked out the words as Aaron walked into the room where Callie and her daughter had slept, his hands jammed on his hips, his lips pulled taut in disgust.

"No sign of her or the girl?" he asked, scanning the room.

Ben shook his head, feeling more alone than he'd ever felt before. And angry. "No. I've checked everywhere and all of their things are missing. It's as if they'd never lived here."

"I'm sorry, Ben. Really I am. I'd hoped it wasn't Callie and her daughter I saw climbing into that wagon earlier."

"Why didn't you stop her?" Ben paced out to the hallway, frustrated, angry and scared.

"I should have. I'm sorry." Aaron followed, a few steps behind.

He imagined her leaving town, head held high, face set with steady resolve toward what, he had no earthly idea. "Well, I'm glad that you at least came to get me."

"I had a feeling she'd do something like this to you. I just didn't think it would be so soon. I tried to tell—"

"Are you trying to make me feel better?" he spat.

"The truth usually doesn't feel good."

Ben had tried to ignore the gut-wrenching feeling that had eaten at him the past twenty-four hours, that Callie would do something like this. This evening he'd ridden hard all the way home from his last house call because of it, and when Aaron had met him on the edge of town, Ben's heart had ceased beating for several seconds.

When he'd kissed Callie last night, she'd seemed so receptive. But just like strays he'd taken in, just as soon as he'd shown love and affection, she'd run off. Usually strays returned, as if giving in to a deep down need for care and love.

But not this time. Not this stray.

"We still don't know she left for good," he muttered, hoping that he was flat-out wrong.

Though he feared his suspicions were true, for some reason he couldn't seem to reveal that deep-seated dread with Aaron. Aaron had had it out for Callie from the day she'd shown up in Boulder.

Ben had no doubt that the man he'd seen her talking with yesterday had as much to do with her disappearance as her desire to run from love. And the idea that she might be in danger sent his pulse stampeding through his veins.

"For Pete's sake, Ben, are you still holdin' to your claim that she's innocent? That her life as a harlot might not be true?"

"Innocent until proven guilty." He stalked toward

the front door, grabbing his bag and an extra blanket. On the way out to saddle his horse and ride out, he held his hand near the stove. "They couldn't have gone far. The woodstove is still hot."

Aaron followed him out the door and matched Ben's long strides. "How much more proof do you need to call her guilty? Seven years ago Max said he'd hooked up with some harlot."

Ben jerked his brother to a stop. "Don't say that."

"That she's a harlot?"

He tightened his fist around Aaron's coat. "You know how Max would say things just to shock all of us. For some reason he enjoyed seeing us flinch."

Aaron brushed Ben's hand away. "Believe what you will. She showed up in a harlot's slinky dress four weeks ago. Remember? You showed it to me. And then with everything else…well, what more do you need for proof?"

Ben turned and strode toward the barn, thankful he hadn't told Aaron about the man he'd seen Callie talking with this morning. Something had kept him tight-lipped. Aaron already had plenty of ammunition against Callie. Ben didn't need to offer him more for his stockpile.

"You just don't want to believe it's true. That Callie could actually sell herself."

"Enough," he bellowed, entering the barn. He immediately regretted his outburst upon hearing his mare's anxious snort. "I don't want to hear another word about this."

Ben stepped up to the stall and spoke in low, soothing tones to his mare as he opened the gate and led her out.

While Aaron hung back, clearly and appropriately wary, Ben had to wonder what had gone through Callie's mind to leave so abruptly. Though the weather conditions weren't bad, in his estimation it was nowhere near fit for traveling at night with a young child.

She had not only herself to think about, but her child, too. And if their departure had anything to do with the man he'd seen with Callie this morning, then Ben would be dead in his grave before he'd allow his brother's child to be raised in some hole of a brothel.

He hauled his saddle up on his horse and cinched it almost as tight as the cord of betrayal that nearly cut off the feeling in his heart.

"I'm heading out." He loosened the cinch a couple of notches and set his focus on his brother. "You can ride along if you want. But if you choose to ride, I'll not have you saying one more thing like that about Callie. Do you hear?"

Aaron spoke not another word as he mounted his mare and spurred his horse alongside Ben in a fast gallop south.

Within an hour, they'd located Callie and her daughter riding in the back of a wagon driven by a traveling salesman. To Ben's great relief, both Callie and Libby seemed sound. To his almost equaled relief, she didn't fight him when he gave her no option but to come back to Boulder.

It almost broke his heart that some of the stubborn tilt to her chin had gone missing. As if some of the fight and determination that defined Callie had been lost between home and the road south. Hesitation, and maybe even a small sense of relief, had hung heavy in her gaze when he lifted her up to ride sidesaddle in front of him.

With little more than a few complacent words said for the sake of Libby, Ben returned in silence with Callie. Her little girl perched in front of her uncle Aaron, stealing sweet, almost worshipful glances in the moon's light over at Ben every minute or so, as if to make sure he was heading the same way. His throat grew raw with the effect that had on him—to know that Callie's little girl looked at him with such awe. He'd be hard-pressed to ever live up to the appreciation he saw in her eyes. He'd failed those he loved more than once, and all he could do was trust that God would work it all out.

When Callie shifted against him, he struggled to ignore the way every nerve ending hummed with instant attraction. Had Ben not been angry with the petite little woman in front of him, he'd have been driven to distraction by the way her body molded to his in the saddle. The way an errant lock of her hair whispered against his cheek. The way her eyes seemed to pool with unshed tears as she gazed with vacant sadness across the milky, moonlit horizon.

After they returned to Boulder, Aaron continued on alone to his cabin outside of town. Ben felt an overwhelming sense of relief when he tucked Libby into bed—not in the room she'd been sleeping in with her mama, but in the extra bedroom in his home.

He found Callie standing in front of his fireplace. As he advanced closer, she trembled slightly as she hugged her arms tight to her chest. Her gaze flickered between shame, stubbornness, sorrow and resolve.

"Why?" He stood back from the fire, irritation still running with heated energy through his veins. "What were you thinking?"

She met his gaze with the same kind of bravery he'd seen in her that very first night. "I didn't have a choice, Ben."

He shook his head, noticing for the first time that the heirloom locket didn't hang there against her creamy white skin, as it had every other time he'd been with her. Had she left it for him?

"You had a choice." He couldn't let that kind of sentimental musing affect his mood. Misplaced mercy wouldn't do him or Callie any good. "We all make choices. Only yours happen to border on irresponsible."

She pinned him with an insolent glare.

He raised his brows. "Well, far be it from me to say… I mean, I am just your brother-in-law, your daughter's uncle, and your employer—"

"Not anymore."

On a frustrated sigh, he jammed a hand through his hair. "What I'm saying is that I care, Callie. I care what happens to you and Libby, and exposing your child to the kind of lifestyle you might lead isn't wise. Or healthy. Or right."

She furrowed her brow, her perfect features crinkling in bewilderment. "What do you mean…the kind of *lifestyle* I might lead?"

"You're single." He took a step closer. "And alone.

Do you think there will be many options for you out there?"

"I'd make it just fine," she retorted with sharp precision. Grabbing her cloak from the chair, she whipped it around her shoulders. "I can do all kinds of work."

"I'm sure you can." He shoved his hands into his pockets and gave his head a slow, sorrowful shake.

Just like that, her stubborn streak had barged in on her vulnerability, taking it over by force. Ben would have to be more forthright if he hoped to get through to Callie. Though he may be a fool, he cared for this woman. Deeply. And if he planned on enjoying any kind of future with her, then he'd have to be up-front about his suspicions.

As irritated as he was with Callie, he also felt sick thinking about how lost he'd feel if something happened to her or her daughter. And how he'd blame himself, too. No matter what her past, he'd hold himself directly responsible for any ill fate that would come their way. The fact that he hadn't been able to keep her here and turn the situation around would only add to the shaming regret eating at his sense of trust in God and himself. It would be the final nail in his coffin.

"How do you think I made it the past seven years?" she asked through clenched teeth, her spirited gaze narrowing.

"I'm afraid I already have an idea." He thought about the medical items that had come up missing along with the other evidence that was piling up against her. "What about your daughter? What will you do with her?"

She glanced down the hallway to where Ben had

tucked Libby into bed, her gaze suddenly filling with doubt and apprehension. "She'll attend school, of course."

Though a small part of him wanted to come right out and accuse her, something else, something bigger and unexplainable, stood like some thick barrier against the accusing thoughts as they made their way to his tongue.

Was he just like those who'd accused her in the past?

He remembered how timid she'd been when he'd taken her to church that first time. She'd feared judgment as though it had already been measured out for her in large doses, and she had only to take it. Sadness had gripped his heart at how petty those in the church could be, and now he wondered if he was being the very same way.

But she'd betrayed him. She'd never been forthright about her past. This whole time he'd felt like maybe he was breaking through, now he wondered if he'd even begun to crack the thick layers.

But she'd been betrayed, too. In the worst way possible, and maybe because of all of that, she was so set on protecting herself that she would walk away from all he could offer.

"Did you like the life you shared with Max?" he finally asked, trying for a more reasoned approach. "Was it anything like you've had here?"

"No." She gave a snort, her gaze briefly sliding to the flames that licked at the dry wood. "But I made the best of it. I had to."

"And I suppose you'll make the best of it again." He

sighed, frustrated by her inability to see things for the way they really were. "You're just going to strike out on your own…with no more than a month's wages to your name. *And* with a child."

Taking a step nearer, he rested his hand on the sturdy, beautifully crafted mantel Joseph had made when Ben had the house built three years ago. "Do you forget how you showed up here?" He dipped his head to get her attention as her long lashes whispered down over her eyes. Ben lowered his voice. "You were half-dead, Callie. If I hadn't come along when I did, you'd be buried in some unmarked grave up on a lonely hillside."

"And I thank you for your care." With an earnest gaze, she peered at him. "But that won't happen again."

"How can you be so sure of that?" More, how could she be so careless with herself or her daughter? Either she was more naive than he'd ever imagined or she had well-laid-out plans. "Is it because you already have a safe, warm place to go where you'll have your meals prepared for you, a wardrobe for your evenings," he bit off, picturing her in the ruby-red dress she'd shown up in, and remembering how his stomach had turned seeing his mother's locket framed in such gaudiness. "Well, I'm sure you'll get *plenty* of attention where you're going."

She shrugged, as though belittling the words he'd just spoken. Words that had come hard, tasting like some bitter draught on his tongue. "Your implication is harsh. Surely you can't believe—"

"I want to believe that the shoe won't fit." He stood to his full height, watching for any kind of remorse or indecision or regret to flit across her face. He really wanted to see at least an inkling of those emotions in her gaze, not because he wanted her to hurt, but because he wanted a reason, a good, solid reason not to believe all of the things he'd questioned in his heart were true.

She looked at him with that blank, unconcerned stare of hers. That stubborn wordless expression that shut off all vulnerability.

Something snapped inside him, the worst of his suspicions now ricocheting through his head with conscience-numbing force.

"I can't stop you from making a bad decision for yourself, but I'll do whatever I have to, to keep you from dragging Libby into a life that no child should have to witness. Or live in." He crossed to the front door and held it open for her. "If you want to go and sell yourself, then you'll do it without your daughter."

Had she stayed in his house a minute longer last night, Callie would've rained down on him like some wild woman on the loose. He'd insulted her dignity, her character, and he'd made himself some self-imposed guardian over her daughter.

Ben was trying to control her life. Just like her father. Just like Max. Just like Mr. Whiteside. The insulting jabs, the questioning of her decision making, the I-know-what's-best-for-you attitude…she'd heard it all before. And until last night she hadn't really believed that Ben was capable of the same kind of behavior.

How could he question her integrity like that? The very thought made her skin crawl.

Last night she'd walked out on him, leaving with those disgusting words resonating in her head like some dread dirge. Even now she felt mad enough to spit. And she was a lady!

Determined to tamp down her irritation before she sought out her daughter at Ben's, she sat out on the front porch of the office. Where she'd huddled, sick and weary, against a blinding snowstorm just four weeks earlier.

Had she known then what she did now, she wouldn't have come anywhere near this place. She would've run as far and as fast as her legs could take her in the opposite direction, staying clear of his control.

Unwanted images of the gentle and tender way he'd cared for her when she'd been sick flashed through her mind. His big, strong hands had sheltered her so that she could breathe and rest for the first time in a long time. His warm, endearing grin had lit her days with promise and hope and anticipation for something more. And his arms had opened like some wonderful refuge when she'd been at her lowest.

But she knew well how people could change. Her kind and patient father had changed dramatically after her mother had died. And wonderful, adventurous Max had changed within a few short months of marrying.

At least she'd found out sooner rather than later with Ben.

When a wagon rolled by the office, she glanced up to see Mrs. Duncan craning her neck, staring at her with that ever-watchful gaze of hers.

Callie forced a smile to her face and waved as though it was a daily occurrence for her to sit outside every November morning. She was unwilling to give the woman one morsel, or even a crumb, to gossip about. If she looked forlorn or angry or irritated, the woman would take that to the bank, invest and build on it before the sun went down.

Callie had to figure out what she would do. There was no way she'd leave Boulder without her daughter, but in less than two days Whiteside would be back. If she didn't have the full amount then he'd make good on his claim and muscle Callie back with him to Denver to live as one of his *girls*.

Her skin crawled with repulsion.

And that Ben had insinuated that she'd already lived some compromised life selling herself sent bile from her stomach burning all the way to her throat, just like his words had burned all the way to her heart. She'd desperately wanted to defend herself, but why would he believe her? Furthermore, she in no way wanted to elicit sympathy from Ben. And if he knew the way she'd had to work in a brothel just to pay off Max's gambling debt, he was sure to treat her with pity. And he was sure to feel worse about what kind of life Max had led. When she'd shown up on Ben's doorstep four weeks ago, she'd been backed into a corner. She'd had nowhere else to turn and had been forced to follow her dying husband's last words back home. To his home.

To Ben.

To comfort.

To a family who really seemed to care.

She couldn't drag Ben or anyone else into the mess she faced. And no matter how unfair it seemed, she couldn't wriggle her way out of the debt Max owed.

When she'd married him, it had been for better or worse.

With a heavy sigh, she wished once again that there'd been some *better* in the mix of it all.

Her silent musings were broken when she heard the awkward clump of boots on the boardwalk, racing this way.

Luke's blond head bobbed a good block down, his thick hair hanging in his eyes.

She rose, and as soon as she saw his frantic wave and heard his frenzied call for help she set off, running to meet the boy.

"Luke? What is it? What's wrong?" she asked when she was halfway down the block.

He almost ran right over her, but stumbled back at the very last moment. His breath came hard. Fast. "Fire. There's a fire."

Callie braced her hands on his shoulders. "Where?"

"My house. My ma—she's still in there." His sweet face contorted in an effort to hold back tears pooling in his wide, fearful gaze. His lower lip trembled. "And the kittens—I tried to get 'em, but the smoke…"

"Where is your ma, Luke? Where is she?" she implored, tugging the boy that direction as she set off at a run. She remembered what Ben had said about Luke's mama, that she was often drunk and had kept a steady stream of men coming and going from her house.

No way for a child to live.

"In the bedroom. I tried to get 'er, but she's too heavy when she's out cold."

"And the kittens?" Callie swallowed hard. She pictured the way Luke would hold his fluffy little charges. Loving them and talking to them as though they were kin.

"I keep 'em up in the loft. So's they don' bother Ma."

Dread crawled up Callie's spine. She willed her expression to stay clear and focused for the boy, but all the while she prayed that God would spare the kittens and his mother.

"Is there anyone else there to help?" Remembering the way the sorry little house sat like some lonely survivor on a forgotten street, she doubted it.

Luke shook his head, his chin trembling.

She skidded to a stop, pulling in a long breath. "Go. Get help. Get Ben." She pushed him that way. "Run fast."

Sprinting toward Luke's house again, she hoped that some merciful soul had arrived. Before she reached the remote, heavily rutted street, she caught a whiff of acrid smoke hanging in the crisp, frosty air.

He'd said his mother was in there. And the kittens. When she turned the corner and saw smoke whispering from cracks in the walls into the morning, her throat seared with instant grief. She pulled up her skirts and ran as fast as she could, her heart faltering with each step when it was clear that no one else was around.

She opened the front door as a wave of thick, gray smoke hit her square in the face like some knock-out blow in a back-alley fight.

Callie pulled her skirt up and held it to her face, peering in vain through the smoke.

Luke's mama. She was in there.

She pulled in a long breath, held it and charged into the burning structure. "Mrs. Ortmeier…are you in here?" She searched frantically through the smoke for the bedroom. "Mrs. Ortmeier…"

The faint sound of a cough sounded to her right. She barged into the bedroom. The caustic air stung her eyes. She groped through billowing, choking smoke. "Are you in here…?"

When the woman grabbed her arm, Callie felt a surge of relief. "Come on, let's get you out of here."

She heaved her to her feet. Having had enough experience with Max when he would straggle home drunk, she couldn't miss the unmistakable scent of hard liquor even through the biting smell of smoke.

"The boy," the woman choked. Grabbed her blanket around her. Fell into Callie, nearly knocking her down.

"He's fine," Callie choked, struggling to pull Luke's mama to safety. "Come on. We need to get you out of here."

Stumbling out of the bedroom door, fear gripped her heart. She could hear the crackle and pop of the fire across the room.

She coughed, her lungs craving fresh air.

When she found the door to the outside, she felt a surge of relief. "Go. Far from the building—" She gave a harsh cough. "I'm going to get the kittens."

Confident that the woman could make it on her own from here, she nudged her outside. Heaved in a gulp of what little fresh air she could grab.

"God, if You're listening, please help me get Luke's kittens," she whispered then held her breath.

The smoke was thicker. She sank lower and felt for

the ladder leading to the loft. She sprang up the ladder, taking the steps two at a time. She crawled forward and located the box of kittens near the thin pallet.

Panic raced through her veins. She'd never be able to manage the cumbersome box down the ladder. And the smoke—its blinding effect had her feeling her way back to the ladder.

Her mind searched frantically for a way as she gave a long, harsh cough. She had to get his kittens out.

Her pulse pounded harder at the crackle of flames.

Grabbing her skirt, she made a sling and scooped all five kittens out of their box, laying them in the makeshift hammock. She pulled it together. Held part of the thick wad in between her teeth to free both hands.

Her heart swelled when she heard small mewing sounds coming from her skirt as she made her way back down the ladder. When her foot reached the floor her legs threatened to buckle beneath her. She coughed hard. Her heartbeat fluttered wildly inside her chest. She was almost outside.

Her hope fell hard as she reached the doorway to find the heat of orange flames barring the way to safety. She had to get out. For the kittens. For Luke. For her daughter.

Libby… She couldn't leave her daughter motherless, again.

And Ben… She couldn't leave this world without him knowing the truth. She couldn't let him believe that she'd been some tramp who thought so little of herself that she'd sell her body.

Turning, she crawled toward the back of the house, groping around in the unfamiliar dwelling for another way out. When her hand touched the wall, she rose to her feet to find the morning's crystal light filtered in a faint, hopeful stream through dense smoke. She blinked hard against the sting burning her eyes, fumbling for a door handle. She tugged it open. Stepping into the fresh air where she was safe, she fell to her knees, coughing, sputtering and thanking God.

Chapter Eighteen

"Callie's in there?" Ben's heart fell hard as he locked his gaze on the bright orange flames leaping at the side of Luke's house. His pulse thundered through his veins at the dark, ominous smoke billowing into the sky like some ill-begotten sacrifice.

"Oh, no…" Luke's strained voice brought Ben's focus around. His face contorted with grief. "What if I kilt her, Ben? What if she died savin' my ma or my kittens?"

Ben took hold of the boy's shoulders and dipped down, eye to eye. "Callie's fine, Luke. We've got to believe that."

Ben ran headlong toward the house, spotting Luke's ma lying on the ground ahead of him, her slumped form barely clad in a flimsy nightdress. He pulled his coat off, rushing over with Luke close at his heels to lay it over her, even as his stinging gaze drifted to the burning structure.

Callie must've gone back in there for Luke's kittens. The thought sent a swell of emotion so deep through him that he had to struggle to catch his breath. "Luke, stay here. I'm going in for Callie."

When he felt a faint touch against his leg, he glanced down to see Luke's ma peering up at him, her heavily painted eyes fluttering open as she let out a harsh, ragged cough. She struggled to pull him close. "T-take care of my boy, won't you?"

Her whispered, ragged words seized his heart. Luke had already suffered so much and now he could face the loss of his only kin. That wasn't fair. Not to Luke. And not to his ma. She'd miss out on raising a young boy with dreams and hopes and love. He wouldn't let her do that.

He braced her with a steady gaze. "You're not going anywhere. You'll see Luke grow up to be a fine, honorable man."

Pushing himself up, he sprinted to the burning dwelling. He broke a window and crawled inside. Glass scraped, shredding his shirt and arms as he lowered himself through the small window.

Flames snapped, angry. Ravenous.

"Callie?" he called above the fire's menacing roar. "Callie, where are you?"

Peering blindly through the thick smoke and searing hot air, his hope nearly caved.

He dropped to his knees to stay low. Inched forward. Braced himself against the heat and smoke. "Callie? Please answer me."

His heart thudded with frantic madness inside his chest.

"Callie, are you in here?"

A large crack sounded above him. He jerked back. Glanced up.

Something heavy cracked over his shoulder and neck. White-hot pain seared through him. He teetered on his hands and knees. Crumpled to the floor, the last glorious image drifting through his mind of Callie.

"Miss Callie!" Luke cried. "Ben found you!"

"Ben?" She coughed, staggering toward the boy.

Luke knelt beside his mama again. "I thought somethin' might'a happened to 'im just now when I heard that crash."

Callie turned and peered at the house, emotion piercing her already raw throat as she recalled hearing the sharp crack followed by a crash. Her breath came in desperate gasps as the boy's words hit her full force.

She blinked against the stinging pain in her eyes as she peered at the broken window. It hung like the mouth of some ravenous predator, poised and ready to devour another soul.

"B-Ben is in there?"

She turned to see Luke's eyes widen to twice their size. He nodded, thick tears springing to his eyes.

Callie knelt and carefully dumped out the kittens from her apron next to where Luke sat with his still, unconscious mother.

"Check your kittens over, Luke. And watch over your mama," she said, her voice sounding all raw and rough from the smoke. She set a hand to his shoulder. "But don't go near your house. Do you hear me?"

"Here, take my coat." Luke grabbed her arm and pulled her to a sudden halt. Tears streamed down his face as he shrugged out of the coat Ben had given him a couple of weeks ago.

"All right."

Spotting an old pan sitting in the yard with a generous melting of snow pooling in the bottom, she ran over and dipped the coat into the pan of icy water. Then dashed toward the broken window.

As she approached the burning building yet again, a sick feeling crept through her at the thought of losing Ben. He'd been nothing but good to her. He'd taken her in, fed her, clothed her, cared for her when she was sick. He'd done more for her these past weeks than Max had done the entire seven years they'd been married.

Yet she'd spurned Ben. At every single turn, she'd spurned him. She'd held Max's reputation over Ben as though it were some instrument of torture passed through the family.

If something happened to him it'd surely be her fault. Had he not gone after her, he'd be safe from the flames and smoke.

Pulling a long breath into her already raw lungs, she climbed into the window, shielding her eyes from the heat and smoke and flames. She nearly landed on Ben. He lay facedown on the floor. Mere feet from where heated flames licked at him.

"Ben? Ben," she called, kneeling down beside him. Fear singed her bravery when he didn't move or speak.

She smothered the flames inching closer to him with Luke's coat. Then through the smoke saw a large beam lying over him. She reached down to lift it off, but the weight of the solid wood wouldn't even budge.

"I won't leave you," she choked out, coughing. "God, please help me… I can't leave him here."

Panic wrapped her tight and suddenly the flames loomed too much. Too hot. Too big a foe for just Callie to take on.

Desperate to free Ben from the weight of the crushing beam and burning flames, she heaved again. In vain.

"Callie…" The voice seemed to come out of nowhere. She started then found Aaron hovering near her shoulder.

Relief so great that she nearly cried washed over her in huge waves.

"Aaron. He's trapped." She coughed, her lungs desperate for a gasp of fresh air.

"I'll lift. You drag him toward the window," he yelled above the roar. Coughed. "Now. Move him now."

With a firm grip on his ankles, Callie tugged him back. Two seconds later, the beam crashed back down and Aaron was beside her lifting Ben in his arms.

"Is there another way out?" he yelled.

Callie motioned with her hand. "This way. There's a back door," she called over the angry fire's fierce roar.

Her face and skin burned. Pulling her skirts up from the fire, she led the way. Beating back flames with Luke's coat as they rushed headlong through the house, desperate for fresh air.

An eerie creaking resounded over the loud crackle and roar. Dread crept down her spine. She fought to stay on her feet, locking her gaze on the slim thread of light coming from the back doorway.

She crossed the threshold, tugging Aaron and Ben with her as a thundering roar sounded. Then a deep, haunting groan. Lunging forward away from the burning structure, Callie looked over her shoulder to see the middle of the house swell as if taking one last dying breath, then sag and cave in a spray of bright orange sparks.

She surged ahead, barely escaping the sparking roar of flames. Aaron followed and knelt next to her, struggling to pull in a gasp of fresh air. Callie's knees began to buckle. She sank to her knees next to Ben as Aaron laid him ever so carefully on the ground. Her burning, smoke-tinged eyes pooled with tears and her throat constricted tight as she peered down at Ben's unconscious form then glanced up at Aaron.

"Tha-thank you," she rasped on a harsh cough.

Her head swam. Chest tightened. She could barely hold a coherent thought as she willed herself to stay focused. Willed her burning eyes to stay open against the corrosive sting. Though her lungs burned and she struggled to capture a full, cleansing breath, she would manage. She had to. She had to make sure Ben was all right. The guilt and condemnation she already lived with would grow to insurmountable proportions. She'd never forgive herself if something happened to him.

"I couldn't have done it without you," she rasped.

On a bellowing cough, Aaron gave her a long, contemplative look. "You're the hero here, Callie. Ben was right about you all along."

It'd been a good six hours since the fire, but it may as well have been a day for the fatigue Callie felt. She peered at the thick bandages she'd wound around Ben's head, arms, and hands.

Those hands had touched her with such tenderness. With such care and concern. They'd healed her. They'd brought her comfort. And his hands had made her feel again. Made her yearn for his touch, his gentle caress calling to life dormant, yet fully innate and glorious, sensations.

She shifted on the padded chair Katie had placed next to Ben's bed. She'd cleaned his wounds, stitched and bandaged them, and all the while Ben had wafted in and out of consciousness, mumbling step-by-step directions that would've put him in the grave, had she followed them.

But since she'd patched him up, he'd been sound asleep, the raspy sound of his breath on each inhale and exhale worrying her. Had he taken in too much smoke?

"He'll be all right, Callie." Joseph settled a hand on her shoulder. "He's too stubborn to die."

She gave a hiccupping chuckle that turned into a cough. She blinked hard against her red eyes. "That's what he said about me." Her voice still sounded and felt raw and scratchy. Her hands bore angry, red burns where she'd tried to lift the beam, and her skin felt stretched tight over her frame.

"I think he mentioned that," Katie added, smiling as she tucked a tendril of hair back from Callie's face. "It was a brave thing you did, going in for Luke's mama and his kittens. And then Ben."

"Very brave." Joseph's voice came out low and choked with emotion.

She smoothed a hand over the fresh, clean dress she'd donned after Katie had insisted she pull herself from Ben long enough to bathe and tend her wounds. "Aaron? How's he doing?"

"Just a few minor cuts and burns, but he'll be fine," Katie assured.

"Did he get some kind of medical attention for them?" Even though there'd been a kind of mutual appreciation after the incident, Callie grew immediately concerned that Aaron might forgo treatment just to stay clear of her.

"He said he did," Joseph remarked.

"And what about Mrs. Ortmeier?"

"She's very grateful to you." Katie grasped Callie's hand in hers. "She feels like she's been given a second chance to make things right. Isn't that wonderful?"

She nodded. Hot tears welled in her stinging eyes.

Anger, deep and grating, had thundered through her veins when she'd realized the woman was drunk. But to know that that same woman now saw this circumstance as a second chance somehow dispelled the anger. Mrs. Ortmeier had hope.

A second chance was all Callie wanted. Was it too much to ask for?

"Miss Callie?" Luke whispered as he peeked around the door. "Think I could come in there?"

"Of course, Luke." She motioned him over, noticing the way he snatched a tentative, worried glance at Ben. "Come on in here."

Luke inched into the room on his toes. When he reached the bed, he snuck a trembling hand out, fingering the quilt with an awkward kind of hesitance. "He gonna be all right?"

"I think he'll be fine." Sympathy pricked at Callie.

Ben had been everything to that boy. He'd been a mentor, a friend and a father. Luke's fragile world would likely cave without him.

Callie shuddered. Her world would likely cave, too, without Ben in it. She'd felt so horribly vulnerable after the fire that she'd almost been unable to calm her quaking hands as she'd stitched his head. She'd had to summon every single ounce of her concentration to do right by him.

Her own scrapes and cuts and aftereffects of inhaling so much smoke were the least of her worries after they'd gotten Ben back here.

"Think I could pray for 'im? I seen Ben do that for his patients lots of times..." He slid Callie a watery gaze. "I seen 'im do it fer you, Miss Callie."

Just knowing that Ben had beseeched God on her behalf made Callie's heart swell with indescribable hope. Like some lifeline lowered down inside a deep, dark pit.

But the idea that he'd prayed for her even as she'd eyed him with such suspicion, assuming him to be just like Max, sent shame slipping through her.

"I'm sure Ben would want you to pray for him." She felt the lifeline jerked out of her reach. She just didn't know—didn't trust that God would welcome her the way she knew He'd welcome Luke or Ben...or anyone else in this room.

Luke pulled in a long breath. "God... I'm prolly not real good at this," he began, his voice quavering, his blond hair hanging in his tightly squeezed eyes. "But Ben, he makes it look real easy, praying. He says it's jest like talkin' to a friend. Anyways, I guess what I'm askin' is that You'd take care of Ben." On a long pause, he sniffled, swiping his sleeve over his nose as Joseph settled a hand on the boy's back. "He's been a real good friend to me, God. Like a pa, even. And I know—well, I know You prolly like 'im, too, but maybe You could let 'im stay here longer. A lot longer."

Callie fought to gain some control over her ragged emotions. She watched as Luke reached out and touched his fingertips to the bandage covering Ben's head.

"That was very nice, Luke," Katie whispered.

"I think he's going to be fine," Joseph assured the boy. "He just needs to rest."

Luke suddenly turned and faced Callie, his earnest gaze a mix of childlike hope and adult caution. "Ma said she's gonna change, Miss Callie." He kept his voice low. "Said she's gonna start being a real good ma fer me after she gets better."

Callie slid her hand around his. "I'm so glad for you, Luke. You deserve that. She'll be so proud of you."

When she spotted Libby standing over by the doorway, peering at her with that hesitant gaze that cut Callie to the quick, sorrow pricked through her heart.

Maybe Ben was right. Maybe she was fooling herself to believe that she could make it on her own while raising a daughter. She didn't want to rely on others. She never again wanted to place herself in such a vulnerable, helpless position.

She had her fiery will. Stubbornness. She was a survivor.

But there was one element she felt sorely lacking deep in her heart...peace. Peace she could trust in. Rely upon. Rest in when her journey took her over rough spots. She could stand on her own two feet, insisting on carving out a new future, but the fact that Mr. Whiteside lurked a day away somehow sealed her bleak fate. As much as she wanted to believe in second chances, she had to wonder if there would ever be hope for her.

Luke stepped over toward Libby and took her by the hand. “I told yer girl here that yer a hero.”

Callie’s breath caught as Luke maneuvered Libby closer.

“You’re right, Luke,” Katie whispered. “Miss Callie is a hero.”

“Yep.” Nodding, he stood behind Libby, his hands perched protectively on her shoulders. “And then she went and asked me what a hero was, so I told ’er. ’Member what I said?” He craned his neck around to look at Libby, eye to eye.

Libby slowly nodded, her sweet innocent gaze flitting to the ceiling as if searching for Luke’s definition there. With a determined nod, she fixed her enthusiastic gaze on Luke. “It’s someone who’s brave and cares ’nough about others that they do something big.”

“And...” he prompted, twirling his finger in a wagon-wheel motion.

“And brave.” Libby’s long-lashed gaze rose to meet Callie’s.

"Don't be shy, silly." Luke gave the girl a tender nudge. "She's yer ma."

Libby took another step closer. Then, as if breaching some wide, yawning gap in time, made a giant leap into Callie's lap. She wrapped her little arms around Callie's neck for a wonderful moment as Callie did the same, struggling to hold back a deep cry.

She barely worked a swallow past the thick lump in her throat. She hadn't allowed herself to feel for years, and in the past few weeks she'd fought to stay one step ahead of the emotions nipping at her heels. The fear, the sorrow, the anger and even the joy all made her feel horribly vulnerable, prey to anyone who'd choose to use it for their own gain.

Her eyes burned with the lingering effects of smoke and heat and unshed tears. Still, she risked crying in front of all of these people she'd come to care so much about, and pulled Libby close, pressing a gentle kiss on her silky, auburn hair. The emptiness that had filled her arms and heart for the past six years seemed to lessen some.

She stroked a trembling hand down her daughter's petite frame, closing her eyes and breathing in the fresh, little girl scent she'd been deprived of for so long.

What would happen tomorrow, when Lyle Whiteside returned for his money?

Libby pulled back, peering intently at Callie. "You're brave, Mama." She carefully settled her hands at Callie's cheeks. "Luke thinks so. And I think so."

"And I think so..." came Ben's smoke-rasped voice.

Callie whipped her focus over to see him, his

searching gaze locked on hers. The unmistakable love she'd seen in his eyes that night at the dance was there again, and sent a tremor shimmying all the way up her spine.

His mouth drew up in that heart-stopping half grin of his. "You were very brave, you know," he rasped with a lazy wink. Then he gave his head a long, slow shake. "But don't *ever* scare me like that again."

"I—I… You'd gone in—" She shifted in her chair to face him, drinking in his easy smile, the way his eyes sparkled, the way a faint shadow already hinted at his strong, masculine jaw. "I couldn't leave you there."

"Thank you." His quietly uttered words whispered over her like the gentle way he trailed his fingertips down her cheek.

It was useless to try and tame the wild beat of her heart.

"How are you feeling?" Joseph stepped closer to the bed.

"Are you havin' pain?" Luke edged his watchful gaze from Ben's head to his quilt-covered toes.

"Not enough to be stuck in this bed." Ben threw back the covers.

Callie yanked her focus to the sturdy pine headboard. "What are you doing?" She craved a small peek at his bare chest, but instead, pinned him to the featherdown mattress with a wide-eyed stare, settled directly on his face. "You need to stay in bed. At least for the time being."

With a sigh, he conceded, lying back as Luke rustled the covers over him and smoothed them back into place again. The creased brow and innocent look Ben flicked to her couldn't have been more than puddle-deep. "Look at what happens… I'm out of commission for a few hours and you've gone from *just* Callie to Doctor Callie?"

"Apparently you can give orders better than you can take them," Katie retorted, sidling down to the end of the bed and nudging his foot.

"Yes, and believe me," Joseph added. "With the instructions you mumbled to Callie as she patched you up, you ought to be glad she knew enough on her own about what she was doing."

The slightest of winces wafted over his face as he held his arms out, surveying the thick, gauze wraps. "I must not have been very coherent. Huh?"

Callie grinned wide. "Umm…not exactly."

"I taught you everything you know. Right?" He gave Callie a pulse-quickening wink then reached out to touch a fingertip to Libby's nose. "How are you, sweetie?"

"Jest fine." Libby scurried to sit on the bed, perching quietly next to Ben, her dainty fingers edging over the bandage wrapped around his head. "Are you gonna be good again?"

"Thanks to your mama and uncle Aaron, I'm going to be fine. I'll probably be up and going before the day's out."

Luke frowned at Ben. "But I thought you said…"

"Yes, what was it that Ben said?" Callie put in, raising her brows and encouraging Luke to continue.

As soon as Luke caught on, he gave his head a single nod then looked down at Ben with eager dedication. "You said that when a body's sick they gotta rest.

So they don' get worse. That's what you say all the time. I heard it with my own ears," he added, plucking his ears for effect.

"Luke's right," Joseph added, chuckling.

Ben huffed. "But I—"

"You got a banged up head, Ben." With great conviction, Luke folded his arms at his chest. "I heard the crash all the way from outside. Scairt me half t'death."

"You've been through quite a lot today," Katie added.

Callie breathed a sigh of relief at that uniquely Ben kind of warm, comforting light that had settled into his gray-blue eyes.

"Why don't I take Libby and Luke home with me?" Katie smoothed a hand over Callie's back as she leaned close. "We'll take care of the kittens and then bake some cookies."

"The kittens are all right, then?" Callie pulled her head around, noticing that Katie's eyes pooled with tears. "They're all healthy?"

"They seem fit to me." Joseph settled his hat back on his head. "Though, as little as they are, they probably wouldn't have made it much longer had you not gotten them out when you did."

Relief washed over her. "I'm so glad they're doing all right."

"Thanks for savin' my kittens, Miss Callie." Luke wrapped her in one huge hug. "Mr. Joseph found me another box to put 'em in, and after Miss Katie warmed up some milk and gave 'em some food they went right t'sleep."

"They did." Libby nodded her vigorous agreement. "They're sleeping now."

"No wakin' 'em this time, Libby." Luke angled a squinty-eyed look at her. "Like Ben says, when ya been through somethin' bad, ya need yer sleep. And the kittens went through somethin' real bad this mornin'. Fact, they're prolly the only kittens who survived a fire like that, I'd think."

With a solemn shake of her head, Libby threaded her little hands together beneath her chin. "Promise. I won't even touch the box."

After Katie and Joseph ushered the children out of the room, Callie was left alone with Ben.

She should be overjoyed right now. Luke's mama had her sights set on the right path, the kittens were safe, Ben was alive and things with her daughter had just taken a miraculous turn for the better.

Deep inside, though, she felt strangely empty. She craved peace as much as she did her next breath. But it seemed so elusive.

Without being able to reconcile her past, the painful history that followed her like some stealthy predator, she'd never fully enjoy the bright outlook of each new day.

But no matter how much Ben would protest and insist otherwise, she'd never leave Boulder without Libby. And she couldn't—wouldn't ask Ben for money to pay off the rest of the debt. He'd already given her so much. As wily as Thomas Blanchard was, Ben had to have paid a generous sum to bring Libby home with him. Scoundrels like Blanchard didn't make gestures like that out of the goodness of their hearts.

Likely, the man didn't even have a heart.

Trapped once again by the decision she faced, she pulled in a long, slow breath. She raised her head to find Ben's crystalline gaze settled on her, the effect penetrating all the way to her core.

"Thank you again, Callie. You did something today that most people wouldn't have considered."

"I'm just glad you're all right," she breathed, slumping in the chair and cradling her head in her hands. Thoughts of how horribly different circumstances could've been rushed through her head, scavenging almost all of the emotional reserve she had left. "I wasn't sure we were going to make it out."

When she felt his hand settle like some warm claim at her back, she fumbled about for control. But as she turned and saw the way his eyes shone with care and unmistakable love, she barely bit off a small cry.

"You came after me. All alone, didn't you?"

Callie threaded her hands together in her lap. "You risked your life, Ben. For me," she breathed, gulping down the sense of shame she felt as her gaze inched from his bandaged hands, to his arms, to his head. "I don't know what I would've done if something had happened to you." She shuddered at the thought that he could've died trying to save her. How could he risk his life, ransom his own fulfilling life to the flames like that? Just for Callie.

Chapter Nineteen

"And I don't know what I would do if you'd been hurt. Or killed," he said, his voice low and choked.

Regret at the caustic words Ben had said to her last night filled his mind. How could he have been so callous? How could he have so easily allowed his frustration to rule his words?

He'd so much as called her a harlot.

Just seeing the vulnerability that weighed her down, the suspicions didn't matter. None of it mattered. Whatever her past, whatever her present, it just didn't matter.

He needed her.

He wanted her.

He loved her.

And if she had some things to overcome, then so be it. Didn't everyone have some kind of secret that loomed too difficult to face?

He'd seen the way God had been softening her heart. The three times she'd been to church with him, and when she'd sat and listened with rapt attention while he'd read to Libby from the Bible, his heart had swelled at the hunger he'd seen in her eyes. As though she wanted so badly to reach out and partake of God's goodness and mercy and unconditional love.

But something always held her at bay.

"I felt so helpless when I called and you didn't answer, and when I couldn't see to find you through the smoke." His breath hitched at the awful memory as he moved a hand to the side of his head where bandages hid a deep, long gash. He blinked against the stinging moisture crowding his eyes. "When I felt the beam hit me, I thought for sure you and I were as good as dead."

Slamming his eyes shut, the same old, haunting regret shook the chains that had held him hostage for so long. He'd failed those dearest to him. He couldn't seem to rescue those he loved the most. What he did, the grand efforts he made, just weren't enough.

"What, Ben? What's wrong?" Callie leaned over him, her hand resting against his cheek. Her light breath whispered feather-light over his face.

He grasped her hand. "In those seconds before I lost consciousness, it was you that I thought of, Callie. And how I wished I could go back and do things differently."

She gave his shoulder a gentle squeeze. "You don't need to do anything differently. You've been good to me, Ben. It's time you let others take care of you for a change."

The way she touched him with such tenderness, and the way she looked at him, as if pleading with him to rescue her from her silent pain, sent his heart into a shuddering frenzy inside his chest.

He'd often pondered that she was much like the strays he'd rescued. Had God really meant all along for him to rescue her? Not just from the here and now with a job and a warm home, but from the pain of her past?

It would be just like God to defy all of Ben's thoughts and plans and assumptions. It would be just like God to bring a woman whose history intertwined his with such delicate force that it would be an undeniable connection. A forever and always bond marked by providential design.

"Your arms and head and hands…do you think they'll heal?" Her concern penetrated his heart.

He nodded, taking in the beautiful, faint way her fingertips trembled against his cheek. "I'm sure they will."

She turned his hand over in hers and stared down at the bandages. "You'll have scars."

"Probably," he agreed, raising her chin with a crooked finger. "But everybody has a scar or two, somewhere."

He couldn't miss the way her hand strayed as if by some involuntary force to her side. And the protective way shame shuttered her vulnerable gaze, leaving him feeling as if she'd stood up and swept out of the room.

If he was going to help her and free her, then he'd have to take a risk. "I know about your scars, Callie."

"What?" She threaded her hands, white-knuckle tight.

"Katie told me about them after she'd helped you with that bath. At first I couldn't imagine the scars were from Max, but now I know. They had to be from him. And I'm sorry." He lifted her gleaming auburn hair from her forehead. When he lightly brushed his fingertips along the red puffy scar marring her hairline, he struggled to reconcile how a man—how Max—could be so cruel. "So sorry you had to endure that kind of treatment."

Her eyes shimmered with unshed tears as she tugged his hand away from the scar. "That's in the past. It's all in the past. And it's surely no fault of yours."

He pushed up to sitting, not quite able to take the words to heart. "Well, I'm not likely to believe that anytime soon. I'm sorry for the things I said last night. I care about you, Callie, and I want to spend every minute I can showing you just how much I care."

He desperately wanted to reach that part of her, the area of her heart held back by some powerful, unseen force. "When I look in your eyes I see things that make me hurt. Right here." He pointed to his heart.

The look she gave him, that look that begged to be rescued, was like some pleading cry he could never, ever ignore.

"I want to help, but I can't if you won't let me," he said, his voice low and tight.

He wondered if he might never be able to unlock that prison. That maybe he had to trust God to reach her and free her from the chains that held her so firmly.

He settled his searching gaze on hers, looked deep enough to see the longing in her eyes, a desire that was meant just for him. He loved Callie. Not because deep down she yearned for love. Not because she was Max's poor, mistreated widow. Not because she needed to be loved.

But because God had led her straight to Ben's heart.

Because she was perfect for him.

Because she was just Callie.

"You're right…the scars are in the past. And Max did plenty wrong, but one thing he did right…he sent you to me."

"What is all of that?" Ben asked, catching the distinct stench of smoke as he peered down into the bag Aaron had dragged in with him. "It smells like you've been digging around in the fire rubble."

"I have." Aaron settled his hat on the back of the chair with a bandaged hand.

"Why would you do something like that? There couldn't have been much worth saving in that house."

From the burlap bag, Aaron pulled the charred remains of a stethoscope and the blackened skeleton of a medicine bottle.

Ben's face flamed hot. And when Aaron hefted out the small scale that had come up missing just last week, his heart skidded to a halt inside his chest.

"These things were in the rubble?" He knelt down across from Aaron, taking the stethoscope in hand.

"Yep. There were other things, too, but some of it was too burned to even recognize." He plucked out the warped remains of tweezers. "The fire was so hot. Even a day out, and some areas were still smoldering."

Ben touched the heat-deformed pan to the scale. "I can't believe it," he whispered.

He'd always seemed to give others the benefit of the doubt, but in this instance he'd listened to whisperings of accusation.

"How did you know to look there?" he asked, perplexed. "I've never said anything to you about the missing items."

"Actually, Luke came to see me." Aaron fiddled with the iodine bottle. "He's been feeling mighty bad, because he'd only borrowed the items."

Ben sighed, sickened at how easy it had been to accuse and condemn—and how very unlike God that was. "Here I thought Callie had taken them."

Aaron met his shame-filled gaze with one of his own. "We've both been guilty of accusing her, Ben."

He gave his head a disgusted shake. "I should've been more trusting. I accused her—silently, but still, I accused her."

"Well, if it's any consolation, you've never done anything but defend her honor—to me, anyway," Aaron said, bracing a hand on Ben's good shoulder. "Luke wanted to tell you himself. But he wouldn't come in here. He thought you'd be mad at him."

Ben eased himself into a chair, his shoulder throbbing. "Please, would you mind getting him for me?"

"Sure." Stashing the items back into the bag, Aaron stood. "Ben, I'm sorry. I was way out of line in the things I said about Callie. It doesn't matter what her past was."

"Her past was with Max. And as far as I'm concerned, that makes her one courageous woman. I just know that she couldn't do what seemed obvious—no matter what proof points that way. She doesn't have it in her."

"She showed more bravery than most men." Aaron cleared his throat. "I don't know why I was so determined to bring her down. I guess maybe she represented Max. And, well… I have some things to take care of as far as that goes."

"Believe me, I think we all probably have a bitter root or two stemming from our last couple of years with Max." He eased a hand over his eyes, feeling the pull of the tight red skin. When he glanced up at his brother, he saw deep regret in Aaron's repentant gaze. "Now that you know that, you can deal with it. And I know you will. You're a good man."

"Thanks." Aaron nodded. "For everything."

Everything? Regret and failure snapped at him as he remembered how incompetent he'd felt, how horrible he'd felt at not being able to turn the events for Aaron's wife and baby. "I wish I could've done more for Ellie and the baby. I wish I could've saved them. For you."

"I know you do." Aaron's mouth formed a tight line. "You did everything you could. I don't blame you, Ben."

Swallowing hard, Ben's eyes filled with hot tears. "Thanks," he ground out, his voice tight and strained with emotion. "Thanks."

Pulling in a slow breath, Aaron's knuckles whitened as he grasped the bag. "Someday, maybe I'll figure out why God thought it was best to take them when He did. Or maybe someday I'll just finally accept that they're gone."

Ben nodded, astonished at his brother's dignity. "You're going to make it. It's going to be all right."

With the locket cradled in her hand, and purposeful strides, Callie walked over to Ben's house where

Libby had been keeping him company. She had to return the locket. And if worse came to worst, she'd have to humble herself enough to ask him for help. She didn't have a choice.

Maybe if she'd made it back home to her father, he might have loaned her the money, but that was a risk she couldn't take. With Libby in her care now, she wouldn't take off for her father's home and risk Whiteside tracking her down and hauling her back with him.

Since the fire yesterday, Callie had felt as if she'd been moving through life in slow motion. The entire Drake family and then some had been together at lunch today—a celebration of sorts. Even Aaron…

He'd taken her by complete surprise and apologized. For being so harsh toward her. For assuming the worst. For hoping to sway Ben's opinion regarding her. She'd felt oddly vindicated, yet still without the peace she craved.

She was surrounded by all of the things she'd ever longed for…a loving family, her beautiful daughter and friends who cared.

But she didn't have peace.

"Your time's up," came Lyle Whiteside's voice.

Steadying herself, Callie turned to find him slinking a heartbeat behind her.

"Did you hear me, girl?" He caught her arm in a meaty fist hold. "I've waited long enough. Either pay up what you owe now or you're comin' with me."

Callie blinked hard, trying to calm the racing beat of her heart. Intimidation snaked around her, threatening to suffocate her will and hope. For a moment, she couldn't seem to grasp a single, coherent thought.

When her frantic thoughts settled on her little girl, a fierce sense of protection rose within her. "I don't have all of it—yet. But I won't go with you."

God, please... I need Your help. Would God hear her this time? Would He help her? All morning long she'd prayed that He would turn the tide. Give her a second chance, just like He'd given Luke's mama a second chance, because Callie would never sell herself. Never that.

"I'm sure you don't want me getting the law involved in this," he cautioned, wrenching her arm so hard she barely bit off a cry. "You wouldn't stand a snowman's chance in a hot box with all the cheatin' that husband of yours did."

"Please, I'll have the rest for you soon," she assured, struggling to keep the fear from her voice.

Feeling the locket in the palm of her hand, she stuffed it inside the pocket on her dress. If Whiteside got his hands on it, she likely would never see it again, and she had every intention of returning it to Ben.

"I have a good job now and the pay is good. I'm doing everything I can to make right on what Max owed you."

He yanked her toward the street. "Not everything. There's plenty more you could *do* for me."

She fought to wrench her arm free. "If you'll just give me another hour..."

"Not another minute." Whiteside tugged her toward the carriage that sat in the street like some fancy, black coffin. "You know me, Callie. I don't like being put off. With the way you ran out on me like you did, you should consider yourself lucky I gave you an extra two days."

"Back away from her." Ben's strong, authoritative voice broke through the nightmare. "Now."

Whiteside glanced over his shoulder and pivoted. "This isn't your concern."

Ben caught Callie's eye with a reassuring look. "She is my concern. And I'm telling you now…you better release your hold and back away."

Whiteside tightened his grip on her arm. "It's not that easy. She's coming with me."

She shook her head. "I won't go with you. I can't."

Ben moved in closer. "As far as I'm concerned, you're taking her against her will. And that could get you into trouble with more than just me."

"That's right." Aaron strode out from behind the house. "You'll be in hot water with me, too. And probably the rest of this town."

"Let her go," Ben commanded.

"I'm telling you. She owes me." Whiteside edged back a step. "And I intend to collect."

Ben stalked up to stand nose to nose with Whiteside. He placed a hand on her arm, like some warm, wonderful claim as he stared the man down. "Get your hands off her. Now."

Callie's eyes grew wide as she shifted her gaze from Ben's calm, collected look to Whiteside's red face and his flaring nostrils. Ben obviously didn't know how vengeful Lyle Whiteside could get—especially when someone dared to cross him.

Ben drew a fistful of Whiteside's crisp white shirt

in a bandaged hand. "If you know what's good for you, you'll step away and leave her alone."

Looping an arm around her waist, Whiteside hauled her against his side. "I'm not going anywhere without my money. And if she can't pay up then she's as good as money to me."

Ben advanced another step. "What are you talking about?"

"He's talking about a gambling debt, Ben," she managed, her voice betraying her with a quaver.

Ben sent her a confused glance.

"It's a long story. But Max…before he died, he'd stacked up a mountain of debt with gambling losses."

"And he's making *you* pay?" Ben nodded toward Whiteside.

She boldly met Ben's gaze. "I was working at his saloon and brothel as a cook and housekeeper to try and pay it off before I came here. But then I—"

"She was lucky I let her do that. I shouldn't have gone easy on her. She could've made me a fortune."

Ben's calm slipped away. She could see it in the way his jaw tensed. His eyes suddenly grew sharp with anger. He drew his grip tighter around Whiteside's shirt. "Is this how you always do business? Swooping down on widows when they're still grieving?"

"She had a roof over her head and decent meals," Whiteside barked, the words causing her stomach to churn.

The tiny closet she slept in and the pitiful, half-eaten leftovers she was allowed were a far cry from decent. That he spoke of them as though he'd let her live in the lap of luxury stirred anger from deep within.

"I suppose you gave her a clothing allotment, too?" Ben's voice was so even and hard, Callie almost didn't want to look at him.

"Why, yes. She could have the best if she'd come back and work for me." Whiteside tugged his head to the side in a useless effort to free himself from Ben's grip. "I'm offering more than that sorry husband of hers ever gave her."

Aaron joined Ben beside the man. Callie didn't think Whiteside stood a chance, but if he had a gun on him, then they were the ones without a chance.

"You're a sick man," Ben confirmed.

Her skin crawled thinking of all the girls back at Whiteside's brothel, and how he'd convinced them that he was doing them a favor in taking care of them.

Aaron gave a derisive snort. "Taking advantage of this situation for your own gain…"

"Let her go," Ben commanded.

"He owed me plenty and I'm going to collect." He hissed a breath through his clenched teeth. "He promised to pay up with her, but he backed out."

She jerked her head around to peer at him, her heart thudding in her throat. "What did you say?"

In spite of his bandaged, injured hands, Ben locked a crushing grip on Whiteside's hand and yanked it free from Callie.

"He must not have thought much of you, girl," Whiteside chided as he stumbled back a step. "'Cause he was willing to pay off his debt with you."

"No… Oh, no…" Bright splotches of light embedded in darkness bombarded her vision. Her head spun. She tried to steady herself. "He w-wouldn't do that."

But even as she uttered the words, she knew that Max could. And probably did. He'd done it with his own daughter.

"Said so himself," he spat with a derisive snort. "Drunk as all get-out when he made the offer, but the idea was very tempting. Too tempting to pass on."

Ben hauled his arm back and pummeled Whiteside's face, sending him toppling backward. An instant later, Ben was straddling him as he seized his coat so tight, Callie was sure Whiteside would suffocate.

Aaron knelt over them, his hands clenched into fists. "You said the wrong thing," he muttered. "I wouldn't want to be you about now."

Through the tears clouding her eyes, Callie noticed Whiteside struggling to edge a hand to his side, under his coat.

Dread shot up her spine. "He's got a gun, Ben!"

In a flash Aaron snatched Whiteside's hand and held it tight as she pulled the gun from the holster and held it in her hands.

"Get the sheriff, Callie," Ben breathed, the pained look he gave her piercing her heart.

He had to be about ready to collapse in his weakened condition. But mostly, he'd said more than once how responsible he felt for Max's failings. This must've come as a horrible shock, as much for him as it was for her, to know that his brother would suggest such a thing.

"If Max wasn't such a white-bellied chicken and gone through with it, he might still be alive." Whiteside angled an intimidating, beady-eyed stare her way.

"I may have felt generous enough to let him have a stab at you. For a reduced rate."

She held her breath. Stared at the man. Max had offered her as payment for a gambling debt, just like he'd offered his own child.

But if he hadn't had second thoughts…maybe he'd still be alive.

She peered at the cold, heartless look in White-side's eyes. "You killed him, didn't you?" she heard herself say.

"Surely you don't think I would do that." He raised his bushy eyebrows. "I will say, though…my establishment's a better place without him."

Chapter Twenty

Unless Whiteside was more forthcoming with the truth, Callie realized that she might never know for sure if Max had been shot because he'd refused to go through with his agreement.

But this was certain… Max had betrayed her more than she probably knew.

And—she swallowed hard—with his dying breath, he'd implored her to find Ben.

Even if the sting of seven years of betrayals never fully waned, she could find comfort in knowing he'd tried to do what was right before his life slipped away.

After the confrontation with Whiteside, Callie had sat for an hour in Ben's office with Sheriff Goodwin and Brodie Lockhart, answering more questions than she'd heard both Libby and Luke ask, combined. Ben had been beside her for most of the questioning, offering her his good arm for support even when he had to be cringing with the information she'd disclosed. About the last few months with Max, the night he was shot, the way Whiteside threatened her if she didn't work for him as a harlot.

Pulling her cloak tighter, she walked next door, the crisp, early evening air invigorating her tired eyes a little. The sheriff had said that with as much time as had gone by since the murder, it might be hard to pin it on him. But the fact that he'd reached for his gun would be enough to put him behind bars for a while, anyway. Maybe with a little encouragement, the right people, those who knew the truth, would be brave enough to come forward and expose Whiteside.

There was no guarantee. But for some reason, Callie didn't have it in her to fret about that. She'd been through so much over the past days, she was spent.

And the debt...well, Whiteside wouldn't need it for a while. Maybe if he managed to wriggle free from the charges, she'd have enough to pay him back by then.

Opening the front door of Ben's house, she quietly entered. She could hear the faint sound of her daughter's sweet voice coming from down the hall.

She tiptoed in that direction and peeked through a crack in the door into the spare bedroom, where Libby had slept that night Ben and Aaron had found them on the roadway south.

Her little girl sat on Ben's lap in the sturdy, walnut rocking chair. She peered up at him, her eyes big and gaze earnest. "And what if someone does something *really* bad?"

"Like..." Ben prompted.

Callie set a hand to her lips, her heart warmed by

Ben's show of patience. As though he had all the time in the world to answer her endless questions, even when he had to be exhausted.

"Well, Luke, he told me he took some doctor stuff of yours." She traced a finger around the top button of Ben's white shirt.

"He told you that?"

She nodded. "He took 'em without asking. And then they burned. That's bad, isn't it?" Her delicate, perfectly shaped eyebrows creased in a sorry frown. Holding one of his hands up, she pressed her small palm to his. "Are you mad at him?"

"No. Luke and I…we got that cleared up a little bit ago. I understand that he was just trying to help his kittens. He knows now that he needs to ask before he borrows something."

"And is God mad at him?" Libby tapped the toes of her new black boots together—boots Ben had insisted on purchasing. "Does He still like Lukey?"

Her throat grew tight at her daughter's heartfelt and innocent questions.

"Of course He does. He loves Luke." Ben held Libby's chin, urging her focus up to him. "And He loves you. There's nothing you can do that will make God love you any less."

Her big blue eyes grew even wider. "Really?"

"No matter how bad you are, no matter how good you are, no matter how old or young you are, God loves you. He loves you, Libby. His love and forgiveness is like a great big blanket that covers over every bad thing." Ben stretched a leg out in front of him. "His love is what leads us to Him."

She shifted to peer at him, eye to eye. "Do you think He's leading me?" She slid a serious gaze around the room. "I don't see Him."

"I'm sure He is."

A fleeting memory flashed through Callie's mind. Of when her own father would look at her, way back before her mama died and grief had turned Callie's happy world upside down. Death had a way of stripping life from more than just the one who passed.

"You'll know He's leading you because you'll feel it right here," Ben promised, tapping on her chest. "In your heart."

Tugging her dress taut, Libby angled her focus to where Ben had pointed. "Is God in there?"

He chuckled, touching a fingertip to her nose. "Only if you ask Him to live there." Tucking a wisp of hair behind her ear, he added, "He wants to live in your heart and be your friend."

Libby gasped. "Oh… I wanna be God's friend. Then I'll have two friends… Luke and God." She threaded her fingers together beneath her chin, looking as if she might burst with delight. After that Ben led her in a prayer that filtered beyond Callie's ears, all the way to her heart.

"I wanna go tell Luke, then he can make God his friend, too." Libby's giggle filled the room. Her little feet bounced with joy.

The warm look of contentment and the undeniable glow of peace coming from Ben's face shook Callie to the core.

Was that it? Could peace be that simple?

As simple as receiving God's forgiveness and love?

"I believe Luke's out in the barn with Aaron," she heard Ben say. "Maybe you should go tell him right now."

Libby jumped down from Ben's lap and bolted to the door, coming to a sliding halt when she found Callie standing on the other side. "Mama…guess what? God's my friend."

"I'm so glad, honey." Before Callie got the words out of her mouth, Libby was already halfway to the front door.

"Is it true?" she whispered in a strangled voice as Ben walked out of the bedroom and stood beside her. "Is all that you told her true? About God's love and forgiveness?"

He ushered her to the living room sofa. "It's true."

Callie stared at him as he sat beside her. "Do you believe that?"

"With all my heart." He grasped one of her hands in his and peered at her. The peace blanketing his face was so tangible she was sure she could almost touch it. "You can't mistake God's love and forgiveness for the ways of His people. Sometimes they're as different as night and day. We all make mistakes," he breathed, his eyes closing for a brief moment before he looked at her again with a reassuring intensity that nearly took her breath away. "We all react wrongly at times, but that doesn't change the way God loves us. Ever."

Her mouth pulled tight in a quiet cry as she wondered how she could've been so wrong for so long. "For years I've thought that because I disobeyed my father and married Max, that all of the bad things that happened were because of that." Struggling to steady the quaver in her voice, she pulled in a deep breath.

"That's not true." He edged closer, settling an arm behind her shoulders.

She pulled the locket from her pocket, remembering how devastated she'd felt when she'd found out that Max had stolen the heirloom from his own brother. "I thought I'd never get free from paying back for the mistake, because one bad thing after another after another kept happening."

Ben shook his head. "There's no paying back to it, Callie. We make mistakes, but there's nothing you can do to pay back for the mistake. You can only ask forgiveness—and that is free."

"But my father's words? That God's fierce wrath is exacted upon those who disobey…" She willed her heart to slow its rapid-fire beat. "When I came here, it seemed like things started changing for me, but then the fire happened and Luke almost lost his mama and his kittens. And I almost lost you…"

"You didn't lose me, Callie. I'm right here." He tugged her closer, his strong, capable arms around her like some mighty fortress. "And I'm not going anywhere."

She pushed away. "Ben, what if all of that happened because I'm here?"

He steadied her quivering chin. "No, Callie. You're stubborn. You're a fighter. You're strong. But—"

"But—" She fought back a cry, hot tears stinging her eyes.

"But you are *not* that powerful." He gave an adamant shake of his head, conviction cloaking every single word.

But could she trust them?

"All of the things you went through with Max were because of his choices. And I'm so sorry that he put you through that. You are far more valuable than that. You have to know it's true. God loves you, Callie."

"His love covers you," he encouraged as he watched one lone tear trickle down her cheek. She was so strong, even when she faced lies and betrayals that were as wounding as anything he'd ever seen. Ben thumbed away the tear, his heart clenching inside his chest. "It's unconditional. It's real. And it's for you."

"Ben..." Uncurling her tightly fisted hand, she revealed the locket. Held it out to him. "I want you to have this back."

"What?" He furrowed his brow.

She pulled her lovely, full lips into a determined line. "I can never repay you. But at least I can give this back."

"No." He held his hand over hers. "This is yours, and you don't have to worry about paying anything back."

Callie's long lashes fluttered momentarily over her eyes. "But—"

"That debt's been paid," he said, catching her gaze in his.

"What?" She gasped then, as if she'd been holding her breath. "What do you mean?"

"Whiteside won't be bothering you for his money again."

The vulnerability he saw there in her wide-eyed gaze, as if she was not fully understanding his meaning, made his heart ache. He'd take care of her for the rest of his days if Callie would have him. And if he was moving too fast for her, then he'd wait. As long as she needed.

"I took care of it," he breathed, his voice catching. "Maybe not in the way Whiteside wanted, but I've arranged to have the money owed him put toward getting those ladies out of there. Getting them some decent clothes. And maybe a place to live."

Her brow rose in shock. She slumped against him, as if a huge weight had been removed. "Y-you did?"

"Yes." With a slow nod, he drew her close and pressed a kiss to her head, breathing in the wonderful, beautiful scent of Callie. "You don't have to worry about the debt."

"You shouldn't have," she squeaked, sniffing. Squaring her shoulders.

"Yes. I should have." He couldn't help but smile at her stubborn insistence even in the face of insurmountable odds. He didn't even want to think about the way things could've turned out had Whiteside gotten to her first. "And I'm glad I did."

"I'll pay you back." Callie wrenched free from his embrace. "I'll work as long as I need to, to pay back every cent, Ben. I promise."

"You don't understand, do you?" He held her cheeks between his hands. "I'd pay that ten million times over, then again and again and again, if it meant freeing you."

"But, Ben—"

He settled a finger to her lips, to stop the willful protests. “I care for you, Callie. And I’ve learned that I can never go back and change the past. I can’t change the loss of Aaron’s wife and baby, or the loss of Joseph’s sight. I can’t change what I did or didn’t do right in raising Max. I can’t change the way he treated you… but I can trust God to work things out,” he breathed, tracing the full pout of her lower lip. “And I can tell you just how much I love you.”

He drew in a ragged sigh. “I love you, Callie.”

“But, Ben, I—” She stopped herself short and stared at him, as if seeing him for the first time. “You what?”

“I said, I love you. I think I did from the moment I found you on my porch.”

The soft, new glow in Callie’s face was all the confirmation he needed to know that she believed him. She really believed him. And she trusted him. She was opening her heart to trust God, as well.

Ben’s heart swelled with that knowledge. The softness and vulnerability in her gaze was fresh and new and wholly attractive.

“I’m crazy about you. I love you and want you to be my wife.” That wonderfully innocent, warmly beckoning look could melt his heart. “I love you. And I’m not going anywhere. I’m going to be here for you, Callie. I’ll rejoice when you rejoice and when you’re sad, I’ll be a shoulder for you to cry on.”

“You would do that? For me?”

“Aww, darlin’… I’d do that and so much more. And if this is all too quick for you, then I’ll wait. I’ll wait however long until you’re ready. Because there’s no one I’d rather spend the rest of my days with than you.”

"Why? Why would you give so much for me? You ransomed me—my life and my daughter's life, too, and you've done it with no thought of return."

"Let me show you." He gently took the locket from her hand and opened it.

Through bright tears, she stared down at the engraving: *All for love.*

"Oh, Ben… I love you. I do. I love you."

The new, tender look of peace growing on her face seemed as if to come from the inside out. As if she had finally grasped not just his love, but the higher revelation of God's love.

With his bandaged hands, he fumbled to clasp the locket around her neck once again, moved by the glowing look of love and tranquility in her unshuttered gaze.

"All for love, Callie. All for love."

Epilogue

"Slow down, Libby," Luke whispered, his voice echoing in the packed church. "Yer goin' too fast."

Callie looked on from the back of the sanctuary, smiling as her little girl came to a stop five rows down the aisle.

Libby peered, with charming devotion, at where Luke stood proudly next to his mama, at the end of the very first pew. She took two slow steps forward as if trying out her feet for the first time. "How's this, Lukey?"

"That's better." He rewarded Libby with a decided wink as he struggled to tuck something inside the new jacket Ben had purchased for him. "Jest remember what I showed ya."

An errant giggle escaped Libby's lips as she clasped one hand to her mouth. "A kitty," she squealed, glancing over her shoulder at Callie. "Mama, look. Lukey brought Beauty to yer wedding."

"I had to," Luke tossed in Callie's direction then

swung his focus back to Libby. "She *is* named after yer mama."

"Yep. For Mama," Libby echoed.

Sliding his hand into his coat, Luke withdrew the fluffy kitten. "'Sides…she wanted to come. She told me so, herself."

The trickle of laughter streaming through the sanctuary was more meaningful and pleasant than a hundred bouquets of fresh flowers to celebrate Callie's trip down the aisle.

"Aww…that's very sweet of you, Luke." Callie glanced to where Ben waited for her at the front of the church, her heart taking flight at the look of complete adoration he'd aimed directly at her.

You're sweet, he mouthed, his affectionate gaze like some gentle caress.

A fresh blush warmed her face. He'd made her cheeks rosy more often that not over the past month with his endearing compliments and oh-so-tender touch. It was as if he knew just what to say and just what to do to coax the last little bits of reservation from her heart.

With the newfound freedom she'd discovered, her smile had been next to impossible to wipe off. All the years of pain and regret had seemed to crumble away since Callie had found true peace with God. The experience had made her feel alive again.

Breathing deeply, Callie slid her gaze over the faces of everyone in attendance. She was surrounded by those she loved. And by a town that had gone out of its way to make sure this wedding was perfect: with a reception hosted by Mrs. Duncan, a lovely wedding dress made by Katie and a hope chest packed as full of gifts as this church was packed with well-wishers.

Gratefulness welled up inside of her, seeing Joseph and Katie, Zach and Aaron positioned there in the first pew, in a show of unconditional, loyal support. She didn't even want to think about how different her life would be had she not finally and desperately sought out her last resort. But Ben and his family…they were so much more than her last resort…they were her only resort.

Yes, this day was perfect.

Callie took it all in as Libby made her way to the front of the church, pausing long enough to pet the kitten Luke held out like some prized possession.

"Come on, Mama," she whispered, motioning Callie forward.

Callie took her first step down the aisle then, glancing at where her father had secured her arm in his. His presence here at her side was yet another testament to Ben's goodness and thoughtfulness. Even though she'd assumed her father had long since written her off, Ben had contacted him two weeks ago about the wedding, and her father had booked passage immediately.

The tears of joy Callie and her father had shed when they embraced far outweighed the tears of regret about so many lost years.

"You look so pretty, honey." The low crack of emotion in his voice belied the steadying comfort she felt as he patted her hand. "Just like your mama."

"Oh, thank you, Daddy," she whispered, her throat growing tight. "Thank you for being here with me."

"I'm just glad I can give you away…." As he pressed

a kiss to the top of her head, tears crowded her gaze. “And to the man of your dreams.”

She squeezed his hand, her heart swelling with deep, pure love as she continued down the aisle, shifting her attention forward and locking gazes with Ben. He was so handsome in his dark gray suit. So noble in the way he treated each and every person.

And he was hers.

The man of her dreams.

He’d been waiting for her all along—that’s what he’d told her. And she believed him.

Not in her wildest dreams did she imagine she’d find such love and comfort in his arms, at least not that night when she’d shown up half-frozen on his doorstep.

Had Max somehow known that, with his last breath, he was sending her straight into Ben’s arms?

Callie’s heart stirred with a poignant awareness as she neared the front of the church where Ben stood, his hand outstretched to meet hers with the pledge of protection. And his ardent gaze…penetrating and capturing her completely, drawing her to his side.

She willed her feet to slow down. Willed her heart to slow its rapid beat inside her chest, but it was useless.

Her head and heart rushed with the glorious promises of today and every single tomorrow she’d share with Ben.

When her daddy placed her hand in Ben’s, blissful peace infused straight through her hand to every part of her being.

“I’ll take good care of her, sir,” Ben breathed, his

voice so true and steady as he entwined his fingers in hers and pulled her a little closer.

"You're beautiful," he whispered. "I'm a blessed man."

"I love you, Ben," Callie responded on a contented sigh. Peering up at him, she was humbled by the powerful love she could see in his gaze…for her. And she knew, just as sure as the sun's rising, that she would forever and ever be safe, secure and loved in Ben's arms.

* * * * *

When a charming rodeo cowboy comes home, will he make amends to an old sweetheart?

Read on for a sneak preview of The Prodigal Cowboy, *the next book in Brenda Minton's miniseries* Mercy Ranch.

Holly saw him enter but she didn't believe it, not at first. It couldn't be Colt, looking rugged but handsome, a few days' growth of whiskers on his too-attractive face as he leaned heavily on a cane and announced his arrival like she might have been waiting for his return.

He removed his hat and pushed a hand through dark hair. For a moment she was eighteen again, meeting up with a guy and not realizing the combined power of attraction and loneliness.

Just like that day twelve years ago she felt it again, hitting her hard, taking her breath for just an instant before she reminded herself that he was a two-timing, no-good piece of work that she wanted nothing to do with.

She couldn't let herself get pulled in by his looks and charm. Not again.

"Holly," he started.

She shook her head and took a step back.

"What are you doing here?" she asked. It wasn't the first time he'd come home. Nor the first time she'd seen him in the past eleven years.

It's just that he never came here, not to the café.

"I just need a few minutes of your time."

"Why?"

He had moved closer and was suddenly in front of her, smelling too good. She nearly groaned at her own weakness for this man.

"Spit it out, Colt."

He motioned her toward a table, even pulled out a chair for her.

She took the seat and he sat across from her. "Get it over with, please. I can't take much more of this. Are you sick? Did that bull hurt you worse than everyone said?"

He grimaced as he leaned back. "I'm not sick. I would tell you not to worry but I doubt worry is the first thing you feel for me."

"I would be upset if something happened to you," she admitted, her voice faltering.

"This isn't about the accident. I'm healing up fine." He leaned back in his chair and studied her face. "You're still beautiful."

"Don't. I don't want your compliments. You're obviously here on business. So why don't we cut to the chase?"

He didn't smile. "Of course, right to the point. Holly, it's about Dixie. That's why I'm here."

Dixie.

He wasn't here about the café or about them. He was here to tell her something concerning Dixie.

Their daughter.

LIEXP0520